VENOM
EPIC ADVENTURE SERIES #8

COLIN FALCONER

Copyright © Colin Falconer

The right of Colin Falconer to be identified as the author of this work has been asserted in accordance with the Copyright, Designs and Patents Act 1988.

All rights reserved. No part of this publication may be reproduced, stored in, or transmitted into any retrieval system, in any form, or by any means (electronic, mechanical, photocopying, recording or otherwise) without the prior written permission of the publisher. Any person who does any unauthorized act in relation to this publication may be liable to criminal prosecution and civil claims for damages. The only exception is by a reviewer, who may quote short excerpts in a review.

This is a work of fiction based on the true story of Charles Sobhraj. Some names, characters, businesses, places, events and incidents have been changed and are either the products of the author's imagination or used in a fictitious manner.

NOTE: This updated edition is different from the original. It has been edited for better readability and includes additional scenes.

PART 1

Adrienne: 1946-52

CHAPTER 1

Saigon
June 1946

It was a sultry afternoon in June. The monsoon season. Rain beat on the roof of the arcade, flooding the street drains and spilling onto the cracked pavements. Adrienne Christian's blue skirt was stained with mud. She hurried past the iron-shuttered shophouses along the Rue Le Loi, the umbrella clutched to her side.

Adrienne had elegantly chiseled features and her hair was long and blue-black. She would toss it back over her shoulder with a casual movement of her head like a young filly. There was a grace and fluidity in her movements that allowed her to fully capitalize on nature's gifts. Her skin was pale as marble, but her eyes were startling green, set in her face like emeralds on cream silk.

The nuns at the convent school prayed for her constantly.

She turned into an alleyway and stopped outside the tiny shop that belonged to the Sikh spice merchant, her senses assaulted by a miasma of cardamom, turmeric and anise. She looked up. Above the narrow, wooden stairs that led up from the street hung a small hand-painted sign:

J.K.S. Krisnan, Tailor

She pulled a scrap of paper from her purse, a note written in her father's precise hand, shook the water from her umbrella and went up the steps.

VENOM

When Adrienne walked into his cramped workroom that steamy afternoon, Joginder Krisnan was bent over an ancient foot-pedal sewing machine, sewing a cotton blouse that a French captain had commissioned for his wife. He looked up and stared at her with frank admiration. His face creased into a lazy smile that he would never have attempted in the presence of any of the French *madames*.

'Can I help you. Mademoiselle?' His voice was velvet soft and he spoke French with a strong accent.

'I've come to pick up a dress jacket,' Adrienne said. 'For *Monsieur* Emmanuel Christian.'

Joginder picked up a small, leather-bound notebook from the workbench and flicked through the pages, pretending to search for the name. In fact, he remembered Emmanuel Christian very well. A grey-haired Frenchman who barked his instructions at him as if he were one of *les jaunes*. Arrogant bastard.

'Ah, yes. *Monsieur* Christian. The white dress jacket.'

'My father said it would be ready today.'

'I finished it this morning,' Joginder said. 'Just a moment.' He disappeared into a small back room.

Adrienne had expected him to look like the Indian spice merchant in the shop below, with a dhoti and silk turban. But Joginder Krisnan wore western clothes, white cotton trousers with an open-necked shirt.

He was not handsome like some of the French officers she had danced with at the Caravelle. Instead, he had the serene expression she had seen on the faces of statues in the temples. His skin was smooth and very light. His eyes were huge and brown, and he had delicate hands with long, tapered fingers.

He reappeared with a bulky, brown-paper package in his arms. He held it out to her, his gaze candid, and allowed his fingers to touch hers.

For a moment their eyes met.

Adrienne stared at him in alarm. She took the parcel and ran from the shop.

'You're quiet tonight.'

'Yes, Father.'

'What's the matter? You've hardly said a word all evening.'

'Nothing.'

Emmanuel Christian pushed his plate away and dabbed at his chin with a napkin. His movements were stiff, as if a lifetime of strict self-discipline had transmuted rigidity into his very soul. The deep lines at the corners of his mouth twisted into a habitual frown.

Through the years he had risen rapidly through the ranks of the public service in Saigon. His career had reinforced in him two convictions: the importance of order and the inherent superiority of his own race. He disliked any circumstance that disturbed the equilibrium of his life.

It was unlike his daughter to be sullen. Indeed, he often found her eloquence a burden, especially during dinner.

Mai Ong, their ancient *boyesse*, removed his plate and disappeared into the kitchen.

It was silent in the room, save for the murmur of the cicadas through the French windows and the delicate tinkle of silver on china as Adrienne pushed a morsel of chicken around her plate.

Emmanuel sighed, leaned back into his chair and waited for Mai Ong to reappear with his cognac. He loved his daughter, but he disliked being with her. He was either irritated by her constant chatter or was uncomfortable with her silences.

So, he was alarmed when she suddenly dropped her knife and fork onto her plate. The noise resounded in the silent room like a crashing drawer.

'I feel unwell,' she said. She threw down her napkin and jumped to her feet. 'I shall go to my room and lie down.'

Adrienne closed her bedroom door and allowed the tension to drain from her with a long sigh. She went to her dressing table and removed the clips from her hair, shaking it loose about her shoulders.

Her bedroom overlooked the garden. Bougainvillea blossom wreathed the veranda outside her window, and she breathed in the perfume as the branches were stirred by the breeze.

It was sticky hot in the room. She turned off the light, stripped off her dress and lay on her bed under the gently moving mosquito net. She stretched her arms above her head and thought of the whispered conversations at school and the confessions, real and imagined, that other girls had made to her. The lure of sin excited and terrified her. She tried to picture herself in bed with a man, wondered what it would feel like.

Her fevered imagination was teased each week when she danced with the young army officers at the Saigon Royal or flirted with the aspiring diplomats and colonialists at the Cercle Sportif. They all wanted to fulfill her fantasies, but Emmanuel Christian was a prudent man and let her go nowhere unescorted.

Now, Joginder Krisnan had provided a new and seductive twist. She imagined a darkened room littered with lotus petals and a bed of carmine silk. Sitar music filtered into the room and the air was thick with incense.

She lay on the bed, as she was now, her arms raised in sensual languor above her head, her hair spread like a fan across the pillow.

Joginder entered the room from behind a veil of thin, gossamer curtains, his body oiled and silk smooth. He lay down beside her on the bed, kissing her neck, her lips and stroking her hair.

The rest of the fantasy faded into mystery behind the shadowy gauze of the unimaginable. As the images faded, she was left alone with the suffocating heat and a nameless longing.

She tossed and turned into the night and threw her pillow over her head to shut out the deafening murmur of the cicadas. It was dawn before she finally fell asleep.

'I want you to see that Indian tailor for me.'

Adrienne looked up from her book. She felt the blood drain from her face.

Emmanuel held out a blue velvet smoking jacket. 'There is a tear in the lining here. And this pocket needs some work.'

'I can mend it for you.'

'You can't even sew on a button. Take it to the Indian. You can drop it on your way to school in the morning.'

She nodded and looked away, afraid the look in her eyes might betray her.

Joginder's face blossomed into a beatific smile when he saw her walk in. 'Bonjour, *Mademoiselle* Christian.'

'My father wants this jacket repaired.'

'Of course.' He held up the garment and inspected the lining. 'This is not difficult. I will have it ready for him in the morning.'

'The pocket is torn also.'

'I will attend to it.' He smiled again.

She hesitated, even though this was her cue to leave. 'You must be very clever,' she heard herself saying. 'I can't even sew a button on.'

'Perhaps I could teach you.'

Her nerve failed her. 'I have to go to school,' she said and raced from the shop.

The next day, Emmanuel decided to collect the jacket himself.

There was no reason for Adrienne to ever return.

But every day, she walked past the shop on her way to and from school, and she looked up at the hand-painted sign.

It was an exciting game, knowing there was something sinful and forbidden up that dark stairway. Sometimes she lay awake at night wondering what might happen were she ever to climb those stairs again.

It was only a little past noon, but the streets were already steaming from the rain. Vietnamese schoolgirls cycled home in their white silk trousers, and dice rattled in the cafes where French soldiers played *quatre-vingt-et-un.*

As usual, Adrienne stopped at the entrance to the alleyway. She bit her lip, one shoe scuffing the dirt. She had thought out an alibi, what she might say to her father if she ever did return to the tailors.

Of course, she would never do anything, even if she did go back. It was just an entertaining puzzle.

But now she had her story prepared, the temptation to go in was overwhelming. She shifted the satchel on her shoulder and took a deep breath, then set off down the alley.

Joginder was at his workbench when she walked in, bent over a machine. He stared at her in surprise.

'I've come for my lessons,' she said.

Two or three times a week, Adrienne ran up the stairs to the shop on her way home from school, to spend half an hour with Joginder working with needle and thread. She was a clumsy student, but he proved a patient teacher. He was charming and gentle. He did not try to touch her, and she was both relieved and disappointed.

One afternoon, they were sitting side by side at the workbench and Joginder was demonstrating his technique for double stitching. His fingers were nimble and practiced.

'Here. Now you.'

'I can't.'

'Adrienne, you must try.'

She took the needle and bent to the task.

She was suddenly aware of his breath on the hairs at the nape of her neck. It startled her and she pierced the tip of her index finger with the needle.

'You've pricked yourself.'

'It's nothing.'

'You're bleeding.' He took her hand in his. Then he placed her forefinger in his mouth and sucked the tiny spill of blood.

She watched him roll her finger round his tongue, fascinated by the startling pink of his mouth against his white teeth. He lowered her hand and pulled her towards him. Suddenly his mouth was on hers.

She tried to push him away, not because she didn't want him to kiss her, but because he was hurting her. But he pressed himself against her even harder, and her stool toppled backwards onto the floor.

He picked her up and carried her into his bedroom. There was a single wooden cot on the floor between a worktable and some bolts of cloth. He threw her onto it, and his hand tore at the buttons of her silk blouse.

Joginder lay quite still beside her, one arm outstretched, the only movement the rhythmic rise and fall of his chest. There were tiny beads of perspiration on his forehead. His eyelids flickered, and he gave a grunt of satisfaction.

'Do it again,' she said.

His eyes blinked open. 'What?'

She rolled on top of him, and her fingernails traced the droplet of sweat that ran down his cheek.

Adrienne put her bag on the hall stand and walked into her father's library, crossing her hands in front of her in an effort to appear contrite.

Emmanuel was sitting in his wing-backed chair. The bookshelves were bright with leather-bound novels. Reproductions of Van Gogh and Gauguin hung on the walls.

He removed the spectacles from his nose and slammed shut the book on his lap. 'You're almost two hours late,' he said.

'Sorry, Father. I was at the cathedral.'

He frowned, puzzled. 'The cathedral?'

'I was praying for mother. It's ten years since she left us.'

'Yes, I remember.' The mention of his dead wife still made him uncomfortable.

'I promised I would light a candle for her each day this week.'

Emmanuel had not expected such devotion from her. He felt his anger evaporate. 'You should have told me. I almost had the police searching for you.'

'I'm sorry. I had no idea you would be worried.'

He picked up his spectacles and returned to his reading. 'Very well. You may go.' He dismissed her with a wave of his hand.

She hurried from the room. She wanted to run, dance, scream. She was no longer a girl. She was a woman, and she was in love.

The next afternoon, a pretty, young French girl with sable-black hair bounded up the stairs next to the Indian spice shop.

The old Sikh heard her footsteps on the wooden staircase and laughter from upstairs. He scratched irritably and mumbled something into his beard.

Ferengi! They were all pigs.

Joginder locked the door to the shop and followed her into the back room. The green shutters were drawn, and the room was dark and hot. He could scarcely believe his good fortune.

It was a moment to savor. Not only did he get to fuck a beautiful girl, he also got to fuck the French.

CHAPTER 2

September 1946

The Notre-Dame Basilica stood in the square opposite the Post and Telegraph Office. Unlike its Parisian namesake, it was a small, plain building built from red brick. Beggars thronged the steps, appealing to the Christian souls of those who came to pray there.

One afternoon, Adrienne crossed the square on her way home from school, and instead of entering the Rue Le Loi, she walked slowly up the steps of the basilica and into the cool sanctuary of the cathedral.

She stood for a long time in the nave to let her eyes grow accustomed to the gloom. Then she walked along the aisle and sat down at one of the pews under the statue of the Blessed Virgin. She slipped to her knees and bowed her head.

'Mother of God,' she said, 'please don't let this happen. I'll do anything. Please take this sin away.' But she knew it was hopeless. In her mind, God and her father had the same face, and both their judgments were cold and stern.

She knelt on the hard stone, staring at the flickering glow of the candles and allowing her despair to wash over her. What could she do? Her father would never accept Joginder as a match for her. He would try to send her away.

'Holy Mother,' she repeated, 'please take this thing away.'

She got to her feet and went out into the bright afternoon sun.

Mai Ong opened the door and grinned, revealing betel-stained teeth. 'Been at Holy God prayers again?'

Adrienne ignored her. She hated the old woman. 'It's none of your business. Where is my father?'

'He sends message. Work late at office tonight. See, maybe okay stay longer at cathedral.'

She knows, Adrienne thought.

'Bring me some tea. I'll be in the garden.'

The old woman disappeared to the kitchen.

Adrienne went to sit on the veranda and watched absently as parrots swooped and played in the banana palms. She could not accept this foul trick her body had played on her. She should have been more careful. Now it was too late.

Well, it's no good crying about it now, she thought. I have to do something.

She ran upstairs to her bedroom, unlocked the top drawer of her dressing table and took out her jewelry box. Inside was a small gold ring, inlaid with emeralds and amethysts. It had been her mother's. She put it into her purse and went back downstairs.

Mai Ong stood in the kitchen doorway, holding a silver tray and a pot of Chinese tea. 'Where you go?'

'Out,' Adrienne said.

She hoped her mother, up there in heaven, would forgive her for what she was about to do. She knew her father wouldn't.

The following afternoon, Adrienne feigned illness and left school early. Instead of going straight home, she made her way to Cholon, the Chinese quarter. In her purse was five thousand piastres and an address one of her school friends had scribbled for her on a bit of paper.

Cholon was Saigon's grotesque twin. It had once been a separate settlement, but the sprawling mass of slums had kept spreading until the border between the two cities was indistinguishable. It was said that Cholon was more Chinese than Shanghai, and at least one Hollywood mogul had chosen to go there to film a China epic.

Big-bellied children squabbled in the mud alleys between the crumbling rows of shanties and shophouses. People ate, played cards, had their fortunes told, their teeth pulled, and even bathed on the streets. Beggars and dogs squatted side by side in the gutters. Coolies straggled along, bowed under heavy loads.

The address Adrienne had been given was on the Su Van Hahn, near the racecourse. It overlooked a crowded alley where hollow-ribbed dogs sniffed among piles of rubbish. She wrinkled her nose in disgust at the pervading stench of rotting fruit and the sour taint of the nearby fish market.

She entered a crumbling shophouse. It was dark inside, and the shelves along the walls were filled with rows of earthenware jars. The desiccated carcasses of bats and snakes lay piled on a wooden counter. There was the dank, fetid smell of things long dead.

The *bac si* was an ancient Tonkin Chinese with sparse, grey hair and huge, betel-stained teeth like old tombstones. Her face was wrinkled. She wore dirty, blue pajamas. She looked up from the table where she was crushing roots with a mortar and pestle. 'What do you want?' she said in French.

'I need help,' Adrienne said.

The old woman got up and came over. As she got closer, Adrienne saw that she had only one eye. The other was blinded with disease, the eyeball covered with the yellow-opaque membrane of a cataract.

The woman patted her stomach. 'Baby, yes?'

'Yes.' Adrienne took a deep breath. 'I want to get rid of it.'

'Bad joss for you, Missee.' She held out her hand. 'Money?'

Adrienne took out her purse and showed her the five thousand piastres.

The woman shook her head and muttered something in Cantonese. 'You wait,' she said and walked off into the gloom at the back of the shop.

When she reappeared, she had a cracked china cup in her hands. She proffered it to Adrienne as if it were a chalice.

Adrienne took the cup. The liquid was brown-black and smelled of the grave.

'Drink,' the woman said.

Adrienne held the cup to her lips, her stomach revolting at the stench of the potion and the knowledge of the terrible thing she was about to do.

This is a mortal sin, she heard the Mother Superior say. There can be no absolution for this.

She threw the cup onto the floor, turned and ran out of the shop.

Joginder leapt to his feet when he heard the familiar footfall on the stairs. He stood beside his workbench and waited.

'My little lotus,' he said when he saw her. He took her in his arms, but she did not respond. 'Where have you been? I haven't seen you for almost a week.'

Her face was as pale. 'I'm pregnant, Jogi.'

'What?'

She pulled away so she could look into his face. 'I'm going to have a baby. Your baby.'

Joginder forced a smile. 'That's wonderful news.'

She searched his face. 'Is it?'

'Of course.'

'Will you marry me?'

'Yes,' he said, knowing her father would never allow it.

Adrienne threw her arms around his neck.

'It's all right,' he said. 'Everything's all right.' He pulled her closer, aroused. He had thought of nothing but her all week. This was bad news, but he didn't have to do anything about it right now. They had time. He had time.

'Just hold me,' she said.

Joginder locked the door. He led her to the back room and his narrow cot. As soon as they were inside, he began to tear off his clothes.

'Do you love me?' Adrienne said.

'I've never loved anything more.'

'You want this baby, don't you?'

Joginder unbuttoned her blouse. She did not try to resist. 'Yes, my darling, yes,' he said and pushed her back onto the bed.

Downstairs, the old Sikh sat on a stool inside his shop, the metal shutters rolled down against the flattening heat of the afternoon. His somber grey eyes rolled upwards as he heard the bare boards of his ceiling begin to creak once more. For a week, the afternoons had been quiet. Now the girl had come back.

He went to the doorway and spat into the street.

Emmanuel sat in his library in his favorite chair, a leather-bound volume open on his lap. The soft light of the reading lamp accentuated the strands of silver in his neatly combed hair.

Adrienne hovered in the doorway.

He sighed, a long, pained breath. 'What is it, child?'

She had been steeling herself for this moment all day, and now it had come, she didn't know if she could go through with it. How would he react? She couldn't remember seeing him betray any emotion since the day her mother died.

Her hands were clenched so tight she felt her fingernails biting into her palms. The words stuck in her throat.

Emmanuel watched her, his jaw set in a grim line.

'Well, come on, out with it.'

She felt tears welling up, making her eyes sting. 'I'm going to have a baby.'

He sat there, not moving and not saying a word. His face set like stone.

'Say something,' she said.

He rose from his chair, went to the sideboard and poured himself a brandy from a crystal decanter. It was so quiet in the room she could hear the thick, amber liquid swirling around the brandy balloon.

'Whose is it?'

'His name is Joginder.'

'A native. You've been sleeping with one of *les jaunes?*'

He dropped the glass on the cedar floor and took two steps towards her, his hand raised. For a moment she thought he was going to hit her. Her father had never struck her before.

'He's not Vietnamese, he's Indian. And I love him.'

'Love? You don't even know what the word means. How long has this been going on?'

'Ever since I fetched the jacket.'

'The Indian tailor?' He grabbed a fistful of her hair and threw her to the floor. 'You stupid, ungrateful-'

Adrienne stared up at him. A knotted vein bulged at his temple. It was the first time she had ever seen him lose control, and despite her terror, she felt a thrill of satisfaction.

'I love him.'

'You're a shameless little whore!'

There was a long silence.

'Get out,' he said. 'Go to your room.'

She scrambled to her feet. Her knees were shaking. She looked back once and saw her father take her photograph from the sideboard and throw it with force at the wall.

The next morning, Emmanuel sat on the veranda under the heavy wreaths of red and purple bougainvillea, eating one of the croissants he had Mai Ong buy fresh each day from the Givral café. He wore a crisp white tropical suit, and his pith helmet lay on the starched linen tablecloth beside the silver coffee pot. He was reading a week-old copy of *Le Figaro*.

The morning sun filtered through the leaves of the tamarind trees and the garden was vivid with the last of the *flamboyants*.

Adrienne sat down and waited as Mai Ong filled her cup with steaming black coffee.

'Do you want breakfast?' Emmanuel said.

'I'm not hungry.'

He removed his spectacles and leaned back in his chair. 'I am sending you back to France,' he said. 'I will tell your teachers you have gone back for a holiday. When this thing is born, I will arrange for it to be adopted. Afterwards, you may return, and it will be as if nothing has happened.'

'I don't want to go back to France.'

'You should have thought of that before you whored yourself with a native. You have made your bed and now you must lie in it.'

'No.'

'Don't think you can defy me. I will not allow you to shame me in front of all of Saigon. If you want to remain my daughter, you will do precisely as I say.'

He took a fob watch from his waistcoat and glanced at it. Then he leaned forward and drained his coffee cup. 'I will make the arrangements this morning. There is a boat leaving for Marseilles next week.'

'I won't go'.

He picked up his newspaper and slammed it down on the table. Coffee spilled onto the virginal white cloth. 'I will not allow this madness to continue a moment longer. You will remain in this house until it is time for you to leave. I forbid you to see this man again.'

'I want to marry him.'

'And live the rest of your life in one stinking little room?'

'He will be a rich man one day. He has plans. He is going to have shops in Hong Kong and Bombay and-'

'He's a filthy darkie and that's what he will always be.'

She shook her head.

'Do as I say or else you can leave this house and never come back. I will forget that I ever had a daughter.'

Adrienne got to her feet, drawing back her shoulders. 'Very well and I will forget I ever had a father.'

Emmanuel watched her run back up the stairs, his fists clenched in fury.

Let her protest about love all she wants, he thought. This time next week she would be on that boat for France.

He would not have her make him a laughingstock. She might scream and shout but, in the end, she would not give up her fine home to live in squalor with that Indian coolie and his sewing machines.

Joginder was at his workbench by the window, bent over the seams of a new jacket. When he heard footfall on the steps he looked up, assuming the obsequious smile he reserved for his customers.

When he saw that it was Adrienne, his smile fell away. What was she doing here at this hour of the day?

She settled her brown leather suitcase on the floor.

'I need your help.'

He stood up and came towards her. 'Have you told your father-'

'He threw me out,' she said. It was a lie. In fact, he did not yet know she was gone.

'Perhaps he will change his mind when he sees how much you... how much we love each other.'

'Who cares? We don't need him, Jogi. We have each other.'

Joginder took her in his arms. They could not marry, of course. But he did not want it to end, not yet. One day he would have to give up her perfect, white body. But not yet.

It was just a question of how long he could play out the game.

May 1947

The night Michel was born, a storm swept across the city from the China Sea. Adrienne arched her back as another contraction racked her, her screams drowned by the rolling of thunder overhead. She had long ago surrendered her humanity to the pain. The world had become a surreal, nightmare place of unrelenting agony.

For two days, she had labored on the wooden cot, bathed in her own sweat, trying to push the child from her body. But the child would not come, and Adrienne wanted only to die.

Her cries brought one of the nuns.

Her pinched face swam in front of Adrienne's eyes, illuminated by a flash of lightning. The storm was directly above them. Something moved on the roof.

'This is God's judgment on you,' the sister said. 'You must pray for his forgiveness.'

'Please,' Adrienne gasped, 'please do something. Find a doctor!'

'It is God's will,' the sister shouted over the roar of the storm. A doctor? This was a charity ward and there were few enough doctors even for the good hospitals.

The spasm passed and Adrienne gulped in a mouthful of air. There was no escape. The baby was killing her. For forty hours she had been straining and screaming in this stinking charity ward. She didn't care about the baby anymore. She just wanted to be free of the terrible pain.

She felt the onset of another contraction. She crammed her knuckles into her mouth and bit down.

'Pray God for forgiveness,' she heard the nun say, and then she was gone.

She was left alone with her agony and the desolate sound of the rain beating against the window. She sunk her nails into the flesh of her thighs, screamed herself hoarse and cursed the child and the man whose seed it was.

VENOM

The boy was a mirror image of his father. He had the same complexion, with brown eyes and a down of black hair. When Adrienne put him to her breast, he stared back at her the whole time, greedy for her attention and her love.

She wiped away the tears that smeared her cheeks.

'What's wrong, child?'

Soeur Odile was different from the other sisters. She was a kindly woman with florid cheeks and horn-rimmed spectacles.

'Every infant is a gift from God, you know.'

Adrienne wanted to laugh in her face. But when she looked into the old nun's eyes, she realized she meant what she said.

'There are other gifts I would have liked better.'

Odile patted her hand. 'You are fretting. It is not just the baby, is it?'

Adrienne had seen young men visiting the other girls, smiling at their babies, bringing flowers and chocolate. 'Has there been anyone asking for me? An Indian. He's tall. You couldn't forget him if you saw him. He's very handsome.'

Odile shook her head. The sad eyes looked owlish behind the thick lenses of her spectacles.

'His name is Joginder. Joginder Krisnan.'

'No one has been here asking for you, my child. I am sorry.'

Adrienne gripped the nun's hand. 'Can you do something for me?'

'If I can.'

'He has a tailor's shop, near the main square.'

'You want me to go there?'

'Would you? Please. It's not far.'

Odile sighed. 'Very well. I'll see if I can get away later this afternoon. Now you must rest. You have to regain your strength.'

It was evening when *Soeur* Odile returned. She stood by the bed and picked up Adrienne's hand.

Adrienne saw genuine regret in her face.

'I'm sorry,' Odile said. 'I spoke to him. But he says he cannot come at the moment. He is too busy.'

Adrienne nodded and turned her face to the wall.

CHAPTER 3

November 1951

Saigon had once been a quiet village nestling on the banks of the Mekong River. Now its streets bristled with barbed wire and machine guns.

As the war in Tonkin dragged on, a campaign of terror was taking place against the colonial French. Their buildings were bombed, and bloated corpses began to appear in the river. Grenades were thrown into cafés and into cinemas, and each night after the curfew, mortar fire from the surrounding hills crunched into the suburbs.

In the French quarter they barricaded the doors and windows of their villas and settled to a life under siege.

Each day, there was news of some fresh atrocity. A French major staying at the Saigon Royal hired a Vietnamese barber to shave him in his room. Unfortunately for the major, the barber was a Viet Minh agent. The man took the opportunity to draw the cold razor across the officer's throat.

When the proprietor ran into the room, he found the major gurgling and flapping on the floor like a beached fish, surrounded by a widening pool of his own blood.

And that was just the start of it.

Adrienne lay on the narrow bed staring at the flaking paint of the ceiling, its patterns forming grotesque shapes in the shadowy darkness. The fan creaked overhead, almost useless in the thick, damp air. The room was suffocatingly hot even with the shutters thrown wide open, and the sheets were damp with sweat.

Michel gave a small cry, restless in his cot in the corner.

It was past midnight. Joginder turned off the lamp in the workshop and crept in. She watched his silhouette against the shuttered window as he took off his clothes. He was running to fat. Too many long hours at the workbench. And there was a glistening brown patch on his scalp where his hair had begun to thin.

Business was flourishing though, and he had more work than he could handle. He had taught Adrienne to sew buttonholes and measure seams, and now he employed another seamstress at the shop, Sai, a smooth-skinned Vietnamese girl. But even with all the new customers, there never seemed to be enough money.

One day, he promised her, he would be a rich man. It was the only fragment of their dream that had survived.

She wondered when they had stopped loving each other, or even if Joginder had ever truly loved her at all. For a while, after Michel's birth, she thought they had rediscovered the spark. But he had never shown any interest in their son, and as Michel grew, Joginder became more distant.

She told herself it was because he was working so hard, but deep in her heart, she knew the terrible mistake she had made. She stayed with him now out of stubborn pride. She could not bring herself to go back to her father, beg his forgiveness and ask for his help.

She sniffed the gamey taint of sweat as Joginder slipped into the bed beside her. She felt besieged by her own loneliness. She ached for someone to hold her and love her. It had been so long.

'Jogi.'

'I'm tired.'

She reached under the bedclothes an rubbed herself against him. He pushed her away.

'You work too hard,' she said, stung by the rejection.

'A man has to work hard if he's going to succeed.'

'You're ruining your health.'

He didn't answer her, and she thought that he had fallen asleep.

But then he said, 'It's what I've been wanting to tell you. I've bought a ticket on a ship going to Bombay next week. I want to visit my family. I haven't seen them for nearly six years.'

'Your family?'

'I need you to stay here and look after the shop.'

'No, I want to come with you.'

'The voyage will be too difficult. Besides, I cannot close the shop. You are the only one I can trust.'

'How long will you be gone?'

'A month. Perhaps two.'

'I didn't know you had a family there.'

'Everyone has a family. Now, go to sleep.'

'You said that when we get married-'

'I said, go to sleep. We'll talk about it in the morning.'

He rolled away from her.

She listened to the fan creaking overhead and felt as if she was burning up. She thought of her bedroom on the Rue Catinat, the crisp cotton sheets, the smell of the bougainvillea blossom that wreathed the veranda outside her window. The cooling fans on the ceilings.

And she cursed herself for trading all that for a cramped room and an uncaring husband.

Joginder had been away for two weeks when Adrienne finally made up her mind.

She awoke early one morning and bathed before Sai arrived at the shop for the day. She stood naked in the tiny, white-tiled washroom and splashed cold water over her head with the long-handled dipper.

Afterwards, she peered into the cracked mirror and examined her reflection critically. She was twenty-three now. She was not as taut or as supple as she had been before Michel, but she knew she was a very desirable woman. She could still turn men's heads in the street.

But these last few years with Joginder had hollowed her cheeks, and there were tiny lines etched around her eyes. She couldn't afford to waste any more time on him. Her beauty could be her passport back to the life of ease and luxury that she had once so recklessly surrendered.

What a fool she had been. Her romantic daring had been nothing more than a schoolgirl fantasy. It was time to put her pride away and take back all she had lost.

She put on the pale green dress she had last worn the day she had come to live with Joginder and splashed some Joie perfume behind her ears. Then she went to the iron cot in the corner to dress Michel in his best clothes. Two arms reached out eagerly towards her.

The boy's resemblance to his father was startling. Even after four years, she couldn't believe he was hers.

'Come on, little Michel,' she said. '*Maman* is not going to work today. You and I are going out.'

'Where?

'We are going to visit someone very special. You must promise to be on your best behavior. You mustn't shout or scream, and you must remember the manners I taught you. Do you promise?'

He nodded.

She dressed him in a white cotton shirt and blue shorts, then stood back and nodded, satisfied.

She had passed her father's villa on the Rue Catinat every day for the past four years on her way to the market. Sometimes she saw a shadow move behind one of the windows and wondered if her father was watching her. Twice she had passed him on the street, but he had not spoken to her or even looked in her direction. She had been tempted to grab him by the shoulders and make him talk to her, but her pride wouldn't allow it.

Now, as she walked up the long drive between the banana palms, she felt a familiar pang. The neat gardens were rimmed with pale orange and yellow tiger flowers. So beautiful.

She stood on the porte-cochere and took a deep breath to steady her nerves. She wondered what her father would do when he saw her.

'Shoulders back,' she said to Michel. The boy thrust out his chest and gripped her hand even tighter.

She set down her suitcase and rang the bell.

Mai Ong opened the door. Her face twisted into a malicious grin. 'So, missy, you come back?'

Adrienne drew herself up to her full height. 'Tell my father I'm here.'

The *boyesse* looked down at Michel. 'This belong you now?'

Adrienne took a step forward. She wanted to slap her. 'Just tell my father I want to see him.'

'You still damn fine manners.'

Mai Ong turned and shuffled across the marble-floored hallway. 'You wait. Master on veranda, breakfast time. Maybe he not want to see you.'

So, it's come to this, Adrienne thought. Begging the help for an interview with my own father. Treated like a tramp, which is what everyone thinks I am.

She peered inside, trying to remember. The door to the library was open, and she could see her father's chair and the shelves of leather-bound history books. It was cool, and the house had a cathedral quiet. She suddenly missed it all so much that she could hardly breathe. She fought back tears of self-pity.

'So. You've come back.'

Emmanuel was standing in the hallway, his hands clasped behind his back. He wore a crisply starched white tropical suit, and his silver-grey hair was meticulously parted.

'Hello, Father.'

He looked down at the child beside her and frowned. 'Is this your brat?'

'His name is Michel.'

'It's a French name. The child is obviously not.'

'I want to come back.'

'Oh, I see. You've finally come to your senses.'

I had forgotten how much I detest you, she thought. Just one smile, one moment of tenderness, and I would have dissolved in tears at your feet. 'I won't beg,' she said.

He sighed. 'Your experience of the seamier side of life hasn't changed you.' He stood there, tapping his foot, pretending to make up his mind. 'Very well. Not the child, though.'

'What do you mean?'

'He's a darkie. You can't bring him into this house.'

Adrienne tightened her grip on Michel's hand. 'But I'm his mother.'

'Yes, that's the whole problem, isn't it? You can come back if that is what you wish. But you must leave the child with its father.'

Adrienne wanted to protest but no words would come. It had never occurred to her that he would make such a demand.

She couldn't do it. Michel was her son. She picked up her suitcase. 'As you wish.' She dragged Michel away.

'Adrienne!'

She turned around, hoping that he was about to relent. But the expression on his face crushed any false hope.

'When you have had enough, give the urchin back to its father or to the orphanage, whatever you wish. Then you can come home.'

She hurried away, clutching Michel's hand, the little boy running to keep up.

Sai was bent over the Singer when Adrienne got back to the shop.

'You have been crying,' she said.

'It's nothing.'

Sai frowned. 'Joginder should have taken you with him.'

She's goading me, Adrienne thought. Something in the girl's tone alarmed her. 'It's none of your business what Mr. Krisnan wishes to do. Get on with your work.'

Sai shrugged and pouted at her.

Adrienne went into the suffocating bedroom and closed the door behind her. She dropped her case onto the floor, threw herself down on the bed and slammed both her fists into her pillow.

'That cold, bloody bastard!'

'*Maman*, what is wrong?' Michel stood beside the bed, his eyes wide. 'Why are you crying?' His fingers stroked her hair.

What am I going to do with this child, she thought. He has no legal father, no nationality, no existence outside the handwritten entry in the records of the Catholic hospital.

She pulled him close and felt the beat of his heart against her cheek.

'What am I going to do with you?' she said aloud.

There was a knock on the door. It inched opened.

'What are you doing here?' Adrienne said. 'Get back to work.'

But Sai didn't move. 'I have to talk to you,' she said. 'It's about Joginder.'

'What about him?'

'You know what he's doing, don't you? He has a wife in Bombay. That's why he went back.'

Adrienne felt a chill run through her. 'What are you talking about?'

'He told me all about her. Her name is Sushila.'

'Why should he tell you anything?'

Sai did not answer. But as Adrienne stared at her pretty face and soft willowy figure, she understood.

'I just want to help you, *mademoiselle*.'

'I'm sure you do.'

'I'll get back to work now.' Sai closed the door. A few moments later, the sewing machine clattered back to life in the shop.

Adrienne stared at the flaking plaster of the walls and saw her father's face in the grim patterns. He was smiling.

Two weeks later Joginder returned. He got back one night and slipped silently into bed beside her. A few minutes later, he was snoring.

The next morning, he got up at dawn and went to work in the shop without a word.

Adrienne put on her green dress and went to stand beside him at the workbench.

He lifted his eyes from the half-finished shirt on the table and put down his needle and thread. 'My little lotus. Do you have a kiss for your husband?'

'No.'

'Are you still angry with me?'

'I want to know if you have a wife.'

'Where did you get such an idea?'

'From Sai.'

'She's been talking about me while I've been away, has she?' He reached for her hand. 'We'll discuss it later.'

She pushed him away. 'I want to know the truth.'

He sighed. 'Of course, I have a wife. We were married in India when I was thirteen years old.'

'Why didn't you tell me?'

'Because it doesn't matter.'

'You denied me marriage all these years.'

'It was arranged by my family. I don't love her. She's fat and has a sharp tongue.'

'Then why don't you divorce her?'

'I can't.'

She suddenly understood why there had never been any money. He had been sending it all back to India.

'But you said you loved me.'

'I do love you. But I have my sons to think of. My real sons.'

'Your sons?'

'I told you. We were thirteen when we were married.'

'You pig.'

His face underwent a change. When he spoke again his voice was quiet. 'Do not speak to me that way again.'

'You knew you couldn't marry me. You let me make a fool of myself.'

'You are not Hindu. My religion forbids it.'

For a moment she was too stunned to speak. She had sacrificed everything for him, even turned her back on her own prejudices to be with him. She had lowered herself. Now he was telling *her* she wasn't good enough.

'You ignorant coolie,' she said. 'What have you done to me?'

Joginder jumped to his feet and smashed his fist into her face. She hurtled back across the floor and blacked out.

When she opened her eyes, he was standing over her, his face contorted with rage. 'Don't you ever call me that, you French whore!' He hit her again, this time with the back of his hand. She tasted blood in her mouth.

She scrambled to her feet. Her fingers closed around a pair of scissors on the workbench. He tried to stop her, but he was too slow. She slashed at him.

His brought his arm up to protect himself and her hand struck his forearm, knocking the scissors out of her grasp. They clattered out of sight under the workbench. He grabbed her and twisted her hand behind her back. She thought her arm was going to break.

'You little bitch!' he hissed. 'I'll teach you a lesson.' He pulled her towards the bedroom.

'Get off me!'

She managed to wriggle away, but then he hit her again, a savage blow that put her on her knees. He dragged her across the floor and threw her face-down onto the bed. He pulled up her nightgown and pinned her with his own weight.

'This is what you wanted, isn't it?' he whispered in her ear. 'A black lover?'

He coiled his fingers in her hair and forced her head back.

She felt herself gagging, choking for breath. There was a sharp, terrible agony as he forced himself inside her. She clawed at the sheets and tried to roll away from him, but he pulled her head further back until she begged him to stop.

As he pounded at her, she thought about her father's library, the drifting aroma of his Havana cigars, the summer birds in the garden among the yellow tiger flowers, the smell of fresh-ground coffee and her soft bed with its clean, white cotton sheets.

He ground his hips into her and gave a dry scream, then collapsed, panting, on top of her.

She heard a child crying. Michel was watching them through the bars of his cot. She reached out a hand to try to comfort him, but it was Sai who hurried into the room to pick him up and gentle him. Her face was creased into a secret smile.

Adrienne's humiliation was complete.

CHAPTER 4

Michel stood up in his cot and watched his mother step naked from the bed. His large, solemn eyes followed her to the dressing table in the corner. He adored his mother. He loved watching her dress, loved the strange, magic smell of her. She was the only beautiful thing in the whole world.

Sometimes at night he watched her sleeping next to his father. Yesterday he had hurt her again. He remembered the noises and his mother's face turned towards him, her eyes tight shut, her lips working in a silent scream. Once before, he had cried out in the middle of it and they had stopped, so he tried hard every night from then on to stay awake and protect her from him.

He hated him.

The times he loved best were when they were alone, as they were now. Joginder had gone to the temple to pray to Ganesh. The sun had not yet risen, and the sky was stained a smoky violet. It was already oppressively hot. A droplet of perspiration trickled between his mother's breasts.

He watched contentedly as she combed out the long, silky hair that fell around her bare shoulders. She slipped on her green dress and threw some clothes into a suitcase.

'Where are we going, *Maman?*'

'Michel, I didn't know you were awake.'

'Are we going to see grandfather?'

'Not today. I have to go out.'

'Can I come?'

'No, you must stay here and be good boy for me.' She bent down next to his cot. 'I have to go away for a little while. You'll be all right. Your father will take good care of you.'

He stared at her in shock. He knew he had to stop her, but he was trapped by the iron bars of the cot.

'No, *Maman!* No!'

She picked up her suitcase and hurried to the door.

He could not believe this was happening. The only beautiful thing in the world was leaving him.

She stood in the doorway, her face wet with tears. For a moment, he thought she was going to come back for him, and he held out his arms to her. Then the door slammed shut and he heard her clatter down the wooden stairs in her high heels and out into the alley.

His shrieks of despair echoed around the tiny room long after she was gone.

When Joginder returned from his devotions later that morning, he could hear the boy's screams from the street.

The fat Sikh merchant was rolling up the iron shutters of his shop-house. 'Your little brat's been screaming like that all morning,' he said.

'I'll see to it, I'll see to it,' Joginder said. He ran up the wooden steps to the shop.

Sai was at her place at the workbench, bent over the foot-pedal Singer machine.

'What's going on?' Joginder said. 'What's that row?'

'I tried to gentle him, but he won't let me near him. He bit me.' She showed him the angry red mark on her arm.

'Where is Adrienne?'

'She's gone.'

'Gone where?'

'I saw her on the stairs when I got here this morning. She had a suitcase with her. She said to tell you that she was never coming back.'

Joginder threw open the bedroom door. Michel was standing up in the iron-framed cot, his face flushed beet-red from his screaming. His eyes were wild like an animal's. When he saw Joginder, he threw himself backwards and banged his head against the bars, over and over.

'Shut up!' Joginder shouted.

Michel kept screaming and banging his head, so Joginder slapped him as hard as he could with the flat of his hand. It only silenced him for a moment. Then he started howling again.

'She's gone back to her father,' Sai said.

Joginder whirled around. 'Why didn't you try to stop her?'

'It was what we wanted.'

'It was what *you* wanted.'

The bitch had abandoned him with her brat. Well, if she thought he was going to take care of him, she was very wrong.

'What are you going to do?' Sai said.

Joginder's nose wrinkled in disgust. The boy had soiled his pajamas. 'Get him out of here.'

'And take him where?'

'I don't care what you do with him, just get him out of here.'

'You mean, the orphanage?'

'If you like. Or you can throw him in the street. Just get rid of him.'

Later that morning, when the boy was gone, Joginder's good humor returned. He felt as if a huge burden had been lifted from his shoulders. He whispered some prayers of thanks to the picture of Ganesh that hung on the wall over his workbench and lit incense beneath the image as a token of his appreciation.

December 1951

It was a Sunday afternoon and the heat hung in a misty haze. The peal of the cathedral bells drifted across the city. The broad tamarind-shaded streets were crowded with trundling *cyclopousses* and horse-drawn traps, the clatter of horses' hooves drowning out the cries of the street hawkers. In the far distance the grey sprawl of Cholon melted into the limpid indigo of the sea.

Adrienne and Emmanuel sat under the slow fans on the terrace of the Continental Hotel, looking over the Rue Catinat. Adrienne sipped her *vin blanc*, ignoring the stares from around the restaurant.

The French colony, like every bastion of expatriates, thrived on gossip, and Emmanuel Christian's infamous daughter had become a major topic of conversation in every salon and club.

Emmanuel, immaculate as always in his tropical whites, appeared oblivious to the stares and whispers. But she knew he would be dying inside.

'You are very quiet,' he said.

'Am I?'

'I'm sorry if you find my company tiresome. It is perhaps not as exotic as you are accustomed to.'

'What do you want from me? You insist on parading me in public in this fashion. Do you want me to laugh and giggle with you like a schoolgirl?'

'Of course, I do not expect gratitude. That would be foolish of me.'

'Gratitude?'

'Yes, gratitude. Please be good enough to keep your voice down.'

'What am I supposed to be grateful for? Do you want me to thank you for throwing me out of my own home and forcing me to abandon my-'

She could not bring herself to say it. She sipped her *citron pressé* and composed herself. The glass trembled in her hand.

'You left me no choice. And you can't hide away for the rest of your life. It is best you are seen in polite company again. Let them talk all they want. They'll soon get tired of it. Anyway, it is not the past I wish to discuss with you. It is the future.'

'Oh?'

'You are young. You can still make something of your life.'

'My life? Is it really mine?'

Emmanuel sighed. 'Look at you. You used to be such a pretty girl. What are you doing to yourself? You don't eat enough and there are rings under your eyes.'

'I can't sleep.'

'Do you want to see a doctor?'

She shook her head, feeling the tears coming again.

'You look pale and thin.'

It was true. She had let herself go a little, but she couldn't summon the strength for anything anymore. She woke most nights, thinking she could hear Michel crying. Sometimes, in her half-sleep, she stumbled out of bed and fumbled around the bedroom looking for his cot, before she remembered where she was, and that Michel was not really there.

Whenever she closed her eyes, she could see the look on his face the day she left and hear his screams as she ran down the steps away from him.

Now there were other things to worry about. She had missed her period. Had Joginder's final insult been the planting of another seed?

She looked over the balustrade at the traffic below. A bus swerved out of a side street and sent a cyclist sprawling headlong onto the road. There was a chorus of yells, klaxon horns and cycle bells as rickshaws and Renaults swerved around him. The bus driver leapt out, screaming and gesticulating.

Miraculously, the fallen man picked himself up and retrieved his crumpled bicycle. The bus driver ran over, laughing, and patted him on the back, congratulating him on his lucky escape. The cyclist grinned back, shook his hand and trotted away, pushing his wrecked machine.

'That's the difference between the Westerner and the Asiatic,' Emmanuel said. 'It is impossible for them to take responsibility for their own actions. The bus driver was to blame, yet he and the poor wretch he knocked into the road treated that whole incident as if it was an act of God. The one on the bicycle thinks the gods are in his side now and will go home and bet his last piastre in a card game.'

'You sound like a professor.'

'I'm merely trying to point out to you, as gently as possible, why your love affair with that loathsome Indian was doomed from the start. You were just another bicycle on his road, my dear.'

A shadow fell across the table. Adrienne looked up.

'*Monsieur* Christian,' a man said.

Emmanuel turned around. 'Ah, Jean-Claude. *Ca va?*'

'*Oui, ça va bien.*'

'I believe you have not had the pleasure of meeting my daughter. Adrienne, this is Jean-Claude Breton. He is on my staff at the bureau.'

The man bowed.

'Won't you join us for a glass of wine?' Emmanuel said.

'Thank you, but no,' Jean-Claude said. 'I am here on business. An important journalist from *Le Figaro* arrived in Saigon today. I have to meet him and brief him on the situation in Tonkin. *Desolé.*'

'You work too hard,' Emmanuel chided gently. 'Well done.'

Jean-Claude looked at Adrienne. She waited, thinking he was about to say something to her.

Instead, he blushed and looked away. 'Well, I must go,' he said. 'Until this evening, then.' He walked quickly towards the stairs, tripping on the top step.

'A very bright young man,' Emmanuel said. 'I have invited him for dinner. He wants to meet you.'

Mai Ong placed the saffron-colored chicken on the table and scurried out of the room to fetch the rice.

Emmanuel picked up a bottle of red burgundy and refilled Jean-Claude's glass. 'To France,' he said.

'To France,' Jean-Claude said. They drank.

Adrienne watched their guest over the rim of her glass. Jean-Claude Breton was younger than she had first thought. He had delicate, pale skin that would have made him appear almost feminine but for the wispy moustache on his upper lip. He had a sparse frame and his cream double-breasted suit hung loosely on his shoulders. He directed his conversation at her father, but at times during the meal she looked up and found him staring at her. As soon as she caught his eye, he looked away again, flustered.

She knew, of course, why her father had invited him. He wanted to marry her off and finally wash his hands of her. She wondered that he could be so desperate as to choose this one.

She ate slowly, trying to appear interested in the conversation. They were discussing the reporter who had arrived at the Continental that morning. She stifled a yawn.

But nothing escaped Emmanuel. 'I hope we're not boring you with all this talk,' he said.

'No, of course not,' she said. 'It's fascinating.'

'Jean-Claude is one of my best officers. I shall be sorry to lose him.'

She turned to Jean-Claude. 'You have been promoted?'

'I am to take over our office in Dakar. In Senegal.'

'He is one of the youngest men ever to head a regional bureau,' Emmanuel said. 'He has a great future.'

'My congratulations.' She smiled and raised her glass in toast. Africa, she thought. He really does want me out of the way.

After the coffee, Emmanuel excused himself to smoke a cigar on the veranda.

'I'll join you, sir,' Jean-Claude said.

'No, no. Stay here and keep my daughter company. I shan't be long.'

They listened to his footfall on the stone flags outside.

Jean-Claude drummed on the polished teak of the table with his fingertips. Adrienne sat back in her chair, and on an impulse, she folded her arms, accentuating the creamy swell of her cleavage against the blue *crêpe-de-chine* of her evening gown. She watched a rash of perspiration, like tiny blisters, erupt on Jean-Claude's forehead.

'That's a very pretty dress,' he said finally.

'Thank you.'

His gambits were exhausted. He looked nervously around the room. She felt suddenly sorry for him. 'When do you go to Dakar?'

'Three more weeks.' Then he added, 'I shall be sorry to go now.'

'Oh, why?'

'I should like to see you again.'

'Perhaps you shall,' she said, knowing it was out of the question. 'May I have some more wine?'

His hands were shaking, and he poured too quickly. The burgundy splashed into the glass and some of it spilled on her dress. She jumped up and hurried to the bathroom to wash off the stains. She didn't wait to listen to his mumbled apology.

***

'He's clumsy and he's impossible to talk to,' Adrienne said. 'I don't know why you ever invited him here.'

'It seems you have not learned your lesson after all.'

'What lesson?'

'That romance does not put a roof over your head or food on your table. Jean-Claude is a decent young man with a great career ahead of him. And for some reason he thinks you are the apex of femininity.'

'He may be a pleasant enough gentleman. I want something more in a man.'

'Someone who can mend a suit perhaps.' Emmanuel picked up a crystal decanter and poured himself a brandy. He eased himself into his wing-back chair.

'I will find my own husband.'

'You don't understand a thing, do you? You cannot stay in Saigon. Everyone knows about you here. You have a reputation. It is precisely why Jean-Claude Breton is such an excellent choice. In three weeks, he will be in Dakar. You can start a new life without insults and innuendo following you wherever you go.'

'No one has insulted me.'

'I have not given them the opportunity. But Saigon is a provincial French village surrounded by Asians. You will never outlive your past. Not here.'

She got up. 'I'm tired, I think I shall go to bed.'

He put a hand on her arm. 'If you won't do it for your own sake, think about me.'

She gave him a bitter smile. 'I wondered when we'd get to that.'

CHAPTER 5

Emmanuel made his way along the Rue Pasteur, a tall and arresting figure among the junior Vietnamese clerks in ill-fitting white shirts, all heading home from the government offices after their day's work. Old women in conical straw hats sold balloons on the footpath, while their daughters hawked cigarettes. A lorry full of Algerian soldiers rumbled past.

He was lost to his own thoughts. He wondered what it was he had done to deserve such a willful and immoral daughter. He had given her everything, sent her to a fine school, bought her the best clothes, taught her the impeccable manners that could have been her passport to the highest strata of French society. In return she had disgraced him, blighted his career, turned him into an outcast and a pariah in the community where he had once been so respected and admired.

After all she had done, he had still forgiven her and allowed her to return to his home. And how had she repaid him? With ingratitude. She was utterly impossible. There was no reasoning with her.

He passed the Café Givral. Its windows were covered with a fine mesh grille to prevent a repetition of the previous month's catastrophe when a grenade had been tossed inside. Six soldiers had been killed and sixteen others seriously wounded.

It was the hour of the aperitif. The crowds had returned, and the café was packed with *fonctionnaires* like himself and a few officers from the French Expeditionary Corps. It was now considered a good spot to eat as people believed that lightning never struck twice in the same place. A German legionnaire sat at one of the bentwood tables on the pavement, clicking his fingers imperiously for service.

The evening sky was lemon-grey, the shadows long.

Emmanuel did not see the Vietnamese in the grey cotton shirt step out from the alley beside the Givral and toss a grenade casually into a doorway a few yards away.

There was a thunderous explosion, and a bright sheet of light hurt his eyes. Something hit him hard in the side of the chest. He fell on his back. He thought that a cyclist had run up on the pavement and collided with him. He started to swear at his unseen assailant but the words would not come. He could not even move.

The sky turned black. He did not know he was dying, nor did he hear the screams of the injured lying beside him on the pavement, writhing in pools of their own blood.

Adrienne sat on the veranda, her face empty.

She still expected him to walk through the French windows at any moment, wearing his velvet smoking jacket or his white topee, clutching a copy of *Le Figaro*, his face set in that frown of disapproval. She supposed she should feel some remorse for the way she had treated him or at least a sense of relief that he could no longer exercise his will over her. Instead, she just felt numb.

He had been dead for a fortnight. His funeral had come and gone in a blur. The lawyer had read the will. She had been shocked to learn that her father had placed conditions on his estate, stipulating that she would not receive a single franc until the day of her marriage to a French national. Without such a match, the money would remain in trust.

If that was not enough bad news, she was now certain that she was pregnant again. The French administration was preparing to repatriate her to France. By the time she returned to Paris, she would be four months along and with no private means.

'Who's going to want you when you're carrying some dirty native's child?' she heard her father say from somewhere beyond the grave.

Mai Ong appeared suddenly from inside the house. 'Missy, *Monsieur* Breton here to see you.'

Jean-Claude wore a black suit and tie, enduring his discomfort out of respect for her father. Perspiration glistened on his forehead, and his cheeks were flushed pink in the heat. He dabbed at his face with a white handkerchief.

'*Mademoiselle*,' he said and bowed. 'I've come to pay my respects and see how you are. The loss of your father was a tragedy. He was one of the most respected men in the department.'

'Thank you, *Monsieur* Breton,' she said. 'Won't you sit down?' She looked at Mai Ong. 'Bring us a jug of *citron pressé*.'

The old woman went inside, mumbling under her breath.

'I don't think she approves of me,' Jean-Claude said.

'She doesn't approve of anyone. My father was the only one who could do anything with her.'

'Your poor *papa*. It was a barbaric attack. It must be terrible for you.'

She nodded. He is so earnest, so sincere, she thought. It is a pity he is also so dull.

'What will you do now?'

'They are sending me back to France.'

'Do you have family there?'

She shrugged her shoulders. 'An uncle, but I haven't seen him for more than twelve years. I do not even know if he is still alive.'

'I am sure your father has provided for you.'

She forced a smile. 'Yes, he made provisions.'

Mai Ong hobbled back carrying a tray with a pitcher of lemonade and two glasses.

After she had gone, Adrienne said, 'Why did you come, really?'

He seemed startled by her directness. 'I wanted to make sure you were all right. If see there is anything I can do.'

'It is very kind of you,' she said and gave him the benefit of a radiant smile. 'I appreciate it, Jean-Claude.' She reached out and lightly touched his hand.

It pleased him so much he sent the pitcher of lemonade crashing to the floor.

Adrienne saw Jean-Claude every day for the next week. There were lunches at the Ramuncho and the Valenco, dinners at the Continental and the Caravelle. He was attentive and courteous. He did not once try to kiss her.

She grew impatient. Time was running out. She had received notification that her ship would sail the following Wednesday. She calculated that she had four days to become *Madame* Breton.

It was not a decision she had taken lightly. But her father's machinations and a cruel twist of fate had left her no choice.

If she married Jean-Claude now, before she began to show, she would have the security of a husband as well as satisfy the conditions of her father's will. Of course, when he found out about the baby, she would have some talking to do. But by then it would be too late for him to reconsider.

She was shocked at her own pragmatism. She was no longer the dewy-eyed romantic she had been at eighteen. Her father had been right all along, she could see that now. She had been a fool. Besides, even if she didn't love Jean-Claude, she was sure she could learn to be fond of him. And it was clear that he wanted her.

If only he would hurry up and say so.

That Sunday, they strolled hand-in-hand through the *Jardins Botaniques*. Vietnamese girls in flowing silk *ao-dai* rode their bicycles along the shaded paths, their boyfriends looking slightly ridiculous beside them, dressed in shorts, cotton shirts and trilby hats. High above them, cranes built their nests in the topmost branches of the trees.

The park had a Sunday school atmosphere. There were kiosks selling tributes of artificial flowers. White-bearded fortune tellers sat on cane chairs peering into their customers' eyes with magnifying glasses.

Jean-Claude steered her towards a shaded path, his heart hammering in his chest. He had never felt this nervous in his whole life.

He took a deep breath. 'Adrienne, there is something I want to say to you.' His mouth was so dry, he could hardly speak. 'Soon you'll be leaving to go back to France, and I will be going to Dakar. We may never meet again.'

'Will you miss me?'

'Oh yes,' he said, looking down at the wonderful, dark-haired girl at his side. He had never seen anything so beautiful. 'Oh yes, very much.'

'What about your other girls? Will you miss them too?'

He flushed. 'There are no others.'

'I don't believe you.'

'I mean it. I love only you.' There, it was said. He hurried on, 'I've never felt this way about any woman before.' He waited for her to turn away.

Instead, she looked intently into his eyes. 'Do you really love me?'

'You know I do.'

'There are many things about me you do not know.'

'Nothing that could make me feel differently about you.'

Of course, he had heard the stories. Everyone in Saigon had heard about Emmanuel Christian's daughter. There were even rumors of a love child with one of the natives.

Jean-Claude did not care. It was this stigma that had attracted him. It gave him an advantage over her. It made her attainable in a way that other beautiful women were not.

Just last night, on the terrace of the Continental Hotel, he had seen two young men, foreign newspapermen, steal glances in her direction. He had seen the envy in their faces. Jean-Claude had been clumsy around women all his life and having a woman that other men wanted was a new experience for him.

'What are you saying?'

'Adrienne,' he began and swallowed hard. 'Will you marry me?' Before she could say anything, he added, 'You do not have to answer straight away.'

She took his hands in hers and smiled.

'I already know my answer.'

Adrienne watched Joginder assume his usual expression of servility as she ascended the stairs. It quickly changed to surprise and then contempt. Behind him, Sai's foot-pedal machine stammered into silence.

She folded the parasol she had brought with her to protect herself from the worst of the noon day sun and looked around the room. It was filled with the ghosts of sour memories. The reek of cardamom and turmeric made her want to vomit.

It had taken all her resolve to come back here. She had to see her son just once more, try to explain things to him, make sure he was all right.

'What are you doing here?' Joginder said.

'I am leaving Saigon. I am to be married.'

He shrugged his indifference.

'I want to see Michel before I go.'

He scratched at his belly. 'Why?'

'I want to say goodbye.'

'I don't know where he is.'

'What do you mean, you don't know?'

'I warned you. It's not my fault. If you wanted him so badly, you should have taken him with you.'

Adrienne stared at the snarling face of the man she once thought she had loved. 'No,' she said, 'you didn't.'

'He was your brat. I never wanted him. You knew that.'

'He was your son.'

'I already have two sons. What do I want with another one?'

She slumped against the wall. 'Oh, God, where is he?'

'I told you. I don't know. Now go on, go. I don't want you here anymore.'

She stumbled back down the stairs and stood on the Rue Catinat, numb, as Saigon bustled around her.

What had she done.

June 1952

Soeur Gabrielle watched a small boy walk across the quadrangle below and throw himself into a corner. It was the one called Michel. He had been brought there, pale and starving, six months before. The Vietnamese woman who brought him said he was French, for Heaven's sake.

VENOM

Sometimes Gabrielle found it hard to keep her faith in a loving God amongst so much misery. She had been born in Saigon and seen suffering every day in all its squalid forms. Two of her brothers had been opium addicts, and she had watched them waste away to skeletons. She had looked on as three of her fellow nuns were raped and butchered by invading Japanese soldiers at Hue.

Despair had been in her blood long before that. Her grandfather had been beaten to death while working as a contract laborer on a plantation in the Rung Sat during the rubber boom of the 1920s. Violence and degradation were as much a part of Vietnam as *nuoc mam* and *ao-dai*.

Now the on-going war between the Viet Minh and the French had made so many orphans. Here, at least, the children had a little food and some shelter. Still, she wondered what she was saving them for. It was sinful to think that way, she knew. One must have faith.

But that little boy down there would never survive. He hardly ate and had made no friends among the other children. He spoke to no one. She could scarcely guess at what he thought of the world and his place in it. She watched his head drop between his knees. He looked like a beaten dog.

No, that one wouldn't survive.

PART 2

Michel and Valentine: 1954-64

CHAPTER 6

'The boy is an animal. A beast. I do not know what we are to do with him.' The *canonesse* gripped the rosary beads in her lap. 'Well, go on. Speak your mind.'

Soeur Gabrielle had never seen her as agitated as this. 'I do not know what to say, Mother. I know the boy is difficult, but I'm sure that-'

'He has been with us more than three years. In that time, he has caused us more trouble than all the hundreds of children who have been here.'

Gabrielle bowed her head. 'Yes, Mother.'

The *canonesse* tapped impatiently on the edge of her desk. 'I look in his eyes and I see evil.'

'He is only a boy, Mother.'

'Yes, but one day he will be a man.'

The older nun got to her feet and went to the window. She listened to the sweet sound of the children's voices singing 'O Holy Night' in the chapel. She was proud of Le Sacré-Coeur. The orphanage provided shelter for a hundred and fifty children, orphans of the war or the unwanted half-caste *métis* of French soldiers.

There was a name for them, *bui doi,* the dust of life. The beaten, the starving, the crippled.

The nuns had given shelter and succor to as many as they could. But this one was different. He spat their kindness back into their faces, refused food as often as he took it, even though his bones were visible through his skin, and he cursed and struck at them with his fists. Only *Soeur* Gabrielle could get anywhere near him.

'What do you wish me to do?' Gabrielle said.

'I don't know. I pray for him constantly. As yet I have not heard the answer.'

'He suffers, Mother.'

'All these children suffer. Yet I have never seen such hatred, such venom in a child. I am worried about the other children here. His presence is having a poisonous effect on them.'

Gabrielle looked up at the wall. A small, white lizard darted from a crack in the ceiling and dashed for cover behind a cheap print of the Blessed Virgin. 'Have you heard any more from the French Immigration, Mother?'

Two years ago, they had applied to have the boy repatriated to France, because of his obviously European blood.

The *canonesse* shook her head. Such processes were notoriously slow.

'Perhaps soon.'

'Perhaps, Sister. That may be the answer for us, but I fear it will not be the answer for whoever else his life touches.'

Shouts echoed across the quadrangle from one of the classrooms. Moments later there was the sound of running feet on the cloister and *Soeur* Thérèse threw open the door.

'Mother, come quickly!'

'What is it? What has happened?'

'Michel has stabbed Kam with a knife!'

Michel sat on a stool in the empty classroom staring at the dull, red terracotta tiles. There was a bright splash of blood by the window.

Gabrielle watched the *canonesse* approach the small boy. She was holding a bone-handled knife in her right hand.

'Where did you get this?'

Michel looked up at her, his expression sullen. 'I stole it from the kitchen.'

'In God's name, what were you doing? You could have killed your classmate.'

'They were reciting their lessons, Mother,' Thérèse said. 'Michel was having difficulty with his reading.'

'You stabbed Kam because he laughed at you?'

Michel didn't answer. The hooded eyes stared back at her, dark and malevolent.

The *canonesse* turned to Thérèse. 'How is Kam?'

'The knife cut his arm. It is not serious.'

'Take the knife back to the kitchen.'

After she had gone, the *canonesse* looked at Gabrielle. 'I must send him away.'

'Please, Mother. Give him one more chance. For the love of God.'

The *canonesse*'s hand went to the wooden crucifix at her neck. For a moment she seemed undecided. 'You shame me, Sister,' she said at last. 'Very well. I hope your faith will prove justified.'

Gabrielle bowed her head in gratitude. She knelt down in front of the boy. The ragged white T-shirt looked oversized on his loose frame, and the legs stuck out of his baggy shorts like stalks.

'Michel,' she said softly, 'you must understand, we want to help you. We love you. The *canonesse* loves you. I love you.'

'You love everyone.'

'Yes. Yes, I do.'

'So what good is your love to me?'

She did not know how to answer that. Finally, she said, 'You must trust us, Michel.'

The boy hawked deep in his throat and spat in her face.

The *canonesse* gasped.

Gabrielle bowed her head and very deliberately wiped the spittle from her forehead with the hem of her robe. Then she leaned forward and kissed Michel's cheek.

There was never a time that Michel decided his mother was not coming back for him. He convinced himself that one day she would appear at the gates to fetch him and explain how it had all been a terrible mistake.

The realization of her betrayal did not come to him suddenly. His psyche would not allow it. It grew slowly, a bitter seed that took slow root deep in his soul and blossomed, like all terrible hurts, into a venomous rage.

The nuns were kind to him, but that only made him despise them more. He knew they were only trying to make him like them, so they could hurt him too. They were women and women could not be trusted.

The other children learned to leave him alone, terrified of his sudden, violent outbursts. Even the nuns were frightened of him.

Except *Soeur* Gabrielle. She didn't seem to mind his curses and insults. No matter what he did, she took his part. Michel decided she must be crazy.

But then, today, she had shaken him.

He could still see her, the fleck of spittle running down her smooth forehead, her face set in that half-smile, the sunlight from the window glinting on her spectacles. He saw her wipe away his spit with her *ao-dai*, could feel the tenderness with which she kissed him. She might as well have kicked him in the chest.

Now, as he lay on his back in the darkened dormitory and listened to the sobs of the smaller children, crying like they did every night, like he had done when he first came here, he felt the stirrings of doubt. He stared at the moon, framed by the open window beside his bed, and made up his mind.

The line of children snaked across the cobbled courtyard. Gabrielle stood in the shade of the cloister, behind a wooden trestle, spooning watery rice porridge into the children's enamel bowls with a ladle. The sun had barely risen, but already the street beyond the gates was crowded with bicycles, *cyclopousses* and bent women in straw hats pushing their hand carts to the market.

She was about to pour another spoonful of the porridge and stopped. The little boy standing in front of her did not have his bowl with him. It was Michel. He always kept his head down, but this morning he looked openly into her face. Suddenly he reached out, grabbed her hand and kissed it. Then he turned and fled.

Gabrielle stared after him in amazement.

'The Lord be praised.'

She turned around. It was Thérèse.

'You see, Sister,' Gabrielle said, 'miracles can happen.'

From that moment on, she gained a second shadow. Michel would be at her side first thing every morning, helping her dole out the rice porridge for breakfast, and then silently trailing her from classroom to classroom until the midday siesta. Even then, instead of going back to the dormitory, he would sleep in the cloister outside her room.

Every afternoon she would sit down with him in the classroom and help him with his reading. He would even watch in the evenings while she knelt at her prayers in the chapel. On Sundays, he helped her prepare the wine and wafers for the Mass.

All the other sisters at the Sacré-Coeur considered his transformation a miracle.

Only the old *canonesse* was dubious. 'You should take care with that child,' she said, 'the change in him may not be as great as you think.'

'I do not understand, Mother.'

The old lady fingered the wooden crucifix at her neck. 'Don't you find his attentions exhausting?'

'A little.'

'Does he show the same devotion to any of the other sisters?'

'No. With the others, he is just the same.'

'For many years, I worked at the Hôpital Miséricorde. I learned that if you cut the skin, the veins will bleed, but after a while the blood will clot. This is normal, yes? But at the hospital I saw a few rare cases of children who were born without this healing in them. They cannot stop bleeding. Their wounds never heal.' She shook her head.

'But last year when Michel fell in the courtyard-'

'I do not mean his physical body. He has a soul that bleeds. You have staunched the flow, for now. But you must be careful not to make him dependent on you, or when he loses you he will hurt worse than before. Who will heal him then?'

When Gabrielle stepped out of the *canonesse*'s study, Michel was waiting for her. He fell in step behind her.

'Where are you going?' he said.

'To the chapel.'

'To pray?'

'Yes, to pray.'

'Why?'

'It is what God expects.'

'What did the *canonesse* say about me?'

Gabrielle stopped and looked down at him. The huge brown eyes stared frankly back at her. She was impressed, as she always was, by the power that seemed to lurk behind them. 'How do you know we were talking about you?'

He shrugged. 'I listened at the window.'

'It is wrong to eavesdrop. I've told you before.'

'Yes, Sister.'

She turned and made her way towards the chapel.

'But what did she say?'

'If you were listening, then you should know.'

'I heard, but I didn't understand.'

'Thank the Lord for that, then.'

They went into the chapel. It was dark, and the face of Christ on the large crucifix above the altar stared at them in mute agony.

'You must do penance,' Gabrielle said.

'Why?'

'For eavesdropping. Twenty Hail Marys. You can kneel beside me while I pray.'

'Yes, *Maman*.'

Gabrielle stopped. It was as if someone had poured ice water on her soul. 'What did you say?'

'Nothing.'

She caught his shoulder, span him around. 'I'm not your mother. Do you understand? I love you, Michel, but I can never be your mother.'

'Yes, of course. I understand.'

But as he walked away down the aisle of the chapel, Gabrielle thought about what the Mother Superior had said, and she realized the old nun was right.

He was still bleeding. He would never stop.

CHAPTER 7

May 1955

The *canonesse* summoned Gabrielle to her office. As she walked in, she indicated the ancient rattan chair on the other side of her desk. 'Please sit down, Sister.'

'Thank you, Mother.'

'I'm afraid I have some bad news.' The old nun took a pair of wire spectacles from her drawer and put them on. She glanced quickly at the letter in front of her and slid it across the desk. 'It is from Père Jean-Paul in Hue.'

Gabrielle read the letter quickly, the onion-skin paper trembling in her hand. She made the sign of the cross. 'May her soul find peace in heaven,' she murmured.

'I am sorry. Still, there was no pain. The Lord was merciful.'

Gabrielle fought back tears. 'Yes, Mother.'

'Is there anyone to look after your father now?'

'I am the only daughter.'

'The abbess says he is a sick man.'

Gabrielle nodded. She did not trust herself to speak.

'You must go home. You will be excused your duties here for as long as is necessary.'

'But Mother-'

'Your father needs you.'

Gabrielle got up to leave.

'We will say Mass for your mother this Sunday.'

When Gabrielle reached the cloister, she found Michel crouched down by the open window outside the office. He had heard every word.

'You won't leave me?' he said.

Gabrielle tried to walk past him. 'Please, Michel. Don't do this.'

'*Maman,* you can't leave me!' he shouted. He clutched at her leg, making her stumble.

The *canonesse* appeared in the doorway. 'For the love of God, let her be.' She grabbed his arm, but he twisted away from her, trembling with rage.

His face contorted like a wild animal. 'I hate you,' he screamed. 'I hate all of you. I hope you die!'

By 1955, the French soldiers had gone, but the war continued to rage. The battle of Dien Bien Phu, almost a year before, ended with the rout of the French military on the Plain of Jars, and should have ended the conflict in Indochina.

Instead, President Diem took power in Saigon with the full backing of the United States of America. He declared war on the Viet Cong and prepared to take on the Binh Xuyen, an army of bandits who had risen to prominence under the protection of the departed French administration. Jealous of their power and their wealth, Diem set out to break them.

And so, on March 28th, he sent paratroopers to attack their stronghold at the Saigon police headquarters. The Binh Xuyen, backed by the remaining French officers of the *Deuxième Bureau* and the SDECE, responded the following night with a mortar attack on the presidential palace. Sporadic street fighting continued around the capital for the next month.

Life in the orphanage remained largely unaffected by the battle that was going on in the rest of Saigon. Sometimes at night, Michel heard the rattle of machine-gun fire or the distant crump of mortars, but he ignored them. They were as much a part of the background hubbub of his world as the cries of the street vendors outside the gate, or the blaring klaxon horns of the old Peugeot taxis.

But the morning of May 2nd was different. It was on that day that Diem's ARVN made their final push to drive the Binh Xuyen out of the city.

The din from the city center was continuous. The nuns spoke in whispers, fingering their rosary beads and looking nervously at the city skyline, as skeins of smoke trailed into the sky. The street was choked with cars, motor scooters and bicycles.

Michel stood at the gates and watched the chaos of refugees, their pathetic bundles of possessions tied to the frames of bicycles or piled high on hand carts. Pots and wicker baskets of ducks wobbled crazily beside screaming, runny-nosed children.

The fighting was getting closer.

Suddenly, a group of armed soldiers ran by, shoving people aside with their rifle butts. They had snarling tiger badges on their black berets: Binh Xuyen.

One old man riding an ancient bicycle was too slow, and the bandit shouldered him into the gutter. The bamboo cage teetering on the back split open, and two ducks spilled out, squawking and spluttering on the pavement.

Michel heard the hollow thud-thud of mortars. Plumes of black smoke rose into the sky close by. Another crump. Another thud. Debris clattered into the courtyard. The people in the street started to wail, scrambling over each other to get away.

'Michel!'

He turned. It was *Soeur* Gabrielle. She was standing at the doorway of the chapel, her arms held out towards him.

'Quickly now.'

He realized he was the only one still in the courtyard. The other children had already been ushered inside. He ran towards her.

There was a high-pitched wail overhead. Instinctively he threw himself onto the ground.

The explosion lifted his body off the cobblestones, dropping it again with such force that it smashed his nose. He felt a stinging pain as debris smacked down on his back and legs.

Then there was an unnatural silence.

He got slowly to his feet, patting down his shirt and shorts. Except for a nosebleed, he was unharmed. He shook his head like a wet dog, his ears still ringing from the blast of the exploding mortar shell.

The orphanage was gone. In its place was a pile of smoking, flaming rubble. Then the moaning began, the weeping of those still beneath the hot stones and burning timbers.

Another shell exploded a hundred yards away, and more debris clattered into the courtyard around him. He ignored it. He walked towards the chapel, or what was left of it. The heat from the flames was intense and scorched his face.

He saw an arm protruding from the rubble, rosary beads still clutched between the fingers. He fell on his knees and scrabbled at the bricks, clearing away whatever he could.

Soeur Gabrielle's face was white, except for the deep gash on her temple. He was surprised how little she had bled. He pulled at her arm, tried to drag her clear. It was much easier than he expected. He felt her body coming free.

He fell backwards and lay there for a few moments, stunned, staring at the disembodied arm in his hands. Blood seeped from the stump and spilled onto his shirt. He yelled and threw the terrible thing away from him into the jumble of masonry.

It occurred to him then, with absolute clarity, what had happened. He had wanted them dead and some power within him had destroyed them. He need not be afraid anymore. He had the power to judge.

Saigon was inured to war. Only three days after the fighting ended, even while the sweet, cloying stench of death still hung over the city, the street cafés reopened for business.

Michel stood outside the Café Seine, and the smell of hot food made his stomach growl. He had eaten nothing for three days. On the day of the bombing, he had found fresh water in a jar, miraculously untouched in the ruins of a house. Later he had found a little rice in the wreckage of a godown near the river, but he had nothing to boil it in, so he tried to eat it raw. It had made his intestines bleed.

They were mostly Americans in the café. There was only one Corsican at the pavement tables, a tough-looking man in a white tropical suit, drinking Pernod. At the next table was a bony, crew-cut man in an MACV uniform devouring a plate of grilled fish and rice. Michel watched, hypnotized.

The waiter saw him and shooed him away as if he were a dog. He made to go, but when the waiter moved off to serve another customer, he came back. He had to eat. He had to have food.

The American leaped to his feet to greet a Vietnamese girl in a silk *ao-dai*.

Michel knew it was his chance. He hopped across the little border of potted plants that divided the footpath from the tables and snatched the

American's plate off the table. Then he leapt back into the street and started to run.

'Wait, you!'

He knew someone was chasing him, but he didn't look back. If he could slip into the maze of alleyways off the Tu Do he would be safe. As he ran, he stuffed the remains of the fish into his mouth.

Something hit him hard in the chest and he dropped onto his back, choking on the food. The plate clattered into the street, and even before he could get his breath someone grabbed him by the collar and pulled him to his feet.

He looked up. A policeman. He must have run straight into him. He tried to squirm away, but the *flic* took a firm hold of his arm and he yelled out in pain.

The American ran up, panting. His face was flushed. 'That's him, that's the thieving little cocksucker!'

The slap caught Michel hard across the side of the face. His eyes watered and blood leaked from his injured nose. He howled, not with pain but with frustration. The force of the slap had knocked the rest of the fish out of his mouth before he could swallow it.

A green police jeep pulled up and he was bundled into the back. The policeman said something to the American which seemed to mollify him. A second policeman sat in the back of the jeep with a boot on Michel's neck.

He gave up struggling. He hoped, wherever they were taking him, they might think to give him some rice.

The children's prison was on the outskirts of the city, on Cach Mang, the main highway to Tan Son Nhut airport. It was a two-storey, red brick building, originally built by the French a decade before. It was surrounded by seven-foot-high walls, surmounted with barbed wire and broken glass.

Michel was bundled out of the jeep and marched across the boiling yard into the chief warden's office.

Pham Chi Thien was a hollow-cheeked ex-army officer, with graying hair and a neat, black moustache. Michel was shoved across the room towards his desk.

Thien stared at him, his hands folded on the desktop, the long fingers restless as butterflies. 'What's this one here for?' he said.

'He tried to steal food from a café,' the policeman said. 'Be careful. He tried to bite my hand.'

Thien got up and walked around the desk. He smiled like a kindly uncle, revealing two gold teeth. 'Leave us,' he said to the man who had brought him in.

He towered over Michel. 'What is your name?'

'Michel.'

'Ah, a *métis*. A Frenchman's bastard.'

Michel said nothing.

Thien lit a cigarette. 'You have a choice. Your stay here can be very easy or very hard. You must understand. No one cares what happens to you. Nobody. You are dust. If you die, no one cares. Do you understand?'

Michel understood this part perfectly. This was not news.

'If you are nice to me, I will be nice to you.'

Michel didn't know what Thien meant, even when the warden started to unbutton the front of his khaki drill pants.

'In this place I am God. You should always do everything you can to make God pleased with you.'

Michel hawked the bile from deep in the back of his throat and spat expertly in Thien's face. The globule of saliva tracked down his cheek.

For a moment Thien's eyes blazed. 'You choose that way? Alright then, little *métis*. I don't mind. Either way, I will enjoy myself.'

There were no windows in the room and the walls were bare concrete. In the corner, a chain had been suspended from a hook in the ceiling.

Michel hung upside-down, his feet manacled to the chain, his arms cuffed behind his back. He was naked. He saw Thien's grinning face swing in and out of his vision. His body jerked as he tried to free himself.

'It is pointless to struggle,' Thien said. 'It will only make it worse.'

Michel closed his eyes and concentrated on the pain. He bit his lip and willed himself not to cry out. Whatever happened he would not give Thien the satisfaction.

Thien unfastened the clasp of his belt. It was leather with a solid silver clasp. 'Now I will show you how we treat thieves here at Van Trang.'

He wrapped the two loops of the leather around his palm so that the silver buckle dangled loose by the side of his leg, twitching like a snake. He swung Michel around on the end of the chain, so that his back and buttocks were towards him.

Michel heard the belt whistle through the air. It was as if someone had taken a knife and slashed cleanly through the muscles of his back down to the bone. The spasmodic contraction of his ribs forced a sob through his lips.

I won't scream, he promised himself. I won't scream.

He waited for the next stroke, but it did not come. Thien was too clever. He allowed him to twitch and groan on the end of the chain for a while, before the belt sliced through the air once again.

Michel heard the wet slap of the buckle against his skin, and this time he bit down hard on his tongue to keep from crying out. He tasted his own blood in his mouth. It felt as if his whole body were on fire. He realized with despair that if Thien hit him again he would not be able to keep silent.

The belt sliced and hissed.

Michel screamed.

But it was not the cry of a small boy. It was a bellowing roar that filled his own ears, drowning out all his other senses.

He screamed again and again and again, and his screams continued to echo around the stone walls long after Thien had finally tired of his game and left him hanging alone in the cell.

'*Maman!*'

CHAPTER 8

The boy knelt over him. 'He beat you, huh?'

Michel opened his eyes. He was lying on the stone floor of a narrow cell. He tried to sit up, but the sudden slash of pain across his back and buttocks made him gasp. Instead, he eased himself carefully onto his side and looked around.

There were four other boys in the cell. One of them lay on his back, his eyes rolled back in his head. There were needle tracks along the veins of his arms and legs and flecks of foam on his lips.

The boy opposite him was asleep, his legs splayed, skeletal and useless. Polio, Michel decided.

The other two boys were both older. They sat against the far wall, staring at him with casual indifference.

The first boy shoved a metal pannikin into his chest. 'I saved you some rice. You can pay me back tomorrow out of your ration.'

Michel snatched the bowl from him and fisted the rice into his mouth.

'You've got a pretty face,' the boy said. 'Thien likes the ones with pretty faces. That's what got you into this mess.'

'Number ten motherfucking bastard,' Michel grunted, using the worst words he knew.

'They call me No Name. What about you?'

'Michel.'

'French, huh? A Round Eye. That's how you got the pretty nose?'

'My mother was French. Number ten whore.'

No Name nodded. He was a cherub faced Tonkinese with crab-apple cheeks and quick, darting eyes. His hair was shaved close to his scalp.

'What did you do?'

'I stole an American's dinner.' Michel shoveled the last few grains of rice into his mouth. Then he put his fingers gingerly underneath his shirt, felt the swollen and raised wheals on his back, and the crusts of blood where the buckle had ripped his flesh.

'Don't worry about that. He always beats the new kids. Especially the ones who won't play little woman games with him.'

'What is this place?'

'Van Trang. It's the kids' prison.'

'How long will they keep us here?'

'Long as they want. How old are you, huh?'

'I don't know. How old are you?'

'Nine maybe. How long you been on the street?'

Michel toyed with a lie. He decided on the truth. 'Three days.'

'Shit. A virgin.' No Name put his hand on Michel's shoulder. 'It's all right, Round Eye. I'll look after you.'

Michel had his hair shaved for lice and was given a metal bowl and a tin cup. Twice a day he stood in line for his rice ration and a small piece of salty, bony fish. It was barely edible and, even when he managed to force it down, he got a rash on his body which itched unbearably. After a few days, he threw away the fish and just ate the rice.

He found out that the women who cooked in the prison kitchens received a weekly allowance to buy the food for the inmates. They bought the cheapest rice and never bothered to clean or scale the fish. They pocketed the extra money themselves.

The daily rations, meager enough for the Vietnamese children, were barely enough to keep him alive. He grew even thinner. The wounds on his back became infected and began to ooze.

At night he slept on the hard, stone floor in his cell, listening to the maddening whine of the mosquitoes. He tried to stay awake. He had woken up the first night and found himself staring at the whiskered maw of a small, grey kitten. He reached out for it, and it scampered away. It was only then that he realized it was a rat.

There were plenty of others just like it. At night they would come skittering out of the drains to gnaw at toes and shins.

Every day there was drill. Thien stood them in line and paraded them like soldiers in the hot midday sun. It would continue until at least a dozen boys had fainted. They were earmarked for further duty in the afternoon, cleaning out the kitchens and the toilets. Thien said he was teaching them discipline.

Michel never fainted, although there were times when the sky and the buildings and the ground swam in his vision in a gelatin blur. If it was discipline, then he learned it well. He stumbled many times but didn't fall.

It made no difference. Thien never forgave him for that mouthful of spit. Once every two or three days, the guards came to his cell, dragged him down the corridor to Thien's office and beat him with bamboo sticks while Thien watched, blowing smoke rings at the ceiling.

The weeks and months blurred to a nightmare of pain, hunger and despair. Then two things happened very suddenly that changed the routine of life at Van Trang.

It began with a long, piercing scream from Thien's office.

It was a hot, oppressive afternoon, the rains beating on the roof and raising steam from the asphalt on the drill ground. As they cowered in their cells, the boys heard footsteps running up and down the corridor and heard Thien's panicked shouts. Much later there was the clang of the ambulance bell.

No Name unraveled the mystery for them.

'Thien had a new boy in there this afternoon,' he told them, his eyes shining with excitement, 'another pretty one like Michel, huh.'

'What happened to him?' Michel said.

'He bit it off,' No Name slapped the floor with the palms of his hands in excitement. 'Thien took his pants down and the boy put it in his mouth and bit it off!'

The other boys clapped and cheered. All except Michel.

'What's the matter with you, huh?' No Name said.

'I wanted to hurt him myself,' Michel said. 'I wanted to see him scream.'

They never found out what happened to the new boy.

When the new chief warden arrived, the gratuitous beatings stopped. A Round Eye nurse from Saigon Hospital was allowed to visit them every few days and she handed out clothes and soap and medicines. When Phuong, one the boys in Michel's cell, got diarrhea and started vomiting, Michel asked the nurse to look after him.

She was from a place called Australia, a country Michel had never heard of. She was tall, with bony arms and legs, and pale, freckled skin. She spoke some French, but her voice had a curious accent that Michel could not understand.

He and No Name watched as she bent down to examine Phuong, her long fingers probing his abdomen, then feeling for the pulse at his wrist. She put a silver thermometer under his tongue and when she took it out again, she shook her head in concern. She frowned at the festering sores from the rat bites on his ankles and at the dirt encrusted in his hair and on his face.

When she stood up, she said something to the new warden, who shrugged and shook his head. Half an hour later, one of the guards carried Phuong out of the cell. From the barred window they watched him being put in the nurse's battered Peugeot.

'They're taking him to the hospital,' No Name said.

Michel smiled.

'Thien's coming back.'

They were on their hands and knees in the corridor outside the warden's office, scrubbing the stone floor with stiff wire brushes. They had a bucket of water and a bar of thick soap between them.

'How do you know?' Michel said.

No Name lowered his voice. 'One of the guards told me.'

Michel was horrified. 'If he's coming back, we have to get out of here. That vicious bastard will take it out on all of us.'

'Especially you, huh?'

Michel did not need to be reminded. After the new warden had taken over at the prison, he had been happy enough to remain here. At least they were fed, even if the rations were meager. He did not know if he could survive back on the street.

But if Thien was coming back, he had to get away.

'If I get out of here, will you come with me?'

'How will you survive without me, huh?'

Michel reached into the bucket and took out the soap. He broke it in half and gave one piece to No Name. Then he put his half in his mouth and started to chew.

'Eat it,' he said.

'Are you fucking crazy?'

'Eat it.'

'This stuff will make you sick.'

Michel forced himself to swallow the first mouthful. 'Yes, it will make us sick. If we have enough, it will make us sick enough for them to send for the Round Eye nurse.'

No Name understood. He hesitated, then put the hard lye soap in his mouth. He gagged once but managed to keep himself from vomiting. Then he swallowed.

After they had eaten the soap, they went to one of the guards and told him they needed more. He took them to the storeroom and gave them another bar. While he was not looking Michel slipped two more into the pockets of his shorts.

Then they went back to their work, scrubbing the floors while they slowly chewed their way through three bars of lye soap.

Michel rolled onto his side and dry-retched. He had long ago emptied the contents of his stomach, and all that was left was bile. His own stench filled his nostrils. The Australian nurse touched his forehead with her cool, moist hand and then slipped the little silver thermometer under his tongue.

No Name lay doubled over on the other side of the cell. His face was knotted in agony from the cramps. 'Fuck you,' he said. 'You're fucking crazy.'

'Shut up!' Michel said.

'We're going to die.'

The nurse got up and left the cell. A few minutes later she came back in, followed by the warden.

Michel could not understand much of what she said, but he recognized the two words he wanted to hear most of all: Saigon Hospital.

The hospital was in the city center near the market, and it was the poorest and most crowded in Saigon. The entrance hall served as the emergency room and consisted of half a dozen stretchers on wooden stands. When the stretchers were full, patients needing treatment were left to lie on the floor.

When they arrived, there were just two nurses and a young, fresh-faced medical student on duty. The doctors had all gone home. The student and nurses were crowded around one of the stretchers, where an old man lay heaving and choking, clawing at the empty air like he was drowning.

The prison nurse squatted beside them on the floor and watched. Then the young Vietnamese medic said something to her in English and she got up to help him.

Michel twisted his head around. No Name lay on the stretcher beside him, his face white with pain.

'How are you feeling?'

'I just want to die. How about you?'

Michel nodded. 'Think you can move?'

'Now?'

'Why not?' Michel raised himself on one elbow, fought back a wave of nausea and looked around for their nurse. She was busy, bent over the stretcher doing something to the old man's chest.

He got onto his knees and crawled to the door. He broke out in a cold sweat and had to close his eyes and hold onto the wall as the world spun and dipped around him.

Finally, the nausea passed. He felt light-headed but knew he could make it to the gates. He beckoned to No Name to follow.

No one was paying them any attention. They staggered out of the door. A few moments later, they were back in the streets of Saigon.

The smell of wood smoke from a thousand cooking fires drifted across the city. The shells of bombed-out buildings were silhouetted against a mauve dusk.

'Where now?' Michel said.

'Follow me,' No Name said. 'I will take you to my home.'

No Name picked his way through the dark as if it were the middle of the day. Michel panted, struggling to keep up as he darted and twisted through narrow alleys into the rubble-strewn streets of the Arroyo Chinois, where the worst of the fighting between the ARVN and the Binh Xuyen had taken place a few months before.

As night fell, the crumbling skeletons of houses and godowns rose ghostly and desolate against the glow of a yellow moon.

No Name suddenly stopped and caught Michel's arm. 'Down here.' He jumped into the blackened maw of a crater and was immediately lost from sight in the shadows. 'Come on, jump!' he said from the darkness.

Michel took a deep breath and followed, landing with a jolt and twisting his ankle on a piece of rubble.

No Name helped him to his feet. 'Nearly there.'

They were in the ruins of what had once been a cellar. Half the floor had caved in, leaving a scree slope that led down to the basement floor. From the blackness of this desperate cave came an eerie glow of light from a small, orange fire. There were three tiny shapes huddled around it.

One of the figures leapt to its feet and rushed towards them. Michel saw something glinting in the darkness, a knife.

'Three Finger!' No Name shouted. 'Dinh, Tiger Eye, it's me!'

The figure stopped in its tracks.

'No Name?' It was a girl's voice.

'Yes, it's me.'

'Who's that?'

'I've brought a friend with me.'

'A friend?' a voice said from around the tiny fire. 'Shit, that's less food for the rest of us.'

'Come on,' No Name said, pushing Michel ahead of him. 'Sit down. Make yourself at home.'

Michel slumped down among the bricks and chunks of mortar. No Name crouched next to him. His friends were cooking something over the tiny fire. They had skewered it on a long stick and were roasting it over the flames. Fat from the charred creature sizzled on the coals.

Michel suddenly realized what it was. 'A rat,' he said.

'Out here it's our turn,' No Name said cheerfully. 'In Van Trang, they bite us. Out here, we bite them.'

The girl lifted it off the fire and cut it into portions with her knife. Michel hung his head, exhausted, and listened to the rustle of lizards and mice in the rubble around him.

No Name nudged him and proffered a piece of smoke-blackened meat. 'Here, eat it,' he said.

Michel took it. He picked gingerly at it with his fingers.

'Not like that. Like this.' No Name put his share of the rat in his mouth and bit down. 'A boy who can eat soap can manage a piece of good home-cooked meat, huh?'

Michel heard the bones crunching between his teeth and a rivulet of grease flowed down his chin and glowed in the firelight. He put the rat in his mouth and chewed. It's just another kind of meat, he told himself. What does my stomach care when I'm this hungry?

He closed his eyes and snuggled into a niche in the rubble, as if it were a soft feather bolster. He could hear gunfire in the distance and cats crying like babies as they scavenged in a rubbish heap.

He thought about his mother.

He wondered what she was doing now. Sleeping in soft sheets somewhere, he supposed, with good food, warm and safe. While she abandoned him to this.

Well, I will survive, he promised the black silence. I will survive and come back to haunt you. All of you.

'But especially you, *Maman*,' he said aloud. 'Especially you.'

CHAPTER 9

Dakar, West Africa
1960

Dakar was the showpiece of French West Africa. The common language was French. There were French restaurants everywhere. And the *fonctionnaires'* wives could buy fashion direct from the Faubourg St-Honoré.

Modern skyscrapers rose above the minarets and clustered shanties of the native medina. Gangly Senegalese strode through the streets in bright *djellabas.* The women wore rakish turban-like *moussoires,* their flowing *bous-bous* swirling in a kaleidoscope of color.

For eight months of the year the sun shone every day in a cloudless sky, reflecting from the whitewashed buildings and sparkling in the blue of the harbor.

The villa of Jean-Claude and Adrienne Breton stood on the plateau in the neat and prosperous French section of the town, looking over Bernard Bay and Cap Manuel.

It was late afternoon. Adrienne dozed on the shaded porch in a wicker chair, listening to the sleepy drone of insects in the garden. The ocean breeze touched her face, bringing with it the aroma of *cacahouites* - roasted peanuts - from one of the mills outside the town. Swallows darted in and out of the eaves.

She heard footsteps on the porch.

'Bonjour, *Maman*.'

Adrienne opened her eyes. 'Ah, *ma petite*, it is you. Come here and give me a kiss.'

Valentine obediently kissed her mother's cheek. Then she sat down on one of the cane deckchairs beside her.

Adrienne lay there and admired her daughter. She was a stunningly pretty little girl, tall for her age, and with hair as black and glossy as the feathers of a raven. Today she wore it tied in a ponytail at the back of her head, leaving two long bangs to dance at her cheeks. Her skin had tanned to mahogany in the African sun, and it accentuated the astonishing whiteness of her teeth when she smiled.

Strange to think that eight years ago, her first glimpse of the child had filled her with terror. They had laid her in her arms, the umbilicus still pulsing, and she had wanted to cry. The baby had olive skin and a shock of thick, black hair. Even the doctor had appeared embarrassed.

She had waited in her bed at the military hospital in dread, anticipating the scene when Jean-Claude arrived to see his new-born daughter. He must have already known the child was not his, though they had never spoken of it. It was barely six months since they had married in Saigon, and the child was a healthy seven pounds.

But Jean-Claude had not wanted to break the spell. 'She has my father's black hair,' he had crooned, 'but she has my features.'

Adrienne had breathed sigh of relief. She knew what he was doing. There was no solace to be gained from the truth, not for either of them. If she had deceived him at first, then later he had complied with it. She had gained the husband she needed; he had the wife he wanted. She had realized with a surge of gratitude that he didn't care whose child it was.

And in the end, everything had worked out.

'Stay and talk to me for a while,' she said. 'How was school? Did you work hard?'

'Yes, *Maman*.'

'Tell me what you did.'

Valentine began to talk, stroking Adrienne's hair, the sound of her voice soothing her like a drug. Adrienne drifted back to sleep, taking refuge from the specters that haunted her every day.

Valentine watched the little pool of saliva, that had collected at the corner of her mother's lips, overflow and bead slowly down to her chin. Safe now from her mother's gaze, she allowed herself a frown of distaste as she sniffed the sour smell of wine on her mother's breath. Her eyes fell on the empty bottle of vin ordinaire beside the chair.

She could not remember when it had ever been different. Ever since she was a little girl, her mother had been this way – slow and fat and lazy like an old cat. She wondered what her father had ever seen in her.

And there was the wine. Even at eight years old, Valentine was old enough to know that her mother was addled by it. She felt sorry for her, but she hated her as well. She looked longingly towards the garden and the cliffs beyond. Once Adrienne was asleep, she could escape.

'Michel,' Adrienne murmured, her eyes flickering in half-sleep. 'Michel.'

Valentine started at the unfamiliar name. '*Maman?*' She leaned closer.

She waited, but Adrienne did not say anything more, and the secret she had so tantalizingly glimpsed was locked away again in the world of her dreams. She let her mother's hand slip back onto the day bed and ran out into the warm sunshine.

When Jean-Claude got home that afternoon, Adrienne was asleep in the wicker chair, her mouth open. He noted with disappointment that she was still in her nightgown.

'Jemal, where are you?'

The houseboy appeared. *'M'sieur?'*

'How long has Madame Breton been out here?'

'Since it is twelve hours and thirty,' Jemal said. 'So sorry. So sorry.'

Jean-Claude handed him his topee and cane. 'Don't apologize, it's not your fault.' He waved him away and turned back to his wife. He gripped her by the shoulders and shook her.

She opened one eye and then her head fell back on her chest.

He shook her again.

She roused herself and wiped her mouth with the back of her hand.

He was reminded of the opium addicts he had seen in Saigon. They had those same empty eyes and drooping lips.

'What do you think you're doing?' he said. 'If you want to sleep, go to your room. Don't loll out here in front of the servants like a Left Bank drunk.'

'I'll do whatever I want,' she said. 'I need a drink. Jemal!'

The houseboy appeared instantly.

Jean-Claude span around. 'Go back to the kitchen.'

'Jemal, get me a drink!' Adrienne shouted.

Jemal looked in bewilderment from one to the other, then fled.

Jean-Claude looked down at his wife. 'You've had enough to drink. We need to talk.'

'I don't want to talk. Just leave me alone.'

'Can't you see what you're doing to yourself?'

'Go to hell.' She staggered to her feet and tried to push past him.

He caught her arm and pushed her down again. He leaned over her, his face inches from hers. 'Please, Adrienne. Stop this.'

'What are you talking about?'

'What is wrong? You sit here day after day drinking yourself into a stupor.'

'What do you care? All you care about is your work.'

'That's not true. I care about us.'

'Do you really want to know what's wrong? I'm bored. Bored with Dakar. Bored with life.'

'And the way you rave and mutter in your sleep? The headaches? Is that because you're bored?'

'Perhaps.'

'And what about me? Are you bored with me too?'

'I've always been bored with you.'

Jean-Claude felt something snap inside him. He slapped her face with such force that her head snapped back.

She put her hand to her mouth and stared at the red smear on her fingers.

'Oh, God,' he whispered. 'I'm sorry.' He fell to his knees, pulled a large, white handkerchief from his pocket and tried to wipe her face.

She pushed him away, tears welling in her eyes. 'Just leave me alone. There's nothing to be done.'

The python was sleeping in the shade of a cypress tree, near the mudhole where the hippopotamus lived. The way it had curled around itself made it appear like a garden hose, carelessly discarded. Valentine crept closer through the scrub for a better view.

The beauty of the creature took her breath away. She was fascinated by the slick brown sheen of the scales, the sinuous power of its body. She crouched on her haunches, watching, hardly daring to breathe.

The hard, white ground burned her bare feet and she fidgeted against the discomfort. She was so very close, the closest she had ever come to a fully grown one.

The creature was far too big for her collection. She wondered how long its body might be with those massive coils unwound. She shivered at the delicious thrill of being so near to it.

She took another crouching step towards it. One of her toes caught the sharp edge of a stone and she fell onto her knees.

The serpent sensed, rather than heard, the vibrations. Immediately it uncoiled itself and slithered away through the tall grass.

'*Zut!*' She slapped her hand on the ground in frustration and then bent to examine her toe. Blood oozed out from under the nail.

She got up and hobbled back to the villa. The sun was already low over Bernard Bay. It must be later than she thought.

She hoped her papa was not home yet. He got so upset when she went off alone. He worried too much.

The sun lay flat on the sea. Valentine limped across the garden, favoring her injured foot. There was no sign of Jean-Claude. With any luck he was working late at the office again.

But as she darted around the side of the house, hoping to slip unnoticed through the kitchen, she heard him bark at her from the drawing room window.

The cream shutter banged open, and he leaned out. 'Valentine, come here!'

She stopped and slunk back, avoiding his eyes. 'What's wrong, Papa?'

'You are supposed to stay in your room after school and do your homework.'

'Yes, Papa.'

'I've told you before about wandering off on your own. There are some dangerous snakes in that long grass.'

'*Desolé.*'

Already his anger had spent itself. He sighed. 'You've hurt yourself,' he said.

Valentine looked down. Blood still oozed from her big toe.

'You should be more careful,' he said. Then, in a gentler voice. 'Come inside, we'll put something on it. Hurry. You must get dressed for dinner.'

The evening meal was the time of day that Valentine hated the most. Adrienne rarely rose before noon, so at breakfast Valentine had her father all to herself. She ate her lunch at school. Dinner was the only time the three of them were together.

They sat in silence as Jemal spooned aromatic chicken and rice onto the white china plates. Valentine fidgeted with the lace border of the tablecloth, the starched white cotton of her dress biting the skin under her arms.

'Sit up straight, Valentine,' Jean-Claude said.

She was sitting opposite her mother. She noticed that tonight there was too much rouge on her cheeks, and her lipstick was smeared into the corners of her mouth.

Adrienne picked up the bottle of Burgundy and poured herself another glass. Some of the wine splashed onto the tablecloth, the stain blossoming quickly.

'Don't you think you've had enough?' Jean-Claude said.

'You know I like a glass of wine with my dinner,' Adrienne said. 'Don't be such a bore.'

Valentine picked up her heavy silver knife and fork and started to bolt down the chicken. If she finished her dinner quickly, she could escape to her room on the pretext of doing her homework.

'Valentine has been playing in the bush again,' Jean-Claude said.

'Let her do what she wants.'

'It's dangerous. I expect you to be able to control her when I am not here.'

'Oh, for goodness' sake, leave the child alone. Did you have a good day at school, *chérie?*'

Valentine nodded, her head down. She hated it when they fought. She tried to think of something to say to make them forget their squabbles. 'What is mixed blood?' she said.

There was a sudden, shocked silence. She knew she had said something terrible, but she could not understand what it was. Jean-Claude stared at his wife, ashen.

Adrienne pushed her plate away. She had barely touched her food. 'I think I'll go to bed,' she said. She gripped the edge of the table for balance as she got to her feet and weaved towards the doorway.

Valentine listened to her retreating footsteps on the stairs. 'What's wrong, Papa?'

He forced a weak smile. 'Where did you hear that expression? Mixed blood.'

'One of the boys at school. André Gondet. He was teasing me. He said his father had told him that I had mixed blood.'

'Ignore him. It doesn't mean anything. He was just being silly, that's all.'

That night as she lay in her room, watching the breeze play with the curtains through the French windows, she wondered why Jean-Claude had lied to her.

CHAPTER 10

The following Sunday, Jean-Claude and Valentine went to Mass. They went every week. Valentine wore her best white frock and carried a parasol to keep off the sun. Sometimes they went by pony and trap, but usually Jean-Claude preferred to walk.

Adrienne had not been to Mass with them for some time, and Jean-Claude had long ceased asking her to accompany them.

It was a clear day with a sun-washed blue sky. The road back from the church crossed the park near the Palais de Justice and led to the pathway along the cliffs above Madeleine Beach.

Valentine recognized a group of children sitting under the trees. Some of them were her classmates from the French school. Most of them were friends of André, the boy who had been teasing her. She gripped her father's hand a little tighter.

André wasn't with them. She later decided he must have been hiding behind the bushes waiting for them.

As they passed, he rushed out, whooping like a banshee, a white sheet wrapped around him like a skirt, his face blackened with boot polish.

'Valentine's a nigger!' he chanted. 'Valentine's a nigger!' He danced up and down in front of her while the other children cheered and laughed.

She felt her face blush to the roots of her hair with shock and embarrassment.

Jean-Claude took a long time to react. The sheer audacity of it took him by surprise. By the time he went after him, it was too late. André had run off, the rest of his mates scattering in all directions, leaving Jean-Claude staring helplessly after them, banging his walking cane against the ground in frustration.

'*Petits salauds!*' he screamed after them. 'You little bastards!'

Valentine had never heard her father swear before. She lowered her eyes.

When he turned back to her, his face was pale, and he was shaking with anger and humiliation. He grabbed her hand and marched her back to the villa. She had to run to keep up with him.

It wasn't until they were home that he let her go and stamped inside. She took off her white glove and rubbed her hand. He had gripped it so tight all the blood had drained from her fingers.

She found him in the garden at the back of the house, slumped in a wicker chair. He was crying.

'I'm sorry, Valentine. I'm so sorry.'

'Please, don't cry.'

She was astounded how such a stupid, childish prank could have wounded him so deeply. For her own part she was embarrassed, but not hurt. She did not really understand how André mattered so much. What mattered was that it had hurt her father. She laid a hand on his shoulder and felt her childhood disappear as she absorbed his pain. As she patted him, her heart burned with a terrible flame. She swore she would make André Gondet pay.

And she knew just the way to do it.

She arranged to meet him under one of the acacia trees in the garden. A fresh ocean breeze blew across the Plateau from Bernard Bay. Goree Island stood sentinel among the whitecaps in a sea of metallic blue.

The bright sun beating on the whitewashed villas of Cap Manuel hurt her eyes and she had to squint to see him coming. He shuffled towards her from the dusty road, his hands thrust into the deep pockets of his shorts.

'What's the matter?' he said. 'Are you still mad about the other day? It was just a joke.'

'It doesn't bother me,' she said.

'Really?' He looked disappointed. 'What did you want to see me about?'

Valentine looked at the ground. 'Have you ever kissed a girl before?'

'Lots of times.'

'Will you kiss me?'

He took his hands out of his shorts.

She grabbed him by the arm. 'Come on.'

The cellar smelled of mold. The steps that led down from the garden felt cool under her bare feet. The only light was filtered through the cracks in the heavy cedar door and the tiny grilled window set high in the stone wall.

André baulked at the top of the stairs. 'It's creepy,' he said.

'Are you scared?'

He hesitated, then followed her down. 'What is this place?'

'It's the cellar. See, that's Papa's wine stacked along that wall. But he never comes down here. Only Jemal. He won't tell.'

'Tell what?'

She took his hand and led him to the far end of the cellar. Something stirred in the blackness, and there was a faint rustling sound like leaves blowing across a wooden porch.

He stopped, his eyes still not accustomed to the gloom after the bright sunlight. He made out what appeared to be a number of boxes stacked against the wall. Valentine stooped down next to one of them.

He realized that they weren't boxes, they were cages, and they contained living, moving things. He wanted to run but he wasn't going to let a girl frighten him.

He took a step closer. 'You've got snakes in there.'

'They're beautiful, aren't they?' Valentine whispered.

He gasped. He recognized that dark satiny sheen. His father had pointed them out to him in the market. He sucked in his breath in alarm. '*Putain!* Valentine, that one's a mamba!'

She grinned at him in the darkness. '*T'as peur?*'

'I'm not scared. I'm just saying. How the hell did you get a mamba?'

'I caught him myself. He was asleep under the banyan tree. I used a forked stick to trap his head.'

'Liar.'

'It's true. I won't keep him always. I'll let him go soon. I just like to come down here and stare at him. He's so strong, so beautiful. Don't you think so?'

'Yes, and if he bites you, you're dead. That's how beautiful he is.'

Valentine stood up suddenly and opened one of the cages. She put her hand inside and came towards him, two small orange eyes glinting between her fingers.

André thought he was going to wet himself. 'What are you doing?'

'I'm going to teach you a lesson. You aren't going to make fun of me in front of my father ever again.'

'It was just a joke!'

'You've had your laugh. Now I'll have mine.'

He stumbled backwards and fell on his back. 'No!' It came out shrill, echoing around the cellar and up through the house. 'Please!'

She stood over him. He knew he was helpless. The snake's head danced in front of his eyes, and he saw its tongue flick out.

'Papa cried, that's how funny your little joke was.'

'Stop it! I'm sorry!'

Suddenly Jean-Claude's voice echoed around the cellar. 'Valentine!'

She looked up and saw her father silhouetted in the doorway.

'What in God's name are you doing?'

She took the snake back to its cage and dropped it inside, slamming the lid.

André saw his opportunity. He clambered to his feet and ran out without looking back.

When Adrienne announced that she was pregnant just a few weeks after they were married, Jean-Claude was stunned. A childhood glandular disease had left him sterile, but he had baulked at telling her, afraid that she might refuse the marriage even in her straitened circumstance. So, if he was going to ever raise a child, it was always going to be someone else's.

He was a practical man, and he knew what he was getting into. What was unexpected, when the doctors ushered him into the white-painted hospital room where Adrienne lay exhausted on the bed, was his sheer joy at the first glimpse of his daughter. She was exquisite beyond belief. He really didn't care what Adrienne had done nine months before to conceive the child. She was his now. And that was why the smile he offered Adrienne in the labor ward that night was absolutely genuine.

He displayed the baby proudly to all his friends, though no one else was allowed to hold her. If anyone ever frowned at the color of her skin, he never noticed. He fretted over her constantly. She would only have to utter the smallest cry from her bassinet, and he would be there, scooping her up in his arms to comfort her. He would sit with her for hours and gaze at her perfect face and silky hair and marvel at the unlikely circumstances that had contrived to give him such a beautiful daughter.

It was some consolation for the inexplicable transformation that had overtaken the woman he loved. He had long ago stopped asking the fates why his once beautiful wife had been transformed into a plump and frowsy alcoholic, or why she could no longer speak even a few words to him without insult.

He learned instead to live only for Valentine.

But now, as he stood in his study, he wondered at this little angel, whom he had found just a few minutes before waving a snake in the face of a school friend.

'Well, what have you got to say for yourself?'

'I'm sorry,' Valentine mumbled.

'Sorry? You put a snake in that boy's face.'

'It was a baby rock python. It wouldn't have hurt him. I keep it as a pet.'

'He didn't know that.'

Valentine grinned. 'No, he didn't. Peed in his pants, didn't he?'

Jean-Claude took a deep breath, trying to control himself. Her contrition was entirely feigned, he realized. 'How long have you had those things under the house?'

'I never keep any of them longer than six months.'

He shut his mind to the enormity of what she had just told him. The dangers his daughter had exposed herself to did not bear thinking about. 'Some of those snakes are deadly poisonous. There's a black mamba in one of the cages.'

'He's my favorite. He's beautiful.'

Jean-Claude had never heard anyone call a mamba beautiful. 'It's the deadliest snake in Africa.'

'I'm very careful. Jemal showed me how to catch them. You have to use a special kind of stick.'

'What were you doing to that boy?'

'He upset you. He was the one making fun of me in the park the other day. He made you cry.'

Jean-Claude felt his anger snuff out like a candle flame.

When he walked into the bedroom, he found Adrienne lying on the bed, still in her dressing gown, sipping white wine and gazing at a magazine. It was exactly what she had been doing when he had left that morning.

She had been so beautiful once, lovely and assured. He tried to think when it had all changed between them. Whatever had happened to her in Saigon had followed her to Dakar, and the clear blue skies of the African colony had done nothing to heal her. He remembered the stories that were whispered about her before they got married, and now he cursed himself for a fool for ignoring them.

He had tried to talk to her about it many times, but she just got upset. He had told himself that it would pass. But it only got worse. Now he felt overcome by a sense of loss.

He sat down on the edge of the bed. 'My love,' he said.

Adrienne peered up at him. She seemed unable to focus properly. My God, he thought. Has she been drunk all day?

He took her hand. 'She knows, Adrienne. I had to tell her. The children are teasing her at school and-'

'What are you talking about?'

'Valentine. I told her that I am not her real father.'

Adrienne caught her breath.

'She has a right to know. She's old enough now.'

She tried to turn away from him. The wine spilled onto the bed sheet.

'So, you had a child by another man,' he said. 'It doesn't matter to me now. It never mattered to me.'

'I don't care if it matters to you.'

'We have to talk about this. We'll be going back to France soon.'

She shook her head. 'I don't want to go to France. I like it here.'

'The *Dakarois* will have their independence this year. The administration is to be dismantled. It is not my decision; I go where they send me.'

'Yes, of course. Run, Jean-Claude. Stand still, Jean-Claude. Jump through the hoop, Jean-Claude.'

'Jumping through hoops got us this villa.' He patted her hand, hoping to soothe her. 'It will be for the better. They have good doctors in France.'

'Why do we need doctors?'

'There are experts who understand the mind.'

'You think I'm mad, is that it? There's nothing wrong with me. You made me do it.'

'Made you do what?'

'Just leave me alone.' She closed her eyes.

Jean-Claude shut the door gently behind him. He heard muffled sobs from the other side as his wife wept into her pillow.

Adrienne watched the shadows creep across the wall. A mosquito whined at the netting above her head.

'Michel,' she whispered into the gathering darkness, 'please forgive me.'

Was he alive? No. More likely dead, starved in a Saigon street years ago. Her eyes went to the crucifix on the wall. Jesus hung there in the half-light, his face twisted into a snarl of contempt. There was no forgiveness there. She had not even made her confession in the church. Better that there was no absolution. She wanted to suffer. She deserved it.

Jean-Claude had to suffer too. He was the reason she left. He had offered a way out, and she could never forgive him for that.

She had given up her son for a life of ease and luxury. How ironic that things had turned out this way. She had thought she could leave Saigon behind, but it had followed her here all the same.

Now she just wanted to sleep and never have to face herself again.

CHAPTER 11

Saigon

Saigon had become a whore of a city. It had shone the shoes of the Japanese and French soldiers and sold them its women. In return, the war had fed the *cyclopousse* drivers, the beggars, the tailors and the forgers of ancient works of art.

Once, it had been a city of bicycles. They had been replaced by noisy Lambrettas, army lorries and tanks spewing gasoline fumes.

Graffiti was scrawled everywhere on the white-painted, stucco walls: **Support President Diem!**

Like any whore, Saigon used her cosmetic charms to conceal the ugliness beneath. Beautiful Vietnamese women, in sheath-tight *ao-dai*, strolled along the broad, tree-lined boulevards of the Tu Do. Monks still begged for alms every morning at dawn, serene in their saffron robes.

Beyond the flowered gardens and cream walls of the old colonial French villas were the shanties and cardboard shacks of the Cholon slums. Street urchins hung at every corner and swarmed outside the hotels and markets with outstretched hands - a generation of orphaned and abandoned children without homes, without food and without hope.

Michel was thirteen years old. Already, he knew four languages: French, English, Vietnamese and *chiu chao*, the Chinese dialect of Cholon.

In addition to these skills, he was an expert shoplifter and pocket thief. He could slit open a shopping bag with a razor, to take a purse, and snatch shopping bags from the back of moving Hondas around the markets in Ham Nghi Street.

He had his own network of fences and was on friendly terms with half a dozen black-market dealers.

The street was his home.

His light brown skin and smooth features helped him to blend into the background, and only his height hinted at his European blood. He was a head taller than No Name and the other Vietnamese boys his own age. He was thin, but the spare muscles of his body were hard and taut as rope. He wore a Brooklyn Dodgers baseball cap and a white t-shirt with a packet of Lucky Strike cigarettes tucked under the left sleeve. He kept a Zippo lighter and a flick knife in the back pocket of his shorts.

But his most memorable feature was his eyes. They were not quite evenly matched. This gave the impression that the two sides of his face had been minted separately and then brought together. The effect was disturbing and hypnotic.

'Look what I scored today,' he said. He reached into the voluminous pockets of his US army-issue shorts and took out a heavy Rolex with a chunky silver band.

No Name whistled softly. 'Where did you get it, huh?'

'A big American outside the Caravelle. Took it straight off his wrist and ran like the wind.'

Three Finger emptied his wicker basket onto the ground. There were six bars of Lux soap, a dozen tins of Carnation milk and some tubes of Colgate toothpaste. 'I went to the refugee camp. Here, look. A gift from the people of America.'

Tiger Eye reached into the blouse pocket of her khaki shirt and threw some crumpled blue notes onto the ground.

No Name picked them up and examined them critically. 'Make them pay you in dollars.'

Tiger Eye snatched them back. 'You want dollars, you fuck them.'

Three Finger scooped up the soap and the toothpaste. 'I'm going to sell these in the market.'

Michel tossed the watch into the basket. 'Here. Sell this for me too.'

No Name nodded his head towards Dinh, who lay on his back under a lean-to of corrugated iron and matting set against the crumbling wall of the building. 'Perhaps we can buy some medicine, huh?'

Dinh was moaning. A rat bite on his thigh had become infected. This morning it was swollen and hot, and a scabrous crust had formed over the wound. A custard-yellow putrefaction oozed from beneath.

'We'll get him some pills from the refugee camp,' Michel said.

'That's just for head devils. We need stronger medicine.'

'Medicine's expensive. We need food more.'

No Name spat into the dirt. 'Sometimes,' he said slowly, 'you talk like a round eye.'

'Sometimes, you talk like an old woman.'

'We have to look after each other.'

'He's going to die. Why waste money on him?'

No Name shook his head. 'I was wrong about you. You'll never be one of us. I should have left you in Van Trang.'

'If it weren't for me, you'd still be there.'

No Name jumped to his feet. A knife appeared in his hand. 'I say we buy medicine.'

Michel stood up slowly. He towered over the little Tonkinese. He reached into his shorts and took out his switchblade. 'I say we don't.'

They started to circle each other, and the others backed off to give them room.

A hollow boom shook the ground under their feet. Both boys turned, startled, forgetting their fight.

'That was close,' Michel said.

No Name slipped the knife away. 'Let's go.'

The bar was a favorite haunt of American engineers from the Caravelle. But the grenade mesh across the windows had been little help this time. A Viet Cong had left a *plastique* under one of the tables.

When Michel and No Name got there, the street was still littered with bodies, and the air was filled with the terrible moans of the injured. The whole ground floor of the building had been blown out, the walls peeling outwards and raining bricks and masonry into the shops either side. Flames licked at the blackened embers. Ambulance bells clanged in the distance.

A green ARVN jeep arrived and one of the soldiers began to cordon off the area with plastic ribbons.

'We'll wait,' Michel said.

That evening, they picked their way through the rubble like jackals after a kill. Three Finger found a watch. The steel band was warped and twisted, and the glass face was smashed, but the mechanism still worked. He would be able to sell it at the market for a few piastres. Tiger Eye found a disembodied finger and slipped the thin gold band from the bloodied relic into her shorts.

The apothecary next to the café was deserted, one wall blown away, shelves and drawers smashed and splintered among the rubble. Michel picked his way through it, his hands raw and blistered from pulling at the timbers and bricks which were blackened but still fire hot.

The shop had catered to the American as well as the traditional market. Among the broken jars of dried herbs and desiccated insects and plants, he found a store of Western medicines, little vials of pills with long indecipherable names. He put half a dozen bottles in his pockets.

When they got back to their makeshift shelter, he tossed them onto the tiny pile of treasure they had salvaged. 'Medicine for Dinh,' he said.

No Name weighed one of the bottles in the palm of his hand. 'Man-drax,' he read, slowly. 'What does it do, huh?'

Michel shrugged. 'It's medicine.'

No Name unscrewed the cap and poured some of the white pills into his palm. 'How many shall we give him?'

'Two,' Tiger Eye said. 'At the refugee camp they always make you take two.'

'But Dinh's very sick,' Three Finger said. 'Better make it four.'

The smoke from their fire drifted upwards. The shadows under the skeletal walls of the godown broadened and deepened.

'His leg's worse,' No Name said. 'It stinks. The skin around the scab looks green. The medicine didn't work.'

'Let's give him something else,' Three Finger said. He was holding another one of the little glass bottles. 'What about these?'

No Name took them from him. 'Co-deine. Sure. Why not?'

'Is he still asleep?' Tiger Eye said.

No Name nodded.

'Maybe he's dying.'

'Or maybe it was the medicine,' Michel said. 'The Americans have pills that make you go to sleep.'

'If he doesn't wake up soon, we can't give him any more of the tablets,' No Name said.

Michel stared into the fire. 'It must be very strong medicine. He's been asleep for nearly two days.'

'It's no good if all it does is make you sleep. Throw it away.'

Michel shook his head. 'Sometimes you can be so stupid.'

'All right, you're so smart. What good is this Mandrax to us?'

Michel told him.

Tiger Eye called it turning tricks. She had No Name or Three Finger pimp for her on the street, hitting on the American engineers and contractors in their Hawaiian shirts or badly fitting MACV greens. The transaction would be finalized in an alley, and then she would take them to a small Chinese hotel, where she would pay for a room at an hourly rate.

The Americans were big and heavy, and they hurt her, but it was easier than stealing. If she pretended to be a virgin, they paid her twice as much. Some of them liked her to scream a little, and she didn't have to pretend. Others were kind to her and gave her Camel cigarettes, Hershey Bars and bottles of Coca-Cola.

It had been Michel's idea to raise the stakes in the game. She watched him work the street. After a few minutes, he found a customer. He was eating noodles at one of the cafés.

'Hey, Mister, you want to sleep with my sister? Number one girl. Tight pussy.'

The American picked at the remains of his lunch with a small wooden toothpick. 'Is this number one girl your little sister or your grandmother?'

Although Michel could speak English perfectly, he affected the stilted patois of the street. He found it was good for business if the Americans thought he was just another hustler. 'Very young. Number one. Come and see.' He tugged at the man's shirt. It had electric-yellow bananas and bright orange pineapples overlaid on a bed of green palm trees.

'How much?'

'Come and see. Number one girl. This way, Mister.'

The man followed Michel into the alley. Tiger Eye was leaning against the wall. Her arms and legs looked as fragile as twigs. Her hooded eyes stared back at the American with casual indifference.

The American stopped, surprised. He took the toothpick out of his mouth and ran a hand through his thinning, ginger hair. 'How old is she?'

Tiger Eye was thirteen and told her customers she was sixteen. Michel saw the American's small, pink tongue flicking between his lips like a lizard sizing up its next meal. Something told him this man was different from most of the others. 'She's eleven,' he said.

The man pushed past him and put a huge hand on Tiger Eye's breast. 'Hell, she ain't hardly got any titties yet.' It was not a rebuke, he seemed pleased.

Michel watched him. The man's scalp gleamed under the spare thatch of curls. Once, he may have been a powerful man, but now his stomach lolled over the belt of his pants.

'Your little sister a virgin?'

Michel nodded. 'Of course.'

Michel and Tiger Eye went ahead, the American shambling along behind.

Outside the hotel, Michel gave Tiger Eye a bottle of Michelob beer and four of the Mandrax. 'When you give him the beer, crush these up and slip them in the bottle,' he said.

'All right.' She looked over her shoulder. The American was still ten paces behind them.

'And don't forget to make a noise. You're supposed to be a virgin.'

Tiger Eye shook her head, offended. 'Don't tell me my business. I know what to do. I've been a virgin more times than you could count.'

When she came out of the hotel an hour later, there was a curious bulge at her waist and her eyes glistened with excitement. She had the American's wallet tucked inside her underpants. They dashed into a side alley, and she hitched up her dress and pulled it out. Michel snatched it from her.

'At first, he didn't want the beer,' she said, 'but I made him drink it. I said it was a Vietnamese custom. Then he started pulling off his clothes.' she grimaced. 'He had a stomach like a whale. But would you believe it, his thing was like this.' She held up her little finger, 'Then he got on top of me, and I thought maybe we hadn't given him enough medicine. Then, you know, he just fell asleep. Right on top of me. I thought I was going to suffocate.'

While she spilled out her story, Michel emptied the wallet into his lap. There was a photograph of the American with a woman and two smiling girls with long, neatly combed brown hair. Not much older than Tiger Eye, Michel thought, surprised. There were some business cards and a membership to a private club in San Francisco. He tossed them into the alley.

He unzipped one of the pockets and a sheaf of American dollar bills and Vietnamese piastres tumbled out. He counted them quickly. 'Fifty-two United States dollars and two thousand piastres.'

Tiger Eye banged the ground with her fists and giggled.

Michel shook his head in wonderment. Today, he had learned two important lessons from life: The power of sex and the power of American medicine.

CHAPTER 12

Two yellow-fanged cats squabbled and fought for scraps in a pile of rubbish. Three Finger picked up a half-brick and hurled it at them, sending them shrieking away along the alley.

Tiger Eye cradled Dinh's head in her lap. Sweat shone on his face, soaking her dress. Dinh tossed and moaned with the fever. She stroked his hair, rocking gently back and forward on her haunches.

'His leg is rotten,' No Name said. 'We should take him to the hospital, huh?'

Michel lit a Lucky Strike, blowing smoke from the side of his mouth as he saw some of the American soldiers do at the Caravelle. 'Why? He's dead anyway.'

'Maybe they can give him medicine,' Tiger Eye said.

'No, they won't. They'll just leave him in the corner to rot with all the others.'

'We can't leave him like this.'

'Why not?'

No Name spat on the ground. 'You're a Number ten motherfucker.'

Michel shrugged. 'I still say you're wasting your time.'

VENOM

The Nhi Dong Children's Hospital was on the Su Van Hahn, near the racecourse. The street was heavy with the stench of rotting fruit, and an occasional breath of wind carried with it the taint of the nearby fish market.

Michel waited in the street while the others carried Dinh into the hospital. He saw a man in a khaki uniform come out carrying a small bundle wrapped in a ragged blanket. An old Vietnamese woman in black pajamas was waiting patiently by the gates. The man held the bundle out to her. As she reached for it, the blanket fell away, and Michel saw it was the body of a teenage boy, about the same age as himself.

The woman took the corpse and walked away, cradling the child in her arms.

'Might be you one day, huh?'

Michel whirled around. It was No Name.

'No, I won't die. Not till I've evened the score.'

'What score?'

'You'll see.'

'You're crazy. There's something wrong in your head.'

'Maybe.'

'Don't you want to know what happened to Dinh?'

'No.'

Michel walked away. No Name stared after him. He turned to Three Finger and Tiger Eye and pointed to his temple.

Three Finger shrugged. Crazy, yes. But Michel was still the smartest and the biggest. They might need him someday.

They followed him back up the street.

Dinh did not die. A few months later he was back on the street, another one-legged beggar among the city's hordes. He might have starved, but the band pooled everything they had and shared it out. Even Michel agreed to the arrangement. Besides, Tiger Eye was making more money than any of them, and she insisted that if the others wanted to pimp for her and share in the profits, then Dinh was to get an equal share.

Tiger Eye was fourteen years old now, rail-thin, small-boned and fragile as rice paper. But her face was astonishingly pretty. She had velvet skin and straight, white teeth. She never bothered with the padded bras and stiletto heels that the other street girls wore. She knew that there were some men who liked young girls, and already, even before puberty, she was lying about her age. She told her customers she was twelve.

One night, Michel waited for her in the alley beside the Eighty-Eight Hotel in Cholon. She was with one of her regulars, a small, owl-eyed catering contractor from Texas. Michel was impatient. The man always brought extra gifts as well as cash, and he was eager to see what they had scored.

An hour later, Tiger Eye sauntered down the alley carrying a heavy cane basket.

Michel grabbed it off her shoulder. 'What did you get?'

'That crazy motherfucker,' she said. He noticed a fleck of blood on her lip. 'Slaps me around then crawls on the floor in his underpants and tells me he's sorry. Then he shows me photographs of his children in America. I tell him that's the last time. I don't need number ten cocksucker like him.'

Michel wasn't listening. He tipped the contents of the basket onto the ground. There were a dozen Hershey bars, half a dozen packets of Lucky Strike cigarettes, two bottles of Seven-Up and a half-bottle of Jack Daniels whiskey.

'How much did he pay you?'

Tiger Eye hitched up the long khaki t-shirt she wore as a dress, put her hand down the front of her pants and pulled out a bundle of notes. She threw them at Michel.

He grinned. 'Look at this! Worth a fat lip any day.'

'Let's go back. I don't want to turn any more tricks tonight. Must be close to curfew.'

He started to throw everything back into the basket. 'What's it like?'

'What?'

'Screwing these guys. Do you like it?'

'It used to hurt. Now I don't feel anything.' She cocked her head to one side. 'Ever done it?'

Michel looked away. 'Sure.'

'Want to do it to me?'

His mouth went suddenly dry.

'Want to boom-boom my sister, Mister?' she said, imitating him. 'Number one girl. Very clean, virgin.' She snatched the basket out of his hand and dropped it on the ground. She spun him around, so her back was against the wall. 'Take your pants down.'

He could see the cars and bicycles on the Tu Do, heard an American's voice booming over the din in the street.

'No one can see us,' she said. 'Are you scared?'

He eased down his shorts. He gasped with shock as her fingers clamped around his penis.

'You're soft.'

He didn't know what to say. He knew what he was supposed to do, but he couldn't do it. He leaned in to kiss her. She turned her face away. He felt her tug and knead at his penis. It hurt.

He heard the sampan horns out on the Saigon River and was suddenly aware of the alley smell of rubbish, kerosene and urine.

He placed a tentative hand to her chest and felt the swollen lump of her nipple against her ribs. He felt his chest growing tight and a burning ache in his groin.

'That's better,' she whispered. She slipped down her pants. 'You'll have to hold me up.'

He put his hands under her armpits and lifted her easily. He was amazed how light she was. She put her legs around his waist and then reached down with her right hand and guided him inside her.

'Push. Come on, push, push!'

'Is that all right?'

'Yes, yes,' she whispered. 'It's nice and small. The Americans are too big. They hurt me.'

He was stung by the comparison. Angry, he began to push into her as hard as he could. He gasped at these new sensations. This felt good.

He found himself thinking of a small room above the Rue Le Loi, of a hard wooden cot and a sewing table, long bolts of cloth under the window. He saw the dark sheen of sweat on his father's back, and he saw his mother, her face contorted into a grimace with this same pleasure-pain, her lips working in a silent scream.

Adrienne.

But when he opened his eyes, it wasn't her. It was just a skinny little Vietnamese girl, her eyes half-closed in concentration.

And he felt an upwelling of rage such as he had never known in his life.

No Name was ecstatic. He had hung around outside the Cafe Givral all night, waiting for his opportunity. He watched a fat American in a tropical suit sitting at one of the tables getting drunk on Martell brandy, and every time he pulled out his wallet, he could see thick wads of greenbacks and Vietnamese piastres.

When the man staggered outside, he barely felt the bump as No Name ran into him. It wasn't until he got in the back seat of his taxi that he realized what had happened, and by then No Name was two blocks away.

No Name made his way to the Eighty-Eight Hotel to share his good fortune. He found Michel standing at the end of the alley with Tiger Eye's cane basket over his shoulder.

'Hey Round Eye, ask me how much money I scored tonight. Fifty American dollars and five thousand piastres! Huh?'

Michel didn't seem to hear him. He looked dazed.

'You all right? You been smoking *ma thuy* huh?'

'I'm all right.'

'What's the matter with you? Hey, snap out of it. Where's Tiger Eye? Turning a trick, huh?'

'She's hurt.'

'Where is she?'

Michel looked down the alley. No Name pushed him aside and ran down there.

Tiger Eye lay slumped against the wall. It was dark, and No Name couldn't see her face. He bent down and put out a hand to touch her, immediately pulled it away again as if he'd been stung.

'Holy fucking shit!' There was a warm, sticky mess on his fingers.

'It was her American trick,' Michel said. 'He came out of the hotel after her. He said she stole his money. He just went crazy. I couldn't stop him.'

'Fucking number ten round eye cocksuckers!'

'He just kept hitting her.'

No Name fumbled for her pulse, then put his ear against her bony chest.

'Shall we take her to the hospital?' Michel said.

'What's the point, huh? She's dead.' He stood up. 'Why didn't you use your knife?'

Michel didn't answer.

No Name shook his head. What was the point of having a big bastard like Michel around if he couldn't protect them when they needed it? He was all bluff. Maybe he was a coward after all.

'Come on, leave her,' he said. 'It's back to stealing handbags for us.'

CHAPTER 13

By the time Michel was seventeen, the angular youth had become a lean and attractive young man. He was aware of how some women looked at him. He oozed sexuality in the way that he moved. He was tall and sinuous, and he dressed well. No one who saw him in the street would have guessed that he was *bui doi*. His frame and features were European, his skin and liquid brown eyes were Asian. Like a chameleon, he moved easily from the cafés in the French quarter to the Chinese slums of Cholon.

One morning outside the Caravelle Hotel, he discovered that he had other talents besides bag-snatching and picking pockets.

The Caravelle was nine stories of concrete and glass. Polished stone steps led up to a foyer furnished in mock-Oriental plastic. The hotel was patronized by the Americans, who preferred its gaudy charms to the more traditional comforts of the Continental Hotel just across the square.

Michel was sitting on his Vespa at the curbside watching out for police while No Name worked the street, hawking *ma thuy* to the American soldiers. He noticed a girl sitting alone on the terrace, drinking coffee. She looked over at him and he smiled.

An American, he thought. She wasn't pretty, but she was slim with striking curly black hair that flowed halfway down her back. She wore a pink blouse and khaki-green slacks. A reporter. All the American reporters sported at least one piece of army issue. Even the women.

He watched her finish her coffee. As she came out, he waved at her. 'Hi. You want a lift?'

She ignored him and walked off down the street.

He left the scooter on its stand and followed her. 'Hey, sexy!'

She wheeled around, her face crimson. 'I don't want to buy anything.'

'I'm not selling.'

'Please go away.'

'You're new in Saigon, aren't you?'

She bit her lip. 'So?'

'Nothing. You look scared, that's all. Like you need someone to show you around.'

The girl pushed back a wisp of hair from her face. 'How old are you?' she said.

'Nineteen.'

'Shouldn't you be in the army?'

'Why? I'm not Vietnamese. I'm French.'

She turned away. 'I don't let men pick me up in the street.'

Michel shrugged. 'Where do you want to be picked up? I'll meet you there.'

She hesitated. 'The Caravelle. Eleven o'clock.'

She was an hour late. Michel waited for her in the corner with a bottle of 33 beer. He was about to leave when she walked in, her face flushed, damp patches along the back of her blouse.

She smiled when she saw him. 'I didn't think you'd wait.'

'I would wait forever for a pretty girl.'

She ignored the obvious deceit. 'I was getting my accreditation. They tell me it takes even longer to get your MACV from the Embassy. Christ, it's hot.'

He ordered two more beers.

She pulled a packet of Lucky Strike from her bag and lit one, throwing back her head and blowing smoke in a long plume towards the ceiling.

He watched her. She was a little older than he had thought at first, twenty-five or twenty-six. She had a freckled nose and hazel-brown eyes. She looked nervous. He lounged back against the wall.

'I don't know your name,' she said.

'Michel.'

'Mine's Susan. Susan Howard.' She gave him a tight smile. 'How did you know I'd just arrived here?'

'I told you. You looked scared. Everyone looks scared when they first come to Saigon. It's all right. You'll get used to it.'

'If you must know, it's my first overseas assignment. I've never been out of America before.'

'That's okay. I've never been out of Saigon before.'

'You were born here then?'

'My father's French. He has his business here.'

The beers arrived. Susan took a long draught from her glass, her tongue licking away the froth on her upper lip. 'I don't even know why I talked to you. Perhaps it's because I'm a long way from home.'

'Perhaps.'

'That doesn't mean I'm going to let you sleep with me.'

'It never crossed my mind.'

Two more beers, he thought. Two more beers and I'll have her on her back.

Michel padded out of the bathroom, still wet from the shower. He was naked except for the towel at his waist. This was his first time in a hotel room. He had never seen a bathroom that had running hot water. He was overawed by the luxury of it, by the feel of soft carpet under his bare feet, astonished by the chill of the air-conditioned rooms.

One day, he promised himself, one day I will live like this all the time. I will live in big hotels and sleep in soft sheets and take long showers whenever I want. I will look down on the streets instead of living on them.

Susan lay on her back, covered by a single cotton sheet. She stretched like a cat.

He sat down on the edge of the bed and held up the medicine bottle in his hand. 'What's this?'

'Jesus!' She snatched it away from him. 'Have you been going through the cabinet?'

'Just curious.'

'It's dye, okay?'

'What's it for?'

She stared at him, not sure whether he was making fun of her. 'It's for my hair. It's not really this color. It's ginger and I hate it.' She grinned. 'But you know that already.' She put the bottle down on the bedside table, and the sheet fell away.

Michel dropped his gaze to her body. 'That's all right,' he said. 'I'm not really nineteen.' He reached out and lazily cupped her breast in his hand, his thumb tracing the contour of her nipple. He pulled away the towel and eased himself onto the bed beside her.

Susan shuddered and lay back on the pillow. 'Don't make me regret this,' she whispered.

'She's dead, Michel. She's dead!'

They were outside the main bus station on Petrusky Street. Michel had stolen a melon from the market and was perched on a low wall, carefully dissecting it with his pocketknife. He took a bite and wiped the juice off his mouth with the back of his hand. 'Who's dead?'

'That American journalist, the one you were talking to outside the Caravelle yesterday. They found her in her room and-'

'Slow down. What are you talking about?'

'She's dead.' No Name took a breath. 'There's police swarming all over the hotel. Everyone's talking about it. She was strangled in her bed.'

'So?' he cut off another slice of melon with his knife.

'So, they're looking for you, motherfucker. Every fucking American journalist in Saigon saw you in the Caravelle with her. You're fucked!'

'Don't look so happy about it.'

'You didn't have to murder her, you idiot.'

'There was one hundred dollars in her purse. And the watch and rings were worth another hundred. What was I supposed to do?'

'Just take them. You didn't have to kill her, huh?'

'I didn't mean to kill her. She was struggling, I just tried to calm her down.'

Yes, she had struggled. Even before his hands closed around her throat, she guessed what he was going to do, and she had fought him with her fists and nails. But he was too strong for her, and in the end it had been very easy. Her neck had snapped like a twig.

He still wasn't sure what had made him do it, but he remembered that feeling of release. It was better than sex and its afterglow had stayed with him for hours, an almost trance-like serenity.

'You can't murder an American in her room and get away with it,' No Name said, 'they'll turn the whole city upside-down to find you.'

'Maybe.'

'I always knew you were a dangerous motherfucker. I didn't think you were stupid, huh.'

'You're gibbering like an old woman.'

'If you want to save your neck, you'd better get out of Saigon.'

'I'm not going anywhere.' Michel hacked off another slice of melon. 'Want some breakfast?'

No Name turned away. Well, he'd warned him. If the idiot was going to wait around for the police to find him, that was his problem. He didn't want to be there when they did.

Later that afternoon, No Name was back outside the Caravelle looking for customers. Two cigarette girls were squabbling with each other at the entrance, each claiming the territory as her own.

A crew-cut American walked out, pushing his way through the shoeshine boys, beggars, and cripples hawking Capstan cigarettes and Juicy Fruit.

No Name fell into step beside him and affected the theatrical whisper that he used to add urgency to his pitch. 'Hey, Mister, you want to buy smack, huh? Want to boom-boom my sister? What do you want, Mister, huh?'

The young man kept walking.

'Hey, Mister, what do you want, huh?'

The man stopped and wheeled around. 'I want you to look at me.'

No Name took a step back. What the hell was this?

The American took off his sunglasses and grinned. 'Still think I should get out of Saigon?'

'Jesus Christ, Round Eye!'

Michel ran his hand across his head. 'Didn't you recognize me?'

'How did you-'

'Amazing what a haircut can do. Then I put on a pair of sunglasses and a leisure suit and ordered a beer in the front bar. Not one of the stupid bastards looked twice at me. They're all telling each other how they'd like to get their hands on the son of a bitch who murdered the girl. And I was standing right next to them.'

No Name shook his head. The transformation was incredible, but it was more than just the hair and the sunglasses. Michel had changed the language of his body, the set of his shoulders, the way he held his head, the way he walked. He had shrugged off his Asian blood like a serpent shedding its skin.

'You went back to the same bar?'

'I cursed that gook murdering cocksucker right along with them. I even bought one of the fat bastards a drink. Guess whose money it was?'

'You're really crazy.'

'I'm not crazy, I'm invisible. I can be whatever I like, East or West, whenever I want. It's my birthright.' He laughed and walked away, disappearing among the press of bodies along the Tu Do and ignoring the street beggars who jostled and pulled at his shirt.

No Name shuddered. He didn't give a damn about the American girl, but murder was a dangerous game to play. Michel had raised the stakes. He wasn't sure he could afford to play.

PART 3

Birthright: 1967-72

CHAPTER 14

Paris
August 1967

'Shhh!' Valentine whispered, and fell heavily up the wooden stairs, shrieking with laughter.

The boy bent down and pulled her to her feet. Suddenly her arms were around his neck, and he felt her warm, wine-sweet mouth on his. The kiss electrified him. He groaned as his belly tightened, and he was suddenly hard and ready for her. He pushed her against the wall, but she wriggled away and clambered, giggling, to the top-floor apartment.

A door edged open on one of the landings and a grey-haired woman in a black smock peered out. The boy wrinkled his nose at the smell of boiled cabbage and cheap scent. He hurried up the stairs after Valentine.

All that *vin ordinaire* they had drunk in the schoolyard slowed him down. By the time he caught up with her, she was already fumbling for her key. She had stolen it that afternoon from her mother's purse.

'I love you,' he said, knowing he sounded utterly foolish.

She looked up smiling, put her hands on his shoulders and kissed him again.

Suddenly the door to her apartment swung open, spilling light onto the landing. The boy pulled away, startled.

Valentine pushed him towards the stairs. 'Go!' she hissed.

He hesitated for only a moment, then took off. He looked back just once, from the second-floor landing, but already Valentine and her father had gone. He heard the apartment door slam.

'Do you know what time it is?'

'I'm sorry, Papa.'

Jean-Claude sniffed. 'You've been drinking.'

'Yes.'

'Is that it?' He wanted - expected - her contrition. He had spent the last two hours pacing the floor of the apartment, frantic with worry. Instead, her face showed neither remorse nor guilt. 'Who was that boy?'

'He is in my class at school.'

'What were you doing?'

'We were kissing, that's all.'

'You're only fifteen years old!'

'So?' She raised her chin at him in defiance.

So much like her mother in so many ways. She even looked like her - or how she used to look. 'You are my daughter. I expect you to behave like a lady.'

'What is all the noise?'

He turned around. Adrienne stood in the doorway of their bedroom, her silhouette framed by the bedside lamp. Her hair was mussed from sleep. She had been drinking again, he could smell it. Two drunks in the house.

'Nothing is wrong, go back to bed.'

'You were shouting.'

'It's all right, *Maman,*' Valentine said. She took her mother's arm and led her back to the bedroom. The door closed.

Jean-Claude slumped into a tall-backed chair by the window. His wife lived her life closeted in her bedroom with a wine bottle. They had spent most of the last seven years in clinics and hospitals, seeing doctor after doctor, looking for someone who might exorcise her demons. None of them did any good.

And soon his daughter would be gone, too. He would lose her to some boy.

Valentine came out of the bedroom, shutting the door gently behind her. 'I'm sorry. I won't do it again.'

'You're a good girl,' he said, but as he looked into her eyes - two dark pools surrounded by shallows of pale green - he shivered.

She was Adrienne's daughter. There was no doubt about it.

CHAPTER 15

Saigon

Michel leaned on the handlebars of his Honda motor scooter, his eyes trained on the press of humanity on the sidewalk. It was early afternoon and the streets were crowded. Schoolchildren in white and blue uniforms mingled with fresh-faced ARVN. Vietnamese women, in black pajamas and conical straw hats, carried mangoes and pineapples to the market in wicker baskets.

He revved the engine and waited.

No Name leaned forward on the seat behind him. 'Over there,' he said.

Michel looked where he was pointing. A middle-aged and plump Vietnamese woman in a flowing *ao-dai* was making her way along the arcade close to the road. A heavy, leather handbag bounced on her arm.

He revved the motor again with a flick of his right wrist. Then he swooped across the flow of the traffic, ignoring the blaring horns of the motorbikes and taxis. He maneuvered the scooter next to the curbside, his eyes fixed on the woman.

As they roared past, No Name threw out an arm, his fingers clutching the straps of the bag and wrenching it free. The woman screamed, attempted to grab it back, then fell forwards onto her knees.

'Go!' No Name shouted.

Michel revved the Honda to full throttle and weaved away through the press of taxis and bikes. He looked back over his shoulder and cursed. A bottle-green and white police jeep had appeared from a side street. A cop got out, pulling his service revolver from the holster at his hip.

He cut across the line of traffic in front of a sputtering Lambretta, spilling the rider, his wife and three children on to the road.

The first two gunshots were muted by the blaring of horns.

Michel couldn't believe the cop would fire into a crowded street. These guys don't give a shit about anyone anymore, he thought.

A small boy on the sidewalk a few feet away collapsed onto the ground. A Vietnamese woman, probably his mother, shrieked and rushed over to him.

Michel weaved down the street looking for an alleyway that would take them to safety. He heard another gunshot and felt No Name slump forward and slip sideways off the pillion seat. The scooter skewed beneath him, the handlebars twisting around. He dropped the machine and threw himself clear. The Honda crashed into a food stall, spilling boiling soup and barbecued ducks onto the pavement.

No Name lay face-down in the middle of the street. There was a large red stain on the back of his white t-shirt.

Too bad, Michel thought. But better you than me. He jumped to his feet and ran through the screaming crowd, favoring his left foot, blocking out the pain in his twisted ankle. He could hear the wail of police sirens.

He limped into a side street, ignoring the startled, frightened faces, and tried to lose himself among the press of secretaries, schoolchildren, beggars, hawkers and businessmen. He ran until the breath burned in his lungs and black spots appeared in front of his eyes. Soon, he was in a part of Saigon even he did not know.

But the police whistles were still too close.

He looked up. The crude hand-painted sign over his head proclaimed in a gold lettering: THE SAIGON AND BOMBAY TAILORING COMPANY

He stumbled inside.

It was quiet, cool and dim. A heavy brass fan labored overhead. Racks of jackets and suits hung on a rail on the wall, partly concealed behind a thick, red velvet drape. Behind the counter, a handsome young man with wild eyes and denim jeans stared at him in mute surprise. He started, then realized it was his own reflection.

Suddenly, a curtain at the back of the shop was thrown aside and a fat, balding Indian appeared. The two men stared at each other.

Joginder, anticipating a customer, had assumed a greasy smile. Seeing this thug in his shop, the smile vanished. 'What do you want?' he said.

Michel had already figured it out. He had lost a lot of hair and blown up like a balloon, but when some bastard rapes your mother in front of you and turns you onto the street, there's something about him you don't forget.

'What do you want?' Joginder repeated. 'Who are you?'

Michel heard the blasts of the police whistles fading into the distance. It was safe now. He could double back across the canal, disappear in the maze of Cholon city.

He turned for the door.

'I said what do you want?' Joginder said. 'What are you doing here?'

Michel smiled at him, gave a mocking salute and left.

Joginder Krisnan should have been a happy man. He had just delivered a new suit to an American colonel at the Caravelle. The colonel was an important man who had promised to recommend Joginder to his colleagues and associates. On any other day he would have been celebrating his good fortune.

Instead, as he made his way back to his shop through the darkening streets, his fleshy face was furrowed with concern. He ignored the outstretched palms of the beggars - he usually slipped them a few coins for good karma – and hurried along, head down, sweat staining his white silk shirt. He did not enjoy the aromas of burning joss from the pagoda as he usually did and was not tempted by the tang of garlic and anise from the roadside stalls.

He took inventory of his life, as he liked to do at the end of every day.

He now owned three shops: two in Bombay and one in Saigon on the Ngo Duc Ke. He had a large, six-room flat above his shop, staffed with two servants. He still had Sai to cook, clean and minister to him. When he tired of her, he had money enough to engage the talents of the prettier Chinese whores of Cholon, though he had found his carnal needs decreasing of late. He preferred a good *bhel puri*.

On the debit side of the ledger, his wife in Bombay was a harridan with betel-stained lips and a body like a concertina, but he had so contrived his affairs that he no longer had to spend more than a month or two every few years in her company.

Yes, Joginder Krisnan should have been a happy man.

Until two days ago, so had he been. But the appearance of that desperate looking young man in his shop had disturbed his tranquility. He had tried to tell himself it was just his imagination, but something about that face was too familiar. It was like looking at himself, twenty years ago.

The Germans had a word for it. Doppelgänger. That was it. But there was nothing paranormal about this event. It could be him. It must be him.

He had not thought about it in a long time. He remembered that French whore and that brat of hers that Sai had taken away, when he was still living in the dog hole on the Rue Le Loi. He should have died long ago. How could he have survived? What was more absurd - what if he had recognized him?

He turned down the alleyway beside his shop. Stop worrying, he told himself. He was four years old the last time he saw you.

A hand closed over his mouth from behind and pulled him off his feet. He felt his bowels turn to water. He struggled feebly against the arm at his throat, but it was no good. Whoever it was, they were strong.

A switchblade glinted in the dark.

'I ought to cut your throat.'

Joginder tried to say something, tried to plead with his assailant, but the hand clamped his jaw shut tight.

'Don't struggle. It won't do you any good,' the voice said. 'God, you're like a sack of blubber. It would be like opening up a whale.'

The man took his hand away. But then his arm curled around Joginder's throat, squeezing so hard he thought his eyes would burst out of his head. He pushed him onto the ground.

Joginder rolled over. 'Don't hurt me! I have money! Please don't kill me!' The knife blade glittered a few inches from his face.

'You disgust me,' the man said.

A fleck of spittle spilled from Joginder's lips and ran down his chin.

'Yes. You recognize me, don't you? You know who I am.'

'I don't know-'

The toe of Michel's shoe hit him just under his chin, snapping his neck back. He groaned, spat blood out of his mouth.

Michel expertly emptied his pockets of a thick wad of bank notes. He bent down. 'Thank you for the allowance, Father. I'll be back.'

Joginder didn't doubt it for a moment.

Paris

November 1967

The two cigarettes glowed in the dark. It was late evening, and the streetlamps were on, throwing arcs of sodium light onto the pavement. The two girls, crouched in the doorway of the apartment building, seemed to shrink from it.

'What will you do after the *baccalauréat*' Valentine said.

Madeleine blew a smoke ring. 'I want to be a model.'

'Really?'

'I know what you're thinking. You're right, I suppose. I don't have the figure for it.'

'I wasn't thinking that.'

'We can't all be built like you. You could be a movie star.'

'Don't be stupid.'

'It's true. Boys go crazy after you. So, what will you do, after school?'

'I don't know. I haven't thought about it.'

'Everybody thinks about it. What if you could do anything, go anywhere you wanted?'

Valentine shivered. It was getting late. In the distance the lights on the tip of the Tour Eiffel glowed red against the night.

'I want to travel. Not just in Europe. To exotic places, like India and Siam.'

Madeleine laughed. 'Oh, you want to be a hippie. Wear flowers in your hair.'

'No, not that kind of travelling. I want to stay in expensive hotels and travel around in big limousines.'

'What about men? Will you take a lot of lovers?'

Valentine frowned. 'I want just one man. Someone tall and dark and a little wild. Someone dangerous and romantic. That's what I want.' She stubbed out the cigarette on the stone doorstep. 'Can I have another cigarette?'

They smoked in silence for a while, relishing the illicit act more than the bitter taste of the smoke.

'How are things at home?' Madeleine said.

'Bad.'

On cue, they heard a woman screaming from the top-floor apartment.

Valentine sighed. The cigarette tumbled end over end into the street. She got to her feet. 'I have to go. I'll see you tomorrow at school.'

CHAPTER 16

Saigon

Joginder Krisnan's life had been changed very little by a war that, for twenty years, had become as much a backdrop to the country as the jungle itself. Despite having to pay VC tax - every merchant in Saigon was obliged to pay off the local Viet Cong cadres - he had twenty million piastres in his safe in the corner of his office.

For the past three years, he had stopped sending his money back to Bombay because he suspected his brother-in-law was cheating him, and he did not trust him with such enormous amounts. The next time he returned to India, his money would travel with him to help purchase the villa he had always promised himself, high above Back Bay.

He thought about his dream as he sat naked on the edge of the bed. He watched a droplet of perspiration trickle down his chest and into the thick folds of his belly. It was stifling hot in the tiny room.

The girl lying beside him stifled a yawn and sat up. 'Baby, want to fuck me now,' she crooned in a Texan drawl. 'You number thirty-five!' Thirty-five was the Vietnamese symbol for virility.

Joginder pushed her away.

She shrugged and picked up a nail file from the bedside table. She started to manicure her nails.

A bed creaked on the other side of the thin wall, and Joginder listened to the theatrical groans of some other girl servicing a captain in the 7th US Cavalry. A tiny chin-chook lizard darted, ever watchful, along the exposed beams of the roof.

His impotence was all the girl's fault, of course. They were saving the really pretty ones for the Americans these days. Now the girls chewed gum and wore electric-pink skirts and make-up. He wished he'd gone to the café instead and read the newspaper.

He found himself thinking about Adrienne. He never had trouble getting hard back then. He wondered if he should have been kinder to her. But she would be old and fat by now, just like his wife. Besides, she was too demanding. She had treated him like a coolie.

Well, she'd had her revenge.

Joginder had thought that after Michel stole his money, he might be satisfied. But one night, as Joginder sat in his favorite restaurant, Michel had shown up again. He had calmly pulled up a chair as if he was his dinner guest. He was wearing reflector sunglasses and a white t-shirt.

A handsome young man, Joginder had to admit, as he himself had once been. He saw how the pretty Vietnamese cashier looked at him. The manager saw her and cuffed her smartly behind the ear.

'You don't seem pleased to see me,' Michel said.

'Get away from me.'

He lounged in his chair. 'I'm sorry about our last meeting, Father. My emotions get away from me sometimes.'

'Don't call me that, I'm not your father. I'll have you arrested.'

The smile vanished instantly, and Michel leaned across the table, lowering his voice to a whisper. 'Listen to me. I know who you are. We are blood, you and me. You owe me. Oh, you owe me so much.'

'I don't know what you're talking about.'

'A hundred thousand piastres. Have it ready for me. A hundred thousand piastres, and you will never see me again.'

'I'm a poor man,' Joginder said. The thought of giving away so much money made him feel physically sick.

'Just have the money ready,' Michel said. 'I'll give you a week.' He walked away and in seconds he was lost among the press of ARVN and American soldiers along Nguyen Van Thieu.

A week passed, nothing.

After a month, Joginder began to hope that Michel had forgotten about him.

Then one day, he suddenly appeared beside him on the Tu Do. Joginder felt a friendly arm go around his shoulders.

'Do you have my inheritance?'

He did not recognize Michel immediately. He had dyed his hair blonde and could have passed for a Frenchman or a German. The boy was a chameleon.

Joginder fumbled in his breast pocket and took out the thick manila envelope he had carried with him everywhere for weeks. 'Here, take it and leave me alone,' he said.

'That's it? After all I have suffered?'

'Just go, for God's sake!'

Michel stuffed the envelope into his linen jacket. Then he was gone, melting away as quickly as he had come.

Joginder was glad it was finally all over.

But it had only just begun. Michel came back again and again, dogging him wherever he went. Always he wanted more money.

Joginder thought of going to the police, but he knew there was nothing they could - or would - do. All they cared about was finding Viet Cong cadres in Cholon.

Still, Michel was cautious. He never showed up in the same place twice. Sometimes Joginder would not see him for three days, sometimes three weeks. But he would always come back.

Always asking for more money.

Joginder heaved himself to his feet and started to dress. He looked at the girl preening and fussing over her crimson-painted nails. Women. They were nothing but trouble. Why couldn't Adrienne have cared for her little brat like a real mother?

Still, what was done was done. It was pointless raking over the past. A solution would have to be found. Otherwise, Michel might soon be asking him to take out adoption papers.

Yes, he thought. That's it!

Suddenly he knew what he had to do. It was so simple that he stopped halfway through buttoning his shirt and laughed out loud. The girl looked up, alarmed.

Joginder felt his depression lift. He clapped his hands and began to unbutton his shirt. Why hadn't he thought of it before?

He crawled on all fours across the bed, his monstrous belly swinging beneath him. At least one part of him was hard.

'All right you dog-faced little Chinese slut,' he chortled, couching his insults in Hindi, 'the jewel has once again found its sparkle.'

As Joginder stepped out into the hot afternoon sun, Michel was waiting for him in the back of a *cyclopousse*.

'Can I offer you a lift, Father?'

Joginder caught his breath, startled. Well, speak of the Devil. He eased his bulk onto the cracked leatherette seat.

The Vietnamese driver stood on his pedals and guided his substantial cargo into the snarl of traffic.

'You don't seem pleased to see me, Father.'

'All you ever want is money. You never give me the chance to talk to you.'

The vapid smile slipped away. 'A bit late for a fatherly chat, isn't it?'

'I've wronged you. I do not deny it. If you give me a chance, I can make up for it.'

Michel sat forward so violently their driver had to jerk the handlebars to the left to prevent them from crashing into the curbstones. 'Make up for it. Make up for throwing a helpless little boy out onto the street?'

'It was a long time ago. Everyone changes. As I said, I do not deny that I've wronged you.'

There it was. A flicker of hope in Michel's eyes. You're all bluff, Joginder thought.

'Well then,' Michel said, 'you can start with another hundred thousand piastres. Perhaps that will help assuage your guilt.'

They were caught in the sprawl of traffic beside the Saigon River. Big-bellied children and thin-ribbed dogs squabbled in the mud alleys between the wooden shanties.

Michel pointed. 'Look, that was what you condemned me to. While you were growing fat on chicken grease, I was fighting with pi-dogs for scraps of food in Cholon. Now it's your turn to pay.' He started to climb down into the road.

Joginder caught him by the wrist. 'Wait, I have something to say.'

Michel shrugged and sat down again.

'Look, Michel, every man makes mistakes when he is younger. Only a few of us ever have the chance to right them again. I'm not asking for your forgiveness. All I want is the chance to atone for the wrong I have done.'

'What are you talking about?'

'I can do more than give you a few thousand piastres. I can give you a new life.'

'Go on.'

Joginder licked his lips. 'I will be leaving Saigon. Things are bad here. The Viet Cong are making life miserable for everyone. I will close the shop and go back to India. I have two more shops in Bombay and my family is there, I have a wife and four sons.' He took a deep breath. 'I want you to come with me.'

'Why would I do that?'

'I need an extra pair of hands to help me run the shops. You are young. I can teach you. I don't want to work for ever. You will be my adopted son. You will finally have a family, somewhere you belong.'

Michel looked at the crumbling shophouses, the bars and street stalls, the bootblacks and war-crippled beggars, and everywhere the battle greens of the ARVN and the American soldiers.

Joginder pressed his point. 'Don't you want to get away from here?'

'How can I trust you?'

'Give me one more chance. Please.'

Michel launched himself from the back of the *cyclopousse*, almost spilling it onto its side. He walked straight into the path of a Vespa and sent it swerving into a taxi. The rider dropped the machine into the gutter and got to his feet screaming abuse at the *cyclopousse* driver and at Joginder.

When Joginder looked around, Michel was gone.

One night, a week later, Joginder was at his workbench stitching the seams of a dress jacket he was tailoring for a Marine staff officer. The oil lamp hissed and spluttered. He resettled the half-moon spectacles on his nose and adjusted the bobbin on the ancient Singer. There was a soft tapping at the door.

He got up, rubbing his eyes with the balls of his fists. 'Who is it?'

There was no answer. It's him, he thought. He took a moment to compose himself and threw open the door.

'Hello, Father.'

'You want money?'

'No. I want to go to Bombay.'

Joginder grinned and flung open his arms. 'Welcome home,' he said.

'Why can't I stay here?'

'Because the soldiers will find you, and you will be drafted into the army. You can avoid them on the streets, but they come here at least once a week looking for draft dodgers.'

'What about you then? When will you go back to India?'

'I don't know. One day soon. While the Americans are still here, there is a lot of money to be made. War is good for men like me. But when it is over, I will go back to Bombay and retire. I will let my family run my businesses.'

They were sitting in Joginder's cool and shuttered office above his shop on Ngo Duc Ke. The office faced a Chinese cinema. Through a half-open shutter, Michel stared at a hand-painted poster of a Chinese in a Stetson massacring Red Indians with an AK-47. The lurid reds and greens of the poster hurt his eyes.

He looked back at Joginder. He was pouring black tea into two small and tannin-stained china cups.

'You have no identity,' Joginder was saying, 'no papers. Without papers you do not exist in this world.'

'I'm your son. You can get me an Indian passport.'

'It's not as easy as that. The hospital did not keep records. I have been to the Indian consulate, and they insist that you spend twelve months in India and learn one of the languages before they will give citizenship.'

'I don't understand. How will I get to Bombay?'

'Don't worry. I have prepared everything.' Joginder reached into a drawer and threw some papers onto the desk. 'I have arranged a safe-transit document from Vietnam to India. You travel on the SS Siam.'

'And then?'

'After a year in Bombay, you will get your papers. You will become a citizen of India like myself. Then perhaps, you can come and work here with me and learn the business until I am ready to retire. The important thing is you will have an identity.' He put a hand to his chest in a gesture of contrition. 'And I will be able to sleep easy again in my bed.'

It would have been so easy to kill you, Michel thought. That night in the alley, he had planned to cut his throat. Something had held him back. It wasn't pity. He just wanted him to suffer more.

It was only later that he had realized Joginder was rich. He had used the money to indulge his gambling habits at the cockfights and at the racetrack on the Su Van Hahn. He didn't have to hustle and steal any more. One day, he would settle with him for good. For now, he was still useful.

'I hated you so much,' he said.

'I understand,' Joginder said, 'and I am not asking you to forget the past. Only to weigh it against the future.'

'All right. When do I leave?'

Joginder smiled. 'The day after tomorrow. That is when you start your new life.'

The Gage Roads, Bombay

Michel stared at the dirty, milk chocolate water. As they sailed closer to the mainland, the air became tainted with the smells of the vast city. The stench of decay and pollution carried on the offshore breeze.

Bombay lay just beyond the indigo horizon. By morning, their rusty freighter would be anchored within sight of the Gateway wall and the crumbling Gothic and colonial buildings of the waterfront.

Two weeks since they had sailed out of the docks at Saigon. He had stood at the guardrail that last evening and solemnly said his farewells to his father. It had all seemed unreal, a fantasy come to life.

'My brother will be there to meet you in Bombay,' Joginder had said. 'I have written and told him all about you. He will take good care of you.' He reached into his pocket and handed Michel an envelope. 'Here is a little money to tide you over.'

There was two thousand piastres inside.

'I hope to hear good reports of you.' He held out his hand.

Michel took it. It was soft, like a woman's. 'When will I see you again?'

'How many times must I tell you? As soon as you have your citizenship papers, you can return whenever you want. I look forward to that day.'

'In case I don't... in case something happens. I want you to tell me my mother's name. I remember she was called Adrienne. What was her last name?'

Joginder's smile faded. 'Can't you forget about that? It was such a long time ago. Think only about tomorrow.'

'Tell me.'

Joginder sighed. 'Adrienne Christian.'

'What was she like?'

Joginder's face shone with sweat. He dabbed at it with his handkerchief. 'I can't remember her. It was over twenty years ago now. She had long black hair and she was very pretty.'

'Did you love her?'

'She was a devil. All women are devils.'

'But you must have loved her once.'

'I don't want to talk about this.'

'I want to know about her.'

'Why, what does it matter to you now?"

'The past is everything. It is with us always.'

'Well, I've forgotten all about it,' Joginder said. 'I'd better be going. The boat will be leaving soon.'

Michel put a hand on his arm. 'Where is she now?'

'How should I know? I never saw her again.'

'You must have heard something.'

'All I know is she left Saigon a few months after she abandoned you.'

'Did she get married?'

'I don't know. I think so.'

'One day, I will find her.'

'And do what?'

'She owes me a debt. And she will repay it, like you are repaying yours.'

Suddenly, Michel threw his arms around his father's shoulders and embraced him. His lips brushed the older man's cheek. 'Thank you, Father. You have saved me. You have given me a home again.'

Joginder seemed stunned by the sudden display of affection. He loosened the collar of his shirt. 'I'm only doing what I should have done a long time ago. Goodbye, Michel.'

'Au revoir,' Michel said.

An hour later, the SS Siam steamed out into the South China Sea, and its lights were swallowed up by the deepening night.

Michel woke moments before they came for him. On the street he had developed a sixth sense that alerted him to danger, to the slightest noise, and he sat upright in his bunk and looked around. It was dark in the cabin. The North Star was framed in the tiny porthole, a needlepoint of brilliant white. He knew something was wrong. He swung his legs out of his bunk and fumbled for his clothes.

Before he could dress, the door crashed open, and he felt an arm go around his throat. He struck behind him with an elbow, then lashed out with his heel. In the darkness, a man screamed.

But there were more of them, how many he couldn't tell. He was wrestled to the deck, struggling with the desperation of a wild animal, biting, clawing, kicking out at his unseen assailants.

A fist smashed into his face, stunning him. Then a knee hammered into his groin, and he heard himself scream. He curled into a ball on the cabin floor to protect himself from further blows. One of the attackers knelt on his back, pulling his hands behind him, and he felt a thin cord biting into his wrists. Someone else took a handful of his hair and smashed his head repeatedly against the metal decking until he passed out.

When he opened his eyes, he found himself lying in storage, a space barely wide enough to stretch his legs. One wall curved with the hull of the ship, and foul oil-stained water slopped on the floor. There were no windows, so he guessed he was somewhere below the waterline.

His arms were tied behind him and the barest movement sent spasms of pain through his shoulders and wrists. He hawked into the bilges and tried to sit upright. He couldn't do it. He allowed his body to sink back into the lapping rust-stained water.

He tried to think, make sense of this nightmare.

What had happened? He had a valid ticket. The captain must be in on this. But what did he want? He wouldn't do this just for the two thousand piastres he had in his bag.

For now, there was nothing he could do. He conserved his strength and waited.

January in India is the dry season. Around Bombay it is only slightly cooler than the mid-year monsoon, the temperature hovering in the eighties, day after day. By late afternoon, the sun has scorched all the oxygen from the air. It is like living inside a pressure cooker.

When they finally dragged Michel out of the storage hold, the heat below decks had reached a hundred and ten degrees. He was already dehydrated, and his tongue had swollen in his mouth like a bruised plum. They threw him onto the floor in the captain's cabin and stood aside.

Captain Parwit Charankorn studied the young man and swallowed down his feelings of regret. He earned thirty dollars a month for navigating this rust bucket between Saigon and Bombay, and he had a wife and nine children in Bangkok. When the Indian tailor had waved the fistful of rupees under his nose, he could hardly have refused.

Still, he was not by nature a cruel man, and he didn't enjoy seeing another man suffer. He turned to one of the crewmen who had dragged Michel up from the holds. 'Give him some water,' he said.

The man went out and returned a few moments later with a metal cup. He held Michel's head back and tipped the water into his mouth.

Michel looked into the unsmiling face of Captain Parwit. He tried to speak, but the words would not come out.

'You are a stowaway,' Captain Parwit said slowly in halting English.

Michel shook his head desperately. 'No,' he said. 'My father paid for my tickets in Saigon.' He recognized the three crewmen who had done this to him. He had seen them every day of the voyage. He had seen the captain only twice, but the captain had certainly seen him.

'What is your father's name?'

'Joginder Krisnan.' His head ached. It felt as if it were splitting apart.

'I know nobody of that name. Where are your papers?'

'In my cabin.'

'You do not have a cabin.'

'But my father-' Michel began and stopped. In that moment he saw it all with absolute clarity.

'You are a stowaway,' Captain Parwit repeated. 'I must hand you over to the authorities in Bombay. Do you understand?'

'How much did my father pay you?'

'I don't know what you're talking about. Take him up. The police launch will be alongside any moment.'

Michel went for him, or he would have done if he had the strength left in his body. But it wasn't the Thai captain he imagined in front of him, it was Joginder. He wanted to tear his throat out with his teeth.

As it was, the crewmen grabbed him easily before he could reach the captain, and then kicked him till he lay still.

White-faced and trembling, Captain Parwit got to his feet. 'Take him away,' he said. 'Quickly. He's a madman.'

Michel smelled the Port of Bombay jail long before he first saw it. He was handcuffed to three other men, all Indians, in the back of a prison van. Through the mesh grille of the rear window, he stared at the press of traffic as it honked and jostled. Oxcarts, buses, cyclists, trucks and battered hand carts competed with the yells of the balloon sellers and the chants of the *saddhus*. The sour odor of decay and stale urine hung over everything.

The man at his side nudged him. 'That is the prison,' he said, revealing the brown stumps that were all that remained of his teeth. 'What did you do?'

'Nothing,' Michel said. 'My father-' he stopped, still too bitter to recount the betrayal. 'I have no papers.'

The man rubbed his fingers together in a pantomime of counting notes. 'You have money?'

'I have two thousand piastres.'

'What are they?'

'It's Vietnamese money.'

The man laughed. He turned to the others and said something in Hindi. They laughed as well.

'What's so funny?'

'Keep the money. It will be very useful. For lighting a fire, perhaps.' He laughed again. He was starting to get on Michel's nerves. 'Unless you have rupees or American money, you might as well have nothing.'

Michel kicked the side of the van in fury. 'The bastard. When I get out, I'll cut out his liver and shove it down his fucking throat!'

'If you get out,' the man said.

'I'm only a stowaway. They'll ship me back to Vietnam, won't they?'

'First you must be brought to trial.'

'What do you mean?'

'You should have murdered someone,' the man said. 'Like I did. It would have been easier for you.'

'What are you talking about?'

'Take a last glimpse at the world, friend.'

'How long will they give me?'

'Six months. But that is not the problem. As I said, first you must get to court.'

'So?'

'You do not understand. To get to court you need a lawyer. Lawyers must be paid. Without a lawyer, you can wait a very long time for justice in India. Otherwise, you will rot and die in jail. Many do. No one cares'

CHAPTER 17

Port of Bombay Prison

Vultures squatted on the walls in grotesque malevolence preening their grease-black feathers. They craned their pink necks at the shuffling humanity in the compound below. A pall of dust clung to the scorched air. Families clustered around the medieval wooden gates clutching pannikins of curries and boiled rice for the inmates. The guards in their shabby uniforms looked on, silent and unmoved.

Andrew Rosen sat in the shade outside the mud hut in the Western section, listening to the footfall of the guard on the wall. Lank, blond hair curled around his shoulders, and his goatee beard accentuated, rather than disguised, his youthfulness. He was pale and thin. The filthy, embroidered shirt he wore had been bought in a bazaar in Kabul.

He had been in Bombay prison for seven months, ever since he had been arrested on the street buying hashish from a snaggle-toothed Indian boy - a police informer. He had sent an urgent telegram to his father in San Francisco.

This time his father had refused to bail him out.

Jack Rosen had wanted his son to go into the family business, become the third generation of Rosen Marine. Instead, Andy had grown his hair, dropped out of high school, and played Rolling Stones and Beatles records day and night. One night, Jack told his indolent son to get out of the house.

He hadn't meant it, but two days later young Andy was gone. It had been the first time in a very long while that he had obeyed one of his father's instructions.

Jack did not hear from his son again until he received a postcard picture of the Parthenon. There was one word scrawled on the back: Athens.

Two weeks later, Andy wrote again. He was in prison in Istanbul. He needed money.

Twice more, in Tehran and Kabul, Jack bought his errant son out of trouble. Each time, he extracted written promises that Andy would use the rest of the money to buy an air ticket back to the United States. Instead, Andy kept going further along the pot trail in Asia.

This time Jack had decided to teach his son a lesson.

Andy had accepted his punishment with equanimity. He knew that when his father considered he had done a suitable penance, he would get him out. He always did.

He watched with idle curiosity as the new prisoner was led across the compound, escorted by two khaki-clad soldiers.

He was tall, with shoulder length blond hair and startling brown eyes that didn't quite match. His clothes, a t-shirt and blue denim jeans, were filthy and sweat-stained, but the man who wore them had a panther-like grace about him. He looked around at his new surroundings with an arrogant calm.

Even when the two guards pitched him forward onto the ground, he seemed unperturbed. He got nimbly to his feet and brushed himself off.

'Welcome to the Bombay Hilton,' Andy said.

'Thanks. I won't be staying long.'

The young American laughed. 'Andy Rosen.' He held out a pale, bony hand.

'Michel.' For the first time Michel used the surname he had discovered just two weeks ago. 'Michel Christian.'

'You're French?'

'My mother was.' Michel looked up at the Sikh guard patrolling the five-meter-high wall, an ancient Enfield carbine slung over his shoulder. 'What's the best way out of here?'

Andy followed his gaze to the wall. 'Think you can jump that high?'

'There are other ways,' Michel said.

'Sure. You can buy your way out. Or die. What are you in for?'

'They say I'm a stowaway.'

'That's not too bad. You have money?'

'Not enough.'

'Then you must get some. Where are your family?'

'I don't have a family.'

'There must be someone. Everyone has a family.'

'No. I have no one.'

'Then you're a dead man, pal.'

Michel was still looking at the prison wall. The *bazaaris* were haggling in the market just on the other side. 'How far is it to the wall, do you think?'

'Who cares?'

'It can't be more than twenty meters.'

'Go anywhere near that wall, and they'll shoot you down like a dog.'

'No, they won't, because they won't see me.'

'Why? Are you going to make yourself invisible?'

'No,' Michel said. 'I'm going to dig a tunnel.'

There were two other prisoners sharing the hut - another American and a French-Canadian.

Freak had been a freshman at UCLA when the Beatles held the first five positions on the US Billboard charts, and the US Congress passed the Gulf of Tonkin resolution. Soon after, he discovered acid and the Rolling Stones, grew his hair, dropped out of college and went to live in Haight-Ashbury. In 1965 he had been drafted into the US army. In 1966, just north of Da Nang, he lost his right arm below the elbow.

He had developed a taste for the strong Afghan hash he bribed the guards to smuggle into his cell. Most days he drifted in and out of a psychedelic haze, mumbling unintelligibly into his beard.

The French-Canadian was known as Belmondo. His real name was Serge Duval, but he had earned his nickname because of his resemblance to the French actor. He claimed to own a two-storey house in Quebec and somehow managed to retain an appearance of sartorial elegance. It was an illusion of personality, for his silk shirt was ripped under each arm, and his cream cotton slacks were dirt-smeared and patched.

He had been arrested by the Indian police for fraud. When they opened his luggage at Bombay airport, they found twenty-three passports.

He was scornful when Michel told him about his plan.

'The earth here, see. It's baked hard.' He beat his hand on the floor to emphasize his point. 'You might as well try to dig through solid rock with your fingernails.'

'I didn't ask if you thought it was possible,' Michel said evenly. 'Only if you wanted to help.'

'I have bribed a lawyer to get me out of here. Why risk everything on a craziness like this?'

Michel turned to Freak, who was rocking gently on his heels in the corner. 'I'm going to dig a tunnel from the corner of the hut under the wall and into the bazaar. Do you understand?'

Freak giggled and waved the stump of his arm at him. 'No shit.'

'Do you want to help?'

Freak continued to rock back and forward.

Andy tugged at Michel's sleeve. 'You won't get any sense out of him tonight. We'll talk to him in the morning.'

Michel shrugged. 'All right.' He held out his hand. 'Give me your spoon. I need something to dig with.'

Belmondo shook his head. 'By the time you reach the wall, they'll have to get you out of the hole in a wheelchair.'

Andy unwrapped his flimsy bundle of possessions and handed Michel his metal spoon. He had paid one of the guards a *ghusa* - a bribe - to buy it for him in the bazaar. He didn't want to part with it, but he didn't see how he could say no.

Michel went to the far corner of the hut and began to scrape at the dirt.

'Give him an hour,' Belmondo said to Andy, 'he'll have had enough. Then we'll have enough talk about tunnels.'

But Belmondo had underestimated his man. As he dug, Michel thought of Joginder and Adrienne. With each scrape of the brick-hard earth, he made a silent promise that they would both live to regret what they had done to him.

He dug all through the night, waiting when the guard's footsteps came close, then beginning again as soon as the steady tramp-tramp continued along the wall. He kept working until the first light.

When Belmondo and Andy woke, they found that Michel had dug down almost three feet.

'Four days,' he said. 'Four days and we'll be out of here.'

'If the guards find the hole, we're all for it,' Belmondo said. 'He is going to ruin everything for me!'

'They won't find it,' Michel said. 'We'll cover it with our sleeping mats.'

'What about the dirt? What will you do? Leave it in a pile outside the hut and hope no one will notice?'

'No,' Michel said. 'We'll spread it over the floor of the hut. We can take the big rocks to the outhouse toilet inside our shirts and empty them there.'

Andy smiled.

Belmondo hauled Michel to his feet. 'I'm not going to let you fuck things up for me.'

Michel's knee jerked into Belmondo's groin, and his hands moved so swiftly Andy did not even see the blows.

Suddenly Belmondo lay flat on his back, thick blood oozing from his nose and teeth. He put a hand to his mouth and found one of his front teeth in his palm. 'What the fuck is wrong with you?'

'Don't ever touch me again,' Michel said. He bent down, his voice low and chill. 'I'm getting out of here. And nothing is going to stop me.'

Freak sat outside the door of the hut, tapping on a cheap Indian drum. It covered any noise from Michel's excavations inside.

Andy went in with a pannikin of slimy rice and a half-raw chapati. Michel's feet protruded just out of the hole. He knelt down and tapped him on the ankle. 'Michel. Here, you gotta eat.' He helped him out of the hole.

Michel had toiled for eighteen hours without a break. He took the rice from Andy and wolfed it down. 'Are you coming with me?'

'If I don't, the guards will beat the shit out of the rest of us.'

'What about the other two?'

'The hippie wants in. But I haven't seen your friend Belmondo since this morning.'

'Where is he?'

'I don't know. Probably sulking because you bruised his pretty face. Where did you learn to fight like that?'

'At school.' Michel wiped his mouth with the back of his hand. 'I went to a very tough school. It was as big as a city, and everyone was a teacher. It was called Cholon.'

Andy looked at the hole. He couldn't believe how big it was getting. Michel's determination astonished him. 'You must want to get out pretty bad.'

'Oh, yes, I want to get out very badly. There is someone I have to see again. Every day away is a day too long.'

'A girl?'

'No. My father.'

'Your old man?'

'He is in Saigon, right now, fucking his whores, counting his money and laughing at the way he tricked me. He put me on a boat and paid the captain to turn me in as a stowaway. He thinks he has got rid of me.'

'Jesus, man. This is a joke, right?'

'Yes, it's a sort of joke. On me. But when I get out of here the joke will not be so funny anymore because I'm going to kill him.'

The tap-tap of the drums stopped abruptly. It was their warning signal. Freak had spotted a guard heading their way.

'Shit,' Andy said.

Michel was on his feet in an instant, spreading his bamboo sleeping mat across the hole in the floor. Andy went to the doorway, thinking to stall the guard somehow. He didn't get more than a couple of paces. The chief head warden and •two guards burst in, and one of the guards shoved Andy off his feet with the butt of his rifle.

Michel was already squatting on the mat, the pannikin and spoon in his lap. He took a spoonful of rice, looked up at the warden and offered him a beatific smile.

'Where is it?' the warden said in English.

'I don't understand,' Michel said.

The warden looked at the bamboo mat and kicked Michel off it. Then he bent down and whipped it away with a flick of his wrist. The dark mouth of the hole yawned back at him.

Michel hawked the phlegm from deep in his throat and spat on the floor. Belmondo.

'Oh, Jesus Christ,' Andy said and then the first boot thumped into his ribs.

The chief head warden was a tall, ramrod-straight Sikh. He wore the uniform of a major in the Indian army. He had a full and luxurious beard and all the arrogance of a career officer sent to exile in a demeaning job. He prided himself that no one had ever escaped from the prison while he had been the warden and the discovery of the tunnel had outraged him.

He had the guards drag all three of them into his office.

'Take off your clothes,' he said.

'These two men had nothing to do with the tunnel,' Michel said. 'It was my idea. I did it all.'

The warden drove his fist into his stomach and was disappointed to feel the youth's hard muscles absorb the blow.

Michel gasped and doubled over, but he didn't fall.

'I said, take off your clothes.'

He waited as the three men stripped down. He smiled. The American hippie was trembling like a girl. A yellow rope of urine spurted from him.

His knees gave way. One of the guards stepped forward to catch him, holding him up by the hair.

'Oh, shit,' Freak said. 'Christ all fucking mighty!'

The warden took off the thick, leather belt at his waist and wrapped it around his fist. He left the heavy buckle resting across the knuckles. 'Now, I am going to teach you a lesson. I will show you what happens when you try to escape from my prison. I am going to make you curse your mothers for bringing you into the world.'

When Andy woke up, he was lying in a bed in the hospital. A prison guard - one of the men who had beaten him - sat by the door sipping a cup of tea, his rifle resting across his knees.

He tried to move his arms and discovered his left wrist was manacled to the iron rail of the cot. There was an intense rhythmic pain behind his eyes, and when he tried to sit up, a sharp pain knifed through his lower abdomen. He abandoned the effort. He groaned and closed his eyes.

Later, a doctor examined him and told him in faltering English, 'You have concussion and a ruptured hernia. Someone has misused you very badly.' The man had a concerned frown on his face. 'I will try and persuade them to remove the handcuffs.'

Good as his word, that night the cuffs were removed.

Andy stayed in the hospital for three weeks. When he came back to the prison, the white of one eye was still the color of an overripe plum, and the scabrous wounds on his lips and above his right eye were infected. He had lost ten pounds and looked a wreck. The guards left him at the door of the hut and marched away.

Michel struggled to his feet and embraced him. Then he put his mouth to his ear. 'I've started another tunnel,' he whispered. 'We're halfway to the wall already. We're getting out of here!'

CHAPTER 18

Freak squatted in the corner, tears leaking down his cheeks and into his beard. He looked like a grotesque and withered gnome. He was sobbing and muttering to himself. None of them could make out what he was saying.

'What's the matter with him?' Andy said.

Michel shrugged. 'He's been like that since they found the first tunnel. He's frightened of the warden.'

'What are we going to do?'

'He smokes too much shit. And he's weak. It's not our problem.'

Andy persisted. 'We have to do something.'

'Why?' Michel sat in the doorway, spooning down some watery *lopsi* - a porridge made from flour and salt - his breakfast ration.

'Because we can't just sit here and watch him die.'

Michel did not answer.

Andy heard the spoon scraping the tin bottom of the pannikin. 'You don't give a damn, do you?'

'There are two kinds of people in the world,' Michel said. 'There are the weak and there are the strong. The weak give in when they are faced with a problem, and they die. The strong conquer life and survive. Your American friend is weak. It doesn't matter what we do. He's not going to make it.'

Freak mumbled something else and started to laugh. He waved the milk-white stump of his arm at them. One of the guards had stamped his boot on it during the beating.

'He's scared the guards are going to find the new tunnel,' Andy said.

'So, they'll beat us again. It's not important. What is important is getting out of here.'

'Christ, you mean it, don't you?'

'You can stay behind if you want to. Unless you're thinking of reporting our new tunnel to the warden, like Belmondo?'

'You know I wouldn't do that.' In fact, he had thought about it several times. 'Where is he? Did his lawyer get him out, after all?'

'He's dead.'

'What?'

'He had a fall in the shithouse. Smashed his head on a concrete trough.'

'Jesus Christ.'

Michel put down the pannikin, got to his feet and went to the corner. He pulled back his bamboo mat. 'Time to get back to work.'

'It wasn't you, was it? Did you kill him?'

'Of course not.' Michel stared at him. 'Do I look like a murderer to you?'

Freak was dead. He lay inside the hut, curled in a fetal position, his right arm tucked beneath him.

Andy squatted down beside him and prised the glass pill bottle out of his fingers. 'Jesus.'

'What are they?' Michel said.

'Mandrax. Sleeping tablets. Couple of these will put you out for the night. Looks like he swallowed half the bottle.'

Michel took them. He was more interested in the pills than the corpse. 'Where did he get them?'

'Bribed a guard I suppose. Same way we get anything in here.'

Michel emptied the remaining pills into his hand and put them into the pocket of his jeans.

'What are you doing?' Andy said.

'He won't be wanting them anymore.' Michel grabbed Freak's feet and started to drag him out of the hut. 'Let's get him out of here before he starts to stink.'

The tunnel was nine feet deep and fifteen feet long. The detritus from the hole had raised the floor of the hut four inches so that Michel and Andy had to step up to get inside. But the chief head warden, thinking that he had taught the two Westerners a lesson, no longer bothered to visit them.

Each morning and evening Michel jogged around the exercise yard, running the stiffness out of his muscles. The bemused faces of the other prisoners followed him as he completed his laps of the compound. Occasionally, one of the guards would yell something at him in Hindi and there would be a short bark of humorless laughter from his comrades.

Michel paid them no attention. For him, they did not exist.

One evening, soon after his return from hospital, Andy decided to join him as therapy for his broken body. He found it hard to keep up with him.

'Tonight,' Michel said.

'It's finished?'

'Yes. Are you coming?'

'Can you wait a few days?'

Michel stopped. Andy stopped too, resting his hands on his knees, out of breath. The beating and the three weeks in hospital had taken more out of him than he thought.

'Why do you want me to wait?'

'I got a letter from my old man today. He's organizing bail for me. I'll be out of here in a couple of days. No more than a week, anyway.' Andy looked pleadingly at him. 'I can't take the risk. Not now.'

'All right, then. Stay here.'

'You'll wait?'

'No, I've already waited too long.'

'Please!'

Michel grabbed his arm. 'Every hour that goes by is an hour too long. What if one of the guards walks behind the hut to take a piss and falls through that fucking hole? No. I go tonight.' He looked up at the wall. One of the guards in the watchtower was staring at them. 'Keep running.' He set off again.

Andy jogged along miserably behind him. 'I'm frightened.'

'I'll tell you what to do. I'll give you a couple of Mandrax. Once you're asleep, I'll call the guard. They'll think you've had a relapse and send you back to the hospital. So, you won't even be here when I escape.'

Andy exhaled in relief.

They reached the hut. Michel waved cheerfully to the guards on the wall. One of them flicked the stub of his cigarette at him and turned away, scowling.

Michel crawled on his belly through the burrow he had scraped from the hard earth. He'd calculated it to twenty feet. He tried not to think about it giving way. He could think of better ways to die than to suffocate under four feet of baked clay.

It took no more than two minutes to wriggle the length of the tunnel, a journey he had made countless times in the last few weeks.

At last, he reached the upward curve at the far end and began to punch free the last few inches of earth. The dirt cascaded onto his head. It got in his eyes and mouth and nose. He spat it out. When he looked back, he saw the sparkle of the night stars welcoming him. He smiled and started to crawl out of the hole.

Someone lit a match very close by. Michel looked up into the shocked face of a turbaned Sikh who was patrolling the perimeter outside the wall.

For a moment, they stared at each other in astonishment, and then the guard dropped the match on the ground and fumbled for his rifle. He fired. The bullet whistled a foot over Michel's head.

There was no choice. He pushed himself back down the hole and began to scramble back, feet first. The dirt showered on his head as the guard caved in the hole with his rifle butt.

He inched back along the tunnel, hoping the guards on this side of the wall didn't realize what was happening and try to collapse the whole tunnel in on him. He said a silent prayer and kept going.

When Andy woke up in the hospital the morning after he took the Mandrax, everyone was talking about Michel's attempted escape. Two attempts inside a month. It was unheard of. But no one seemed to know if Michel was alive or dead.

When he got back to the prison, a guard told him Michel was in maximum security, a euphemism for a bare earth dungeon deep under the main prison building. Andy bribed one of the guards to let him visit him.

Michel lay inside a dirt cage, three feet wide and four feet long, scarcely big enough for a man to squat.

As Andy's eyes grew accustomed to the dark, he felt his stomach turn. 'Sweet Jesus Michel. What have they done to you?'

Michel's eyes opened. 'It's all right,' he said. 'Nothing broken.' There were dark stains on his shirt, and his speech was slurred as if he were drunk. He stretched out a hand between the bars and gripped Andy's wrist. He still retained an astonishing strength. 'I have to get out of here.'

'Fuck's sake, you have to be kidding me!'

'I want you to get something for me.'

Andy shook his head. The man wasn't human. 'What is it you want?'

The chief head warden looked up, annoyed, as one of the guards threw open the door to his office. The insolent bastard had forgotten to knock.

'What is it?'

The man fired off a sloppy salute. 'It's the prisoner in maximum security, sir. He's dying.'

The warden threw his pen on the desk in disgust. He was busy composing a letter to the Minister congratulating himself on preventing two attempted escapes. He didn't like interruptions. 'What's wrong with him?'

'There's blood everywhere, sir. He won't stop screaming.'

The warden listened. Well, now that he mentioned it, he could hear something.

He was not sure whether he should be concerned. The prisoner had a French name, though he looked either Greek or Spanish, and had been arrested on board a Thai freighter enroute from a Vietnamese port. What nationality was he? His file did not make it clear. If it transpired that Michel was a European - and with a name like that, how could he not be - there might be serious repercussions if he died. Only a few days ago an American had died in his cell, and the US consul in Bombay was already raising hell.

Then there was the Canadian who had fallen in the latrines and smashed his skull. Already two deaths within a few weeks of each other. Another one would not look good on his record.

He made up his mind. 'All right,' he said, 'I suppose I'd better have a look.'

He strode down the stone steps leading to the cellars. He could hear the screams much more clearly now. He smiled at the irony of it. He had beaten the clever little bastard unconscious two nights ago and he hadn't uttered a sound. Perhaps if he had, he would not have been tempted to hit him so hard. The man's intransigence had been his inspiration.

Now the prick was screaming his lungs out.

He stopped in front of the heavy, metal door that led to maximum security and waited while the guard fumbled with the keys. It was dark and his nostrils quivered at the stench of putrefaction.

The guard swung open the door, and the warden stepped through, allowing his eyes a few moments to get accustomed to the gloom. There were six cages in all, three on each side of the narrow passage. Michel was the sole occupant, in the cage on the right at the end of the row. The warden crouched down and peered in. He asked the guard for his torch.

Michel's shirt was dark with blood. It dripped from his mouth and nose in cloying drops, staining his teeth and lips. There were great gouts of it on the dirt floor. He was still screaming.

'Hemorrhage,' the warden said. 'Handcuff him and take him to the hospital. Hurry!'

The doctor at Bombay hospital looked down at the patient on the stretcher and made no attempt to conceal his disgust from the prison guards who had brought him. 'Another one? What are you people doing over there?' He bent down to examine the man. He was semi-conscious. 'What happened to him?'

'A fall,' one of the guards said.

'The floors at the prison must be very slippery.'

The guard shrugged.

'Take his handcuffs off,' the doctor said.

'But the major said–'

The doctor wheeled on him, white-faced with fury. 'Take them off! Look at him. This man isn't going to run anywhere in that condition. Take them off!'

The guard did as he was told.

Michel opened one eye and looked around. A shoe box of a room. A guard sat on a chair by the door, his chin resting on his hands. His .303 rifle was cradled between his knees. He kept dozing off and waking himself again.

Neanderthal, Michel thought.

So far everything had gone well. But this time he would not be quite so eager to stick his head out of the hole. This time he would judge his moment.

Andy had kept his promise. The day after his first visit, he had returned with the tin cup and the syringe Michel had asked for. He had bribed a guard to get the syringe. Drugs and their prerequisites were in popular demand in the jail. The tin cup had once belonged to Freak.

'What are you going to do?' Andy had asked him.

'The best way to get out of any prison is to let the guards carry you out themselves.'

'How?'

'The less you know about it, the better.'

Andy turned to go. 'If my father doesn't get me out, send me some money, will you?'

'Yes, all right.'

'Promise me?'

'Yes, I promise.'

'Okay. Good luck, man.'

After he had gone, Michel waited half an hour then plunged the needle into a vein in his left arm. He siphoned off a syringe of his own blood and emptied it into the cup. He did it again and again until the cup was full.

Then he raised the cup to his lips and threw back his head. He made himself choke on the blood so that it went everywhere. It sprayed up the wall, over his shirt, through his nose.

Then he began to scream.

He smiled at how easy it had been. So much easier than scraping away that tunnel with a spoon.

It was night. The hospital corridors were quiet after the pandemonium of the day, when the hospital was filled with a shuffling mass of desperate people, some carrying listless infants in their arms, hands held out in supplication to the harassed, white-coated doctors.

There was a familiar clatter from outside. The guard looked up, hopefully. It was the night boy. The guard glanced at Michel, who feigned sleep. He got up and went out into the corridor to get a pot of chai.

As soon as he left the room, Michel stretched his arm out and pulled open the wooden locker by the side of the bed. His t-shirt and jeans had been tossed inside. He reached into the pocket of his jeans and brought out a handful of Mandrax pills.

He lay back on the bed with the tablets clutched in his right fist. Through slitted eyelids he watched the guard bring the teapot back into the room and settle it on the floor at his feet.

Michel groaned. The guard looked up.

He twisted and groaned again. The guard came over still clutching the rifle, unsure what to do. Michel gave a sudden yelp of pain, and the man took a step back, startled. He hesitated a moment and then went back into the corridor to fetch a nurse.

Michel leaned out of the bed and reached for the teapot. It was only just within reach. He felt the cuffs bite into the flesh of his ankles as he dragged it towards him. He dropped the Mandrax into the brown, milky liquid. Then he pushed it back towards the guard's chair.

When the guard and nurse ran back into the room Michel was lying on his back, sleeping peacefully.

'You said he was screaming,' the nurse said in Hindi.

'He was,' the guard said. 'He was white as a sheet.'

The nurse picked up Michel's wrist and checked his pulse, holding her other hand to his forehead. 'Pulse and temperature are both normal. Perhaps he was just shouting out in his sleep.' She frowned in irritation. 'There's nothing wrong with him,' she said and left the room.

The guard shrugged, sat down and picked up the pot of chai. He poured some into a tin cup. He sipped it and resumed his position, with his chin on his hands, rifle between his knees. He yawned. It was going to be a long night.

Ten minutes later, he slumped from the chair, falling heavily forwards onto his face, his rifle clattering onto the tiled floor beside him.

Michel leaned out of bed, reached for the key ring attached to the guard's belt and twisted it free. He prayed the nurse did not come back on her rounds in the next few minutes. He unlocked the shackles around his ankles and pulled the jeans and the bloodied t-shirt from the cupboard.

A few minutes later, he walked out of the front gates of the hospital. It had been six weeks to the day since he had been arrested.

CHAPTER 19

Bombay

The city of Bombay was built on the narrow neck of a peninsula jutting into the Arabian Sea. Crowded bazaars and ragged, squalid slums clustered beneath the gleaming plate-glass of the high rises on Nariman Point. The air was clamorous with the blaring horns of the traffic snarled in its streets, and the pavements were pockmarked with rotting garbage. Sacred cows jostled for space alongside the scabrous beggars, women in twirling saris, and businessmen in western suits scurrying to appointments.

Gaudy, garlanded images of Ganesh were everywhere. The plump and baby-limbed god with the head of an elephant was the Hindu god of money, luck and prosperity, and Bombay's icon.

Bombay was India's New York.

The sprawling tenement *chawls* and pavement hovels were home to the millions who came to the city in search of their dreams and found only disease and despair. They poured in from the surrounding countryside at a rate of six thousand new families per day. The population was cosmopolitan, drawn from every race in India. There were churches and shrines for Hindus, Moslems, Catholics, Buddhists, Jains, Parsees, Sikhs and Jews.

VENOM

Foreigners came from everywhere: wealthy Arabs from the Gulf States, hippies from San Francisco, plump tourists from the Mid-West, and elegantly tailored businessmen from France and Germany.

In such a melting pot of humanity, Michel Christian became instantly invisible. He sauntered out of the gates and walked for about an hour through the night streets, putting distance between himself and the hospital. Then he curled up on the pavement, at the end of a long line of huddled, blanketed shapes, and fell into a deep sleep.

He woke to a grey and sticky dawn.

Ragged toddlers, doe-eyed and solemn, played in the street beside their still-sleeping parents. Bodies rose from the shadowy lines of blankets like ghosts and joined the crowd of people milling around a street pump, collecting water for the day in bowls and empty kerosene tins. Shopkeepers urinated in the gutters and cleaned their teeth with their fingers using white monkey powder. Mission workers collected the night's dead and dumped them outside the taxi rank, while a frail nun in a blue habit walked along the line making the sign of the cross.

Within an hour, the sleeping city had been transformed into a honking, chanting kaleidoscope of sun, traffic and smog.

Michel found his way to the Victoria terminus, Bombay's central railway station. It was a dirty, Victorian Gothic edifice, impossibly ornate and surrounded by hordes of beggars and black and yellow taxis. He fought his way through the chaos and went inside.

It was packed with travelers, rich and poor. They struggled through the crowds with their luggage or lay wherever there was space, exhausted by the delays. Within a few minutes, Michel had quickly and expertly rifled the backpack of a sleeping Canadian student.

When he walked out, he had travelers' checks worth a hundred Canadian dollars and a cheap Instamatic camera. He sold them on the street an hour later and bought himself some new clothes - jeans, sandals and an embroidered shirt - then wolfed down three helpings of shrimp curry and *pau bhaji*.

Now he was ready to begin.

In a city of four million people, Michel knew that he could not find his father with just a name, but he suspected there would be only one Saigon and Bombay Tailoring Company.

In fact there were two. They both belonged to his father.

The pock-skinned Hindu youth in the white linen shirt and fresh blue *dhoti* studied him with suspicion. 'My father's not here,' he said, in crisp, Oxford English. 'Who are you?'

Michel looked over the boy's shoulder to the cool shadows of the tailor's shop. He saw a short, plump Indian woman, a brace of tiny rubies glinting from her left nostril, and some seamstresses bent over their work.

He ignored the question. 'Where is he?'

'He went back to Saigon. Two days ago.'

So, Joginder had been here. Michel shrugged away his disappointment. Their joyful reunion would be slightly delayed, that's all.

'Who are you?' the youth repeated.

'No one,' Michel answered, and he realized with hollow irony that it was true.

He threaded his way through the maze of cheap hotels and restaurants in Colaba at the south end of Back Bay. It was the travelers' quarter of the city, a colony of hippies in bright-patterned clothes, head bands, beads and bracelets. He was fascinated by them.

The only Westerners he had ever seen were rich, self-assured and arrogant. These young people were different. Some of them were young and fresh-faced, others looked worn and hardened by drugs and the road. They would be easy prey for a practiced pocket thief, but he discounted them as a solution to the problem he now faced.

It was no longer a question of just surviving. He could not stay in Bombay. The police would be looking for him and if they sent him back to the prison, he wouldn't get out alive. Not this time.

He needed money, and he needed a lot of it.

The red-domed Taj overlooked the Gateway of India. Porters in festive turbans fussed around the Mercedes and BMW's that pulled up in its forecourt day and night. Oil-rich Arabs and Western businessmen in silk suits strolled the lobby. The place reeked of money.

Michel put his hands in his pockets and climbed the huge granite staircase to the Harbor Bar. He sat down, ordered a Golden Eagle beer and waited. The windows afforded a panoramic view of Elephanta Island and the rusting ships anchored in the roadstead. He wondered if the SS Siam was one of them.

He took stock. All he had left in the world were the crumbled remains of the Mandrax and those unique talents he had learned on the streets of Saigon. He reckoned they would be more than enough.

He looked across the room. There was a girl sitting in the corner, watching him. She turned away as soon as he saw her, but he knew enough by now to know what that look meant. He got up and went over.

Alana Regan was not a pretty girl in the classic sense. Her nose was a little too broad and her mousy hair was dyed black. But nature had compensated in other ways. She had narrow hips and extravagantly heavy breasts. She had learned to exaggerate their effect by wearing very tight white t-shirts.

Despite this apparent brazenness, Alana's closeted upbringing, as the only daughter of a widowed matron in Baton Rouge, meant she could be shy around men. She had followed in her mother's footsteps and become a nurse at the local hospital.

But when Alana was twenty-three, she had applied and been accepted for the position of a private nurse to an Arabian oil sheikh in Oman. Her mother was horrified. Over her objections, Alana left Baton Rouge and spent the next twelve months in the Middle East. She loved every moment of it. The Arabian men had made her feel like a movie star.

When her contract expired, she decided to see a little more of the world before returning to Louisiana. She had fallen briefly and tempestuously in love with a diplomat's son in Beirut, a handsome Spaniard with a husky voice, sweet-scented skin and sensuously drooping eyelids. He was different from any other man she had known. Or so she thought. But just like the clumsy and beer-breathed boys at home, he dumped her like a used Kleenex. The love of her life lasted just three weeks.

Won't I ever learn? she asked herself. If there was a user in the room, that was the one she seemed to go for.

She flew to India just to see the Taj Mahal. Then she meandered south, delaying the inevitable return to a regular life. When she got to Bombay, she decided to pamper herself with an overnight stay at the famous Taj Hotel, even though she heard that just one night cost more than an Indian laborer earned in a year. But she could afford it. She had earned big dollars in Oman.

After checking into her room, she wandered for a while around the Apollo Bunder, but finally, too tired and too hot to be bothered with the hawkers and beggars that pestered her every step, she retreated to the Harbor Bar for a cold drink.

She noticed the young man in the blue jeans straight away. Who wouldn't? For one thing he was outrageously good-looking, with smooth skin, flowing dark hair and hypnotic brown eyes. But he was no pretty boy. He had been in a fight not too long ago, and his face had not quite healed. It made him look dangerous.

It was a combination she had always found hard to resist.

He sat alone at the bar with a bottle of beer, and Alana wondered who, or what, he was. He could have been Greek, but his eyes were too narrow. He might have been Japanese, but he was too tall. He could have been Indian, a film star like the ones that lived in those white palaces on Malabar Hill. Except film stars didn't get bruises on their face like that.

Suddenly, he turned around, saw her and smiled. Instinctively she looked away. It didn't matter, he came over anyway.

'Hello,' he said, his voice heavily accented with French, 'are you alone?'

She nodded.

He sat down, took the packet of Stuyvesant off the table in front of her, and without asking, shook one out of the packet. He lit it with one of the cardboard matches she had brought from her hotel room.

'Michel,' he said.

Her throat was suddenly very dry. 'Alana.'

He smiled and leaned towards her. 'Tell me, Alana,' he said, 'do you believe in Fate?'

'Room 210,' Michel said sleepily into the phone. 'Send up two Western-style breakfasts and a large pot of coffee.'

He put the phone down and padded naked to the bathroom. He took a long hot shower, leaning his head against the smooth tiles, eyes tight shut.

There was a knock at the door. He wrapped a towel around his waist, and still dripping, took the breakfast tray from an elderly Indian in a pressed white uniform.

'Wait a moment,' he said. He went to Alana's purse, took out two small coins and tossed them at the Indian. The man caught one. The other fell on the carpet. Michel enjoyed watching him scramble to pick it up.

He closed the door, went to a table by the window and unfolded a crisp copy of the *Times of India*. He looked for the news from Saigon. It was Tet in Vietnam. This year, the truce had been called for just thirty-six hours. It had ended that morning. The reports consisted of the usual claims and counterclaims of truce-breaking from both sides.

He read while steadily eating his way through the two breakfasts of rolls, eggs, bacon and cereals. He poured himself another cup of coffee from the ornate silver pot and went to stand by the bed.

The girl was dead. She lay on her stomach, one arm hanging limp over the side of the bed. She could have been asleep except for the blueish tinge to her lips.

He shrugged. It was a pity. He supposed he must have put too much Mandrax in her wine. It was French and inordinately expensive, but she had insisted on paying for it. In the end, it had cost her more than she had bargained for.

He dressed leisurely then went to the dressing table and sorted through her leather shoulder bag, spilling its contents onto the polished surface. He pocketed the travelers' checks and four hundred rupees in cash.

There was even a round-the-world air ticket. Perfect.

Then he found the real treasure. He caressed the smooth green cover of the passport as tenderly as a lover and slid it into the back pocket of his jeans.

'Thank you, Alana,' he said aloud. 'A most enjoyable night.'

For some reason he found himself thinking of his mother. She had been slim, dark and very, very pretty. This girl was none of those things.

Still, he was somehow glad she was dead.

Early next morning a Pan Am 747 touched down at Tan Son Nhut airbase in Saigon and an American national named Alana Regan stepped on to the boiling tarmac.

Inside the terminal, the uniformed Vietnamese official at passport control glanced at the photograph, then back at the man on the other side of the counter and waved him through. He did not ask why he had a girl's name in his passport. Foreign names were unintelligible to him.

So, a few minutes later, Michel climbed into a taxi outside Tan Son Nhut, anticipating a joyful reunion with his father.

CHAPTER 20

Saigon

In Vietnam, Tet was the year's major festival - Christmas and Easter packed into four days. The Vietnamese did not celebrate individual birthdays. At Tet, everyone became one year older.

No one went to work, the markets were closed, houses were filled with flowers, and everyone dressed in new clothes. Even the street children begged or stole a new shirt or a new pair of pants.

The air was filled with flashes and bangs from the firecrackers that chased away evil spirits. Merchants spent vast sums hanging long strings of them outside their shops, believing the more they had, the more business they would attract in the coming year.

Tet was a time to celebrate and to feast. A time to visit family and to pay off all old debts. A time to honor one's ancestors.

It was a hot, desolate afternoon. Nguyen Hue street, the Street of Flowers, was a mass of color. The appearance of these flowers every year seemed almost miraculous in a country pocked with bomb craters, vast expanses of defoliated jungle, and rice paddies with barbed wire perimeters.

Michel took a suite at the Continental Hotel. When he retired that evening, he could hear the distant *crump-crump-crump* of shellfire, but it was mostly drowned out by the whirring of the ceiling fan. The war was like a bad habit, and it seemed a long way away. He was accustomed to it. Everyone called it Saigon Night Music.

He had heard the rumors of an impending attack on Saigon by the VC, but he had discounted them. He didn't see how it was possible.

He woke around two in the morning to the sound of sharp, whip-like explosions from the street outside. At first, he thought it was firecrackers, but then there was another, bigger blast, and his bedroom window turned white and fell in, showering the bed with shards of glass. He rolled off the bed and lay flat on the floor.

Another explosion rolled across the square and the curtains billowed in the blast.

Keeping low, he went to the balcony and peered down into the street. He saw half a dozen Vietnamese pour out of a manhole cover like ants from a crumbled nest. They were dressed in black pajamas and carried AK- 47s. They ran off in the direction of the US embassy.

Viet Cong! So, for once the rumors were true.

He heard more gunfire from across the street and saw one of the Viet Cong stumble and fall. A grenade exploded in the square and a piece of shrapnel slapped into the wall of the hotel, just a few feet above his head.

He crawled back inside, fumbling in the darkness for his clothes. He supposed most people in the city tonight were terrified by what was happening in the street. But he was not like most people. There was opportunity here.

A night like this, with guns and explosions going off everywhere, a man could get away with murder.

As dawn broke, the Saigon streets were utterly deserted. The usual clamor of horns, bicycle bells and hawkers had been replaced by the clatter of small arms fire and the sudden, ear-shattering explosions of mortars and rockets.

Joginder saw a squad of Marines crouching behind an overturned jeep. Shadowy figures in black pajamas ducked into an alleyway further down the street. He hurried along the arcade, a white handkerchief flapping in his right fist.

When the attack had started, he had been asleep in his favorite brothel five blocks away. He would have cowered there all week if he had to, but he was worried about leaving his shop unattended. His twenty million piastres were in the small, iron safe upstairs.

A Citroen was skewed across the middle of the street, its coachwork punched through with bullet holes. Joginder stepped over the bodies of three VC sprawled on the footpath. He noticed they wore white, cotton shirts and even jewelry underneath their black pajamas. They must be cadres, ordinary Saigonese who had just been waiting for a chance to fight.

He saw the glitter of a gold chain at one of their throats and bent down to rip it off, before hurrying on.

There was firing from the direction of the US embassy. He would have to get off the main street. It would take him longer to get home, but it might be safer. On the Tu Do he was too tempting a target for Viet Cong snipers as well as nervous Marines.

Get me home, he prayed silently. O Ganesh, get me home, and I will make a great sacrifice in your honor!

When he finally reached his shop, he didn't risk the street entrance. Instead, he went down the alley and hammered on the side door with his fists.

'Sai, it is me, Joginder. Let me in!'

There was no answer from inside. He tried the handle and to his surprise it swung open. He almost fainted with alarm. He was sure he had locked it when he went out the previous evening. It had been forced. Someone had broken in during the night.

Viet Cong!

His first instinct was to run. But where to? And what about the safe? He eased the door open with his foot. It swung half-way and stopped. Something was blocking it. He peered inside.

One of the servants lay face down on the floor. There was blood everywhere. He put his handkerchief to his mouth and retched.

'Jogi, up here!' It was Sai. She was upstairs.

'What's happening?' he shouted.

'The VC were here. Quickly!'

'Have they gone?'

'Yes, it's safe now.'

He ran up the stairs and tripped over another body. Shivering with fright, he stared at the smear of blood on his hands. Savages. They had murdered both the servants. He wiped off the blood with his handkerchief and stumbled the rest of the way to his office.

Sai was sitting behind his desk, white as chalk.

'What has happened?' he said.

She didn't answer him.

He ignored her and rushed across the room to the safe. It was still securely locked. He groaned with relief. He was afraid the VC might have tried to blast it open.

He felt something hard nestle into the small indentation at the base of his skull. Then he heard a familiar voice, very close to his ear.

'Father. How nice to see you again. Are you surprised to see me?'

Joginder thought he was going to lose control of his bowels. This was impossible. Michel was in the Port of Bombay jail, and no one ever got out of there.

Michel grabbed him by the collar and dragged him across the room. 'Get out of the way,' he said to Sai.

She ran to a corner of the room, relieved that she was no longer the one this madman was pointing his gun at.

He threw Joginder into the chair. He was holding the service revolver he had taken from the holster of a dead ARVN on Tu Do Street. He pulled back the hammer and rammed the barrel between his father's eyes.

'No!' Joginder shrieked. 'Please! I'll do anything. Do you want money? I'll pay you.'

'Shut up.' Michel looked at Sai. 'Come here,' he said. He threw her the length of wire twine he had taken from one of the rolls of cloth in the shop. 'Tie his wrists behind his back. Make sure it's tight. If his fingers don't turn white, I'll shoot off one of your toes.'

Sai did as she was told.

Joginder yelped with pain. 'You're hurting me, you bitch!'

Michel gave Sai a humorless smile. 'I don't think you like him any more than I do. Now, step back against the wall.'

She backed off, her eyes never leaving the gun. She had watched this monster gun down the servants. She knew he wouldn't hesitate to do the same to her.

Michel perched on the corner of the desk.

'Please, Michel-' Joginder said.

'Shut up.' Michel hit him with the barrel to make his point. Blood started to leak down his face from his scalp. 'I have often asked myself why you did what you did. Now I know. There are few fathers who have the opportunity to abandon their children twice.'

'I have money. Name your price.'

'How much is in the safe?'

Joginder swallowed hard. Twenty million piastres! He had to try to stall him. 'How much do you want?'

'Everything you have.' Michel held the barrel against Joginder's crotch.

'Open the safe,' Joginder said to Sai. He recited the numbers to her, breathless with terror. 'Seven-three-to the right. Ninety-five-to the right. Sixty-three-to the left. Now back again. Eighty-eight.' He heard the tumblers click and fall. The door swung open.

'Put it on the table,' Michel said.

Sai obliged, piling the bundles of notes on the desk like bricks.

All that money, Joginder thought, all that work gone. That damned French whore was going to cost him everything.

Michel threw an airline bag at Sai. 'Put it in there,' he said. 'His passport as well.'

'Please, not all of it,' Joginder said.

'Take off his rings,' Michel said. The gun shook in his hand.

Sai pulled the fat, emerald-cut ruby from the little finger of Joginder's left hand and the ruby signet ring from the third finger of the other.

'Take it and go!' Joginder cried.

'This is not repayment. This is my inheritance. You sent me to hell, Father. If it weren't for the nuns, I would have starved. I spent years sleeping in bombed-out buildings with rats eating my feet. Even that was better than the Indian prison. Do you know what they did to me in there? The warden spread-eagled me naked across a desk and beat me for two hours with a rubber hose and a brass belt buckle.'

Sai finished packing the thick bundles of paper money into the bag.

Michel snatched it from her, keeping the gun aimed at Joginder's head. 'What sort of man would do that to his own son?'

Joginder tried to speak, but all that came out was a squeak. Saliva spilled from his bottom lip and dribbled down his chin. A vague plan formed in his mind, where he would launch himself from his chair and snatch the gun away. But his legs wouldn't obey. He felt paralyzed.

'So many nights I lay awake dreaming of this moment, Father.'

Joginder closed his eyes. There was a loud bang, and he screamed, waiting for the pain.

He opened his eyes.

Michel was laughing. 'Just a grenade, Father. The VC have their war. I have mine.' He looked at Sai and casually shot her in the head. Joginder heard her heels rattle on the floor.

Another grenade exploded in the street.

'The VC are taking over the whole city,' Michel said. 'There are dead and dying everywhere. I am the only one in all Saigon who takes the festival seriously, who wants to forget about the war with the Americans and simply give my ancestors their due.'

He held the gun low at his hip. He fired once into Joginder's right knee, and then as he lay howling on the floor, he casually fired another round into the other one.

He picked up the airline bag and went back down the stairs into the war-ravaged streets.

It was a week before civilian aircraft were once again cleared to fly out of Tan Son Nhut. During that time, Michel took refuge inside the Continental Hotel.

On the other side of the city, Joginder Krisnan lay in a hospital bed, heavily sedated. During his few lucid moments, he raved to the doctors and nurses about a man who had murdered his family and then tied him up and tortured him. No one took any notice. The medical staff supposed it was a side effect of the strong narcotics. Anyway, the police and the military were fully occupied with tracking down the last of the Viet Cong cells.

And so, Alana Regan flew unmolested out of Saigon aboard a Cathay Pacific flight for Hong Kong.

Once in Kowloon, Michel booked into a luxury suite in the Peninsula Hotel and toasted his inheritance with fine French champagne while he pondered his next move.

He made himself two promises: He would never be poor again and he would find his mother.

Wherever she was in the world. No matter the cost.

PART 4

Reunion: 1972

CHAPTER 21

Paris

Some people think that Interpol is an international police force whose bailiwick transcends national boundaries. Nothing could be further from the truth. It would be more accurately described as an international clearing house dedicated to police work.

Its agents, however, are powerless to make arrests or even interrogate suspects. They merely act as advisers and intermediaries to the police forces of other nations.

Its headquarters is in St Cloud, a suburb of Paris about three kilometers from the Eiffel Tower. It is a drab, grey building near the Longchamps racecourse. An occasional commuter train, rumbling past on the nearby tracks, is all that disturbs the peaceful, leafy calm. Inside, the office exhibits the Spartan anonymity of police stations the world over - metal desks piled high with papers, plastic chairs and cramped cubicles.

The organization has three divisions: General Administration, Research and Study, and International Police Co-operation. This last division is further divided into five groups: international fraud, counterfeiting, bank fraud and forgery, drug trafficking, and murder and theft. Each group has a number of liaison officers responsible for co-ordinating police efforts in specific global areas.

The Liaison Officer for South-East Asia that cold, March afternoon was Captain René Budjinski.

Budjinski had served seventeen years working homicide in the sixth *arrondissement*. Before that, he had been a member of the French SDECE in Indochina. He had nicotine-stained fingers, and his face was pockmarked with ancient acne pits. He wore a crumpled oyster-grey suit, the seat and elbows shiny with wear. His collar was open and his tie pulled down. Anyone who saw him on the street would have been excused for mistaking him for a poorly paid insurance clerk.

But Interpol did not pay Budjinski for his dress sense. His talent was for chasing down information with the tenacity of a bulldog and then sifting an enormous amount of detail into a few important and significant facts.

That afternoon, he sat at his cluttered, ash-strewn desk and stared at a cable he had received an hour earlier from Singapore.

He leaned back in his chair and lit another *Gauloise*. By itself it meant nothing, an act of desperation from a beleaguered detective without a single lead. Hundreds of similar cables flooded into St Cloud every week.

```
28/12/71
TO: IP PARIS
WE WISH TO INFORM YOU OF A ROBBERY REPORTED
ON 28/12/71 AT MANDARIN HOTEL STOP ROBBERY
PERPETRATED BY PERSON OR PERSONS UNKNOWN STOP
OWNER OF ARCADE JEWELRY STORE LURED TO ROOM
AND KNOCKED UNCONSCIOUS STOP OCCUPIER OF ROOM
MURDERED STOP NOW POSITIVELY IDENTIFIED AS
AMERICAN TOURIST SUSAN CONNORS OF HOUSTON TEXAS
STOP
```

WE STILL WISH TO QUESTION A MAN SUSPECTED OF
INVOLVEMENT IN THIS CRIME STOP PROBABLE FOREIGN
NATIONAL 20-25 YEARS OF LATIN DESCENT SIX FOOT
DARK HAIR USES THE NAME ALAN REGAN STOP
  REQUEST URGENT ASSISTANCE IN LOCATING THIS
PERSON STOP IF DETAINED EXTRADITION WILL BE
REQUESTED STOP
  END IP SINGAPORE
  SIGNED: ROLAND TAN (CHIEF SUPERINTENDENT)
  SINGAPORE POLICE (INTERPOL DIVISION)

Budjinski checked the date again, December 28th. Three months ago. Another report delayed by some oversight or bureaucratic bungling. Not that it made much difference.

He would put out an all-stations alert and then send the cable upstairs to Records. He put it to one side, stubbed out his *Gauloise,* and moved on to the next message.

Serge Renard rented a small office on the Rue St Lazare, up two flights of narrow steps. He was a stocky Breton with a thick cap of very black hair, cut close to the skull. He sat at his desk and weighed a thin manila folder in his hands. Four years and this was all they had to show. He wondered how long his client would continue to pay his retainer.

He remembered the first day the man had come to his office. It was clear that money was not going to be a problem. He wore a Piaget wristwatch with diamonds inlaid in the face - worth two thousand dollars at least by his reckoning - a Pierre Cardin suit and a burgundy silk shirt. He looked very young to have so much money.

It had been difficult to guess the man's nationality. He spoke French perfectly, but his dark complexion and those hypnotic brown eyes suggested mixed blood. Renard knew straight off that this case would be outside the normal round of jealous husbands or suspicious employers.

'I need to find someone,' the man had said.

'Why?'

'That is my business.'

'As you wish.'

'Her maiden name is Adrienne Christian. Her father was an official in the *Service Publique* in Saigon in the late forties. She left in 1951 or 52.'

Renard scribbled some notes on a pad. 'And then?'

'That is all I know.'

'Excuse me?'

'It's all I have.'

'*M'sieur,* excuse me, but that is not very much to go on. When did you last see this woman?'

'Is that relevant?'

'Then may I at least ask her relation to you?'

'Will that help you find her?'

'It might.'

'How?'

Renard tossed his pencil onto his pad. 'Is she married?'

'She was only 23 or 24 when she left Saigon. I should think so.'

'And you do not know the name of the man she married?'

'If I did, I would have told you.'

'Is this woman living here in France?'

'Perhaps.'

Renard leaned back, his index finger tapping out a tattoo on the arm of his chair. 'I have connections in Saigon who could perhaps look through the birth and marriage records for me. If they exist. Many were lost after Partition. If we can find her new name, I may be able to do something for you. But it will be expensive.'

The young man reached into his wallet and produced a thick bundle of notes. He threw them across the desk. 'I don't care what it costs. Find her.'

Renard counted how much was there and raised an eyebrow. 'You must want to find this woman very badly.'

'You have no idea,' the man had said and walked out.

That was four years ago. As Renard had predicted, both the birth and marriage records had been lost or destroyed in the chaos of 1954 when the French pulled out of Saigon. After many weeks of fruitless research, he had tracked down an Emmanuel Christian through public service records. The man had been a *fonctionnaire* in the colonial administration and was killed in a bombing there in 1951.

After that, nothing. For three years, he had found only false trails.

Renard wondered how much this fruitless investigation had been worth to him. Hundreds of thousands of francs, certainly. What was so important about this woman that this man would continue to pay such huge sums to a private investigator?

Each month, an envelope would arrive at his office with an Asian postmark. Inside would be a check covering his retainer. His mysterious client would not give a forwarding address. But every few months, Renard would get a long-distance phone call from him. Occasionally he would just appear in his reception, unannounced, and enquire about his progress.

Renard put the file into a drawer and moved on to his other business.

A fascinating case and certainly his most difficult. In some ways he would be glad to have finished with it. But he would miss the money.

CHAPTER 22

New Delhi

Noelle Giresse sat in the shaded garden of the Ashoka Hotel sipping a gin and tonic. The Ashoka had been built by Nehru to celebrate the birth of the new nation and impress the world leaders who had come to India to court him. Noelle loved its faded charm. It was like being back in the days of the Raj.

It was the beginning of the dry season, when the sun broiled the dun, skillet-hard earth until it crumbled and cracked. Not the best time to visit India. And yet as soon as she had stepped off the 747 at Palam international airport, she felt as if she was coming home.

It had been seventeen years since she was last here. At thirty-seven she still turned heads. She was slim and graceful, with ash-blonde hair and soft, hazel-brown eyes. In her youth she had been called beautiful. Now, she suspected she might be called attractive.

An attractive French divorcee.

The divorce had been a bitter and protracted affair. She had had no illusions about what it was going to be like when she begun the proceedings, of course. She had watched her parents tear each other apart when she was sixteen. She had not expected her own separation to be any different.

Both parents had opposed the match. Her husband's family said he was marrying beneath his class. Her own father was a little more blunt. He told her that Jacques was selfish, obstinate and self-obsessed.

You should know, she thought at the time.

When it ended, just as they said it would, her father resisted the urge to gloat. The marriage had lasted much longer than he had predicted. He helped her deal with Jacques' lawyers and gave her a place to stay and a shoulder to cry on.

The one good thing to come from it all was the rebuilding of bridges between them. He had always seemed so cold, but when she needed him, he had come through for her.

Coming back to Asia had been partly his idea. There had been a substantial settlement, and he suggested that now it was over she should take a long holiday. She had always loved India. Her father had been attached to the embassy in New Delhi for many years when he was with the diplomatic service.

She suddenly became aware of someone standing by her shoulder. She assumed it was the waiter. She drained her glass and held it out without looking up from the letter in her hand.

'Yes, I'll have another,' she said in English.

'*Mon plaîsir,*' a voice answered in French.

Noelle looked up in confusion. 'I'm sorry, I thought-'

The man was tall, dark-skinned and very handsome. He disappeared inside.

She watched him go to the bar and order her another drink. What should she do? She could go back to her room to head off the inevitable pick-up, but that would be rude. When he returned, she would thank him for the drink, make some polite conversation and leave. There needn't be any more to it than that.

She put down the letter and smoothed her dress with her hands. She suddenly felt nervous. This was ridiculous.

'A gin and tonic.' He put the glass in front of her and eased himself into the cane chair opposite. He wore an open-necked, white silk Cardin shirt and Givenchy jeans. There was a fat emerald-cut ruby on his little finger. The watch on his wrist looked as if it was studded with diamonds. He looked like a movie star.

'Tell me, do I look like a drinks waiter? Is it this white shirt?'

'I apologize. It was the way you were standing there looking at me.'

'I was admiring you.'

You were undressing me with your eyes, she thought. She picked up her gin and tonic, then quickly put it back on the table when she realized her hands were shaking. A long time since she had let a man seduce her. She fumbled in her handbag for a cigarette and tried to recover her poise.

'Am I supposed to be flattered?'

'You are, aren't you?' He reached into his pocket and took out a gold Dupont lighter. He lit her cigarette for her.

He certainly didn't lack self-confidence. He was young, ten years younger than her. It was obvious what he wanted. Perhaps it's what I want too, she thought. All those years I was faithful to Jacques, and he practically flaunted his mistresses in my face.

'You haven't told me your name,' she said.

'Michel.'

'That's French, isn't it? You don't look French.'

'I'm a citizen of the world.' He looked down at the letter on the table. 'Is that from your husband?'

'No, my father. My husband and I were divorced last month.'

'So, you are a single woman again.' He leaned towards her and took one of her hands in his. 'Tell me, do you believe in Fate?'

That evening, Noelle stood on the balcony of her room, smoking a cigarette and watching the moon rise over the old city. It hung low over the Red Fort, the color of blood. The air was scented with flowers and dust.

There was a knock on the door. She turned on the bedside lamp and checked herself in the mirror.

'Who is it?'

'Michel.'

She felt a rush of excitement and apprehension. If you hadn't wanted him to come up, she thought, you wouldn't have given him your room number.

His voice again, more urgent now. 'Noelle?'

She took a deep breath and opened the door.

He was leaning on the door jamb. He gave her a mocking smile. 'Did I wake you up?'

'It's only early.'

He brushed past her and stood in the middle of the room. He began to unbutton his shirt.

'Turn off the light.'

She hesitated. Perhaps she had been married too long. She was out of practice. She turned off the lamp and heard the rustle of his clothes as they fell to the floor. The moon had risen higher in the sky, framed by the French windows.

He led her into the bedroom and sat down beside her on the bed, letting her touch him first. His skin felt cool and smooth, the muscles taut and hard. She liked that. Her husband had been fleshy and soft. She traced the flat contours of his belly down to his thigh and her fingers brushed against his penis. He was hard already.

He untied the cord of her dressing gown. He eased it off her shoulders and tied her wrists to the bed. His tongue traced the curve of her belly.

Jacques had never liked doing this. He only liked her doing it to him. She felt his lips on her throat and breasts and gasped aloud. Oh, he was good. He was very good. Young, hard and a nimble tongue, in and out of bed. A girlfriend had been telling her for years that all she needed was a good fuck. It looked as if she had found it.

She closed her eyes and surrendered.

When she woke up, the bed was empty. She reached out for him, and when she realized he was gone she felt both disappointed and relieved.

The curtains were drawn, but she could see the sun through the gap. It must be late. She shivered. Before he had left, he had shut the window and turned on the air conditioning.

She stretched and yawned, replaying the previous night in her mind. She felt as if she had lost her virginity for the second time. She had no illusions about it being the beginning of some great love affair. It was more like being worked over by a professional. The idea made her smile. It hadn't happened nearly enough in her life.

She rolled over. Suddenly she realized he had not gone back to his room. He was sitting in the chair beside the bed, fully dressed, staring at her.

'Good morning,' he said. There was a gun pointed at her face. 'Don't make any noise and you won't get hurt.'

'What are you doing?'

He smiled. 'Do exactly what I tell you. I won't hesitate to use this if you don't.'

Noelle looked into the fathomless, unmatched eyes. She believed him.

CHAPTER 23

The management of the Ashoka Hotel leased the dozen or so shops in its arcade to carefully selected merchants for the convenience of the guests. The Jaipur Emporium was one of those chosen. It was one of the finest jewelry stores in Delhi, owned by a Mister Ramesh Patel.

That morning, at a little after ten o'clock, Mister Patel received a phone call.

'This is Madame Giresse. Room 289. I am interested in buying some jewelry from you,' a woman's voice said.

'Certainly, Madam. Here in the Emporium, we have the finest selection of-'

'No, I am sorry', she said. 'I am unwell. I can't leave my suite.'

'That is most unfortunate.'

'Yes, it is. So, you'll have to come to me.'

'Of course.'

'I don't expect to see anything of inferior quality.'

Patel bridled. Who did these people think they were? 'Certainly, Madam. I shall send someone up to your room presently.'

'Immediately.'

'Of course, Madam. I am sure you will be most satisfied.'

He put the phone down and turned to one of his assistants. 'Sanji, put these three trays into a case, then take them to room 289. A Madame Giresse.'

Sanji nodded and did as he was told. He turned to go.

'Oh, and Sanji, don't haggle. If she thinks she's Queen of Bloody India, she can pay top price.'

Noelle's hands were shaking so badly she was unable to replace the phone on its cradle. Michel had to do it for her.

'Bravo,' he said. 'A fine performance.'

She felt the warm metal of the gun barrel pressed against her neck. 'Please don't hurt me,' she said.

'There is no need for anyone to get hurt as long as you do what I say.'

'What are you going to do?'

'Don't worry about that. Just make sure you play your part, like I tell you. Now, you must get dressed.'

Noelle could barely stand up. Her knees were shaking. She had never been so terrified. She couldn't think, and her throat was so tight she could barely speak.

'I want you to look pretty for me.' He took a handful of dresses from the robe and threw them onto the bed. 'Choose something. Put it on. Here, that one.'

'It's an evening gown.'

'Do it.'

She slipped the dressing gown off her shoulders and let it fall to the floor. She fumbled in the drawers for her underwear. He watched her dispassionately, the pistol in his right hand. Suddenly he laughed.

'What is it?'

'You're blushing like a virgin.'

'Don't look at me.'

'If I don't look at you, you will scream and run for the door.'

She slipped into her pants, fumbled with the strap of her brassiere. It was as if the previous night had never happened. She wondered what sort of man could make love to a woman and then casually humiliate her like this.

He was still staring at her. 'You are very beautiful.'

'Please, let me go.'

He picked up the evening gown from the bed and threw it to her. Then he took off his ruby ring and put it on her finger. 'You'll need this as well.'

'Why?'

'It's a working prop to impress our friends downstairs.'

'I don't understand.'

'You don't have to. But if you perform your next role as well as your first, then perhaps I shall let you keep it. Now, put on a pair of shoes. You look a mess. You'd better go in the bathroom and try to do something with yourself. You can't answer the door looking like that.'

She pushed open the bathroom door, but before she could close it, he followed her inside.

'But I need to pee.'

'Then I'll watch. But hurry up. You need to fix your hair and get some make-up on before our friend arrives.'

Sanji bowed. 'Good morning, Madam. I am from the Jaipur Emporium.'

Noelle looked him up and down as if he were inferior goods, the way Michel had told her to do.

As if he's something you just found on the sole of your shoe. You have to be arrogant. Otherwise, they'll think you don't have any money.

'Come in,' she said. She wondered if there was any way she could warn the man. But she knew Michel was watching through a crack in the bathroom door, the Beretta trained on the back of her head.

'Mister Patel sends his apologies. I am Sanji Viswanath.'

Michel had said this might happen. She turned and walked imperiously back into the room. Sanji followed, carrying the rosewood case with the three trays of gems Patel had selected.

She sat down in the armchair facing the bathroom door, as Michel had instructed. From there she could see the black eye of the silenced pistol.

'Sit down,' she said. She indicated the other chair.

'Thank you, Madam.'

If he was wondering why the blinds were drawn and the room in semi-darkness, he did not show it.

He placed the rosewood case on the coffee table between them and unlocked it. 'I think you will agree that what I have here are some of the finest creations in Delhi.'

Noelle reached into the case and took out a diamond ring. She rolled it between her thumb and forefinger under the light of the table lamp.

Sanji leaned eagerly forward. 'A most exquisite piece,' he said.

She dropped it back into the tray with studied indifference and looked into the salesman's face. She wanted to scream at him. *For God's sake, don't you realize what's going on? Are you blind? Look at me, see how my hands are shaking! Do you think this is because of something I've eaten?*

Sanji frowned. 'Is something wrong?'

She glanced quickly towards the bathroom. 'I feel a little unwell, that's all. What else do you have to show me?'

He picked up an emerald necklace and held it out. 'This is a most exquisite piece. Surely one of the finest necklaces in all Asia.'

She took it from him. She knew nothing about jewelry, but Michel had told her that didn't matter. Their first jewels will be mediocre at best. When you throw them back in their face, they will respect you, and then they will open the safe for you. She dropped it carelessly into its bed of green velvet, leaned back in her chair and toyed with the ruby on her finger.

'Surely you didn't think I'd be interested in these trinkets?'

Sanji looked at the ring. He was impressed. 'But Madam-'

'I am most disappointed.' She looked into the ugly mouth of the silencer barrel. Could she warn this man about what was happening without Michel being aware of it? She could feel him watching from the bathroom. She dared not risk it.

'Tell Mister Patel if he cannot do better than this, then I shall take my business elsewhere.' She dropped a platinum American Express card on the table. Michel had given it to her. She wondered how he had come by it and shuddered. 'My husband gave me his credit card,' she said.

Sanji licked his lips. 'We do have some pieces downstairs that we reserve for our most discerning clients. If you will permit me to return to the shop.'

Noelle waved a hand dismissively. 'Yes, yes. Go ahead.' She felt suddenly light-headed. This was what Michel had told her he would do.

Sanji closed his case, bowed and went to the door. Noelle heard it shut gently behind him.

Michel came out of the bathroom and gave her a silent round of applause.

Sanji put the case on the desk.

Patel unlocked it and counted the pieces. 'She didn't buy anything?'

'Mister Patel, sir, she says she does not like anything in here.'

'Why not?'

'They were not what she had expected.'

'What was she expecting?'

'Something a little more exclusive.'

Patel raised his eyebrows. He had misjudged the Frenchwoman. He was prepared to revise his estimate of anyone who wished to make him richer.

'She told me she was too ill to come downstairs.'

Sanji nodded. 'The blinds are drawn, she is very pale, and she shivers as if she has a fever.'

'But you think she has means?'

'She has a platinum credit card. And she was wearing a ring, a Burmese ruby, emerald cut on white gold. Most expensive.'

'Very well. We shall see if we can accommodate her.' Patel smiled. 'Mind the shop for me. I shall attend to Madame Giresse myself.'

He went to the safe in the corner and unlocked it.

Michel lit a cigarette. He had the pistol cradled in his lap. 'You would have made a wonderful actress,' he said.

Noelle wondered how she could have once found this man so attractive. 'What now?'

'Now we wait for Mr. Patel.'

'Why do you need me for this?'

'This way they do not see me.'

It was suddenly obvious to her. Whatever happened, he was going to kill her. She was the only way anyone could link him to the crime.

He picked up the gun. 'If you do what I say, nothing will happen to you. Or you could come with me. You could be my partner.'

She knew that was a lie. She looked into his eyes. There was nothing there but cunning. How easily we are all swayed by charm, she thought. Because someone is funny or attractive or sophisticated, we assume they are good people, when the truth is that the devil always smiles, and he always sweeps you off your feet. It's the best disguise there is.

'Please let me go,' she said.

'Once I have what I want.'

'I can't take this-' Her eyes rolled back in her head. She started to pitch forwards onto the carpet.

Instinctively, he put the gun down and reached out to catch her. But she did not faint. Instead, she pushed him away and picked up the gun. She twisted around on her knees, aimed the pistol and pulled the trigger.

Patel stood outside room 289. He cleared his throat, straightened his tie and knocked twice.

A man opened the door.

Patel frowned. 'I'm sorry. I was looking for Madame Giresse.'

'I am her husband. Come in.' The man stepped aside.

Patel wondered why Sanji had not told him about a husband. He hesitated. The room was in semi-darkness as Sanji had said.

He could see Madame Giresse sitting in an armchair facing away from him. She twisted around. She had a gag in her mouth. Her hands were tied behind her back and her feet were tied to the legs of the chair with pieces of torn bed sheet. There was blood in her hair.

Before he had time to react, the man had grabbed him by the collar and hauled him into the room. The door slammed shut behind him and he saw the man swing something at his head. His legs gave way beneath him, and the world went black.

Michel dragged Patel into the bathroom. A few moments later, he came out, wiping his hands on a towel.

Noelle's eyes followed him around the room. She could only see out of one eye. The other was blinded by the sticky blood weeping from the gash on her forehead where he had hit her with the ashtray.

He bent down and picked up Patel's rosewood case. He unlocked it and took out one of the pieces, a jade brooch in the shape of an elephant with a sunburst of rubies.

'Look at this. It could have been yours.' He pulled up a chair and sat down beside her. 'I offered you riches and in return you tried to kill me. You women are all the same. You give a man love, and then you try to destroy him.' He reached out a hand to caress her neck.

She braced her feet on the floor and tried to throw the chair backwards.

He held the chair with one hand while his fingers tightened around her throat. 'I gave you the best night of your whole life. All I asked was a little help in return. Instead, you nearly spoiled everything. What should I do with you?'

She was making small mewing noises through the gag.

He watched her, his face ugly with disgust.

Women. You couldn't trust any of them.

CHAPTER 24

Montmartre, Paris

'All right, Valentine, over here, walk towards me. Swing your skirt, that's it. That's it.'

Click-whirr.

'Now over by the wall. Look away, look away. Beautiful.'

Armand Poleski was excited. Occasionally, he knew the photographs he was taking were special even before he developed them. This was one of those times. There was gooseflesh on his skin, but it was not the chill of the afternoon making him shiver.

Yes, these were very good.

In the background, a group of old men sat at one of the tables and watched. They laughed among themselves, *Gauloises* clamped between their teeth. The white-jacketed proprietor sat at one of his own tables, his eyes riveted on Valentine's legs.

That would make a great shot, Armand thought, bringing the man's face completely into frame.

Click-whirr.

'Danielle, Isabella, over here.'

The other two models had changed into their dresses. One was wearing a Dior midriff top and black, three-tiered skirt, the other a Givenchy cotton jersey dress. They clambered out of the van, and a dresser threw their fur coats over their shoulders.

The sun appeared for a moment between banks of grey-flecked cumulus. It glistened on the dome of the Sacré-Coeur Basilica on the Montmartre.

'Danielle, take your coat off.'

'It's practically snowing,' the girl said.

'Look, *chérie*, this is the spring collection. Take the coat off.'

'I'll freeze my tits off.'

'If they fall off, I'll be the first to grab them. Now take the coat off.'

The girl did as she was told. Some young men wandered across the street to watch. They whistled and applauded.

Armand snapped a new roll of film into the camera. 'Okay, now look sexy.'

'How can I look sexy in this fucking weather?'

Armand winced. The girl was gorgeous until she opened her mouth. Her thick Breton accent grated on his nerves. Unlike Valentine. Now there was some class.

As he turned around to look for Isabella, he saw that Valentine had wandered away to watch a street entertainer who had braved the chill of the afternoon. He put his hands on his hips. Jesus, where did the agencies get these models from?

A small crowd had gathered around the man. He was a fire-eater, and they all moved back to give him room.

Armand realized the possibilities. He reached for his camera and ran across the street, ignoring the curses of a Citroën driver who had to swerve to avoid him.

Valentine slipped naturally into a pose for him, her lips parted, eyes wide. Behind her, the fire-eater spewed a mushroom of flame into the air.

Armand crouched down for a better angle. Fantastic. 'Put your hands in your hair, toss your head back. That's it, that's it.' He shot frame after frame.

Valentine thrust a hand down her thigh, put her other hand behind her head. The girl was a natural.

The street entertainer ran over. He had been cheated by photographers before. He held out his hand, demanding money. Armand scrabbled in his jeans pocket and threw a handful of notes onto the pavement without counting them.

The busker took another mouthful of the liquid and threw back his head, the bottle outstretched in his left hand, the lighted torch in the other. Another jet of flame.

Armand kept framing shot after shot until the roll was gone. This girl was wonderful. He wondered how he might get her into bed without causing a big scene with Danielle.

Armand stood in the darkroom of his Montmartre studio and stared at the glossy prints drying like laundry over the chemical trays.

He held one of the still-wet prints under an infra-red light. Valentine's scarlet, scalloped dress and the billowing flames shooting from the mouth of the street performer were in dramatic counterpoint to the shadowy crowd of spectators and the grey sky. The fireball lent a devilish tinge to the faces of the men watching from the café tables. In their midst, Valentine appeared pale, angelic.

He smiled. There were still primitives in the world who believed you could capture the soul in a photograph. Maybe they're right, he thought. Sometimes you really can extract the essence of the psyche through the camera lens.

The girl was still a novice, but he recognized raw talent when he saw it. There was something about her that went beyond artifice. He was convinced that *Vogue* would feature the photograph on its front cover. She would soon be in big demand.

He padded through the soft-lit apartment to the phone. He had a long-standing arrangement with a New York modeling agency to spy out exceptional talent. He got a reasonable retainer and a handsome commission when he found a girl they could use.

As he waited for the long-distance connection, he stared at the photograph in his hand. Extraordinary.

The party was in the St Germain apartment of a *Cosmopolitan* fashion editor. When Armand and Valentine arrived, just after nine, the room was buzzing. The crowd was all magazine and fashion people - editors, agents, designers, photographers and models.

Valentine hated fashion parties, hated the cheap talk and the thick undercurrents of envy and muted rage. She would not have come, but Armand had insisted.

He introduced her to a young and upcoming designer, a thin young man in a skin-tight shirt, who made desultory conversation while eyeing a blond-haired man on the other side of the room.

A tall, elegantly dressed man in a navy-blue, double-breasted suit appeared at Armand's side.

'This is John Cassavettes,' Armand said. 'John, this is the girl I told you about. Valentine Breton.'

'*Enchanté*,' the man said. He held out his hand. 'Armand was right. You are exceptionally beautiful.'

Valentine had heard of him. He had built up Fashion Incorporated, his modeling agency, from nothing to the second biggest agency in New York in just six years.

'Thank you,' she said. She heard it all the time. It didn't mean anything. Being beautiful was like wearing a beautiful dress. When you wore it out, people wouldn't notice you anymore. It wasn't you they were looking at. It was the label.

'Armand tells me that *Vogue* are making you their cover girl next month. I am always looking for young women with talent.'

'That's very kind of him to mention me. I'm very flattered. But I don't want to leave Paris.'

'How much do you earn here in France?'

'I'm sure I could earn more in America, but-'

'My girls are the best in the world, Valentine. Their faces are on the front covers of *Vogue* and *Cosmopolitan*. The American editions. They can earn a thousand dollars a day. Can you afford to say no to that?'

'Some things in life are more important than money but thank you for the offer.'

Cassavettes looked at Armand in mock astonishment, then shrugged and gave her his card. 'If you ever change your mind.' He kissed her hand and moved away.

Armand shook his head. 'You must be crazy, Valentine. Most girls would give their right arm for the offer you just turned down.'

'They wouldn't make very good models with one arm.' She touched his hand. 'I don't know how you did it, but thanks anyway.'

'Don't thank me. You just cost me a big commission.' He emptied his champagne glass and grabbed another from a passing tray. 'Out of interest, why did you say no? If you're not interested in the money, what is it you want?'

'I just want to be happy. Look, I have to go. I'm not in a party mood.' Her lips brushed his cheek and then she was gone.

Tehran

A tall, good-looking young man with an Asian complexion and startling bleached-blond hair browsed the news stand at the international terminal as he waited for his connecting flight to Singapore. He picked up a magazine and stared at the cover.

'Adrienne,' he said.

Moving like a man in a trance, he paid for the magazine and folded it into his briefcase. Then he ran to the nearest phone and placed a long-distance call to Serge Renard in Paris.

CHAPTER 25

Paris

The 747 thundered down the runway at Orly airport. The engines roared as the reverse thrust brought the massive machine to a halt.

At last, he had found her. He had rehearsed the scene so many times in his mind. Sometimes the fantasy ended in a tearful reunion. Sometimes it ended in violence. He had imagined recrimination, sorrow, relief, joy, anger and death.

He wondered which it would be.

Paris in the springtime is not like the songs, Renard thought, as he wiped the condensation from his office window and stared at the grey sheets of rain. Traffic snarled along the boulevards. He watched a man struggle with a broken umbrella in the wind.

He heard Monique, his receptionist, walk in. She was early.

'You didn't bring any good weather with you,' he said.

'I didn't come here to discuss the weather.' Michel opened his leather attaché case and took out a copy of *Vogue*. He threw it on the table. 'This is her.'

Renard gaped at him. 'How did you get in?'

'The door was open. You should do something about your security in this place. You're supposed to be a detective.'

'Most of my clients make an appointment.'

'I'm paying you. I'll see you when I want.' Michel pointed to the front cover of the magazine. 'I found her myself in the end. I wasted my money on you.'

Renard picked up the magazine. 'But this girl is so young. The woman we are looking for is in her forties.'

'That is her,' Michel said, stabbing the glossy cover portrait. 'Find her. Find out who she is.' He snapped the briefcase shut and went to the door. 'I give you three days.'

The door shut behind him.

'You were right,' Renard said. He took a manila folder out of his drawer. 'Her name is Valentine Breton. Her mother's name is Adrienne, maiden name Christian. Amazing.' He slid the folder across the desk. 'It's all there. Her name, address, recent family history.'

Michel flicked through the report. 'Breton. Rue St Luc. Jesus Christ, that's only a few blocks from here.'

'I couldn't have known that. I'm a private investigator, not a psychic.' Renard lit a cigarette. 'Do you mind telling me what this is all about now?'

'If you were any detective at all, you'd be able to find out for yourself.'

Arrogant prick, Renard thought. Let's see how you like this next bit of news then. 'I'm afraid it's all a little irrelevant now anyway,' he said.

'What do you mean?'

'Look at the final notation.'

Michel turned to the last page and read it. The folder slipped from his fingers and its contents scattered on the floor.

'It must be a mistake.'

'I don't make mistakes,' Renard said. 'They buried her next to her father in the Père Lachaise.'

'She can't be dead.'

'We all die. *Desolé m'sieur.* I did my best. You asked me to find her for you. I have found her.'

Renard was unprepared for what happened next.

Michel leaped to his feet, grabbed him by the collar and pushed him backwards off the chair. He found himself flat on his back, the knuckles of Michel's left hand at his throat, his knee on his chest.

Michel grabbed a handful of his hair. 'You jerked me around all this time, and she was practically living in your back garden.'

Renard didn't see where the knife came from. Suddenly it was just there in his hand, the point inches from his eyes. He tried to scream but Michel's knuckles choked him. He closed his eyes and prayed.

Just when he thought he was going to pass out, Michel stood up. Renard lay there, gasping for breath.

Michel stood over him, the handsome face screwed into a grimace. 'Fucking dead. Four fucking years, and now you tell me she's dead.' With one quick movement he swept his arm across the desk, sweeping everything onto the floor. A glass ashtray splintered against the filing cabinet. He picked up a chair and threw it across the room. It smashed into the door and one of the legs splintered off.

There was a scream. Monique stood in the doorway, staring wide-eyed at the scene. She screamed again as Michel pushed past her.

Renard got slowly to his feet, straightened his tie and walked out of his office into reception. Monique was already on the telephone.

'What are you doing?' he said. He slammed his fist on the cradle. 'I don't want the fucking *flics* nosing around here. Just make a cup of coffee. Strong and black. He's upset, that's all. Anyway, he still owes me the balance of my fee.'

The gentle slap of the wipers swept away the mist of rain on the windscreen. Michel turned the heater in the rented Mercedes to maximum. He couldn't remember feeling this cold in his whole life.

His mother had abandoned him again. He had always been so sure he would find her. Why did she do this? There was no way to mend the past now. Everything was incomplete. The scars could not heal.

He parked the car and got out, feeling the rain sting his face. There was an imposing square gate in a high white wall. A clutch of tourists huddled outside. He couldn't believe anyone would want to go sightseeing on a day like this. He stumbled blindly along the cobbled paths, past weathered angels, dank vaults, skeletal trees. A woman was taking a photograph of Emmanuel Proust's grave.

It was sprawling metropolis of the dead. He would never find her in here without a map, and already the afternoon was fading to grey. He went back to the car and took out the file Renard had given him. He had misjudged him. The man was thorough. He had marked the grave number and its location on the last page.

It was almost dark when he found her. The grave was unremarkable but had served many generations of her husband's family. Her name had been the last one added, and there were fresh flowers in the vase.

ADRIENNE BRETON

1928-71

A wonderful mother and an adoring wife.

God will keep you a place with the angels.

He stared at it for a long time. Then he threw back his head and laughed. A place with the angels. He turned his face to the heavens allowing the rain to sting his cheeks.

He could never be free of her now. Not until the day he died.

CHAPTER 26

Michel parked in the street. The apartment was in a turn-of-the-century building near the Rue Amali between the Boulevard des Invalides and the Eiffel Tower. There was a charcuterie on one side and an antique dealer on the other. He flicked on the cabin light and checked Renard's folder. The Breton apartment was on the sixth floor.

It was cold inside the car. He shivered. The rain angled down, illuminated by the sodium lights of the streetlamps and driven by a north wind. He looked down at the folder.

Subject had one daughter, Valentine.
Born 23/7/52. No other known offspring.

He closed the folder and turned off the cabin light. He looked at his watch. The dial glowed in the gathering dusk. After six. Well, it didn't matter. He would wait all night if he had to.

An hour later he heard footsteps in the street, the sharp click-click of a woman's heels. It brought back a memory of his mother's footsteps on a wooden staircase a long time ago. She passed within a few feet of the car and hurried across the street into the apartment building. She paused on the steps for a moment to shake the rain off her umbrella. She was mostly in shadow, but he knew it was her by the way she walked, just like her mother.

Their mother.

Then she disappeared inside the foyer.

Adrienne was not dead, after all. There was a part of her living on.

'*Bonsoir, Papa,*' Valentine threw off her coat and scarf and hung them on the back of the door. She hurried over to the fire.

Jean-Claude was huddled in an armchair wearing the same dressing gown as when she had left that morning. He looked sunken and withered. He had aged twenty years since her mother died.

She sat by his chair and put an arm around him. 'How was your day?'

'I feel so tired. I read a little this afternoon.'

'We should go away for a while. A holiday. We can visit Uncle at Nîmes.'

'Maybe soon. I don't feel up to it just now.'

'You need to get out of this apartment. You can't just sit here every day like this.'

'I'm all right.'

'We're going and that's final. I'll write to him tonight and organize everything.' She kissed the top of his head. 'I'll make us dinner.'

He watched her walk into the kitchen. She reminded him so much of her mother at that age. Thank God she wasn't like her in other ways. Adrienne had been cruel, Valentine was kind. Adrienne had punished, Valentine forgave.

She was the reason he never regretted that miserable marriage.

But she couldn't stay here forever. She was famous now, and he saw the way men looked at her in the street. Soon she would be gone. Some man would take her away.

He just prayed that it was the right man.

And not yet.

Please, not yet.

Valentine left for work at seven minutes past eight the next morning. She walked two blocks to the metro at Gare des Invalides. She got off at L'Opéra and went into a building on the Rue de la Paix.

Michel followed her the whole way. There was a directory on the wall inside the foyer. The second and third floors belonged to the Elite modeling agency. He studied the board for a long time, then turned and walked back to the Métro.

It was that grey time of evening that Parisians call *l'heure bleu.* A metallic voice from the tannoy announced the incoming train. Valentine felt a cold draught of air from the black mouth of the tunnel, and the platform shuddered beneath her feet like the first shock of an earthquake.

'*Excusez-moi, Mademoiselle.* Do you have a light?'

She turned around. The man was striking to look at. He had bleached blond hair that jarred with his Asian complexion. His deep brown eyes were direct and unsettling.

'*M'sieur?*'

'A light?'

'I'm sorry. I don't smoke. I've given up.'

'Never mind. Thank you.'

The train thundered into the station, the brakes squealing and setting her teeth on edge. She ducked her head against the icy blast of air pushed in front of it. The doors opened and the crowd surged out of the carriages, jostling her. When she got into the carriage, she looked behind her to see if the man was still there, but he had disappeared.

When she reached Gare des Invalides half an hour later, she was still thinking about him. It had been a very half-hearted attempt at a pass, if that was what it was. She put her hands deeper into her coat and walked a little faster. It had rained again, and the road gleamed in the dusk like the skin of a snake. Tires hissed on the wet bitumen. She turned off the Rue Amali, her head bowed beneath her umbrella against the driving rain.

Once, she thought she heard footsteps running behind her, and she turned around, alarmed. But the street was empty.

That stranger on the platform. What was it about him that had seemed so familiar? She hurried on, almost breaking into a run when she saw her apartment.

Just as she got inside the door, it started to rain. She stood in the foyer and looked back up the street. Was that the man from the Métro? No, just her imagination. There was no one there. She pressed the call button for the lift and hurried inside.

There was cigarette ash spilled over the desk. Budjinski scowled at the mess as if someone else had made it. He emptied the ashtray into his waste basket and lit another *Gauloise.*

He picked up the telex the Singapore police had sent about the robbery and murder at the Mandarin Hotel back in December. He read it again.

Afterwards, he stared out of his window towards the Longchamps Racecourse. It was a race day, and from where he sat, he could make out the grandstand and the distant flash of colored silk as the riders trotted out onto the track.

But his eyes were turned inward, on places very far away from St. Cloud. He was thinking about a man who used a woman to help him rob another jewelry store, in New Delhi.

It had to be the same man.

Were there other similar unsolved crimes gathering dust in police filing cabinets around the world? He could soon find out. He pulled a notepad towards him, lit another cigarette and set to work.

The radio room on the top floor of the Interpol headquarters was never silent. Double glass partitioning muted the endless metallic clatter of the Telex, Teletype and radio telegraph machines. Many of the thousands of messages received each day still arrived in Morse code because the poorer member countries of the organization could not afford more expensive equipment.

In another room, four highly trained operators relayed the five letter combinations that comprised the Interpol code, transmitting in English, Spanish, French or Arabic.

A thin, pale man wearing thick glasses sat down in front of a short-wave radio and placed his index finger over the Morse code key. His hand moved steadily in an easy rolling motion, tapping out an average of thirty-five words a minute.

The words were relayed from one of the antennae on the roof to a pasture outside the village of St Martin d'Abbat, eighty kilometers to the south. From there, a giant transmitter flashed Budjinski's alert to police forces around the world, from Switzerland to the Philippines.

All Budjinski had to do now was wait.

CHAPTER 27

Spring is here at last, Valentine thought. A cool breeze set the *contraventions* fluttering under the windscreen wipers of cars and whipped at the café umbrellas lining the boulevard. She warmed herself in the tepid, noonday sun and ordered *café au lait* and a *croque monsieur*. A group of laughing teenagers roared up to the sidewalk on mopeds.

The waiter brought her lunch. She ate slowly, watching a busker with a flute trying to charm some centimes from the passing tourists. She had just finished her coffee when something made her turn around, and she saw him sitting behind her just two tables away.

He looked up and smiled, folded the newspaper he was reading and came over. 'May I sit down?' he said and did not wait for her to answer.

'Do I know you, *monsieur*?' she said.

'I thought I recognized you from somewhere. Perhaps I am mistaken.'

'We've never met.'

'Didn't we speak briefly the other night, while you were waiting for your train. I needed a light for my cigarette.'

'I'm sorry. I do not remember.'

'My name is Michel Giresse. What's yours?'

'You are very direct, *monsieur*.'

He grinned. 'Yes, I am but I'm afraid I am also very clumsy. You will have to forgive me.

Clumsy like a fox, she thought. 'My name is Valentine.'

'That's a beautiful name. Do you work near here?'

She thought about getting up and walking away. She wouldn't often let herself get picked up like this. She studied him. He was an extraordinary looking man. His clothes were expensive and so was his wristwatch. He wore tinted Bronzini sunglasses, and the ring on his little finger was inlaid with a huge emerald-cut ruby.

'I work in the fashion business.'

'Do you enjoy it? A girl like you deserves the best life can offer.'

'I am quite content with my life, thank you, *monsieur*.'

He sat back in his chair, smiling at her. He looked completely relaxed. His demeanor was at once offensive and compelling. It left her feeling a little off balance like his eyes.

'And what do you do when you are not trying to pick up women shamelessly in cafés?'

'I'm a tourist.'

'And when you are not being a tourist?'

'I travel.'

'You're being very mysterious.'

'That is because the truth is so mundane.' He leaned towards her. 'You know, you are a very beautiful woman.'

Valentine looked at her watch and got up. She had an assignment at a photographic studio at two o'clock. 'You'll have to be a little more original than that.'

The next day at the agency, there were two dozen red roses waiting for her at the front desk. Valentine tore open the card, feeling the receptionist's eyes burning the back of her neck.

To a beautiful lady. From M'sieur. Sorry I couldn't be more original.

She turned back to the girl at the desk. 'Did he bring these himself?'

'Yesterday afternoon. He was very charming.'

She read the card a second time. Who did this man think he was, sending flowers to a woman he had just met casually on the street?

'No one ever sent me long-stemmed roses,' the receptionist said.

'You have them, then,' Valentine said.

He expected her to fall at his feet because he was rich. She met hundreds of men like that every day.

'Valentine, walk towards me. Swing your skirt. That's it. Stand in front of the painter there. Look away, look away. Beautiful.'

The late afternoon was unseasonably warm. The assignment was for *Cosmopolitan*, a new summer collection by Patou.

Armand's idea had been to take the shots among the riotous color of the painters and tourists on the Left Bank, with the Notre-Dame and the Île de la Cité in the background.

'Put your hands in your hair, toss your head back. That's it.'

Valentine looked beyond the camera and froze. It was him. A black Mercedes was double-parked against the curb, and he was sitting on the bonnet. He waved.

'What are you looking at?' Armand turned around. 'Who's that?'

'An acquaintance.' She tried to concentrate but felt suddenly awkward and self-conscious.

When they took a break, Michel sauntered over. 'Hello, Valentine.'

'Hello, *monsieur*,' she said. 'Thank you for the flowers.'

He indicated the car. 'I hired a limousine, so I could take you to lunch after you've finished the shoot.'

'How did you find me?'

'The reception girl at the agency. She won't get into any trouble, will she?' His eyes glittered with amusement.

'What did you say to her?'

'I tortured her with hot irons. She was very brave. But when I told her she had lovely eyes, she caved in completely.'

I bet, Valentine thought. 'She is not supposed to give out private information.'

'Are you angry with her or with me?'

'I'm furious with both of you.'

'Then let me make it up to you. I have booked a table at the Tour d'Argent. Do you think you'll be finished in around half an hour?'

Michel came around the car and held the door open for her. Valentine got in. He took the *contravention* off the windscreen, screwed it up and threw it in the gutter.

He started the engine, then reached into the glove box and produced a small, velvet pouch. He emptied the contents into his palm. It was a diamond necklace and two pearl drop-earrings.

'Here,' he said, 'these are for you.'

She could not hide her astonishment. They would be worth tens of thousands of francs. 'I can't take these.'

'Call it a loan. You can give them back to me afterwards.' He gunned the Mercedes through a red light on the corner of the Rue St Antoine and the Boulevard de Sébastopol. 'You can't go to the Tour d'Argent without jewelry. You might as well be naked.'

'The moment lunch is over, you're getting them back.' She slipped on the heavy necklace. 'Do you always carry this much jewelry in your car?'

'It's my business.'

'You're a burglar?'

'I'm a gem dealer. I export them. From Asia mainly.' He turned onto the Quai Tournelle. 'We're nearly there. I'll tell you about it over lunch.'

The Tour d'Argent was one of the most famous restaurants in Paris. Michel had booked a seat by the window overlooking the Seine and the Île de la Cité. The sommelier brought a bottle of Moët et Chandon, crisp and very cold.

'You look stunning,' he told her. 'Practically every man in the room was staring at you as we walked in.'

She studied him over her glass. 'You speak French perfectly, but I can't place your accent. And you don't look French. So, who are you?'

'My mother was French. My father was a little more exotic. They were unconventional people.'

'How long are you staying in Paris?'

'Until I finish my business. It takes me all over the world.'

'You're lucky.'

'It reads better than it lives. There are times I wish there was someone I could share my life with.'

'Where is your family?'

'I never really knew my father. He left us when I was very young. And my mother died when I was four years old. I grew up in an orphanage in Saigon.'

His playfulness had evaporated, and she found herself revising her first impressions of him. She had thought he was just another spoiled playboy, but his story of loss and deprivation made him fascinating.

'That must have been terrible.' She realized how lame that must sound to him.

'I survived.'

The waiter arrived with the *pâté de foie gras* and the spell was broken. Michel's mood changed abruptly.

He leaned across the table and refilled her glass. 'Now tell me all about you. I want to know where you grew up and what your family was like. Families fascinate me. Probably because I never had one of my own.'

Valentine told him about Dakar and her childhood in the beautiful rambling white villa, and about the shock of moving from a sixteen-bedroom mansion to a cramped two-bedroom apartment in Paris. She talked about her father and how he had been invalided out of the *Service Publique*.

When she had finished, she found that lunch was over, and she had drunk far too much champagne. 'I'm sorry.' she said. 'You must be bored. All we've talked about is me.'

'I'm not bored at all. I want to know everything about you.'

'It must seem very ordinary.'

'Not at all. There is one thing though. In all your stories, you barely mentioned your mother.'

'The truth is, for as long as I can remember, she was an alcoholic. We rarely spoke to each other. She died a few months ago in an asylum. She was both mentally and physically ill. I see I've shocked you. I'm sorry.' She finished her champagne. 'You should take me home now.'

The wine had gone to her head, but she sobered up quickly when they reached the street. They walked back to the car in silence.

Michel opened the door for her. As she went to get in, he caught her arm. He pulled her towards him and kissed her on the mouth. She kissed him back with a passion that surprised them both.

As they drove to his hotel, he watched her from the corner of his eye. It was astonishing. She looked exactly as she had looked, the last time he had seen her. He started to remember things he had tried so hard to forget.

His mother putting on a green dress. 'I have to go out for a little while.'

The whine of the mortar before it fell on the orphanage.

Thien taking off his belt. 'Now I will show you how we treat thieves here at Van Trang.'

The chief head warden at the Port of Bombay prison. 'I am going to make you curse your mothers for bringing you into the world.'

And as he looked at her, he felt the rage growing inside him again.

CHAPTER 28

Michel had a suite at the Bristol, on the Rue du Faubourg St Honoré. It was late afternoon and the lamps had been turned on in the bedroom, throwing his face into shadow. He stood by the window smoking a thin cheroot, watching her undress.

Valentine pulled her t-shirt over her head and kicked off her jeans. She was naked underneath, except for a pair of sheer silk briefs. She slipped them off and crossed the room. She took the cheroot from his fingers and stubbed it out in the heavy onyx ashtray.

'You must think you're very clever. Getting what you want so easily.'

'I don't just want this. I want all of you.'

She put her hands around his neck and pulled his face towards hers.

He picked her up and carried her to the bed. He kissed her lips, her cheeks, her neck. Then he moved slowly down the length of her body, his tongue darting in delicate butterfly motions along her breasts and her stomach. He knelt between her thighs and stripped off his clothes. His body was the color of brandy. He gripped her around the waist and pulled her towards him. She gasped at how easily he entered her.

They coiled and uncoiled in a slow and ancient rhythm. He seemed to know secrets about her body she didn't know herself.

And then he stopped.

She opened her eyes. 'What's wrong?'

He was staring at her, and there was a look on his face she hadn't seen before. His fingers traced the contours of her neck.

'Michel?'

His hand tightened around her throat, but then he kissed her. 'I'll never let you go again,' he said, almost to himself.

She wrapped her arms and legs around his hard, warm body and told him she loved him, which she almost did. She was ready to fall in love with any man who could make her feel like this.

She was asleep. She lay on her side, her knees pulled up and her hands tucked under her chin like a child. His shadow fell across her face.

In the dark it was easy to imagine this was Adrienne. She could have been her twin. He wondered how a small boy could remember so much. Perhaps it was all in his imagination.

He leaned closer and breathed in the scent of her hair. If he closed his eyes, he could still see her combing it out with her pearl-handled brush. He saw her putting on a green dress and walking out of the door.

His lips brushed her cheek. 'Don't leave me again,' he whispered.

Something had happened to him. He had never made love to any woman before without being overcome with rage and contempt. But not Valentine. He couldn't hurt her, not now. She had been waiting for him after all. He didn't care what had happened in the past. All that mattered was she was here, and she would never go away again.

She stirred in her sleep. Her eyes flickered open.

He kissed her tenderly.

'What time is it?'

He reached for his watch on the bedside table. 'Just after midnight.'

'I must get home.'

He slid his hand under the sheet. 'Not yet.'

'Don't do that-'

'Stay a little longer.' He kissed her throat. 'I love you.'

And he started to make love to her again.

When Valentine got back to the apartment, the light was still on in the study. She crept to the doorway.

Jean-Claude was asleep in his big armchair, a book open on his lap. He looked so old. Grey wisps of hair were pulled tight across his scalp, and in the yellow splash of the lamp, his skin looked thin as parchment.

She laid a hand on his shoulder. 'Papa.'

He started awake.

'It's all right, it's only me.'

'Ah, Valentine.'

'What are you doing here? It's late. You should be in bed.'

'I won't ask what you've been doing till this time of the morning.'

'Papa, I'm almost twenty years old. Anyway, I told you I'd be late. Did you get yourself some dinner?'

'I wasn't hungry.'

'Let me help you.'

'I'm all right. I can manage.'

She tried to help him to his feet, but he brushed her hand away.

'I said, I'm all right! I'll have to manage when you're gone, won't I?' He stumbled into his bedroom and shut the door behind him.

She turned off the lamp. 'I won't leave you, Papa,' she whispered. 'I promise you. No matter what, I won't leave you.'

CHAPTER 29

Budjinski stared at the strip light in the ceiling. 'Unbelievable,' he said. He took a deep breath and re-read the batch of cables on his desk.

During the last few weeks, they had flooded into St Cloud from all over Asia - Manila, Kuala Lumpur, Karachi, Tehran, Beirut, Calcutta, Jakarta, Jogjakarta, Tokyo and Osaka. Some of the cases went back as far as 1968.

After he had discarded those that did not seem to fit the pattern he was looking for, the cables fell into two distinct groups. The first group were eerily similar to the murders in Singapore and New Delhi. Like this one from Manila:

```
1114172
TO: IP PARIS
IN RESPONSE TO YOUR REQUEST 514172 WE WISH
TO ADVISE YOU OF AN UNCLOSED FILE OF ROB-
BERY AT SHERATON HOTEL 23/10/70 STOP TOURIST
AND GEM-STONE PROPRIETOR FOUND DEAD IN HOTEL
SUITE STOP TOURIST LATER IDENTIFIED AS TWEN-
TY-THREE-YEAR-OLD UNITED STATES FEMALE JENNY
MARKOWITZ STOP GEMS TO VALUE FIVE HUNDRED
THOUSAND PESOS STILL MISSING STOP
```

REQUEST ASSISTANCE IN LOCATING AND DETAINING POSSIBLE SUSPECTS STOP EXTRADITION WILL BE REQUESTED STOP
  END IP MANILA
  SIGNED: SERGIO OSMENA (COL.)
  PHILIPPINES POLICE DEPARTMENT (INTERPOL DIVISION)
```

But there was a second group of unsolved crimes that, although quite different, also intrigued him. They all involved a woman, usually young, often an employee of a jewelry store. She would use drugs to disable her employer and then flee with the contents of his safe. Like this cable from Hong Kong:

```
1214172
TO: IP PARIS
IN RESPONSE TO YOUR REQUEST 514172 WE WISH TO ADVISE YOU OF OPEN FILE OF ROBBERY REPORTED 18/5/71 AT NG FAT CHOW TRADING PTY LTD 732 NANKING ROAD KOWLOON MISSING JEWELRY AND PRECIOUS STONES VALUE FOUR HUNDRED THOUSAND DOLLARS HONG KONG STOP. ROBBERY PERPETRATED BY EMPLOYEE WHO DRUGGED EMPLOYER WITH UNKNOWN SUBSTANCE STOP SUSPECT IDENTIFIED AS 20 YO FEMALE ROSE KEE STOP BELIEVED TO HAVE FLED HONG KONG STOP PHOTOGRAPH OF SUSPECT AND PHYSICAL DESCRIPTION ATTACHED STOP

```
REQUEST URGENT ASSISTANCE IN LOCATING THIS
PERSON STOP IF DETAINED EXTRADITION WILL BE
REQUESTED STOP
  END IP HONG KONG
  SIGNED: ARTHUR GREAVES (DET. INSPECTOR)
  ROYAL HONG KONG POLICE (INTERPOL DIVISION)
```

There were a dozen similar cables. Only one of the reports indicated the presence of another individual. It identified a Southern European male, 20-25 years old, around six feet, with blond hair, using the name Romeo Bellini. The description did not match the Alan Regan, Latin descent, six-foot, dark hair, wanted by the Singapore police.

And yet.

A man could disguise his appearance. From the sketchy details he now held in his hands, it appeared that there were remarkable similarities in style and execution between all these robberies and murders.

They all involved women. They all involved jewel robberies, and all the women had disappeared.

What if these missing women had not been responsible for the crimes? What if they too had been killed and their bodies disposed of? What if all these crimes were the work of one man?

It was possible.

He stubbed out another *Gauloise* in his ashtray, gathered all the cables into a file and headed for the door.

I've got you, you bastard.

The secretary-general frowned as he looked through the cables on his desk. 'It is all inconclusive. You're guessing.'

'I'm not guessing,' Budjinski said. 'It's obvious. It's staring us right in the face.'

'Nevertheless, it is not enough to justify an expedition to Asia. That is not what you are paid to do.'

'We may have stumbled across a mass murderer here. The first of these cases goes back to February 1968. Over four years and perhaps as many as sixteen murders.'

'Yes, it's possible. But I still do not see how I can justify the expense of anything like what you are proposing. He could be anywhere. We will operate through the normal channels.'

'Sir, I-'

'You've been working too hard lately, René. You should take more time off.'

'I don't need more time off.'

'You came back to work too soon. Even if I thought dispatching an officer to liaise on this case was a good idea - which I don't - you'd be the last one on the list.'

'I'm going to get him, sir.'

'Good. Helping catch criminals is your job. But do it in the usual manner. Assist and inform, Captain. You're not in Homicide now.'

'Yes, sir.' Budjinski picked up the folder and walked out of the office.

CHAPTER 30

'So, when do I meet this boyfriend of yours?' Jean-Claude said.

Valentine examined her reflection in the glass. 'Soon. I promise.'

'You could bring him up here one afternoon for tea.'

'Perhaps when I know him better.'

'You don't want him to meet me, do you? You don't have to be ashamed of me, you know. I know how to behave. I dined with royalty when I was with the *Service Publique*.'

Valentine went to the hall stand and picked up a scarf. 'It's just that afternoon tea isn't quite his thing, you know. Why don't you come downstairs and say hello. He'll be here soon.'

'Why doesn't he ever come up here?'

'How do I look?'

Jean-Claude examined her critically. A change had come over her in the last few weeks, since she had been seeing this latest man. She had become distant and distracted, and her cheeks seemed to glow from some inner radiance.

'Is that all you're wearing? You'll catch your death,' he said.

She kissed him on the cheek. 'Don't wait up.'

'You've seen him every day for practically three weeks.'

A horn sounded in the street.

'That's him!' she said and ran for the door.

Jean-Claude peered down into the street. 'He's got a different car.'

'He hires them. *A bientôt!*'

The door slammed shut behind her.

Jean-Claude watched from the window as she ran across the street and jumped into the black Porsche. It disappeared with a throaty growl. He sighed and turned away. He tried to ignore the sense of foreboding. Just an old man pining for his daughter growing away from him, he told himself. That's all.

The Pont D'Alexandre Trois was silhouetted against a twilight sky. Michel and Valentine walked across, hand-in-hand, towards the floodlit dome of the Invalides.

'I have to leave soon,' he said suddenly. 'Three more days.'

She had known from the beginning it could not be forever. 'I promise I won't make it hard for you.'

He took her by the shoulders. 'You could not make it any harder to leave you. That's why I want you to come with me.'

She stared at him, stunned. 'I can't. Paris is my home.'

'It's your father, isn't it?'

She knew he couldn't understand. A man who had never had a family could never understand. 'He'll die if I leave. I can't just abandon him.'

'We have our whole life in front of us. He's had his.'

'I'm sorry.' She gingerly placed one hand on his. 'We still have three days.'

'I envy him. I wish someone would love me that much.' He looked suddenly like a small boy. He put his head on her shoulder, and she stroked his hair, startled and suddenly very afraid for him.

'What's the matter?'

'Nothing, Papa.'

'Something is wrong. Your coffee's getting cold, and you haven't touched your croissant. You were crying last night.'

'No, I wasn't.'

'I'm not a fool, Valentine. Have you seen yourself this morning? I can tell when a woman's been crying. I'm a man who has had a lot of practice with that.'

Valentine covered her face with her hands. 'He's leaving. He's going to Hong Kong or Singapore or somewhere. He was only in Paris on business. Now he has to go back.'

Jean-Claude reached across the table and put his hand on hers. 'I'm sorry.'

'I think I love him.'

'Does he love you?'

'I think so. He wants me to go with him.'

'And what did you say?'

'I said no, of course.'

'Because of me.'

You selfish old fool, he told himself. She is willing to give up her career, some man that she loves, her whole life, everything, for you.

'Tell him you'll go,' he said. 'Don't worry about me.'

She got up and kissed him on the forehead. 'We'll see. I need to go to work now.'

Michel watched her leave from the doorway of the boulangerie opposite her apartment. He waited a few minutes, then took a pair of black leather gloves from his pocket and slipped them on. He walked quickly across the street. He had taken an impression of her key one afternoon while she slept. He let himself in and decided to take the stairs rather than the elevator.

Jean-Claude heard the front door open and close. He assumed it was his daughter.

'What did you forget?' He looked up from his newspaper and saw a stranger standing in the doorway of his living room. The man had on a knee-length black leather coat and expensive shoes.

'Hello Jean-Claude. May I come in?'

'Who the hell are you?'

'You know who I am.' Michel stood in the middle of the room with his hands in the pockets of his coat and looked around, as if he were thinking of buying the place. 'Have I disturbed your breakfast?'

Jean-Claude let the croissant drop onto his plate. 'What are you doing here?'

Michel bunched Jean-Claude's dressing gown in his fist and picked him up off the chair with one hand. He dragged him across the room and threw him into an armchair.

Jean-Claude would have cried out, but he was so terrified he couldn't speak.

Michel put a boot on the chair between his knees and leaned in. 'Perhaps you don't know who I am.' He looked around the room for the liquor cabinet. He found some pastis, splashed a couple of fingers into a glass and handed it to him. 'Come on, I'm not going to hurt you. I just want to talk.'

Jean-Claude was shaking so hard he could barely hold the glass, never mind drink what was in it. He spilled most of the contents down his pajamas.

Impatient, Michel grabbed the glass and poured what was left down his throat.

Jean-Claude almost choked on it, but by the time he had done coughing, he had at least found his voice again. 'What do you want?'

'Did she ever tell you about me?'

'Valentine said you were-'

'Not Valentine, Adrienne!'

'Adrienne? How do you know about her?'

'You mean she never told you, not even when she was drunk? She was always very forgetful. I seem to have completely slipped her mind when I was four years old.'

'Oh my God.' Jean-Claude said. Suddenly he knew what it was that had destroyed her beauty and her mind. This was the demon she had been trying to escape.

'Ah, now you get it. Yes, I'm your wife's little secret.' Michel leaned over him, his gloved hands resting on each arm of the chair. 'I wasn't going to come. But Valentine has said to me so many times 'Papa is dying to meet you'. So here I am.'

Jean-Claude groaned as the full import of it hit him. 'No, you mustn't! She doesn't know.'

Michel put a hand over his mouth. 'Shut up. Of course, she doesn't know. She's never going to know. She's mine now. There's only one thing standing between us. Do you know what that is?'

Jean-Claude was not listening. He was no longer afraid for himself. He was afraid for his daughter. He had to do something. He kicked out and tried to haul himself out of the chair.

But Michel was far too strong for him. He reached into his pocket and took out a bottle of chloroform and a rag. He clamped it over Jean-Claude's mouth and held it there.

The struggle was over very quickly.

Michel eased Jean-Claude onto the floor. He kept the rag there long after he'd stopped breathing.

CHAPTER 31

It was the release of the Mary Quant summer collection at the Ritz ballroom. Valentine was helping one of the other girls into her dress in the changing room when Marco, the agency's hairdresser, came in and told her that there were two detectives outside asking to speak to her urgently.

They looked uncomfortable in their crumpled suits among the array of glittering gowns. Valentine looked into their faces and knew before they even spoke. She felt her heart lurch.

'I regret to inform you there has been an accident.' one of the men said. 'Your father was found on the concrete outside the sous-sol at about eight o'clock this morning. No one seems to have heard or seen anything. We think he must have fallen from the balcony.'

She felt quite calm, though she knew that wouldn't last. In a way she had been waiting for this to happen ever since her mother died.

They started asking her questions. Had your father been depressed for very long? Had he ever talked about killing himself?

She shook her head. No, he never talked about suicide. But yes, he had been depressed. It's possible it wasn't an accident. Had he done it for her? But why didn't he leave a note?

She remembered nothing of the trip to the hospital. It was a blur.

It was only when she got there that time began to slow down again.

She insisted on seeing his body. A white-coated attendant led the way to the morgue. He opened one of the drawers and pulled back the sheet.

Jean-Claude was grey blue. His right cheek had caved in from the impact of the fall, and the bare, white bone glistened in the harsh strip lighting. His lips were drawn back from his teeth in a silent scream, temporarily frozen in place by rigor.

She kissed him gently on the forehead.

'Are you all right, *Mademoiselle*?' the attendant said.

'I'm fine,' she said. A moment later, she fainted.

It rained the day they buried her father.

Valentine did not remember the service. She leaned against Michel, grateful for his strong arms around her.

The ground looks so damp and cold, she thought. He doesn't like it when it's cold.

She didn't want to go back to the apartment, not now or ever. 'Just get me away from here,' she whispered.

'I will,' Michel said. 'Everything's going to be all right. I'll take care of you now.'

PART 5

The Serpent Strikes: 1972

CHAPTER 32

Michel took her everywhere.

In Athens, they ate red caviar and *taramasalata* on the *teratza* of the famous Grande Bretagne hotel, looking down over the fountains and orange trees of the Syntagma while the setting sun turned the Parthenon the color of honey.

They stayed on a houseboat on the Dal Lake in Kashmir, where lotuses grew on the water like a choking pancake carpet of verdant green. They sat on the deck and watched the *shikaras* glide across the lake while a lady with a twin-set-and-pearls voice read the *All India* news.

Michel hired a limousine to drive them from their hotel at the Oberoi-Intercontinental to see the Taj Mahal at Agra. Valentine was enchanted. A monument to one man's extravagant love and power, it perched on the edge of a cliff like an ice palace floating in the sky.

'It's unbelievable,' she said, 'that one man should do all this for love.'

'Not for love,' he had said. 'For grief. The Shah Jahan did not build it for her while she alive. It was only when he lost her that he realized how much she meant to him. Grief is stronger than love. For grief, a man will do anything.'

In Nepal, they trekked up the Sherpa paths to Nagarkot, alone with the silence of the mountains. The only sounds were the faint tinkling of yak bells and the whip of prayer flags in the Himalayan winds. At dawn the next day, they watched the sun rise over the roof of the world. The mountains spread in panorama before them, from Dhaulagiri in the west to Kanchenjunga in the east.

Michel was like no man she had ever known. He seemed to pulse with energy. Whenever they walked into a room, all eyes turned towards him. And yet he only had eyes for her.

It was like a dream, but like every dream, she wondered when it would end. He spent vast amounts in restaurants and on rental cars, and they always stayed at the best hotels. He had an endless supply of credit cards.

He seemed to have forgotten all about the business that had been urgent enough to make him leave Paris. Whenever she asked him about it, he became evasive and angry. After two months constantly at his side, she still knew almost nothing about him.

She tried not to think about that part of it. She just wanted to enjoy the present. He had got her through those first few miserable weeks after her father's suicide, and she could not get enough of him. He was unpredictable and exciting. At night they fell asleep exhausted in each other's arms, their bodies still intertwined.

One night in Bangkok, as they lay side by side on their hotel bed, he said, 'You are quiet tonight. What are you thinking?'

'I was thinking that I've told you everything about me, but I still know hardly anything about you.'

'There's nothing to know. I'm a simple man, with simple needs.' His hand caressed the silky skin inside her thigh.

'Do you live like this all the time? A five-star gypsy?'

'I have apartments in Hong Kong and Manila. But I hardly ever go there.'

'But what about your business? You must have an office.'

'My business is in my head. As I make money, I spend it. I don't want to build an empire. Is that so wrong?'

'No, I guess not.'

'If you want to live somewhere, we can do that. I'll even rent an office if that will make you happy.'

'You're making fun of me.'

'I'm serious. When I have finished my business here in Bangkok, I will take you to Hong Kong. You can decorate my apartment for me. If you want, we can get married.'

She did not answer him. She sometimes dared to hope the dream was real, but a voice told her to be careful. This was fun, this was spectacular, this was breath-taking. But she sensed that one day soon, it would have to end.

CHAPTER 33

Bangkok, Thailand

Bangkok. Krung Thep to the Thais. The City of Angels. A city of golden temples, redolent with incense, where saffron-robed monks chanted mantras to red-lipped Buddhas.

It was also a city of massage parlors where customers could choose a girl through a one-way mirror by announcing the number of their selection to a stockily built Thai in a tuxedo.

Day-glo colored trucks honked and battled their way through the choked traffic along Ratchadamri Road, their drivers perched uncertainly on the edge of their seats. They reserved the rest of their seat for Buddha, their invisible but essential guardian on the wretched and lethal thoroughfares.

In the distance, the gilded stupas looked cheap and trashy beside the gleaming concrete and glass of the modern hotels.

Grace Somppol lay naked on the bed in the honeymoon suite of the Indra Hotel. She watched Michel take off his clothes.

'I'm frightened,' she said.

'It will take just a few minutes and then you will be richer than you ever imagined. No one will get hurt. Trust me.'

'What if someone walks past the shop and looks in?'

'It will be dark. No one will see you.'

Grace studied him. His body was smooth and lean like the kickboxers she sometimes went to watch at the Lumpini Stadium. 'Can't we just leave here? Now? Tonight?'

'First you must help me.' He crossed the room and sat on the edge of the bed. His hand cupped her breast.

'I don't know if I can do it.'

'Yes, you can. I told you; it will be simple. When old Chaowas wakes up, we will be thousands of miles away. There's nothing to worry about.' He laid himself gently top of her.

'Promise me it will be all right.'

'Shh, now, trust me. I promise you.' He kissed her. 'Everything will be perfect.'

When Michel had walked into the Indra Siam jewelry shop, she had suspected that he was a hustler from the first. She had known enough of them during her short life. It was their eyes that gave them away.

But he was attractive and very rich. A fat ruby glinted on his little finger. There was a burgundy silk handkerchief tucked into the breast pocket of his blazer and a chunky yellow-gold Omega on his wrist. She suspended further judgment.

He had asked to look at some rings and flirted with her as she showed him the displays. He didn't buy any rings, but he did ask her to dinner. She had eagerly accepted.

He took her to the Sheraton, impressed her with his knowledge of gemology and seduced her with talk of life in America. He told her she was beautiful. He told her he would take her to New York and Las Vegas. She believed him because she wanted to.

He pushed inside her. She gave a small cry.

'Tell me about America,' she said.

'There is a big house and a big car. I have my own swimming pool and a telephone.'

'You'll take me to Disneyland?'

'Anywhere you want.'

'Do you really love me?'

'Yes,' he whispered. 'Yes, yes.'

She closed her eyes and concentrated on faking a climax for him. He would screw her all night otherwise.

Valentine stood by the window, watching the lights on Rama I Road. The noise, heat and gasoline stench of the city seemed a world away from her air-conditioned suite. She felt like a queen in an ice tower waiting for her handsome prince to come and claim her.

Michel had stopped dyeing his hair and had cropped it back so that he looked Asian again. Since they had come to Bangkok, he had started leaving early in the morning and coming back late at night, if he came back at all.

She tried to fill her days visiting the temples and shopping in the arcades and the thieves' markets, but soon got bored of sightseeing alone. She toyed with the idea of flying back to Paris. To what? To a lonely, two-bedroom apartment and one-night stands with narcissistic men. Michel had seduced her with his diamond life. He was exciting, passionate and fun. She told herself that when he had finished his business, they would go back to that life. She just had to be patient.

But what sort of business was it? It couldn't be legal, or he wouldn't be so secretive about it. Was it guns, drugs? And if she pretended not to know or to care, what did that make her?

She rang room service and ordered another Scotch and soda. Your mother's daughter all right, she thought. Drown your problems in a bottle.

Michel got back to the Siam Intercontinental just after two in the morning. Valentine was curled up on the leather sofa by the window, her fingers wrapped around an empty glass.

She looked up as he walked into the room. 'What have you been doing?'

'Just business. Why are you still awake?'

'What kind of business?'

He sighed and sat down on the sofa. 'Please, *chérie*, I'm tired. I don't want to fight.'

'It's the middle of the night.' Her voice was slurred. 'Is it another woman?'

'Of course not.'

'You never tell me anything. What is it you actually do?'

'I get gems under the counter, and I sell them. The less you know, the better.'

'But I want to know.'

'I don't talk to you about it because I'm afraid you'll leave me. You weren't born here. But you have to understand, everyone's corrupt here. Yes, I bend the rules a little. No one gets hurt.'

'I think I'll have another Scotch.' She went to get the bottle off the table.

He grabbed her wrist and pulled her back. 'Why do you have to make things so difficult? Everything I do is for you.'

She tried to shake him off. 'You said we'd go to Hong Kong and move into your apartment.'

'I will tie up all the loose ends here tomorrow night. Then we can go. I promise.' He pulled at the cord of her silk pajama shirt and slipped his hand beneath it. 'I would never lie to you. I promise.'

CHAPTER 34

Grace hurried along the hotel arcade to the main lobby, clutching her leather shoulder bag. She tried not to run. A uniformed attendant opened the wide glass doors. She jumped into the Mercedes waiting for her in the forecourt.

'Someone came,' she said breathlessly as she climbed into the car. 'They started peering through the window. I waited until they had gone, and then I got out as quickly as I could.' She told her story as if she was somehow heroic.

'It was probably just one of the guests at the hotel looking at something in the window.' Michel said. 'Why should anyone suspect anything?' He grabbed the bag from her and tipped the contents onto the seat. There were barely a dozen pieces.

'I was so frightened,' Grace said. 'Hold me.'

He held her, his eyes still on the hotel on the other side of the road. There was a fortune in there and it was unguarded.

'Grace, you must go back.'

'No! Please don't make me!'

He thought about doing it himself. But that would be suicidal. The whole point of doing things this way was that he was never seen. There should be nothing to link him with the jewelry store or with her.

'He struggled.'

'What?'

'Chaowas. He knew. The way he looked at me. He tried to get to the door. I had to wrestle with him, right there in his office. You said the powder would knock him out straight away.'

'Perhaps you didn't give him enough.' He put the car into gear and pulled out into the crush of the evening traffic. 'Don't worry. Everything will be all right.'

He headed north out of the city along the black ribbon of the superhighway to Bangkok's Don Muang airport. The 450 SEL purred like a sleek and pampered cat. The dark expanse of rice paddies and tapioca fields was broken occasionally by bright-lit clusters of restaurants that served as fuel stops for the trucks.

The dashboard light lent his face a satanic menace.

He couldn't believe she could walk out of the shop with just the few trinkets she had so proudly handed to him. Not worth more than five thousand dollars, the lot. He had expected at least ten times as much.

Grace curled up on the passenger seat and cried softly.

About ten minutes from Don Muang, he turned off the highway onto an unlit track that ran between the rice paddies.

She looked up. 'Where are we going?'

'We have to hide the diamonds,' he said. 'You can't carry them onto the plane in your shoulder bag.'

He glanced in the rear vision mirror. No one behind them. He stopped the car and turned off the engine.

Grace smiled up at him. 'We did it.'

'Yes, my darling. We did it.'

Stupid bitch. Five thousand dollars would barely pay for dinner in the Hong Kong Peninsula. You think I can live on that?

'What time does our flight leave?' she said.

'One o'clock. Pan Am to San Francisco.'

'I was so frightened,' she repeated.

Michel smiled. Her vacant face smiled back at him. He reached out and held her. He felt the pulse beating in her neck, so tender, so soft, like a tiny bird.

He brushed her hair away from her shoulder to expose her throat completely. It was harder to hate them since Valentine. Now, they were just a nuisance.

'Do you love me?' Grace whispered.

'Of course,' he said.

He had invested so much time and trouble in this silly girl, and she had walked out of the store with a handful of worthless rings. He had wasted his time.

Now he would have to start all over again.

A pale lemon light spread over the gulf. A fisherman pedaled his bicycle beneath the bending palms, just north of the tiny fishing village of Sri Racha. On the back of his bicycle was a bamboo basket piled high with bananas, eggs and vegetables for the market. He rode slowly, for he was very old. Ahead of him, the long, grey strip of beach stretched away into the horizon to Cambodia.

As the light grew stronger, he saw a shape in the sand at the edge of the surf, the white foam sucking around it. At first, he thought it might be a dead turtle. Some turtles grew as big as men and their shells were valuable.

He got off his bicycle and walked down the strand to investigate. His eyesight was poor, so it was not until he was just a few feet away that he realized the turtle was actually the body of a young woman.

She lay on her back, her skin tinged a mottled grey-blue. Her hair waved in the lapping water like seaweed. The crabs had been at work. Her eyes were gone, and her lips.

The old man scrambled back up the beach and pedaled as fast as he could toward Sri Racha. He would have to tell the *puyaiban* to fetch the police.

CHAPTER 35

P aris Budjinski studied the cable the office had just received from Bangkok.

```
1116172
TO: IP PARIS
WE WISH TO INFORM YOU OF A ROBBERY REPORTED ON
5/6/72 AT THE INDRA SIAM JEWELRY STORE AT THE
INDRA HOTEL STOP ROBBERY PERPETRATED BY EMPLOYEE
OF THE PROPRIETOR WHO DRUGGED HIM AFTER CLOSING
THE SHOP STOP THE EMPLOYEE TOOK JEWELRY TO VALUE
OF 10,000 BAHT STOP
   SUSPECT NOW POSITIVELY IDENTIFIED AS A TWEN-
TY-ONE-YEAR-OLD FEMALE GRACE SOMPPOL STOP SUS-
PECT FOUND MURDERED NEAR PATTAYA 7/6/72 STOP
CAUSE OF DEATH BELIEVED TO BE STRANGULATION STOP
SUSPECT NAKED AND NONE OF THE MISSING ITEMS HAVE
BEEN RECOVERED STOP
   NATURE OF CRIME AND MANNER OF DEATH OF
MAIN SUSPECT STRONGLY INDICATES EXISTENCE OF
ACCOMPLICE STOP SUSPECT SEEN IN INDRA HOTEL
```

```
WITH MALE PROBABLE FOREIGN NATIONAL 25-30
YEARS MIDDLE EASTERN OR INDIAN DESCENT SIX
FOOT BLACK HAIR DARK COMPLEXION STOP REQUEST
ASSISTANCE IN LOCATING AND DETAINING POSSIBLE
SUSPECTS STOP
  END IP BANGKOK
  SIGNED: PRENOM TANONGSAK (LT. COL.)
  ROYAL THAILAND POLICE (INTERPOL DIVISION)
```

The ash from his cigarette spilled down his suit. He stood up, sending his chair toppling onto the carpet. With one sweeping motion of his arm, he cleared all the files and papers off his desk onto the floor. Heads turned right around the office.

Clutching the cable in his right fist, he headed towards the elevators and rode to the top floor to ruin the secretary-general's day.

'The answer is no.'

'But-'

'It's out of the question.'

'But it's him. It has to be.'

The secretary-general was a reasonable man. But this last couple of months, his South-East Asia liaison officer had tested his patience.

'Let's suppose you're right, René. Where will you begin your hunt? Bangkok? Delhi? Manila? Singapore? Do you want me to send you off on a tour of Asia?'

'But the trail is fresh,' Budjinski protested. 'We need to conduct a thorough investigation. You know the Thais. They couldn't track a bleeding elephant across a snowfield.'

'Your job is to liaise with them. That means work with them, not tell them how to do their job.'

'But if we could track this man now-'

'No. It's a wild goose chase. We are intelligence gatherers, not storm troopers.'

The secretary-general thought Budjinski looked tired. There were dark pouches under his eyes, and he had lost weight. It seemed he was smoking more, if that was humanly possible. At this rate he would burn himself out long before he was due for retirement.

'This seems to have become a personal obsession,' he said. 'I can't allow that. My job is to ensure that this organization functions along the principles laid down in its charter. I will not authorize you to visit Thailand to pursue this matter. Is that clear? It is futile and desperate.'

'We should be desperate. This man is a psychopath.'

'If indeed it is the work of one man, then you are undoubtedly correct. But we will adhere to the proper procedures.'

Budjinski shrugged. 'Yes, sir, you're right. Perhaps I need to take a break for a while.'

'You're due for leave, René. Take a month off and get out of Paris. Take two months.'

Budjinski nodded, then got up and shuffled to the door.

Bangkok

The Dusit Thani was one of the finest hotels in Bangkok, a gleaming white, ten-storey palace at the southern end of Rama Thai Road. It was patronized by wealthy Asian businessmen, and its lobby and arcades glittered with expensive coffee shops, restaurants, boutiques and jewelry stores.

Mahanorn – she let her customers called her May - worked in the Naree Jewelry Store every day from eight o'clock in the morning until nine o'clock in the evening. She had one Sunday off every four weeks and received 250 baht a month, around a hundred and twenty dollars.

It was a good job. May gave the money to her mother. Together with the money her father earned in his taxi, it helped support her five younger brothers and sisters, and paid some of the rent on their small, wooden house near the airport.

Most of May's customers were Japanese and Malays. But one afternoon she looked up and saw a tall Eurasian man stroll into the shop. The first thing she noticed was his hypnotic brown eyes and white smile. He wore a pearl-grey Cardin suit and shiny leather Gucci loafers.

There were three other girls in the shop, but he walked straight up to her. She couldn't believe her luck.

'Can I help you?' she said in English, the commercial language of the city.

'Possibly. I'm interested in acquiring some diamonds.'

His smile melted her. She wondered if she might be able to interest him in more than a few precious stones. She suspected it might be worth it.

Valentine paused, her finger hovering over the telephone dial. The directory lay open on the bed. The number for Air France had been circled in red ink.

Michel said his business would be finished five days ago. But they were still here in Bangkok, and he stayed out every night until after midnight.

She shook her head and put the phone down. No, she wouldn't just run away. She had to know the truth. She snatched her bag and went out, slamming the door behind her.

The uniformed doorman in the lobby recognized her and smiled.

'Have you seen M'sieur Giresse?' she said.

He nodded. 'He asked me to get a taxi for him.'

'Where to?'

The man hesitated. Valentine took a twenty baht note out of her purse and handed it to him.

'The Sheraton Hotel.'

May looked around the restaurant, awed by the waiters in their immaculate white uniforms, the heavy silver cutlery, the leather-bound wine lists and menus. The other guests were mostly wealthy Europeans, the men in expensive suits - like Michel - the women in designer gowns with emeralds and diamonds sparkling on their wrists and around their necks.

She fidgeted, embarrassed and intimidated, and tried to concentrate on what Michel was saying.

'You seem nervous,' he said.

'I never eat in such a big restaurant,' she said, conscious of her poor English. He had told her that he himself spoke four languages.

'Relax,' he said. 'I will order for you. You just have to enjoy yourself.'

She felt his knee nudge hers beneath the table and caught her breath. She couldn't believe her good fortune. This man was rich, strikingly handsome and sophisticated. Why had he chosen her? She had been told many times that she was beautiful, but she had never thought she might one day attract a man like this. It seemed too good to be true. She hated herself for being so clumsy and tongue-tied.

The wine arrived. It was an expensive French champagne.

He raised his glass in toast. 'To us,' he said.

Her mouth was so dry, she could hardly speak. 'To us.'

This could not be happening. Any moment, she would wake up and realize it had all been a dream.

Paul Herbin came out onto the balcony and stood beside Budjinski. 'An unexpected pleasure, René.' He handed him a glass and poured a beer from a bottle of San Miguel.

'Good to see you again too, Paul.'

They watched the day slip into purple dusk. The setting sun glinted on the golden stupa of a temple, and the ragged coconut palms dotted along Convent Road faded to silhouettes.

'So, it's a holiday, is it?' Herbin said.

Budjinski fumbled for his *Gauloise*s and lit one. 'Sort of.'

'Anyone ever tell you to cut down on those things?'

'Everyone.'

'Why don't you?'

'A few years ago, I was looking at some pretty girls on the Champs Elysées and realized I could have been their father. It meant I was too old to die young, so why worry?'

They had known each other since Saigon, when Herbin was a junior *fonctionnaire* with the Embassy, and Budjinski was with the SDECE.

Herbin had never known his friend to show much emotion. He had been back at his desk in St Cloud the day after his daughter's funeral. It was exactly what Herbin would have expected, why Budjinski had a reputation in the bureau as a callous bastard.

But it was just his way of dealing with things. If he worked superhuman hours, it wasn't because he loved his job, it was because he hated it. He was a crusader who wanted to save the world. Men like Budjinski didn't live long, healthy lives.

There was a story about him. Everyone had heard it.

It had happened in Saigon, just before Dien Bien Phu. A Viet Minh had fired into a cafe with a machine gun and massacred eleven Europeans. One of them was a six-year-old girl. Budjinski had been nearby and had chased the man into an alley. The man's gun had jammed, or Budjinski would have been dead too. Instead, he wrestled the Viet Minh to the ground and beat him to death with his bare hands while the ARVN stood by and watched.

There had been a wife, but she hadn't hung around for long when she realized he was married to the job. His relationship with his daughter had been strained for many years, but he had finally been sorting that out when she was killed. He had called Herbin up from Paris soon after it happened. He had been dead drunk and had wept into the phone.

So much for the callous bastard.

Herbin drained his glass and poured himself another. 'I'm sorry about-'

'I don't want to talk about it.'

'Okay.' There was a difficult silence. 'Is that why the commissariat gave you some time off?'

'No, that was my idea.'

'That doesn't sound like you.'

'Well, the truth is, it's not exactly time off. It's personal.'

'I see. Be careful. If Paris hears about it, you'll be out on a pension the moment you step foot back in France.'

'I don't give a shit.'

Herbin looked at him. 'So, what is this all about?'

'The robbery at the Indra Hotel last week. It's the same guy.'

Budjinski had photocopied the entire dossier before leaving Paris. He had copies of the report on the Indra robbery in his jacket pocket. He took them out, unfolded them, and handed them to his Herbin.

Herbin skimmed them. 'Black hair, dark complexion,' he said. 'That narrows it down to about ten million people in Asia.'

'The man we're looking for is responsible for at least seventeen murders in a dozen different countries. Now, if you were him, how would you travel from one country to another without being detected?'

'I'd use different names.'

'Which means?'

'Different passports.'

'Exactly. I'm going to start tracking down names of people who have had their passports stolen in Bangkok in the last two weeks.'

'Christ, do you know how long that will take?'

'I want to check if any of those names appear on aircraft manifests on the day after the robbery. When I know where he's gone, I can-'

'René, stop. Do you know the odds of finding him this way?'

'It's better than sitting on my ass in St Cloud sending out all-station alerts. *Look out for a tall, dark stranger*. What am I, a gypsy fortune teller? Somebody has to do something.'

Herbin shook his head. 'Well, I wish you luck my friend.'

'I wish you luck too because you're going to help me.' He waited.

Herbin hesitated, then held up both hands in mock surrender. 'What do you need?'

'A list of all passports reported stolen or missing for the two-week period prior to the robbery.'

'That should be simple enough for our embassy. I can have that for you tomorrow.'

'What about the other embassies?'

'That will be a lot more difficult. Some of them will co-operate. Which ones do you want?'

'All the European consulates, plus Malaysia, Singapore, Hong Kong and perhaps India.'

'*Merde*. Anything else? A cure for cancer? World peace?'

'We don't need a miracle, Paul. Just a little bit of luck. I'll do the rest.'

CHAPTER 36

Valentine walked across the lobby of the Sheraton Hotel. Asian businessmen lounged on the leather banquettes while tourists in bright summer shirts milled around, clutching teak carvings and souvenir shells from Phuket or Pattaya.

She went straight to the reception desk. 'Can you tell me if you have a *Monsieur* Michel Giresse staying here?' she said.

The clerk checked the register. 'We do not have anyone of that name.'

Valentine turned away. She checked the downstairs bars, then took the elevator to the top-floor restaurant.

She saw him immediately. He was sitting by the window with a woman. She was young, a Thai with a pretty face. She had on a short, dark skirt, and his hand was resting on her bare thigh under the table.

Valentine felt as if someone had kicked her in the stomach.

He looked up and saw her. He turned back to the girl, whispered something in her ear, and hurried across the room towards her.

Valentine got back into the elevator. She pressed the button for the ground floor.

Just as the doors closed, Michel jumped in beside her. 'What are you doing here?'

'You bastard.'

'She's a business associate.'

'What business are you in, prostitution?'

'Go back to the hotel and wait for me. We'll discuss it later.'

'The three of us?'

The elevator doors opened. He tried to grab her arm. She wrenched herself free and ran across the lobby.

She jumped into a taxi waiting in the forecourt.

Michel leaned in the passenger window. 'It's not what you think.'

'Get away from me.' She turned to the driver. 'Just drive!'

She heard Michel calling her name as they sped away down Rama I Street.

Well, she thought, I've got what I deserve. He's just another smooth-talking bastard with his brains in his pants.

It was over now. The spell was broken.

Valentine took the whisky miniatures from the mini bar and downed three of them, one after the other. Then she stripped off her clothes and ran a shower. She forced herself to endure an ice-cold spray, trying to shock the numbness out of her system, until the needles of water began to hurt.

She didn't hear the key turn in the lock.

When he slid the shower screen aside, she spun around and let out a scream.

'I won't let you leave me.' He turned off the water and pushed her back into the shower.

'How old is she, Michel? Twelve, thirteen?'

'You're tired.'

'Sure, I'm tired of waiting around here all day for you, tired of being made a fool of. Why don't you go and take care of business? I want to get some sleep. I have a long flight tomorrow.'

'You can't leave me.'

'Who do you think I am? Some tart you can use whenever you feel like it?'

'I won't let you walk out on me again.'

'What are you talking about?'

He grabbed her arms and forced her against the tiles. 'You can't get away from me. Wherever you go in the world, I will find you.'

'You're hurting me. Let me go.'

'You can't leave me, and I can't leave you.'

He squeezed her jaw between the steel of his fingers. Then he kissed her violently on the mouth. She couldn't breathe. She clawed at his face, tore his shirt.

He grabbed her arms again and pinned them behind her back. He held them there with one hand while he unzipped his pants.

'Stop it!'

But he didn't stop, not until he had finished with her. Then he left her shivering and sobbing on the floor.

'I love you,' he said as he walked out of the bathroom.

She heard him changing his clothes. A few minutes later, the door slammed behind him.

She curled into a ball. The bastard was mad.

When Michel got back to the restaurant, most of the other diners had left. May almost cried with relief when she saw him. The manager had already asked her twice about the bill. Michel paid the check with a gold American Express card and left a handsome tip.

He ignored May's questions until they were in the elevator. He pressed the button for the sixteenth floor.

'Where are we going?'

'To my room. I want you to see the view.'

'I have to go.'

'No, you don't. It's your day off.'

'Who was that woman?'

The doors opened. Michel put an arm around her waist and guided her out. He led her along the hushed corridor to his room. When they were inside, he closed the door and threw the key onto the bedside table.

May stood in the middle of the room, clutching her electric-pink handbag.

Michel sighed. 'I'm sorry. She has been following me. We were having an affair, and I told her it was over, but now she won't leave me alone.'

'Why you go after her then?'

'I feel responsible. I'm afraid she might do something stupid.'

May knew he was lying. He just wanted to sleep with her. But a man like this, he might be very generous.

She thought about her family and the hovel they all lived in with the jets screaming overhead night and day. This guy paid more for his wristwatch than they paid for rent in a whole year. If she brought home a little extra money her mother would understand. Her father would be sad, but he would be happy to take it.

Michel took off his shirt. There were bloody scratches down his ribs.

'What happened?'

'She got hysterical. She was jealous of you.'

May couldn't imagine a woman like that being jealous of her. She liked the idea of it, even though it seemed unlikely.

He took down his pants. He had a good body, well-muscled and lean. She could do worse things for money.

He kissed her and ran a hand along her arm. 'I can make all your dreams come true. Do you know that?'

'You don't know May's dreams yet.'

'Then you must tell me. I am a very generous man, May. You just have to trust me.'

She let him kiss her. She thought about telling him that she was very nearly a virgin, but she didn't want to spoil it. She had never done anything like this before.

She hoped it would be worth it.

Valentine threw her clothes into her case, then picked up her bag from the table. She quickly checked the contents.

Her passport was gone.

She searched the room, thinking she might have put it in a drawer and forgotten about it. But she knew that was crazy. She always kept her passport in the zipped side pocket of her bag.

He must have taken it to stop her leaving.

But did he have it with him, or had he hidden it in the room?

His crocodile-skin briefcase.

She found the case pushed under the bed. It was locked, naturally. She threw it on the bed in disgust.

Her father had had a briefcase with six tumblers like this one when he was with the *Service Publique*. He had devised a combination from his own birth date. The combination had been 15-12-20. The left-hand lock was 151, the right hand 220. He had told her it was a common system.

Michel did not know when he was born, so he celebrated his birthday at Tet, the Vietnamese New Year. The 31st of January.

She slipped the tumblers on the left-hand lock to 310. It opened.

But how old was he? Had he said twenty-five or twenty-six? She tried twenty-six. She turned the tumblers on the right-hand lock to 146.

No.

She tried 147.

It snapped open.

There were a dozen passports inside: American, Italian, Indian, French. She read some of the names: Jean-Pierre Lebel, Giovanni Carella, Sanjay Das. The names were all different, but the photographs were all of Michel. In a few of the passports his hair was blond, in others it was dark. Sometimes he had a beard, sometimes a moustache and long hair.

But none of the passports was hers.

She put them to one side and stared in confusion at what was underneath. There was a handful of syringes, still in sealed packages, and several small, unmarked glass bottles containing a clear liquid. She unscrewed the cap of one of the bottles. It was odorless. She re-screwed the cap, puzzled.

There were bottles of pills, mostly Mandrax and Mogadon. And money. Ten thousand American dollars in cash, in neat, taped bundles.

She threw the passports back into the case, locked it and put it back under the bed.

Then, terrified, she picked up her case and her shoulder bag and hurried out of the room.

CHAPTER 37

When May opened her eyes, Michel was already awake. He had thrown open the curtains and was sitting at a table by the window. There was a silver tray in front of him with a pot of coffee and orange juice.

He looked over at her and smiled. 'Ah, you're awake.'

'What time?' she said.

'Seven.'

'Must hurry. Eight o'clock I work.'

He brought her a cup of coffee and sat down on the edge of the bed. 'Relax. Have your coffee. I'll call you a taxi after you've had a shower.'

She looked around at the thick, velvet drapes, the leather sofa, the teak paneling on the walls. There was music playing on the clock radio, and the air conditioning kept the room at a perfect temperature. Then she thought about her parent's cramped and suffocating little house near Don Muang.

His hand slipped under the sheet and caressed her thigh. 'Was it good for you?' he said.

She nodded, embarrassed. Thai men did not ask those sorts of questions. It was the woman's place to please the man. He bewildered her. She remembered the European woman who had suddenly appeared in the restaurant. Probably his wife. Still, it had been a good dinner and perhaps he would leave her an expensive gift.

'I must leave Bangkok tomorrow,' he said.

'Yes.' She waited to see what he would offer her in payment.

'You must come with me.'

She almost dropped the cup in her lap. 'Come with you?'

'Of course.' He leaned across the bed, smiling. 'You want to stay here all your life?'

'You tell me true?'

'You are a very special girl. I want you with me always.'

May did not know what to say. Last year, one of her friends, a plump and pleasant-faced girl named Roong, had married an Australian. He looked like an ape. His body was covered with curly, ginger hair and he had an enormous belly. Even so, May had been consumed with envy. Marrying a Westerner was something she had always dreamed about.

Roong had sent her a letter, boasting that she lived in a big house with her own swimming pool. She even had her own car.

May was sure she was lying as the Australian did not seem very rich. Certainly not as rich as this man.

'We make marry?' she said.

'*Merde*, but you're a stupid little peasant,' Michel said in French, still smiling. Then he laughed and said, in English, 'Perhaps. One day.'

'Live in America?'

'If that's what you want.'

She nodded. 'Oh yes. But cannot. Not have passport.'

Michel's jacket was draped over the back of a chair. He took something out of the pocket and threw it onto the bed.

She picked it up.

SURNAME: DANIELS

GIVEN NAMES: MAY

BIRTHPLACE: THAILAND

NATIONALITY: UNITED STATES

She turned it over in her hands. 'What this mean?'

'It's yours. An American passport. All we need is a photograph.'

She looked up at him, then back at the passport. She didn't understand. She pointed to the word Daniels. 'This your name?'

He hesitated. 'Yes.'

She stared at the small, green booklet in her hands in complete awe. She caressed the pages as if they were made from gold leaf. She had always dreamed of getting out of Bangkok, but she never dreamed it could really happen.

He leaned closer. 'Aren't you tired of this life, May? Don't you want lots of money and a nice car? Don't you want to go to America and live in a big house and eat in fancy restaurants every night, to buy jewelry instead of selling it?'

She nodded.

'If I help you, will you help me?'

Suddenly, it all made sense. He wanted something from her, not just sex. She wasn't ever going to marry a man like this. Only fat, ugly men had to buy their wives. Somehow, it reassured her. At last, they were getting down to business. She looked at the passport. What a girl could not do with something like this.

'What is you want?' she said.

Jean-Luc Chirac was second assistant to the deputy commissioner in the French embassy in Bangkok. He was no older than Valentine, but he affected an air of self-importance far above his station. He shook her hand with an air of brisk formality.

The interview room was a tiny office on the first floor, with one small window facing New Street. There was no air conditioning, and the air was stale with tobacco and sweat.

'How can I help you?' Chirac said.

'My passport has been stolen.'

'I see.' He reached into a drawer and took out a white form. 'That is a regrettably common occurrence. First, let me get your details.'

He picked up his pen, a well chewed Bic. He went through the endless questions required by every bureaucracy.

'Now, the passport. Can you tell me where you lost it?'

'I didn't lose it. It was stolen. From my handbag.'

'Where was this?'

'He took it from my room.'

'Who took it?'

'My boyfriend. I told him I was leaving, so he took it out of my bag.'

Chirac frowned. 'You have reported this to the police?'

'Yes, of course. They said they'd look into it. They didn't seem particularly interested.'

'Where is this boyfriend of yours?'

'He's still at the hotel, I suppose. I don't know, I moved out last night.'

He put down his pen. 'We shall look into this, of course. You have funds?'

'Some. But I don't want to stay here another moment. I want to go back to Paris.'

'I am sorry, but these things take time. We cannot simply replace a stolen passport just like that.'

'Can't you arrange an emergency *laissez-passer*?'

'That will take a few days. We will contact you at your hotel.'

Valentine got up to leave.

Chirac hurried to open the door for her. 'It would be easier if you just resolved this situation with your boyfriend.'

'Perhaps. But I'm not going to. I am terrified of him. When I was searching for my passport, I found other things in his briefcase. Drugs. Syringes and sedatives. And money.'

'What did the police say about this?'

'I didn't tell them because I don't trust them. I don't want to get mixed up in anything to do with drugs in a country like this. I am here without a passport, being stalked by a man who is very possibly psychotic. I just want to go home.'

The terrace of the Alliance Française in Bangkok overlooks the Chao Phrya River.

Budjinski joined Herbin on the terrace and watched long wooden skiffs, loaded with rambutans and knobbly durian, motor up and down the sluggish, brown waters. Sampan horns boomed along the river.

The club was quiet at this time of the afternoon. A white-jacketed waiter brought the two men a bottle of San Miguel and two glasses.

'Well, Paul, you have something for me?'

Herbin reached into his jacket pocket and produced a thick manila envelope. 'Some light reading. There's over a hundred names on that list.'

'Thanks. I owe you one.'

'You owe me a hundred.'

Budjinski tore open the envelope and glanced at the typewritten pages: names, nationalities and passport numbers.

'I still think you're wasting your time.' Herbin sipped his beer.

'Why is this name at the top printed in bold?'

'Well, it's the strangest thing. Yesterday afternoon one of my juniors, Chirac, had a young woman come in to report a stolen passport. The interview disturbed him. Not the usual thing at all. He came to me with it.'

'And?'

'The woman told him her passport had been stolen by her boyfriend. She said that when she was searching their hotel room, she came across a handful of passports - none of them hers - and some drugs.'

'Drugs?'

'She didn't seem to know what drugs they were. She said he had syringes and sedatives. Perhaps he's a diabetic with insomnia.'

'She's reported this to the police?'

'She says she's too scared. She's staying at the Erawan under another name. She says she just wants to get back to France as quickly as possible. Chirac said she looked very frightened. I thought you might want to talk to her.'

'Perhaps we've got lucky.'

'If you're right about this, he's the one who's been riding his luck. Sooner or later, it had to run out.'

Budjinski got to his feet, putting the envelope into his jacket pocket.

'You're not going to finish your beer?' Harbin said.

'The next drink we have together will be champagne to toast getting this son of a bitch behind bars. I need to talk to this girl right now.'

Michel looked around the empty room. Her clothes were gone, so was her suitcase. He went into the bathroom. It looked desolate without her makeup and bottles of perfume. Wet towels were scattered around the floor.

No, she wouldn't leave him. She loved him.

It was only business. He had explained that to her.

He went into the bedroom, tore the bedside lamp out of the wall and threw it across the room. He wouldn't let her go, not after it had taken him so long to find her.

Heartless bitch. He had been a fool to trust her a second time. He would find her and bring her back.

This time, she would have to learn her lesson.

CHAPTER 38

Valentine stood at the window and stared out at the Ratchadamri Road. It was choked with *tuk-tuks*, rumbling trucks, and buses so crowded that the passengers clung to the sides and hung out of the doors. The air was thick with exhaust fumes. Even on clear days, it was like looking through smoked glass.

There was a knock at the door.

She froze. She was too scared to move or make the slightest sound. Another knock. Perhaps it was someone from the hotel. She went to the fisheye in the door and peered into the corridor.

'Who are you?'

'Mademoiselle Breton? My name is Captain René Budjinski. I am with Interpol.' He took out an identity card and held it up. 'The embassy told me I could find you here. I have to talk to you urgently.'

She opened the door slowly and found herself looking at a stocky man in a crumpled suit.

'What can I do for you?'

'I'm investigating the murders of these women.' He opened a manila envelope. Inside, bent double, were several Xeroxed pages - badly copied photographs of women with names, nationalities, passport and identity numbers alongside.

She frowned at them, puzzled. 'I don't understand. What has this got to do with me?'

'You made a report to the embassy yesterday afternoon. May I come in?'

She nodded and led him into the room.

'You said that your boyfriend stole your passport. You also told the embassy official that you discovered a cache of other passports and unidentified drugs among his belongings.'

She thought about Michel and the girl in the Sheraton restaurant and felt the blood drain from her face.

'How long have you known this man?'

'A few months, that's all,' she said and sat down, hard. 'You think Michel is a murderer?'

Budjinski nodded.

'Are you going to arrest him?'

'I have no powers of arrest here. I have to work through embassy channels.'

'So, what will happen?'

'The Thai police would certainly arrest him if they found him with all these passports, but if he has the funds for a good lawyer, he will be out on bail within twenty-four hours. He will buy himself another passport and get out of the country.'

'What about the drugs?'

'The police here… many of the senior officers drive a Mercedes Benz even though they are only paid a few hundred baht a month.' He shrugged his shoulders. 'If he has enough money, he will buy his way out of a drug charge.'

She didn't answer. She couldn't take it all in.

'We can ask the Thais to put him under surveillance, but they must catch him actually committing a crime before we can be confident, they will hold him. If he is planning another murder, well that is something he will not be able to talk his way out of. Do you know where he is now?'

'When I left him, he was at the Siam Intercontinental. Suite 203.'

He scribbled this down in his notebook.

'Thank God I got away from him,' she said. She saw the look on his face. 'What is it?'

'There is something else. I have no right to ask it of you, mam'selle Breton, but I must.'

'Ask what of me?'

'I want you to go back to him.'

'I don't think he will hurt you.' Budjinski was saying. He stubbed out his cigarette. 'Think about it. Why hasn't he harmed you when he has used and murdered all these other women?'

Valentine shook her head. 'I don't even want to think about it.'

'Because you do not fit the pattern. All these others were in a position to help him steal something. But you are the wild card. You are also perhaps his weakness.'

'Do murderers have weaknesses?'

'Yes. All of them. Think about it. If he wanted to harm you, he would have done it long before now.'

She pointed to the bruise on her right cheek. 'You see this? It's not a birthmark.'

'I need your help. The police here are notoriously unreliable. This man cannot be allowed to escape, or he will simply disappear, as he has disappeared so many times before.' He tapped a finger on the manila envelope. 'I understand that you don't want to do it for me, some old cop you've never met until today. So, pretend it is not me who is asking. Pretend it is all the women he has murdered. Pretend it is all the women whose lives you could save if you do this.'

She stared at him. Every instinct screamed at her to say no. 'What is it exactly you want me to do?

'Go back, act as if nothing has happened. Just stay with him to make sure we don't lose him.'

She gave an almost imperceptible nod of the head.

'Thank you. In a couple of days, you will get your *laissez-passer* and you can fly back to France. You can forget about all of this.'

'Forget about it? How do you think I will ever be able to do that?'

He pulled out his notebook and scribbled down a phone number. He tore out the leaf. 'Here is the number of my hotel. Ring me any time, day or night. I'll be waiting.'

'All right,' she said. Already, she regretted agreeing to this.

'One other thing. You called him Michel. What name is he using at the moment?'

At the moment, she thought. So, everything about Michel had been a lie, right from the very first. 'Giresse,' she said. 'Michel Giresse.'

Budjinski went pale.

'Is that significant?' she said.

He reached for his cigarettes, but the pack was empty. 'Damn,' he said. He screwed up the cardboard and tossed it away.

He turned back to her. 'A year ago, there was a robbery at the Ashoka Hotel in New Delhi. The woman who helped him carry out the crime was found the next day strangled in her room. Her name was Noelle Giresse.'

His hands shook. 'She was my daughter.'

Valentine stood outside Suite 203. She hesitated. She could still change her mind, get out of here, go back to France and forget this nightmare.

She forced herself to knock.

Michel opened the door. Tears started running down his face. 'Thank God,' he said. 'Please, don't ever leave me again.'

He put his arms tightly around her and pulled her inside.

CHAPTER 39

Sittakorn looked up, his face screwed into a grimace of irritation. 'Hurry up, girl. Get the rest of those trays into the safe.' He returned his attention to the day's accounts.

May did as she was told.

They were alone in the store. That afternoon, the other girl had slipped out to buy herself a bottle of cool drink and had left it under the counter while she attended to a customer. May had slipped the powder that Michel had given her into the bottle. An hour later, the girl had told Sittakorn she felt ill, and he had sent her home early.

May went to her handbag and took out the syringe. She had filled it in the toilets an hour before. Her hands were shaking. She took a deep breath and forced herself to keep calm.

She unlocked one of the display cabinets and took out several trays. She held the syringe in her palm, concealed by the trays. Then she walked back into the office.

'Hurry up,' Sittakorn said again. 'I must do a stock check before I lock up.' He had his back to her and was punching figures into a calculator.

She walked over and plunged the syringe into his arm. He gave a small cry of alarm and twisted around. She emptied the syringe and watched a blossom of dark blood stain his shirtsleeve.

'What are you doing?' He pulled away from her, staring at the syringe that hung from his arm. He swatted it to the floor, his face pale with shock and bewilderment. 'What have you done?'

She backed away.

He tried to get to his feet, but his legs would not support him. His eyes rolled back in his head. He tried to grip the edge of the desk for support but could only claw at the thin air. He toppled sideways onto the floor.

She couldn't believe what she had done. She went back into the shop trying to remember what Michel had told her.

First, she had to empty out her shoulder bag. Everything you take must fit inside, he had said. You can't walk through the lobby carrying a big sack, with a mask over your face. It must look normal.

Take the most expensive items first. Start with the largest stones. It's better to take a few big items than a lot of insignificant rings with tiny chips. Work quickly, then turn off all the lights and lock the door. I will be waiting for you outside. I have rented a black Mercedes, and we'll drive straight to the airport.

She finished clearing away the trays as she did every other night. Then she turned off the lights, went into the office and closed the door.

She put all the largest denomination notes from the day's takings into her bag, then went to the safe. It did not take her long to decide what to take. She had thought of nothing else all day.

Fifteen minutes later, she crossed the lobby of the Dusit Thani, her bag slung casually across her shoulder. She was surprised at how calm she felt. For the first time in her life, she felt superior to everyone – the condescending guests, the concierge who made sex remarks to her every day.

If you all only knew what I'd just done, she thought.

She walked through front doors and across the forecourt. When she reached the street, a Mercedes flashed its headlights at her. Michel had been circling the roundabout for the last ten minutes. He pulled over and she jumped in.

He did not see the blue unmarked Toyota that followed them along Ratchadamri Road.

He thought he had committed the perfect crime, again.

CHAPTER 40

As evening fell, a storm moved in from the south-west. It started to rain, a warm tropical downpour. The city looked grey and filthy during the monsoon. The humidity was stifling. Budjinski felt a trickle of perspiration begin its long, circuitous descent down his spine.

'What do you think, René?' Herbin said. 'Is it him?'

'I'm convinced of it.'

'Did she tell you anything more?'

'No. But I could see it written on her face. She thinks so too.'

They drank their beers in silence. For a long time, the only sounds were the muted roar of the traffic on Suriwongse Road and the drip of water from the eaves.

'What about the Thais?'

'Prenom's men are watching the Siam,' Budjinski said. 'Wherever he goes in Bangkok from now on, he'll have someone watching him.'

'And if it's not him?'

'It's him. She says he has another girlfriend, so he must be planning another heist. This time he's going to get a surprise.'

Michel swung off Ratchadamri Road into an alley that followed the high walls of the Royal Bangkok Sports Club. He glanced quickly in his rear vision mirror to make sure they had not been followed. He drove slowly between the open ditches and rubbish, his headlights dimmed.

Finally, he stopped and turned off the engine.

May sat forward in alarm. 'Why we stop, please?'

'It's all right,' Michel said. He looked around. Good, the alley was deserted.

'We go to airport?'

'Yes, yes. Wait.' He snatched the bag off her lap. It felt gratifyingly heavy. 'You did what I told you?'

'Everything. Yes.'

He opened the glove compartment and tipped the contents of the bag into it. Diamonds, sapphires and emeralds glittered in the muted glow of the dashboard lights.

'Good. You did well, May.'

'Now we go to Don Muang?'

He smiled. He felt sad for her. Valentine had complicated everything. In the past, he would have taken May with him. The ploy had worked well before. Get them out of the country, then dump them. Police in Asia never concerned themselves much with dead foreigners unless they were white.

But now there was Valentine, and he could not leave. May would have to die here in Bangkok. See how she looked at him. He could almost smell her fear, and it made him angry.

'Why we stop here?' May repeated.

'Be quiet. I'm thinking.'

As soon as they found her body, they would start looking for him. He would have to fetch Valentine and get out of the city as soon as possible. They had already found Grace. That was unfortunate. He had hoped her body would be swept offshore by the current.

May panicked suddenly and tried to get out of the car.

He grabbed her, pulling her back into her seat. 'Where are you going?'

She knew. He saw it in her eyes.

He put his hand over her mouth to stop her screaming. She bit him, and he yelled and pulled his hand away. He tried to grab her again, and she butted him in the face and threw herself out of the car.

He caught her wrist. She tried to jerk herself free, but he was too strong. This time, as he pulled her back inside the car, his other hand closed around her neck. She tried to scream, but the sound was choked off as his fingers tightened on her throat. She fell across the front seat, her feet kicking wildly at the air.

Women, he thought. They were such whores.

May's struggles grew feeble. He was about to finish the job, when he saw shadows moving at the end of the alley and heard the soft click as safeties were removed from guns. He let her go and her body slid down the seat.

It had to be the police. Few street thieves in Bangkok carried guns. He thought about driving off and changed his mind. As soon as he turned on the ignition, they would open fire. Besides, the alley was bordered by open sewers. It would be impossible to navigate at speed.

There was another way.

He slipped off his shoes, slid across the seat and dropped out of the open door. He felt May's inert body underneath him.

Lying flat on his belly, he peered back up the alley.

There were three of them moving towards the car in a crouch.

How had they found him?

He crept away from the car, hoping the darkness would shield him. He waited for gunshots, but they didn't come. He ran faster. He was going to make it. Police, they were all idiots.

Suddenly he stopped, blinded, as a car parked at the far end of the alley turned on its headlights. He reeled back. He heard the shouts of men rushing towards him from everywhere telling him to lie down.

He smiled, raised his hands and relaxed. It was over. For now.

The men threw him onto the ground. They pulled his arms behind his back and cuffed him. One of them kicked him. He groaned and brought his knees up to his chest to protect himself from further blows. They dragged him to one of the waiting cars and dumped him in the back seat. Men jumped in on either side.

He had a heel pressed into his neck all the way to the central police headquarters. But he was oblivious to it.

Valentine had betrayed him.

The phone rang.

Valentine snatched it up. 'Have they got him?'

'Yes,' Budjinski said.

She sank onto her haunches on the carpet.

'It's all over,' he said. 'You're safe.'

She let the receiver slip from her fingers. Thank God.

CHAPTER 41

It was stifling hot in the cramped, windowless office. A slow fan labored on the high ceiling, and a fluorescent light flickered and buzzed above their heads.

Major-General Warong Lekchorn was a study in serene indifference.

Michel lounged in a metal chair, his legs-crossed, his hands steepled in an attitude of patient forbearance. They had removed the steel cuffs, but two armed police stood to attention by the door.

'What is your name?' Warong said.

'Lebel. Jean-Pierre Lebel.'

'You are a guest at the Dusit Thani hotel?'

'No, I'm staying at the Sheraton. Look, what is all this about?'

'Tonight your girlfriend drugged and robbed the owner of the Naree Jewelry Store.'

Michel stared at him, open-mouthed. 'She did what?'

'She then came out of the hotel and got into your car.'

Michel reached into his jacket pocket and took out a packet of thin Russian cheroots. 'So?'

'You knew about this?'

'Of course not. I hardly know this girl. We had arranged to go out to dinner, that's all.'

'You deny any knowledge of this crime?'

'I do. This is absurd.'

Warong watched him as he lit his cheroot. A cool one.

'What has the girl said about me?'

'She has said nothing. She is still unconscious.'

'What have you done to her?'

'We have done nothing. My officers report that you tried to strangle her. They also found the missing items in the glove box of your car. You deny that also?'

'Of course. Your men put them there.' Michel blew a long plume of smoke towards the ceiling. 'Look, General, can I go now?'

'I am afraid that is not possible. First, we will get a statement from this girl. When she can talk.'

'When will that be? I have important business in Hong Kong tomorrow.'

'It will have to wait.'

Michel's attitude changed. He leaned forward and lowered his voice, as if about to talk through an intimate problem with an old and trusted friend. 'Look, General, you know how it is. I am a businessman, travelling alone. I went into the jewelry store in the Dusit Thani looking for a gift, and I met this girl. She was very friendly to me, so I took her to dinner a couple of times. I had no idea she was a criminal.'

'I don't think you understand. This is a very serious crime, Mr. Lebel.'

'I do understand, General. And I will do everything in my power to co-operate with your investigation. In fact, I have something to show you that may change the complexion of this case entirely. It is in my briefcase.'

The crocodile-skin case lay in the corner of the room still unopened. The police had retrieved it from the boot of the Mercedes.

Warong had one of his men put it on the desk. He tried to open it. It was locked.

'I would prefer it if we could be alone when it is opened,' Michel said. 'It is very sensitive evidence.'

Warong considered. Then he turned to the two policemen at the door. 'You can go.'

The men saluted and left the room.

'Now then,' Warong said, 'what is it you have to show me?'

Lieutenant-Colonel Prenom Tanongsak was the Interpol liaison officer for Thailand. Budjinski followed him through the grey-walled catacomb of Bangkok central police headquarters to the office of Major-General Warong Lekchorn.

The building was a labyrinth of corridors and windowless offices, where police in drab uniforms tapped away at battered Remingtons, their heads wreathed in cigarette smoke.

Warong had a file open on the desk in front of him, and his head was bowed in concentration as he added some final notes to his report. He waved them to two vinyl chairs.

Budjinski could scarcely contain his excitement. He had run from the foyer to Prenom's office on the second floor. He was wheezing badly and couldn't get his breath. He reached into his pocket, took out his *Gauloises* and lit one.

'You have him?' he said.

Warong raised a hand to indicate that he needed to finish what he was doing. Budjinski glanced at Prenom, who shrugged as if to say we'll have to wait.

Fuck this, Budjinski thought. He leaned across the desk, 'I said, have you got the bastard?'

Warong's spectacles flashed in the strip light. 'He's gone.'

There was a stunned silence.

'Gone? What are you talking about?'

'He escaped from custody.'

Budjinski threw his cigarette onto the floor and leaped to his feet. 'He fucking what?'

'He has escaped from custody. An hour ago.'

'He's a fucking mass murderer! You let him go?'

'I did not let him go. He escaped.'

Budjinski couldn't believe his ears. Prenom put a hand on his arm, worried that the volatile Frenchman might take a swing at the major general.

'How did he escape?'

'He was outside my office in the corridor. He must have run away.'

'You left him in the corridor? Where were the guards?'

'The men responsible for letting him escape will be severely punished.'

'What about his handcuffs?'

'They had been removed. It is not important. We have the girl and the jewelry. He was only an accomplice.'

Budjinski looked at Prenom. 'Didn't you tell him?'

Prenom looked away and found something of intense interest on the ceiling.

'Tell me what?' Warong said.

'Interpol had applied for extradition.'

'I was not advised.' He looked hard at Prenom. 'Was I, Colonel?'

'No, Sir.'

Budjinski could not believe what he was hearing. He leaned across the desk. 'How much did he pay you?'

'Is this an official visit, Captain?'

Budjinski didn't answer.

'Our discussion is finished. Have a good trip back to France.'

Budjinski swept Warong's papers from the desk and on to the floor with one movement. 'You greedy bastard!'

Warong leapt to his feet. 'Get out!'

There was nothing Budjinski could do. He fought back the urge to smash his fist into Warong's face. He turned and slammed out of the room.

'Your superiors will hear about this, Captain!'

I bet they will, Budjinski thought. But I don't give a damn.

CHAPTER 42

She was in a bamboo cage.

She felt eyes watching her in her prison, and when she looked up, she saw a king cobra dancing and swaying around the bars. She was trapped.

Suddenly it stabbed at her with its fangs. She heard herself cry out in pain, and then the cobra's head transformed into a face.

Michel's face.

He was standing over her, holding a flaming torch. She tried to get away, but she couldn't move her arms or her legs.

'You betrayed me,' he said. 'I know it was you. You betrayed me again.'

She sat up in bed, soaked in sweat.

There was someone banging at the door.

She reached for her watch on the bedside table. One-thirty. Who the hell could it be? She slipped on a silk dressing gown and went to the door. Before she could look through the fisheye, she heard a cough. Budjinski.

He brushed past her into the room. He was still wearing the same crumpled suit he wore yesterday, and the pouches under his eyes looked like they had been filled with lead. He slumped onto the leather sofa by the window and groped in his pockets for his *Gauloises*. Instead of lighting one, he threw the pack across the room.

She watched at him and knew. 'It's Michel, isn't it? He's escaped.'

'The pricks let him go.'

'But why?'

'You said he carried a lot of cash with him.'

She nodded. 'United States dollars. There were thick bundles in his case, tied with rubber bands.'

'Well, now you know why.' He sighed. 'They say the Thais have the best police force money can buy.'

'What if he comes back here?'

'That's why I came straight over. You haven't heard from him?'

'No.'

'This fucking country,' he said.

'How could they let him go if he murdered all those women?'

'The Thais have the girl who committed the robbery, and they've recovered all the missing jewelry. The report will show that Michel was merely an accomplice. The getaway driver.'

'But what about the girl? She'll talk, won't she?'

'Not for quite a while. He almost choked her to death. Did a lot of damage. Not that anyone's going to listen to her side of the story.'

'Isn't there anything you can do?'

'I have no authority here. As it is, I'll be in shit up to my ears when my boss finds out about this. Also, I may have just insulted a major general in the Thai police force.'

'But what if he comes back here?'

Budjinski shook his head. 'It's more likely that he went straight to the airport. The police may even have helped him. The general certainly won't want him back here - he would be an embarrassment. He is probably already on a plane out of the country.'

'What are you going to do?'

Budjinski gave her a look.

She shook her head. 'No. I can't do anything else.'

'This isn't going to stop until we get him, you know. And my guess is, if you don't go after him, he'll come after you.'

'I can't.'

'How many more women do you think he will kill before someone catches him?'

She bent to pick up the crumpled pack of *Gauloises* from the floor and lit cigarettes for both of them. Then she went to stand at the window.

I should be thinking about all those girls, she thought, the ones he hasn't found yet. But what really hit her hardest was what Michel had said to her: *You can never get away from me, and I can never get away from you.*

She turned back to him. 'What do you want me to do?'

Valentine watched the sun rise over the city, setting the stupas aflame like molten gold and burning off the mist over the Chao Phrya River. Her eyes were swollen and gritty from lack of sleep.

Budjinski lay sprawled on the sofa, snoring like a bull elephant. He was an unappetizing sight, with two days' grey stubble on his jowls and a button open on his shirt to reveal a great hairy belly. He looked like a hibernating bear.

She ordered breakfast for two from room service and then went into the bathroom. She threw off her clothes and stepped into the shower, letting the boiling water wash away the fear and sweat.

She hoped Budjinski's hunch was wrong, and she would never hear from Michel again.

The room waiter arrived with the breakfasts. After he had gone, she poured a black coffee and set it down on the table next to the sofa. Budjinski was still asleep. She shook him awake and waited out a long coughing fit.

When it was over, he pulled out his cigarettes and lit one. 'That's better.'

'Your wife must be a saint to put up with your snoring.'

'My ex-wife.'

'Ah, that explains it.'

The phone rang. She stared at it, letting it ring. Budjinski frantically gesticulated to her to pick it up.

'Hello?'

'Miss Breton,' the operator said, 'I have a long-distance call for you. Please wait.'

She heard the crackle of the international connection.

'Valentine? Is that you? I'm afraid something has happened. I had to leave urgently.'

'Where are you, Michel?'

'India. Varanasi. Can you join me here?'

He sounds so calm, she thought, as if he's inviting me to his beach house for the weekend. 'What are you doing in India?'

'Do you have a pen?'

Budjinski had laid a fresh pad and two ball-point pens carefully beside the phone the previous night. His prediction had been right.

'Go ahead.'

'Listen carefully.'

A few minutes later, she put down the telephone.

She nodded at Budjinski. It was done.

CHAPTER 43

Varanasi, India

The Ganges springs from its source in the crystalline ice of the Hindu Kush, then runs across two and half thousand miles of the hottest, driest, most densely populated plains anywhere in the world. It finally winds its way to the Bay of Bengal.

Halfway along its route, it flows through the city of Varanasi, the most sacred of all Indian cities. It is a place almost unchanged for forty centuries. Buddha preached his first sermon there, three hundred years before the birth of Christ. It was where Emperor Ashoka erected a temple bearing a sandstone pillar engraved with the dharma chakra, the wheel of law, the emblem still displayed today on the Indian national flag.

By the time it reaches Varanasi, the Ganges is no more than a sluggish and sulfurous sludge. Sewage from the teeming city is pumped directly into the river, and garbage scows, almost hidden behind wheeling and screeching black clouds of jackdaws, dump their stinking cargo of filth and rubbish into it.

Yet to the Hindu, the river is Devi, the Divine Mother, flowing between heaven and earth. Devotees believe that no water is more pure or more sweet. To bathe in the celestial river at Varanasi is to wash away all sin.

Thousands come to the *ghats* each morning to perform their act of faith, stripping to their dhotis and stepping deep into the brown, swirling water, their hands raised in supplication to the fireball sun that rises across the broad bank. It is considered a worthier act than spending one's whole life in meditation and prayer.

And to die in Varanasi is to go straight to heaven.

There are crematoria on the *ghats* all along the river - open pavilions where outcastes, known as *chandals,* ignite the pallets bearing the corpses of the dead. When the body is finally reduced to charred ash and bone, it is committed to the river to be washed away on the current with rose and marigold petals.

It is a riot of beggars, *sadhus* and flower-sellers, backdropped by the dun towers of the ancient city and smudged with the ropes of smoke from funeral pyres.

It was to the bottom step of the Dasaswamedh *ghat* that Michel came, one lemon dawn.

He stripped off his clothes and smeared mustard oil on his chest and arms to help ward off the cold. Then, wearing only a white dhoti, he walked into the murky river. He joined his hands in prayer, bent his knees and dipped his head under the water, staying fully immersed for a long minute.

When he finally emerged, goose-fleshed from the water, he raised his arms in salute to the warming sun, squatting huge and yellow on the far plain.

He had absolved himself of all sin. He was whole again. He was pure.

Don Muang airport, Bangkok

The final boarding call for the Air India flight from Bangkok to Calcutta had been announced. From there Valentine had a connecting flight to Varanasi.

Budjinski pushed his way through the crowds in the terminal, a flight bag thrown across his shoulder. His pearl-grey suit was heavily creased and there were permanent sweat stains under each armpit. He was wheezing.

'Fucking country,' he grunted. 'Too much pollution. Bad for your chest.' He sat down and lit a *Gauloise*. 'Have they called the flight?'

'Just now,' Valentine said. 'Where did you go?'

'I rang the Interpol man in Delhi yesterday. He's an old friend of mine. I asked him to have the Varanasi police check out the hotel where he's meeting you, Clark's. I just rang him to see if he'd come up with anything else.'

'Is he there?'

'They haven't seen anyone answering the description. That doesn't mean anything, of course.'

'So, what happens now?'

'We go ahead as planned. We'll travel together until we reach Varanasi and check into Clark's separately.'

'Will the Indian police help us?'

'Like I said, the Interpol man in Delhi is an old friend of mine. He's told all sorts of lies to the police in Varanasi. They'll help us.'

He looked up at the departure screens on the wall. '*Merde*. Final call. Come on. Don't worry, I won't let you out of my sight. I promise.'

Varanasi, India

Clark's Hotel was on the cantonment near the railway station. It had been built in the 1930s, a grand two-storey Edwardian edifice with showers of bougainvillea screening the white-painted porticoes and terraces. Snake charmers squatted in the shade of banyan trees in the gardens.

Valentine climbed out of the yellow and black Ambassador taxi and went into the lobby. She had expected Michel to meet her at the airport. Although she had not seen him, she had the uneasy feeling that she was being watched. Thinking back on how they had met in Paris, she wondered how many times he had tracked her before.

There was a man sitting in the lobby reading the *Times of India*. He looked up at her as she walked in, then returned to his newspaper. A policeman? She hoped so.

'I'd like a room,' she said to the desk clerk. 'A single.'

'For how many nights?' The man was a handsome Gujarati, with a gold, gap-toothed smile.

'I don't know.'

'That is quite all right,' he said and pushed the register towards her. 'Your name and address please.' He went to the board behind him and got a key.

'Are there any messages for me?' she said. 'My name's Breton. Valentine Breton.'

'Ah, Miss Breton. Yes, yes.' He went back to the row of pigeonholes behind him and produced an envelope. He put it on the desk in front of her.

She recognized Michel's handwriting. 'When was this delivered?'

'This morning.'

'Who delivered it? What did he look like?'

The man shrugged. 'I cannot remember.'

'Not a European?'

'No, definitely not.'

'Thank you,' she said. She took the key and went to her room, the porter hurrying ahead of her with her luggage. She tipped him, then shut the door.

She opened the envelope, her fingers trembling.

Chérie,

I am sorry I could not be here to meet you. It cannot be helped. Meet me tomorrow at noon at the intersection of Raj Bazaar Street and The Mall. I will explain everything.

I adore you, Michel.

Detective Inspector Lai Gupta Singh's office, in Varanasi's crime branch, was cluttered with dusty files. There was a three-tier cabinet on one side of the room, and the drawers hung open, spilling papers onto the floor. More files teetered on the edge of an ink-stained wooden desk.

Gupta Singh studied his visitor. He was unshaven and had the look of a gambler after a long night at the tables. His suit was creased and ash stained. Good Heavens. He must have slept in it.

But Delhi had told him to give Budjinski every co-operation. Detective-Superintendent Engineer himself had hinted that the man responsible for the sensational robbery and double murder at the Ashoka Hotel was now in Varanasi.

It was an unbelievable stroke of good fortune, Gupta Singh thought. A successful conclusion to the case would certainly mean promotion. He might even get his name in the *Times of India*.

'Delhi has informed me of your arrival,' he said, 'all my resources are at your disposal.'

'Thank you, Inspector,' Budjinski said. 'I appreciate it.'

Gupta Singh nodded his head. 'You have a photograph of this criminal?'

Budjinski reached into his pocket. 'Only these. I obtained them from his girlfriend.' He pushed two color photographs across the desk. 'Interpol have at least two outstanding extradition orders for him.'

'What name does he use?'

'He's used several. The Thai police know him as Jean-Pierre Lebel. He told this woman his name was Michel Giresse.'

'Well, if he is in Varanasi, I assure you he will not escape us. Do you have any leads?'

'The woman who took the photographs is here in Varanasi.' He gave the inspector the note that Valentine had received that afternoon.

Gupta Singh smiled. This was going to be easy.

CHAPTER 44

The crumbling shophouses that faced the mall had hand-painted signs in Sanskrit and execrable English. The square was filled with motor scooters and pony rickshaws, bicycles and taxicabs.

Budjinski sat in a shabby street cafe and sipped from a glass of Coca-Cola. He grimaced. Warm. He loosened his tie, feeling fat and uncomfortable in his suit jacket. He did not want to take it off and show all Varanasi that he had a Beretta pistol in a shoulder holster under his arm.

He looked at his watch. Twenty-five past. Something had gone wrong. Valentine was still on the corner, her face hidden under the wide-brimmed straw hat and dark glasses. She had found a little shade under a banyan tree, but she had spent the last half an hour fighting off an endless stream of hawkers and rickshaw drivers. He could see that she was getting anxious.

A wedding procession made its way along Raj Bazaar Street. The clash of cymbals and sousaphones and the deep, booming rhythm of the drums grew louder. Budjinski stared without interest.

The musicians were being pushed along on a gaudy mobile bandstand, their music - if you could call it that, he thought - amplified by loudspeakers. A crowd was milling around the groom, who sat astride a white horse. He was no more than a boy and looked utterly miserable, even in his princely clothes. His yellow turban flashed with cut-glass jewels. The procession wound along the street behind him, on its way to the bride's house. Some of the guests carried chandeliers of acetylene lights. Everyone except the bridegroom seemed to be enjoying themselves immensely.

Budjinski looked at his watch. Half-past.

There were a dozen plain-clothes police posted around the square on foot and in cars, waiting for his signal. The worst that could happen was that Michel would not come. But why would he have left a note and then not been there to meet her?

He looked again.

She was gone.

Valentine had been wondering how long she should wait. He was half an hour late. Something must have happened. He clearly wasn't coming.

She watched the wedding procession making its way towards her along the road. The mood was boisterous. Despite herself, she smiled.

The wedding band, in their frayed white jackets, blue trousers and red caps, were making the most of their moment in the sun. Harmony had been happily sacrificed to volume. The clash of the drums and the trumpets was deafening.

Distracted by the noise and color, she didn't see the Vespa motor scooter until it was almost on top of her. It stopped at the curb a few feet away. The rider, a dark-skinned Hindu in turban and dhoti, was waving at her.

She stared back in astonishment. It was Michel.

'Quick, get on! We're being followed.'

She hesitated. Budjinski was just fifty yards away, on the other side of the square, but the procession had momentarily obscured him from her view. Had he seen what was happening?

'Valentine!'

If she didn't go with him now, he would know what she had done. He would vanish for good.

She jumped onto the back of the scooter. Moments later, they were gone.

Michel weaved expertly through the press of traffic on Grand Trunk Road. He made for the *pakku mahals*, the rabbit warren of medieval *gullies* between the *ghats* and Madanpura Road. He drove too fast down ancient alleyways, sending small children and even an ancient *sadhu* scurrying out of his way. Valentine heard the wail of the police siren in the distance.

Suddenly, he braked to a halt and leapt off. He grabbed her hand. 'This way!' He led her down the noon-dark streets.

Black monsoon thunderheads billowed over the city. A storm was coming.

They reached another narrow *gullie*. It was a dead end, the way to the river blocked by a pile of yellow rubble where a riverfront building had collapsed into the Ganges. He stopped, his chest heaving, sweat running down his face in rivulets.

'Michel?'

He released his grip on her hand. 'Hello Valentine.'

'What's happening?' She felt overwhelmed with terror and panic.

He tore off the turban. She was shocked by his appearance. He had dyed his hair blond again and it emphasized the dark lines etched into his face.

'They are following us,' he said.

'Who?

'The police. Didn't you see them? They were all round the square.'

'I didn't see any police, Michel. What is happening? Why are we here, what have you done?'

He didn't answer her. 'Wait here,' he said. 'I'll make sure we haven't been followed.' He ran back down the *gullie* and was gone.

Valentine stared after him. I must get out of here, she thought. She ran to the corner. Which way?

Two men shuffled past her carrying a white-shrouded body on a pallet, headed for the burning *ghats*. An old, bearded *sadhu* sat cross-legged on the ground, his naked body smeared with white ash.

She set off towards the new town. But it wasn't that easy. The alleyways of the *pakku mahals* twisted between tall, dun-yellow houses, shops that were no more than holes in the wall and anonymous doorways where sightless beggars reached for her. A bare-ribbed cow, vapor streaming from its nostrils, brushed past her forcing her back against a wall.

The sky opened in a torrent.

The further she ran, the deeper she got into the maze. Where was Budjinski?

Budjinski got out of the blue police Fiat and stared at the press of humanity around him – women in homespun saris, men in kurtas and white dhotis, near-naked rickshaw *wallahs*, and tourists returning from the *ghat* loaded down with Nikons and Canons.

No sign of Valentine. He had promised her he would look after her. How had this gone so wrong? Twenty cops in the square and somehow, they'd lost her.

An emaciated Hindu, perched on a stool inside his tiny shop-house, watched her with frank curiosity. He was almost lost among all the *puja* he had for sale: bottles of holy water, colored tilak powder, trays of *lat-i-dana* - the white sweets they offered to their gods. One eye was opaque, covered with a cataract. He nodded his head in her direction, like a genie summoned from one of the dark bottles that surrounded him.

'How do I get back to the street?' Valentine said.

He thrust one of the bottles at her, betel-blackened teeth bared in a smile. 'Clark's Hotel?'

He clutched at her sleeve and tried to push the bottle into her hand.

It was no use. She ran blindly away from the river.

Michel watched her run down a *gullie* towards the Maha Durga temple. This had been her last chance to prove her innocence. If she had waited for him as he had told her, he might have doubted his own instincts. But now he knew for certain that she had betrayed him.

His Madonna was like all the others.

A whore.

The *gullie* led into an open courtyard. Valentine ran inside and leaned against the wall, breathless. The rain ran in torrents down the cobblestones, carrying all manner of filth with it. The air steamed and the city stank like an open sewer.

She was in some sort of temple. She was aware of a face staring back at her from the far wall, a Hindi god. Its shrine was a domed pavilion protected by a brass cage. She took a step closer.

It was hideous. It had a shrunken black head with fang-like teeth and the wild eyes of a madwoman. There was a jeweled ring in its beak. One hand held a noose, another a skull-topped staff. A third hand gripped a severed head that was dripping blood. A clawed foot rested on the body of a black rat.

Strong arms closed around her from behind and held her tight.
She screamed.
'Are you all right?' Michel said. 'I couldn't find you.'
She felt his hot breath on her neck.
She tried to turn round. 'I was frightened. When you didn't come back, I went looking for you.'
'It's easy to get lost in the *pakku mahals*. You're lucky I found you. Do you know who that is?'
'It's horrible. Let's go.' She started to shake.
He kept hold of her. 'It is Bhagwan Bhavani, the Black Mother.'
'It's evil.'
'She is Kali. You have heard of the *thuggee*, the bandits who once lived here in Bengal? She was their goddess. They would befriend travelers on the road, then poison them, strangle them, sometimes burn them alive. Then they would bring their spoils to Kali's temple as an act of devotion. Look there, on the altar.'
A small, black snake had somehow found its way inside the temple. It wound its way up the black mother's leg, through her arms and into her gaping jaws.
'The *naga*,' Michel whispered. 'Here in India, they believe it is the incarnation of one of the gods because of its ability to shed its skin and the hypnotic effect of its eyes. And its bite of course, which is deadly.' He pressed closer and she screamed. He gently stroked a lock of her hair from her face. 'It's all right,' he whispered. 'Don't be afraid. They are gone.'
'Who?'
'The police. They cannot get to us now. We are safe.'
He led her out of the courtyard, her hand clutched tightly in his own. 'This way. I have a room close by. They will never find us there.'

Pilgrims had been coming to Varanasi to bathe in the Ganges for thousands of years. During the late sixties, hippies with tight budgets had started arriving too. Many families had capitalized on this windfall and supplemented their meager incomes by renting out rooms. Some places were clean, most were filthy. They were all cheap.

The room Michel took her to was in a sprawling tenement above the Bedi State Silk Co-op Marketing Federation Ltd. They went up a dark and evil-smelling staircase. The room had peeling plaster and dark stains on the wall. The only furniture was a single iron-framed bed, an old wardrobe and a cane table. Rain dripped from the roof into a puddle in the corner.

A long way from the Siam Intercontinental.

He shut the door behind them. 'Poor Valentine. You're trembling.'

'What's happening? Why were the police after you?'

'Parking offence.'

'Don't make fun of me.'

'I don't want to talk about it now.'

There was a knock on the door. He opened it. It was the landlord, a small, unshaven Hindu with broken teeth. He had brought a pot of tea on an ancient silver tray. He put it on the table next to the window.

After he had gone, Michel poured two cups and held one out to her. 'Here.'

She took it gratefully. Her mouth was so dry she could hardly swallow. The tea was hot and unsweetened. As she sipped it, her mind raced desperately through the options. She had to brazen this out and get away from him as soon as she could.

'What is this place? We can't stay here. It's filthy.'

'I'm sorry, but it's necessary now.'

'Let's go back to my room at Clark's.'

'It's too dangerous.'

She put her cup down on the table. 'I can't stay here, Michel. I'm leaving.'

'You can't.' He grabbed her and pulled her towards him. 'What's wrong? Aren't you pleased to see me again?' He kissed her, forcing her down onto the squalid bed.

Don't fight him, she thought. Make love to him. Afterwards, when he is asleep, you can slip away.

Michel lay beside her, his eyes closed. He looked almost sweet like a little boy.

She tried to get up, but her head felt heavy. The room began to spin. She closed her eyes and waited for the nausea to subside. It was like her arms and legs were full of lead. She broke out in a cold sweat. She couldn't focus.

The tea. Had he put something in her tea?

No. Oh God, no.

There was a buzzing in her ears and her vision filled with a pink gelatin. Michel's eyes blinked open. 'Sleep now,' he said.

CHAPTER 45

Two uniformed policemen went into the Bedi State Silk Co-Op Marketing Federation Ltd.

Bedi appeared from behind a ragged curtain. It partitioned the small, dark room under the stairs that he used as an office.

'What do you want?' he said.

One of the policemen, the sergeant, reached into his pocket and produced a copy of the photograph that Budjinski had brought with him from Thailand. 'We're looking for this man,' he said. 'Have you seen him?'

Bedi took the photograph and stared at it. He shook his head. 'No, I've never seen this man before.'

'Have you anyone staying with you at the moment?'

'Just one person. A very respectable gentleman from Jodhpur.'

The sergeant grunted and put the photograph back in his pocket. 'Well, if you see this man, you must tell us straight away.'

'What has he done?'

'He is a notorious international criminal,' he said proudly. Being involved in such an investigation lent him great importance.

'What sort of criminal?'

'A murderer,' the other policeman said, eager to include himself in the general atmosphere of self-congratulation.

'Remember, if you see him, you must tell us straight away,' the sergeant added.

Bedi followed them outside. He hawked some of the betel juice from the back of his throat and spat on the ground. 'Who did he murder?'

'A woman. In fact, he has murdered many women. Perhaps as many as a hundred,' the sergeant said, embellishing his own information.

They walked away down the street. It would be a long day for them. Inspector Gupta had told them to check all the hotels and boarding houses in Varanasi.

Bedi scratched thoughtfully at his groin and went back inside.

Michel stepped out from behind the curtain. 'You didn't have to ask so many questions,' he said in Hindi.

'I was curious,' Bedi said.

'Well, don't be too curious. It's dangerous.' Michel reached into his pocket and pulled out five one-hundred-rupee notes. 'Here. It's what we agreed.'

Bedi stuffed the money in the pocket of his kurta.

'There's another five hundred rupees when I leave. Just remember - you haven't seen me.' He turned to go.

'They must want you very badly,' Bedi said. 'Perhaps there's a reward.'

Michel frowned in disgust. 'All right, a thousand rupees.'

'Three thousand.'

'It might be cheaper to cut your throat.'

Bedi was terrified but knew an opportunity when he saw one. 'I'm a poor man,' he said. 'I'm doing you a great service.'

'Two thousand rupees. And if you even think of telling the police, you'll meet Shiva a lot sooner than you expect.'

Michel went out and Bedi heard his footsteps cat-soft on the wooden stairs above his head. He scratched his belly. How was he supposed to have known this crazy Westerner was a big criminal? It seemed every policeman in Varanasi was looking for him.

He didn't like this at all.

Michel sat on the edge of the bed and watched her as she slept. He reached out and gently stroked her cheek. How could she have done this to him?

He hadn't wanted to believe it at first, had tried to persuade himself that there must be some mistake. But when he had seen her waiting in the square, seen all those policemen - the idiots, just because they'd left their uniforms in the police station, they thought they were invisible - he knew there was no doubt.

Even then, he had given her one last chance. If she had just waited for him in the *gullie,* he would have been tempted to believe that she had been an unwilling dupe, had not known she was being followed. But instead, she had run like a frightened rabbit.

Bangkok had cost him everything, the profits from the Dusit Thani operation, almost all his cash, all the passports save one. Now even Valentine had turned against him just as Joginder and Adrienne had turned against him. Everything he loved tried to destroy him.

So now he must destroy what he loved.

She had started to wake up. The effect of the Mandrax was wearing off. He picked up her right arm and laid it across his lap. He tied a tourniquet above her elbow and found a pale blue vein in her arm. A syringe lay ready on the bedside table, and he held it up, spilling a little of the drug from the tip of the needle. This would make her sleep through the night. In the morning, everything would be ready.

Budjinski and Gupta Singh conferred in the lobby of the Clark's Hotel.

'We will find him,' Gupta Singh said, 'there is no way he can escape.'

Budjinski dropped his cigarette stub into his cup. It fizzled and sank. Gupta Singh tried to keep the grimace of disgust off his face. As a devout Sikh, he did not smoke and was revolted by the stench of cigarettes. He also did not approve of good Mysore coffee being used as a douse for cigarette ends.

'What makes you think he's still in Varanasi?' Budjinski said.

'We have men at the airport, at the train stations, at the bus stations. He is in this city somewhere.'

'You had men all around the mall and he still snatched her from under your noses.'

'Your nose was present also,' Gupta Singh said, bridling at the criticism.

'We have to offer a reward.'

Gupta Singh spread his hands in a gesture of helplessness. 'I cannot spend government funds on such a thing without permission. A request has been made.'

'By that time, it will be too late.'

'We will find him.'

'So you keep telling me.'

'Why don't you get some sleep. I'll call you as soon as we have a lead. There's nothing more anyone can do.'

'All right,' Budjinski said.

To Gupta Singh's horror, he took a mouthful of the coffee into which he had just tossed his cigarette. He seemed not to notice. He slammed down the cup and shambled off.

'We will find him!' Gupta Singh called after him. 'He cannot escape.'

Budjinski sat alone in his room staring at the wall.

He knew his career was finished. He had insulted a police chief in Bangkok and lied to the Indians about the extradition orders. He had done everything the secretary general had ordered him not to do. They would crucify him when he got back to France.

Risking his own career was one thing, but in his obsession to catch the man who murdered his daughter, he had put one other young life at risk. That was unforgivable.

His hands clenched to fists. 'Oh my God,' he whispered, 'what have I done?'

It was just before dawn. The moon had set, and the night was dark. But even at this hour, thousands of devotees of the three-eyed Lord Shiva shuffled through the dark streets as they did every morning, towards the black, slick tongue of the Ganges.

The Pure. The Eternal. Stairway to Heaven.

They padded barefoot down the ancient stone steps of the *ghats*, as their forefathers had done for four millennia. Despite the chill, they prepared to plunge themselves into the murky waters.

Brahmin sat under bamboo umbrellas selling sandalwood paste and vermilion for the devotees to daub on their foreheads after their ritual immersion. Bells clanged in the temples and a conch shell boomed and echoed along the river.

Sadhus squatted by braziers at the river's edge, their bodies coated with white ash, bright orange garlands of marigolds around their necks. They chanted mantras while the crowd jostled around them, some reverently touching the feet of the holy men, others snatching up a handful of the dust on which the *sadhus* had trodden.

'*Hare Rama, Hare Krisna, Hare Om.*'

They waited for the dawn, the sun's symbolic victory over darkness.

Valentine woke from a black and bitter sleep. She tried to remember what had happened to her. She opened her mouth to cry for help, but no sound came.

'Ah, you're awake,' she heard someone whisper. 'Good. It is almost dawn.'

A face swam into her vision. Dark shadows moved about the walls. A gas lamp flickered and sputtered close by.

She remembered now.

She tried to sit up but couldn't move her arms or legs. She was paralyzed, a prisoner in her own body.

'It's a form of ketamine,' Michel said. 'I purchased it a few months ago in Hong Kong. The chemist who sold it to me said it was the chemical equivalent of a straitjacket.

He stroked her face.

'Do you remember the day you left? You looked beautiful, just like you do now. Except your skin was paler.' He ran a finger along her arm. 'It was just before dawn, like now. This morning it's cool, but that morning was very hot. You had a bead of sweat between your breasts right here. You were beautiful, so beautiful. I adored you, Adrienne. You were my life.'

His voice was so soft. She had to strain to hear him.

'You were wearing a green dress like this one.'

She could not move her head to see what he had done, but she realized he had dressed her while she was unconscious.

What was he talking about?

'Yesterday, I washed away my sins in the Holy River. Now it is your turn. We must make you pure again.'

He threw something across her face, a fine white linen sheet. Then he lifted her effortlessly from the bed and carried her to the door and down the stairs.

She felt the sudden chill when they reached the street and heard him say something to someone in Hindi. A man's voice answered. There was the strong scent of an animal.

A *tonga*, she thought. A pony and trap. Where is he taking me?

He laid her on the soft, leather seat and clambered in beside her. She felt the carriage lurch forward, and then they bumped away through the darkness, the horse's hooves clip-clipping on the cobblestones.

Suddenly, she understood. The pony man did not help her because he thought she was already dead.

The linen sheet was her shroud.

CHAPTER 46

Bedi heard footsteps on the stairs. He got out of his cot and peered through the doorway. He saw the *farang* - foreigner - carry a white-shrouded body down the steps to a waiting *tonga*.

Shiva, he had killed her, here in his own house! If the police caught him now, he would be in big trouble. They might even throw him in prison. He cursed himself for taking the money. He should have gone to the police instead and demanded a reward. This was not good, not good at all.

The *farang* ordered the driver to take him to the *ghats*.

Bedi hesitated, caught between his terror of the *farang* and the certain knowledge of what the police would do to him if they found out he had lied to them. No, he decided. It was too great a risk, even for two thousand rupees.

Moments later, he was running barefoot through the darkened streets to the police sub-station.

Valentine drifted in and out of consciousness. Suddenly, she was aware that the gentle swaying motion of the buggy had stopped, and she felt strong arms lift her out of the seat. She knew it was Michel, knew his smell.

She heard lapping water. They must be on the *ghats*.

'Everything I did was for you,' Michel said. 'I just wanted you to be proud of me, Adrienne.'

Why had he called her that? What in God's name was he doing?

A fragment of memory returned, like a torn page from an old diary.

A pool of saliva collected at the corner of her mother's lips beaded down to her chin. She sniffed the sour smell of wine on her mother's breath. Her eyes fell on the empty bottle of vin ordinaire beside the chair.

'Michel,' *Adrienne murmured, her eyes flickering in half-sleep.* 'Michel.'

Was this the devil that had haunted her mother all those years?

'It's all right, Adrienne,' he said. 'I will take away all your sins.'

Sergeant Dilip Jadeja lay on the wooden cot in the corner of his office in his khaki tunic and shorts, his nightstick resting on his chest. He was exhausted. He had spent all day walking around the city, chasing after this damned *farang,* and he was worn out. He hated night duty. He would rather be at home in bed with his wife.

He drifted off to sleep. He did not hear the first tentative knock on the bolted, wooden door.

Outside, Bedi was growing more frightened and more frustrated. He knocked again, louder. He tried again. And again, this time with his fists.

Sergeant Jadeja opened an eye and sighed.

Suddenly, he remembered where he was. Shiva, perhaps it was the inspector! He leapt to his feet, staggered across the room and threw open the door. He blinked in surprise at the man in the ragged kurta standing in the shadows. He grabbed the kerosene lamp that hung next to the doorway and shone it in his face.

He straightened his uniform and tried to assume a dignified attitude. 'What do you want?'

'The *farang!*' Bedi said. 'I've seen him.'

'What *farang?*' Jadeja said, his mind still woolly from sleep. Then he remembered. 'The murderer?'

'Yes, yes! I came as soon as I could.'

The telephone rang in Budjinski's room at Clark's hotel. He groped for the bedside lamp, turned it on, then snatched the receiver off its cradle.

'Budjinski.'

'We've got him,' Gupta Singh said. "There's a car on its way. Be in the lobby in three minutes.'

Valentine lay in Michel's arms like a rag doll. It was getting light. She heard voices and the fire-crackle of burning reeds. There was an acrid stench of wood smoke.

'Is it ready?' Michel said.

'Yes, sahib,' a voice said.

'Don't be afraid,' Michel said. 'I am going to save you.' She felt his lips brush her cheek through the thin piece of linen that covered her.

'Goodbye, Adrienne.'

Budjinski leapt from the back seat of the Polis Fiat and stared around in confusion. There were police everywhere, shining torches into the faces of the startled pilgrims. Angry shouts echoed along the riverbanks, everyone alarmed by their sudden presence.

Gupta Singh appeared beside him. 'He's somewhere on the *ghats*. We have to hurry.'

Budjinski ran blindly into the darkness towards the Ganges.

The first yellow-bright sliver of sun appeared over the distant horizon throwing specks of gold on the river. A man's voice bellowed from one of the *ghats*. A policeman was frantically blowing his whistle. A skein of smoke rose into the air.

Valentine moaned as a breath of wind blew the sheet back from her face. She saw the tied bundles of sandalwood around her, a heart of orange flame belching smoke.

The billowing yellow clouds parted, and she saw Michel, his head shaved, wearing just a single piece of coarse white mourning cloth. Behind him stood the *chandal*. His face twisted into a frown. He took a step towards her, unsure.

I'm alive, can't you see? I'm alive!

With a supreme effort of will, she moved her hand. It was enough to shift its weight to the edge of the pallet and it fell away and swung loose from under the sheet.

The man roared in alarm, his shouts echoing along the banks of the river. He rushed towards her to pull her clear. Michel blocked his way and she saw the glint of a knife in his right hand.

The *chandal* stopped when he saw Michel was armed. Bellowing like an old bull, he turned and ran up the steps.

Michel threw the sheet back across her face.

She could feel the heat from the flames. She knew it was over.

Budjinski saw him first.

Despite the shaved head and loin cloth, he knew it was him just from the way he was standing, like he was mocking the whole world. It had to be him.

Then he saw the old *chandal* stumbling up the *ghat* and pointing to a white-shrouded figure on a bier, almost invisible now behind the screen of yellow smoke.

Budjinski shouted a warning and ran down the steps.

Michel looked up and saw him. Suddenly he was gone, melting away into the dawn.

Budjinski didn't try to follow. He had to get to Valentine. *Please God let me be in time.*

He threw himself into the smoke and flames and pulled the shrouded body off the bier.

PART 6

The Trial: August 1973

CHAPTER 47

Delhi

Justice in India did not come easily or cheaply. The courts were overburdened, choked by a bloated and indifferent bureaucracy. The system was riddled with delays, bribery and inefficiency. One case initiated in the tenth century was still pending.

After Independence in 1948, the British Common Law system was retained, but the tradition of trial by jury was scrapped. Instead, guilt or innocence was decided by a single judge.

After charges were laid, the police and the public prosecutor prepared a First Information Report. The FIR contained all the evidence pertinent to the case - witness statements, pathologist's reports, records of interviews and even gossip.

The lower court magistrates read the FIR to establish whether a prima facie case existed. If they agreed, the case was brought to trial. The document usually ran to hundreds of pages loosely tied with string, dog-eared, crumpled and stained. Surprise witnesses were rarely produced, new evidence seldom exhibited. Instead, the counsel for the defense set out to discredit the prosecution's case as stated in the FIR.

Michel had been incarcerated behind the thick and ugly walls of the Tihar prison for a year, the monotony broken only by visits to the Parliament Street courts for the preliminary hearings.

Incredibly, he had eluded Gupta Singh's police in Varanasi. He had been arrested in Calcutta four days later and charged with possession of a stolen passport. It took the local authorities three days to realize that they had in their custody the man half the world was looking for.

The case had made headlines around the world. As the list of suspected victims grew, extradition orders arrived almost daily, from the Philippines, Hong Kong, Singapore, Malaysia and finally, Thailand.

Public interest rose to fever pitch. Michel Christian was rumored to be responsible for the deaths of twenty-one women. He was profiled endlessly in India's Sunday papers.

He had become a celebrity.

Now a year later, in the crowded, Hogarthian madness of the Tis Hizari courts, his trial was about to begin.

A few minutes before, standing at the window of his office in the heart of old Delhi, Judge Chandra Reddy watched the crowds pushing and shoving in the street below. It seemed all Delhi wanted to get inside. A *farang* was trying to fight his way through. He recognized him. It was the French Interpol detective.

'Five minutes, Judge,' a face at the half-open door informed him.

He nodded absently and continued to stare across the street. Five minutes before noon, five minutes before a trial that had become the most eagerly awaited in Indian history. Judge Reddy was unused to such publicity. Ordinarily, his little courtroom in the Tis Hizari complex would be almost empty.

But today was different.

First, the man accused was not an Indian citizen. Second, although he was standing trial in this one, rather bizarre case of attempted murder, police in five countries were collecting evidence linking him to unsolved murders. Interpol had a whole inventory of corpses, from the streets of Manila to the lake boats in Kashmir. Most victims had been strangled. Some had had their throats cut.

Such a sensational case was enough on its own to attract the attentions of the Press, but then there was the girl. A French model whose face had appeared on the covers of magazines.

Now, another heady ingredient had been added to this cocktail. The man who was to defend the accused was the Nawab of Pashan, India's most celebrated trial lawyer, a man accustomed to having flashbulbs pop wherever he went.

Yes, it would be a good day for the papers.

Even so Judge Reddy could not suppress a feeling of utter bewilderment as he entered his courtroom. His wife had tried to impress upon him what to expect, but as he looked around at the press of eager, curious faces he was surprised to discover that his hands were shaking. He surveyed his packed chambers. The heat in the room was intense. The ceiling fans moved slowly, as if trying to stir some thick, heavy liquid.

The authorities were taking no chances with their celebrated prisoner. It seemed like half the Indian army had been trucked in. There were soldiers with bayonets everywhere. Even for Delhi, it seemed a little excessive.

Many of the seats were occupied by newspaper and magazine reporters. There were representatives from the *Bangkok Post*, the *Straits Times*, *Paris Match*, *Le Figaro*, even the *New York Times*. Judge Reddy wondered how they would react to seeing Indian justice in action.

He found it incredible that life had chosen him from amongst all the judges in Delhi to preside over such a public spectacle. He knew he would not be remembered by future generations of legal minds for his incisive intellect or his eloquence. He was aware of his own limitations, even comfortable with them. Until now.

In a western courtroom he would have banged a gavel to bring order. But here in India, he just sat down and nodded at the public prosecutor and the trial got under way.

Budjinski did not hear a word of the public prosecutor's opening speech. He stared at the back of the man's head in front of him and watched a bead of sweat squeeze from under his turban and find a wrinkled channel down his neck.

He was reliving those last climactic hours in Varanasi and asking himself, as he had asked himself so many times, if it had all been worth it. The past year had seemed endless, waiting for this day when the sacrifice could be justified.

Was it enough that they had that bastard in chains, that the killing had stopped? What would they do to him? Would any punishment be enough?

He raised his head and searched the mass of faces. Michel was slouched in his chair, his wrists manacled in his lap. Budjinski wondered what he was feeling. Confusion? Fear? Panic? His face betrayed nothing.

Michel caught Budjinski's stare, and a mocking half-smile formed on his lips.

But Budjinski did not see it. He was lost once more in his reverie. He watched a skein of smoke rise over the grey river, heard again the sound of his own screams. Over a year ago, but the horror of it was still fresh in his memory.

He realized that the man next to him was staring.

His hands had tightened into fists on the wooden bench and his body was shaking with the force of his rage. If the Indians did not convict him, he would kill the bastard himself.

Bombay

Joginder Krisnan choked back another wave of pain. From the bed, where he had lain for the past five years, he could tell by the passage of the shadows on the wall that it was time.

There was a mirror on the dressing table, and in it he could see his own reflection distorted by the convex shape of the glass. What he saw filled him with revulsion - an emaciated figure, the legs truncated at the thighs, the hairless body as thin as a girl's under the soiled white vest. Once, he had been tall, with the body of an athlete.

In later years, his body had run to fat, but he had felt a perverse vanity about that, his extra pounds evidence to his burgeoning wealth. He had been anticipating an indolent retirement in a villa somewhere in the shaded hills above the heat, dust and squalor of Maha Amma.

But instead, for the last five years he had lain crippled in this shabby room, the best that his now modest means would allow. That day in Saigon he lost everything: his legs, his money, his livelihood. He had not worked at his sewing table again.

He heard footsteps on the stairs. His youngest son, Ranchi, slouched into the room carrying an enamel plate with rice and a watery curry. Joginder struggled to sit up. The boy watched him, unable or unwilling to conceal the disgust on his face.

'I have brought your lunch, Father.'

'Yes, yes. Put it down.'

The boy dropped the plate on the bedside table, spilling some of the meaty stew onto the floor.

'Be careful, you idiot.'

The boy shrugged his shoulders and left.

Children, Joginder thought. A burden and a curse. They were idle, his sons. Once, he would have put them out on the street. Now he had no choice but to keep them. Who else would run his errands and cook for him now that his wife was dead?

As he reached for the food, he felt a stab of pain in his legs. He gasped, clutching at the iron frame of the bed, a sudden greasy sweat erupting on his forehead. Even after all these years, those two bullets ripped into his flesh anew every day. He had found himself wishing more and more often that he could die. He could not remember the last time he had woken in the morning without a feeling of disappointment.

But before he could rest in his grave, he anticipated that last, slow satisfaction of knowing *he* was dead too.

Since the arrest, he had thought of nothing else. He had read everything that had been written in the papers. It sickened him that some of them made him out to be some sort of hero. That bastard. His one regret was that he was unable to go to Delhi himself, but his crippled legs made the journey impossible.

He promised himself one last pleasure. On the day they hanged him, he would afford himself the extravagance of a bottle of imported French champagne, and he would make a toast at the moment of his son's execution.

May he rot in hell.

Delhi

As the public prosecutor began his opening address, the Nawab of Pashan arrived at the Tis Hizari in all his sartorial splendor, trailing a string of assistants and news reporters like a comet's tail. He feigned an air of indifference to the heads that were craned in his direction as he made his way towards a hastily vacated chair on the right of the judge's bench.

Flustered, the public prosecutor faltered over his speech.

The case had barely begun, and already the Nawab had drawn first blood.

The Nawab was tall and poised, with a luxuriant mane of silver hair combed straight back from his forehead. He was exceptionally fair for an Indian, the kind of man to whom most Indians instinctively deferred. He was one of the founding fathers of the new India, an author of the Constitution, an intimate of Nehru. He had known Gandhi.

Gandhi had not liked him.

His face twisted to a frown as he surveyed the courtroom, the expression of a nobleman confronted with the smell of ordure while passing the hovels of his serfs. He rarely sullied his hands with a case as gross as attempted murder.

He had not troubled himself with the pre-trial hearings and was only scantily familiar with the details of the case. But in India such negligence was unimportant. He might look like an aristocrat, but the Nawab was a playground bully who employed a mordant wit and brutal courtroom tactics in equal measure to devastating effect.

'Why have you taken this case?' one foreign reporter had asked him as he arrived outside.

'Because I feel it is my duty to protect the sanctity of justice in this country. I am outraged by the underhand police tactics used against my client. They have based much of their case on unsubstantiated evidence from foreign countries.'

In truth, his motives were not as pure. He had been drawn to the case like a fly to droppings because he knew it would attract the full glare of public attention. He was hoping Gandhi would appoint him to the High Court.

As he settled himself into the cane-backed chair a few feet from Michel Christian, he didn't afford his client a single glance.

This was his show now.

Paris

Roland Fourget was one of the best plastic surgeons in France, if not Europe. He was attached to the burns unit at the St Jerome Hôpital, and during his short career he had pioneered a number of techniques that were considered breakthroughs in the reconstruction of facial tissue. The tragedy of a disfigurement was never less for any patient. But he privately experienced a unique poignancy in working with patients who had been beautiful before their injuries. For all his expertise, he knew he could never come close to reproducing what nature had once created.

He steeled himself before entering the room. Unlike many of his colleagues, he found it difficult to be dispassionate about his work. It was the reason he had chosen to work with burns victims. Cosmetic surgery for its own sake did not interest him. He was not concerned with vanity, only with healing.

His patient lay quite still, her head swathed in bandages. It was early afternoon, and the blinds were drawn to keep out the bright sunlight, but he knew she was awake by the nervous, sparrow-like movements of her right hand on the sheet.

He sat down on the edge of the bed. After all the operations he had performed, he still felt a chill when he approached this moment of truth. He had done the best he could with what was left of her face, but he had warned her not to expect too much. At this stage, functionality was the best they could hope for.

He had seen a photograph of the girl, torn from the front cover of the French edition of *Vogue,* and had been overcome by unspeakable sadness. How fragile such beauty was.

He carefully removed the dressings, examined the results, and declared himself satisfied. He doubted that she would concur.

If you looked at her from her right side, she was still beautiful, for one half of her face had not been exposed to the heat. Look at her from the other side, and she looked like a wax effigy left too close to a flame.

If only he had had more to work with.

He thought she would ask for a mirror and was grateful when she did not.

'Thank you, Roland.' The words were slurred, the scarring on one side of her mouth blurring her speech.

'Another six months perhaps. We could attempt more surgery.'

She shrugged and looked away. 'The trial begins today. It's time you discharged me, I think.'

CHAPTER 48

Delhi

Public Prosecutor, Mohinder Singh, glared with undisguised resentment as the Nawab of Pashan made his entrance like a maharajah sweeping into his throne room. He was aware that every head had turned in the Great One's direction. No one was listening to his address.

He had anticipated as much.

Mohinder was young, intense and painfully thin. The thick lenses on his spectacles lent him an owl-like intensity. He wore a pair of baggy, black trousers and a black cotton coat, threadbare at the cuff. Perspiration marks already seeped into the cloth between his shoulders. His blue turban was askew and mottled with damp.

By contrast, the Nawab was immaculately tailored in grey striped trousers and a tailored blue serge jacket. What was even more galling, his adversary appeared comfortable in the steamy atmosphere of the courtroom, as if his high caste would not tolerate the appearance of sweat in public.

The Nawab was in no hurry to get to his seat. Mohinder forced himself to look away and continued with his opening address, even though he knew that he was, in effect, speaking to himself.

Mohinder dabbed at his face with a white handkerchief and pushed his spectacles higher on his nose. He bowed to the judge and announced his first witness.

Sanjoy Bedi walked into the courtroom dressed in a long white kurta, blinking owlishly at the press of faces that were suddenly turned towards him. He looked as if he expected that the crowd would turn on him at any moment. There was no dock and no witness box. Bedi stood in the center of the crowd of advocates and junior lawyers clustered around the bench.

Michel sat a few feet away, close enough to touch. He was wearing the *dandaberi* - steel ankle cuffs attached to a bar locked onto his belt. His left wrist was handcuffed to one of the soldiers by a long chain. He glared at Bedi malevolently.

Mohinder tapped an index finger impatiently on the table. He dreaded what his adversary would do to the poor old man.

'What is your name?' he said.

Bedi looked at Michel and shuddered. He had never been in court before. He had not known it would be like this.

'When I get out of here, I'm going to kill you,' Michel said.

'What is your name?' Mohinder repeated.

'B-Bedi, sahib.'

Judge Reddy leaned forward, straining to hear over the hum of the overhead fans.

'Your full name,' Mohinder said.

'Sanjoy Bedi.'

'What did he say?' Judge Reddy said.

'Sanjoy Bedi,' Mohinder said. His patience was legendary. It had to be. His job was purely to coach his witnesses through everything they'd already recited in the FIR.

'What is your occupation?'

Bedi began his speech. He had had plenty of time to rehearse it. Like Michel, he had been kept at Tihar for the past year. It was customary procedure, enabling key witnesses to be produced at will. The suffering this caused an innocent man was never considered.

'I am an honest man, sahib.'

'What was that?' Judge Reddy said.

'He said he is an honest man.'

'Was there ever any other kind?' the Nawab said. He turned to the gallery of spectators for approval. There was a ripple of laughter.

'We are sure you are an honest man. But what is your occupation?' Mohinder said.

'I have a silk emporium.'

'In which city?'

'In Varanasi.'

Judge Reddy assumed a pained expression. 'I can't hear. Tell the witness to stand closer to the bench and speak up.'

Mohinder motioned for Bedi to stand closer to the bench. The old man shuffled forward. He was now standing barefoot in a puddle of water that had dripped through the ceiling when the monsoon storm had broken. He looked ragged and miserable.

'Now then,' Mohinder said, 'can you tell us what happened?'

'Just a minute,' Judge Reddy said, 'start again from the beginning. I haven't heard anything yet.'

Mohinder nodded and smiled. 'Now then,' he said, as loudly as he could, 'what is your full name?'

The rain began again. Mohinder had to shout to make himself heard. He led the old man through a series of biographical questions to get him accustomed to speaking at the right volume and pitch. Finally, he said,

'Now I want you to have a look at the man sitting on your left. Have you seen him before?'

Bedi turned and stared at Michel, thankful that the *farang* was safely restrained in heavy chains. He could feel his hot breath on his arm.

'You're a dead man,' Michel said.

Bedi felt his knees start to give way under him.

'Please answer the question,' Mohinder repeated. 'Have you seen him before?'

'Yes, sahib.'

'Please tell us where and when.'

'He wanted to rent a room from me. I gave him my best room.'

'The lavatory, I should imagine,' the Nawab said.

Mohinder looked towards Judge Reddy, hoping for intervention. There was none.

'This was on the 5th of July 1972.'

Bedi hesitated. 'Yes, sahib.'

'And how was he dressed?'

'He wore a turban. And a dhoti and a white shirt.'

'So, he was in disguise?'

'Objection!' The Nawab leaped to his feet. 'My client was not in disguise. The defense intends to show that the person in question was not my client. Therefore, he was not in disguise.'

Judge Reddy ruminated on this. In Indian courts testimony was not recorded verbatim. Instead, the judge edited and censored it to his personal taste.

'Objection allowed.' He turned to the court clerk. 'On the 5th of July 1972, a man in a turban and dhoti came to my boarding house. He looked a little like the defendant.'

The clerk's ancient Remington clattered to life.

Judge Reddy turned to Mohinder. 'Continue.'

Mohinder sighed. 'Have you seen this woman before?' He picked up a tattered brown folder, withdrew a black and white photograph of Valentine and handed it to Bedi.

It was passed around the court. People in the spectator gallery and in the press corps craned their heads for a glimpse.

'Yes,' Bedi said. 'He brought this woman to the hotel.'

'That must have impressed her,' the Nawab said. His sycophants laughed on cue.

Mohinder looked imploringly at Judge Reddy, who ignored him. Even he's intimidated, he thought. He continued. 'This was on the 7th of July 1972?'

'Yes, sahib.'

'What time?'

'It was in the afternoon. I do not know what time.'

'And what happened?'

'He took her up to the room. I brought them tea. He requested it.'

'A brave man,' the Nawab shouted. More laughter.

'And what happened then?'

'I did not see her again. The next morning-'

'Yes, yes. We'll come to that.' Mohinder paused. They had reached the part in the man's testimony that even he doubted. 'When did the police visit you?'

Bedi mumbled and stared at the floor. Everyone strained to hear over the hammering of the rain and the shouts of two of the Nawab's junior lawyers, who were arguing heatedly between themselves.

'When did the police visit you?'

'I'm not sure.'

'After the defendant brought the girl back to the hotel?'

'Yes, sahib.'

'They showed you a picture of this man?' Mohinder pointed to Michel.

'Yes.'

'Why didn't you tell the police the man they were looking for was staying in your house?'

Bedi looked fearfully at the judge. 'I did not recognize him. In the photograph he had Western clothes, and his hair was very dark. It was only next morning, when he left with the girl, and I saw him without the turban...' His voice trailed off.

Mohinder saw the Nawab grinning in triumph.

Judge Reddy turned to the court clerk. 'The witness states that when the police showed him a photograph, he did not recognize the defendant as the same man who was renting a room from him. Continue.'

The Oberoi Hotel was one of New Delhi's premier hotels. It overlooked the golf links on one side and Humayun's Tomb on the other. It boasted New Delhi's only skyline cocktail bar, the Skylark.

Detective-Superintendent Ravi Engineer led Budjinski to a table by the window and ordered two gin and tonics. They had met many times at police conventions around the world and had become firm friends during Budjinski's two previous visits to the Indian capital on Interpol business.

When Noelle had been murdered, it was Engineer who had handled the case and personally supervised the return of her body to Paris.

Now that Budjinski had returned for the trial, Engineer had invited him to stay with him at his home in Delhi.

He was a Brahmin, a thin ascetic man with pale skin and short, graying hair. He had been educated at Cambridge and still sounded for all the world like a major in the British Army. A clipped moustache added to the effect.

'Well, what do you think of Indian justice, old boy?' he said.

Budjinski swallowed the gin. 'It's not a trial. It's a circus.'

'Oh, I don't know. I thought it was quite dignified in there today. Sometimes it gets out of hand.'

'The prosecutor's a fucking idiot.'

'No, he's just uninspired, that's all. You must be, to do that job. It's not his fault.'

'This could go on for months.'

'It's possible.' Engineer looked out of the window. In the distance, lightning swept and flickered across the night sky.

'If they let him go, I'll kill him myself. I swear it.'

'Oh, my goodness. No bloodshed, old fellow. Let's keep this civilized and make sure he gets hanged.'

'I don't care how it's done.'

'They'll convict him, René. Have another drink and don't worry. Things will go better tomorrow.'

It was the second day of the trial. The Nawab rose slowly from his seat like a bird of prey spreading its black wings. Beneath the gown, he wore an immaculately tailored black coat with grey striped trousers and white choirboy collar. He towered over the old silk merchant and the dichotomy was obvious to everyone. Bedi, already terrified out of his wits, looked as if he were about to faint.

The Nawab looked at Bedi as if he had just crawled out of a drain. Then he threw out a hand and one of his junior assistants placed a photograph into his palm.

'This is the photograph that the police showed you?' he said.

'Yes, sahib.'

'You didn't recognize my client at that time?'

Bedi seemed to be having trouble speaking. 'No, sahib.'

'Why not?'

'His clothes. His hair.'

'What was different about his hair?'

'It was fair.'

'You said he was wearing a turban.'

Bedi looked down at his feet.

'How many times had you seen your boarder before the police visited you?'

'I'm not sure.'

'Once, twice, a dozen times. Three hundred times?'

Bedi was shaking head to foot. Mohinder looked away. He couldn't bear to watch.

'Perhaps a dozen times.'

'He always wore a turban?'

'Yes, sahib.'

'But you knew the color of his hair?'

Bedi did not answer.

The Nawab looked triumphantly around the room. 'All right then, when did you in fact decide that your boarder was the man the police were looking for?'

'The next morning.'

'What time was that?'

'I'm not sure.'

'You got to the police station at five o'clock. You went straight there when you realized your boarder was the man the police were looking for?'

'Yes.'

'But it's dark at that time, correct?'

A nod.

'Weren't you asleep?'

'I woke up. I heard him moving about on the stairs.'

'And you recognized him immediately in the pitch dark, even though you failed to recognize him in broad daylight on a dozen previous occasions? Is that correct? I said - is that correct?'

Bedi looked to be on the point of collapse. He stared resolutely at the floor, unable to utter a word.

Mohinder waited for the Nawab to administer the mortal blow.

'All this happened on the 8th of July 1972. Is that correct?'

When Bedi did not answer, the Nawab shouted, 'It's in your testimony! You said the man you thought was my client took a shrouded body to the *ghats* on the 8th of July 1972.' He waved the tattered FIR in front of Bedi's face. 'It's in here! Well?'

Bedi nodded his head.

'Speak up, the judge can't hear you.'

'Y-yes, sahib.'

'What day is it today?'

'I don't know,' Bedi said.

The Nawab turned to face the courtroom, glowing with triumph. 'He doesn't know.' He took a step closer. 'Your whole testimony is a pack of lies, isn't it?' he shouted.

Bedi nodded. 'Yes, sahib.'

CHAPTER 49

Budjinski sat on the balcony of Engineer's villa in old Delhi. The garden was bright with hibiscus. Mynahs patrolled the high walls, and a bulbul contested the lime tree with a family of sparrows. It was a bright, warm morning, but on the horizon the pillars of cumulus were gathering for the afternoon storms.

A servant brought a pitcher of lemonade. Engineer smiled apologetically. 'I'm sorry. I don't drink in front of the servants.'

Budjinski shrugged, preoccupied with his own thoughts.

Engineer was worried about him. He had lost a lot of weight, but instead of looking fitter, he appeared gaunt and old. He no longer had the same purpose when he walked. Once, René Budjinski had been a battering ram. Now he was an old stick you could break across your knee.

'What do you make of him?' Budjinski said suddenly.

'It is hard to say. I leave psychology to the experts.'

'Women still fawn over him. In court yesterday I saw a girl - a white girl, a Westerner - throw a flower to him. He's killed twenty women! It doesn't seem to matter. Women treat him like a film star.' He ignored the proffered lemonade. 'Can you get me into Tihar?'

'Why?'

'I want to talk to him. I want to know about Noelle. I have to understand, or I'm going to go insane.'

'I'm sorry. It is beyond my power. Even if I could arrange such a thing, I would not let you do that to yourself.'

'What are you talking about?'

'How long would you be able to talk to him before you decided to put your hands round his throat? Then the police would put you in prison too.'

'It would be worth it.'

'I think not.'

Budjinski reached for the cigarettes in his shirt pocket and lit one. His hands were shaking. 'Do you think he's insane?'

'Possibly. A man must be insane to do such a thing. But the robberies have a genius about them. I don't think he's mad. I think he is without a soul. We assume that every man has one, but I don't think it's true.'

'Go on.'

'A man without a soul can learn to be charming and attractive. These are just social skills. He can use his mind more efficiently than most because it is uncluttered with emotion. Yet when it comes to feeling empathy and compassion, he cannot do it. In this way, he is irredeemable.'

'And yet he gave in to emotion with Valentine. That is how he was caught in the end.'

'Ah, the woman. Do you know where she is now?'

'No,' Budjinski said. 'She's disappeared.'

It was the fourth day of the trial. Mohinder had called his second witness, the old *chandal* from Varanasi.

The man was dressed in dirty, cotton pajamas, and his turban was grey with grime. He was a *harijan,* and the gaggle of lawyers and their sycophants shrank back from him.

Mohinder rose with confidence. He was sure today would go much better. 'What is your name?'

'Ranvir Laxman.' The man's voice was rich and deep. Even though he was a from a low caste, he maintained a quiet dignity.

'What is your occupation?'

'I am a *chandal* at the Hari Schandra *ghat*, sahib.'

As with Bedi, Mohinder led the man through a string of routine biographical questions to put him at his ease and establish a rhythm. Then he pointed to Michel. 'Have you seen this man before?'

Laxman turned his head slowly and looked at Michel. 'Yes, sahib.'

'When did you see him?'

'It was the day before he tried to kill the woman.'

The Nawab had been lounging on a wooden bench like a Roman senator at an orgy. He sprang to his feet as if he had been stung. 'Objection!'

The judge nodded. 'Allowed.'

Mohinder nodded. 'The day before the crime was committed. The 7th of July 1972. Is that correct?'

Laxman nodded. 'Yes.'

'And why did he come to see you?'

'He said his wife had died. He wanted her body to be burned on the *ghats* and her ashes spread in the Mother Ganges.'

'You didn't think this was strange? Such a request from a European?'

'I did not know he was European. He wore a turban and dhoti. I thought he was Hindu.'

The Nawab jumped to his feet. 'Objection! The defense maintains that the man the witness is referring to *was* a Hindu.'

'Allowed.'

Mohinder pressed on. 'So, the arrangements were made?'

'Yes, sahib.'

'And when did you next see him?'

'The next morning. He brought the woman. She was wrapped in a white sheet. He carried her down the steps in his arms. I saw nothing amiss.'

'Then what happened?'

Laxman looked at Michel, hawked phlegm from deep in his throat and spat squarely between his feet. The surrounding lawyers craned their necks to stare at the betel-colored blob of spittle as if it were a new exhibit.

'The witness will refrain from expectorating in court,' the judge said.

'Then what happened?' Mohinder said.

'He laid her on the pallet and the fire was lit. It was then that the sheet fell away, and I saw her face. Her lips moved. I realized she was still alive.'

'Did you then try to rescue the woman?'

'Yes, sahib.'

'And did the defendant then step in to prevent you from removing her from the pallet?'

'He threatened me with a knife, so I ran to get help.'

'And it was at this point that the police arrived?'

'Yes, sahib.'

'Thank you. Your witness.'

The Nawab rose imperiously from his perch below the judge's bench and walked towards the press gallery. He stood a moment in profile for the benefit of the court reporters who were hastily making sketches. Then he turned to Laxman. 'You are sure my client is the man you saw that morning at the *ghats*?'

'Yes, sahib.'

'Exactly like him?'

'No, not exactly. He was wearing a turban and dhoti and-'

'He looked quite different then?'

Laxman was not sure how to answer.

Judge Reddy turned to the court stenographer. 'The witness said the man he saw on the day before the crime was quite different from the defendant.'

The Remington clattered into life.

'Continue,' Judge Reddy said.

Mohinder shook his head.

The Nawab pressed on, encouraged. 'How many Hindus come to you each year for your services?'

'I do not know.'

'Hundreds?'

'Very many.'

'Very many. And you remember one unremarkable looking man in a dhoti.'

'You never forget any man who threatens you with a knife.'

The Nawab frowned. 'What you're telling me is you only remember him from the next morning. When this incident took place.'

Laxman hesitated, uncertain. 'Yes,' he said.

'What time was this?'

'Dawn.'

'Dawn, so it was dark?'

'Yes, sahib but-'

'You are saying that you think my client was the man you saw that morning on the *ghat* from your memory of an incident that happened in the dark over twelve months ago?'

'I am certain this is the man.'

'But you have already told us that this crime happened before the sun came up. You must have extraordinary eyesight.' The Nawab turned away and pointed to the clock that hung on the wall above the court entrance. 'What time is it?'

Laxman squinted across the room. 'I don't know.'

'It's a quarter to one. And the clock is only twenty-five yards away. Your eyesight certainly is extraordinary. Extraordinarily deficient. No further questions.'

The American slouched into the courtroom, his lank, fair hair down to his shoulders, a thin beard covering his face. He had lost weight during his long stays in Indian prisons, and the frayed white cotton shirt hung loose on his shoulders. As he took his place in the courtroom, he tried to avoid Michel's eyes.

Mohinder put on his spectacles and consulted his trial notes. 'What is your name?'

'Andrew Rosen.'

'What is your nationality?'

'American.'

'You are from the United States?'

'Yeah.'

'And your occupation?'

'I'm a student.'

'Hah!' The Nawab removed a piece of lint from his jacket and dropped it at the witness's feet.

Mohinder ignored the interruption, having learned by now that he would get no assistance from the judge. He pointed to Michel. 'Look at this man.'

Andy forced himself to turn around.

Michel leaned towards him, 'I'm going to cut off your balls and stuff them down your throat,' he said.

'Do you recognize him?'

Andy struggled to find his voice. They had promised they would release him if he testified. He could not go through another five years in Tihar. He had to do this.

'I said, do you recognize him?'

'Yes.'

'Where have you seen him before?'

'In Bombay. We shared a cell.'

'You were cell mates in the Port of Bombay prison, is that correct?'

'Yeah.'

'Can you tell us what you remember about him?'

'Well, he was pretty violent. He killed this guy. A Canadian.'

'He killed someone?'

The Nawab rose, spreading his gown like a pair of giant wings. 'Objection!'

'Well, I didn't see him do it. It was just a rumor going around the prison. They said he'd cornered a guy in the latrines and smashed his head on a concrete block.'

'What else do you remember about the prisoner?'

'Well, he was pretty anxious to get out of the prison.'

'Was there any particular reason?'

'Yeah. He said he had a score to settle with his old man.'

'His old man?'

'His father. He said he was going to kill him.'

The Nawab half rose from his chair and thought better of it.

Mohinder hooked his thumbs into the pockets of his waistcoat, feeling confident now. 'When did you last see him?'

'Just before he-'

'Speak up.'

'Just before he escaped.'

'Just before he escaped. Is that what you said?'

'Yeah.'

'This man is an escaped convict?'

'They didn't convict him of anything, man.'

'And when did the prisoner make his escape from Bombay jail?'

'It was January 1968.'

'Thank you. Your witness.'

The Nawab seemed to have fallen asleep. After a few moments, he yawned theatrically, stretching out his arms and legs. He rose slowly to his feet. He regarded Andy Rosen for long moments before he began.

'How old are you?'

'Twenty-three, man.'

'Twenty-three. Have you ever worked?'

'What?'

'I said, have you ever worked? Had a job?'

'I told you, I'm a student.'

'What did he say?' Judge Reddy said, craning forward.

'He said he is twenty-three years old and has never done a day's work in his life,' the Nawab said.

Judge Reddy repeated this verbatim to the court stenographer.

'What is your present occupation?'

'Jesus, man, what is this?' Andy appealed to Mohinder, who shrugged helplessly.

'Do you have a present occupation?'

'You know I don't man. I'm in Tihar.'

'You are in prison here in Delhi.'

'Yeah.'

'For what offence?'

'I got busted for possession.'

Judge Reddy frowned and looked at the Nawab.

'He was arrested for possessing hard drugs.'

'They weren't hard drugs, man. It was only a few fuckin' Buddha sticks.'

'The witness was arrested for supplying heroin,' Judge Reddy dictated to the stenographer.

'How long have you been in prison here in Delhi?'

'Two years.'

'And you have five more years to serve.'

'Yeah.'

'And before that you were in prison in Bombay.'

'That was only for a couple of months. I went back to the States after that.'

'And when you came back to India, you were again arrested for drug-taking?'

'Yeah, I got bad karma.'

'How long have you been taking drugs?'

'I don't know, man. Since I was fifteen or sixteen, I guess.'

'Since when?' Judge Reddy said.

'Since he was a small child, your honor,' the Nawab said. He turned back to the young American. 'So, you are a habitual drug user?'

'Isn't everyone?'

'And do you frequently experience hallucinations?'

'No, man, I don't hallucinate. What is this?'

'Why do you take drugs?'

'It's a good trip. Makes you feel good. Makes the world a nicer place, you know?'

'You take drugs because it changes your perception of the world?'

'Yeah, I guess.'

'So, being a habitual drug user, you tend to see things that other people don't?'

'Hey look, man, that's not what I said.'

'You were pressured by the police to become an approver in this case. Is that correct?'

That much was true. There wasn't any other way out. His father had refused to help him anymore. He had made that clear enough. You're a stain on my reputation and a leech on your family, he had told Andy. It's time you learned your lesson. That was two years ago. It might as well have been two hundred. He could not go through another five years in Tihar.

'No, they didn't pressure me.'

The Nawab smiled. 'Really? Describe to me what Tihar prison is like.'

Andy was thrown by the sudden switch. 'It's a shithole.'

'I beg your pardon?'

'It's hell, man.'

'What do they feed you?'

'You get a chapati and half a cup of milk once a day. And maybe some dahl. If you don't have any money, you starve. The guards make you pay for everything.'

'And are your quarters comfortable?'

'I sleep on a stone floor with one lousy blanket, winter and summer. There's rats everywhere.' Andy felt tears welling up. His control was going. 'It's shit, man. You couldn't understand just how bad it is.'

'I imagine a person would do anything to get themselves out of such a place.'

'I'd sell my own mother if-' he stopped. He looked desperately at Mohinder.

'How fortunate you did not have to go that far,' the Nawab said. 'This man doesn't even appear to be a distant relative. No further questions.'

CHAPTER 50

It was the fifth day of the trial. It was not going well. The Nawab had lived up to his reputation, somehow maneuvering and bullying the prosecution witnesses, so that by the time he had finished with them, hard evidence had become mere speculation, fantasy or imagination.

Budjinski sat in the court day after day, feeling an impotent fury building inside him. The bastard looked as if he was going to get away with it.

Something had to happen.

The catacomb of musty offices was filled with stenographers in bright-colored saris, the corridors crowded with white pajama-ed messengers clutching files. Coolies piggybacked lawyers into the entrance hall to save them getting their shoes wet in the rain-deep streets.

Mohinder's office was on the third floor. The sign on the door said simply *Mohinder Singh, Public Prosecutor*. The door was half open and he was at his desk, bent over some papers. His pale blue turban was slightly awry. He was painstakingly sharpening the point of his pencil.

Budjinski pushed the door open and walked in. 'Mister Singh,' he said.

Mohinder did not seem surprised to see him. He waved to a wooden chair. 'Sit down, sir.' He did not get up and continued about his business. 'What can I do for you?'

Budjinski sat down and looked around. The office was cramped, with law books and files crammed on all the shelves. 'I want to know when you're going to call me to the stand,' he said.

'All in good time, sir, all in good time.'

'Let me be blunt.' Budjinski leaned forward and tapped the edge of the table with his forefinger to emphasize his point. 'We're losing this case.'

'We?'

'Look, I've been a cop all my life. I've seen a lot of criminal trials. I know when a case is getting fucked up.'

'Fucked up. I'm not familiar with that term. Is it French?'

'The fish is wriggling off the hook. Every day I sit in that courtroom watching this farce, and I can't believe what is happening. That man is a thief, a murderer and a sadist, and you're letting that smart-arse lawyer run rings round you.'

'You think your testimony will turn the tide then?'

'Yes, I think it will.'

'I see. Tell me something, sir, I hear you were recently dismissed from your employment. You were a captain in the International Police Commission-'

'Interpol.' Budjinski interrupted. 'And I wasn't dismissed. It was early retirement. Health reasons.'

'I see you are still defensive about it, so I won't labor the point. But if I, a plodding public prosecutor, can elicit such a response from you, how will you stand up to my brilliant colleague, the Nawab?'

Budjinski leaned back in his chair, defeated. 'I am sorry. It's just that my daughter...'

'I know that I cannot match the courtroom antics of my illustrious colleague, but do not despair just yet. I still have an ace up my sleeve.'

'Something that's not in the FIR?'

'You will see.'

Budjinski listened to the rain falling on the banana palms. He scratched at the prickly heat that had blossomed under his arms and on his back. Beyond the garden wall, the street was awash with the sudden deluge. He watched a man tuck up his dhoti and wade across the flood, holding a black umbrella over his head with his other hand.

The weather matched his spirits.

He pushed away the bowl of sweet black-rice porridge and stared at the rain. He thought of Noelle and the rage boiled up inside him again. It was all so bloody hopeless.

'Good morning, René.'

He looked up. It was Engineer, cool and dignified in an open-necked shirt and muted grey trousers.

'Seen this?' Engineer threw a copy of that morning's *Times of India* onto the table.

Budjinski picked it up. 'What is it?'

'Front page. Read it.'

VALENTINE BRETON TO RETURN FOR TRIAL

Engineer sat down and poured himself some tea. 'According to the story, she came to them. The Indians gave up on her months ago.'

'I don't believe it.' Budjinski said.

'Neither do I.' Engineer folded a napkin on his lap. 'Neither will the Nawab. Let's see if he can convince the judge that a woman doesn't recognize the man who tried to kill her.' He took a slice of papaya from the plate on the table and picked up his fork. 'Good news always gives me an appetite.'

CHAPTER 51

Valentine had been taken initially to the general infirmary in Varanasi. But the next day, Budjinski arranged for her to be flown to Delhi and then back to Paris. He had paid for this out of his own pocket.

For two weeks she had clung to life in the burns unit at the Hôpital des Invalides. She had second and third-degree burns to the left side of her face, her left arm and shoulder, and the back of her left leg. She had floated on a soft cushion of analgesics, which protected her from the worst of the pain. The doctors ordered four-hourly intramuscular tetracycline to stave off the streptococcal infection that would otherwise have killed her.

When the drugs were stopped and she regained full consciousness, she would not speak to anyone. She did not utter a word to Budjinski, to the doctors, to any of the nurses or to her friends.

A psychologist said it was post-traumatic stress.

Budjinski continued to visit her in the hospital, but she showed no sign of recognition. He feared her psyche had been destroyed by what had happened to her.

Three months later, Valentine discharged herself from hospital and disappeared.

The Indian authorities had hoped to secure a full and damning statement from her. They had been forced to press on with their case against Michel Christian without her.

There were a lot of rumors - she had been admitted to a private psychiatric clinic, she had gone to live with a distant relative in the remote Dordogne, she had even been seen at a Buddhist monastery in Nepal.

Now she was coming back to India.

Budjinski wanted desperately to see her again. He wanted to ask her to forgive him.

Budjinski arrived at the court at twenty minutes before noon. It looked more like the main train station than a court of law.

Naked babies screamed and urinated on the concrete floors, and beggars tugged at his trousers. A desperate-looking man, holding bundles of legal documents, turned this way and that, trying to get the attention of anyone who looked as if he might be a court official.

Budjinski pushed his way through the crowds in the hall and found his way into the courtroom. He took his seat in the section set aside for the press.

Finally, he heard the tramp of soldiers' boots and the clank of iron chains outside. The courtroom doors burst open, and Michel appeared, almost lost behind a wall of khaki. He saw Budjinski and gave a mocking smile. Budjinski looked away.

When he turned back, Michel was whispering to a young American writer, who was crouched beside him scribbling into a notebook. There were rumors that the contract with a New York publisher for his life story was worth fifty thousand dollars.

'He's gorgeous, isn't he?'

Budjinski turned around. There were two young girls, wearing t-shirts and jeans, in the row of chairs behind him. Their eyes, bright with excitement, were fixed on Michel.

'He's a cold-blooded killer,' Budjinski said. He turned his back on them.

Michel had noticed the two girls and was smiling at them.

They gasped and fluttered. 'He's beautiful,' one of them said. 'He couldn't have done it!'

'The prosecution calls Valentine Breton.'

For the first time in a week, a hush fell over the courtroom. Even the circus of lawyers fell silent. Like the sweating gaggle of spectators and reporters, they were desperate for a glimpse of the woman about whom they had heard and read so much.

Valentine walked in wearing a pure white sari, stitched with gold. Her head and face were covered in the style of the Moslem *chauderei*. She was ushered into the court by half a dozen khaki-clad soldiers, who helped her force a way through the press.

Budjinski craned his neck for a glimpse of her. She was led towards the bench, to the place reserved for her among the tight press of lawyers.

Even the Nawab was on his feet, staring with frank curiosity.

Mohinder waited, impassive. The only sound in the room was the hum of the electric fans.

Budjinski wiped the perspiration from his face. Valentine had her back to him now, lost among the jostling crowd of reporters and lawyers.

This was a rare event in an Indian courtroom. The witness had not previously made a statement in the FIR, and what she would say was unknown to anyone except the public prosecutor.

Mohinder went to stand next to her. He whispered something to her, then said aloud, 'Please tell us your name.'

Valentine removed her veil. She turned her head as if she were looking for someone. There was an audible gasp.

'Oh God,' Budjinski murmured. One side of her face was as perfect as he remembered it. But the other was raw with fresh scar tissue that blurred the lines of her nose, lips and cheek.

She turned back to Mohinder.

'Please tell us your name,' he repeated.

'Valentine Breton.'

'How old are you, Miss Breton?'

'Twenty-one.'

'And your nationality?'

'French.'

Budjinski concentrated on the cadence of the voices, Mohinder's monotone, Valentine's lilting accent, repeating the usual formalities.

'How long have you known the defendant?'

'I met him about eighteen months ago in Paris.'

'And what was your relationship to him?'

Valentine looked at Michel for the first time. They were close enough to touch. His eyes were half closed, his head lolling back in an attitude of arrogant passivity as if he were listening to a young child reading a story.

'We were lovers.'

'Is it not true that when you were with the defendant in Bangkok, you were approached by a Captain René Budjinski from Interpol and asked to stay in contact with the accused as he was under suspicion for a series of murders?'

The Nawab leaped to his feet. 'Objection!'

Judge Reddy leaned forward. 'Is this pertinent?'

'Yes, your honor,' Mohinder said, 'It is to establish the motive for the crime.'

'Objection overruled.'

The Nawab sank back into his seat, his face turned in exasperation to the gods.

'I was told Michel was under suspicion,' Valentine said.

'And so, you followed him to Varanasi at the request of Captain Budjinski?'

'I would have gone anyway.'

Mohinder shrugged this elaboration away. 'And what happened when you arrived in Varanasi?'

'There was a note at my hotel from Michel. He wanted me to meet him the next day.'

'And Captain Budjinski advised you to make this rendezvous?'

'Yes. But, as I said, I would have gone anyway.'

'Did you know the police were intending to arrest him? That a warrant for his arrest had been issued in connection with...' Mohinder bent to examine his notes.

'Yes, I knew that. I warned him.'

Mohinder was startled. 'You warned him?'

'The police were harassing him. He was innocent. When I saw him, I shouted to him that we were being watched and that we should get away as quickly as possible.'

Mohinder fumbled in the pocket of his jacket for his handkerchief. He mopped the perspiration from his forehead and resettled the spectacles on his nose.

'Then he took you to the boarding house owned by Mister Bedi.'

'That is correct.'

'This is where he drugged you.'

The Nawab was on his feet again, alert now, sensing blood. 'Objection! Leading the witness.'

'Allowed.'

Mohinder frowned. 'Can you tell us in your own words what happened at the boarding house?'

'Michel and I decided that it would be best if he got out of Varanasi immediately.'

Budjinski could not see Valentine's face, but he could see Mohinder. The prosecutor was perspiring freely now. He had begun to falter.

'You decided he should leave?'

'Yes. I decided to stay behind. He had a better chance of escaping on his own.'

'Why are you lying?'

'I'm not lying.'

The Nawab leaned back against the judge's bench and clapped his hands in silent applause.

'Please tell us what happened then,' Mohinder said.

'Someone broke into my room.'

'Who?'

'I don't know.'

'You're lying.'

The Nawab leaped to his feet. 'The prosecutor is badgering his own witness!'

Judge Reddy was astonished. The counsel for the defense seemed to be protecting a prosecution witness. He turned to Mohinder. 'Objection allowed.'

Mohinder pressed on. 'What happened when this unknown person broke into your room?'

'He put a cloth over my mouth. There was a strong smell, so I imagine there was some chemical on the cloth. Chloroform perhaps. That's all I can remember. I must have passed out. The next thing I remember was waking up at the *ghats*. The man was carrying me down to the water's edge.'

'It was this man!' Mohinder shouted, pointing at Michel.

'No.' Valentine said, perfectly calm. 'I told you, the man who did it was holding me in his arms. I got a good look at his face. He was an Indian. It wasn't Michel. It was someone else. Michel wouldn't do that to me. He loved me.'

The courtroom exploded. The prosecution's case had just been shredded by the victim of the crime. The trial was over. The reporters dashed for the door.

Michel Christian would go free.

The Nawab leaped to his feet and started to pound Valentine on the back. 'Well done!' he shouted. 'Justice has been done here today!'

Budjinski tried to reach her, but her frail, white-clad figure was lost among the crowd.

Michel was the only one in the courtroom who had not moved. He sat perfectly still in his chains.

He was smiling.

The black and yellow Ambassador pulled up in the street. Budjinski watched its arrival from the balcony above. A slender figure in a white sari got out of the car and hurried through the garden to the *porte cochère.*

'Kapil will show her up,' Engineer said. 'I'll leave you alone, old chap.'

A few moments later the door opened, and Kapil ushered Valentine into the room.

Budjinski took a step towards her, uncertain what to do, how to greet her. 'Hello, Valentine.'

She went to sit in one of the cane armchairs, her eyes watching him from behind the gossamer veil.

There was a silver teapot on the carved mahogany table. He poured two cups of unsweetened tea. 'I didn't think I'd ever see you again. After you left the hospital-'

'I could not stay in France. There's a place Michel took me to, once. It is in Nepal. I went there.' She took the cup from him. 'How have you been?'

'All right. Thanks for coming.'

'I heard you wanted to see me.'

'Of course.'

'You want to know why I did it.'

She couldn't still love him, he thought. Not after what he did to her.

'Yes.'

'I'm sorry. I can't tell you that. Perhaps one day.'

It wasn't the answer he was looking for. He thought about the journalist taking down Michel's story in the courtroom, the two girls who had been sitting in the courtroom flirting with the bastard.

'Just tell me that you don't still love him.'

'There are some things that it's better not to know.'

'He's not getting out of there, you know. There are extradition orders from Singapore and the Philippines. And if they don't get him, I'll finish that bastard myself.'

'Please, Captain-'

'I'm not a captain anymore. They kicked me out.'

'I'm sorry.'

'Don't be. I did what I had to do.' He lit a cigarette. 'I've been meaning to give these up, but there really hasn't been a good time to do it in the last twelve months.'

'Perhaps now?'

'No, this doesn't seem like a good time either.'

She sipped her tea. 'Is that the only reason you wanted to see me?'

He got up and went to stand on the balcony. 'I don't know how to say this.'

'You want absolution?'

'I was never a very good Catholic. I just want you to know I am sorry. It was all my fault. It will haunt me till the day I die.'

'When I was in Nepal, the monks there explained karma to me. It is like a debt that must be paid. Sometimes it is our debt. Sometimes it is a debt from another lifetime. It can even be a debt we inherit from our parents. Whatever debt there is, I have now paid mine.'

She stood up and put a hand on his shoulder. 'Don't torment yourself. What I did was my decision and my destiny. If I had not gone after him in Varanasi, he would have followed me back to France. He told me once that our destinies were entwined. He was right.'

'Just say you forgive me.'

'There's nothing to forgive. I never blamed you in the first place.'

'Where will you go now?'

'I don't know. That depends on what happens to Michel.'

'Did you know the Paris police have reopened the file on your father's death?'

For a moment, he thought she was going to faint. She seemed to sway on her feet.

'I thought you ought to know.'

'Michel?'

He nodded. 'Can you still love him now?'

'I cannot ever explain to you what I feel for Michel,' she said. She put down her cup and got to her feet. '*Au revoir*, Captain.'

The door closed gently behind her. He wondered if he would ever see her again.

CHAPTER 52

Michel was ushered into the empty room. A guard pushed him down onto a bench. They had chained him in the *dandaberi* again so that he could receive his visitor.

For the past year, he had lived and slept in a cramped cell, three paces wide and five deep, on a starvation diet. Each day he received one chapati, a half cup of soured milk, a dish of watery green dahl and some mashed bean soup. He had been allowed no visitors, no radio, no newspapers. He slept on a hard stone floor with a greasy, woolen blanket to cover him, enduring the moans and babbles of those driven insane by their incarceration. At night he had to cope with hordes of black rats.

A rusty pipe jutted from one wall, and brownish water occasionally belched from it. But it was the only water he had, so he cupped his hands for this meager and infrequent offering, whatever hour of the day or night.

His legs and wrists were raw and festering from the scraping of the steel manacles that he was made to wear whenever they took him from his cell. His body was covered in sores, where lice and flea bites had become infected.

Privately, he had hoped the Indian court would convict him on attempted murder. They would sentence him to seven years, maybe ten. It didn't matter. He would receive the advance on the book the American publisher wanted him to write and buy his way out of Tihar.

But now, if he was extradited to Singapore or Thailand on murder charges, they might convene a quick trial and execute him.

He needed a miracle.

The door opened and Valentine entered, flanked by two guards. She sat down at the table opposite him and drew back her veil. She regarded him coolly, though the left eye stared from a shapeless putty of scar tissue. One side of her mouth was frozen, the other curled in a smile of regret.

'Hello Michel,' she said.

'You're the last person I expected to see.'

'Why? There's a bond between you and me, *chèri*. You said that yourself.'

'Have you come to gloat?'

'No. I've come to say I'm sorry.'

'For Bangkok or for yesterday?'

'I helped you. I saved you.'

'Saved me for what? For the Thais?'

'The Thais?'

'I'm to be extradited.'

She switched quickly from English to French, so the guards would not understand. 'That's why I came. I have a plan.'

Michel narrowed his eyes. 'Go on.'

'It's my fault you're here. So, it's up to me to get you out.'

'How?'

'I can get you a uniform and a disguise. And some money to bribe the guards.'

'You're crazy.'

'Am I? The warden here earns three hundred rupees a month. How much do you think it will cost to make it all sound a little less crazy?'

'You can organize all this?'

'Of course.'

'What happens if I get out?'

'I'll be waiting near the front gate. I'll have transport and we'll drive straight to the Nepalese border at Raxaul. I'll hide you in the back until we get out of the city.'

'When?'

'Tomorrow night. Eleven o'clock. No one will know you are gone till the next morning. From Nepal we will fly to South America. I've arranged it all - a passport, new clothes, everything. In two days, you will be safe, and we can start our life again.'

'I've underestimated you,' he said. 'I thought you hated me.'

She stood up to leave. 'I did. For a long time, when I was in the hospital, all I did was dream of a thousand different ways for you to die. But then I realized that if I killed you, I'd be killing a part of myself. We belong together.'

The door shut behind her.

Michel stared after her. My God, he thought. She actually thinks I'd take her back after all she's done and looking like that. He shuddered at the thought of making love to such a horror.

It was a pity she had not died that morning in Varanasi.

Now he would have to kill her all over again.

Valentine made her way to the Chandni Chowk, the famous flea bazaar between the Jama Masjid Mosque and the Red Fort.

It was a maze of covered arcades and winding alleys, where you could buy anything from parts for a 1956 Austin Healey to ammunition for a .38 Smith and Wesson revolver. Small, green snakes were charmed from brass spittoons, and sacred cows ambled past the painted doors of tiny shops. There was a pervading fug of spice and excrement.

She purchased a khaki uniform, gold braid, a wig, a false beard and a khaki turban separately. She found military insignia - ribbons and medals – in a small jewelry shop nearby. It was the last item on her list that caused her the most trouble.

She finally found what she was looking for in a crumbling *haveli* at the end of a deserted alleyway. The purchase was an expensive one and impossible to carry. She would have to collect it later.

The van was obtained at considerably less expense from a gold-toothed Jain. Valentine guessed that it was stolen. It was of no importance. It would only be required for a few hours.

Finally, everything was ready. She paid five hundred rupees to one of the guards at the Tihar to have the cardboard box delivered to Michel in his cell.

Soon he would be free.

The guard unlocked the door and pushed Andy Rosen inside. It slammed shut again behind him. The only light came from the kerosene lantern that hung on the wall outside the barred window.

Michel lay slumped in the corner, sleeping.

Andy crept towards him. 'Michel.' There was no answer. He moved closer. 'Michel!'

There was a blur of movement, and Andy found himself on his back, Michel's elbow pressed on his throat.

'How do you want me to kill you? Shall I snap your neck or choke you slowly with my fingers?'

Andy tore desperately at the arm that was choking him. 'No, got some thing...woman...'

Suddenly, he could breathe again. Michel grabbed his hair and jerked his head up from the floor. 'Talk.'

'One of the guards gave me something from the woman, Valentine. A box.'

'Where is it?'

Andy scrabbled on the floor in the darkness. He pushed it towards him. 'I haven't opened it, I swear.'

Michel tore open the string bindings in the tiny square of yellow light under the window. He sorted through the contents. There was everything she had promised, even a cheap watch. There was also a note scribbled in her hand: *Main gate. Eleven o'clock. Listen for horn. One long, two short.*

'Michel, I'm sorry about what happened in court,' Andy said somewhere in the darkness, 'I had to do it. I can't take any more in here. Anyway, I knew you'd find a way out.'

Michel didn't answer.

'I did okay, huh? I told the woman I'd get these things to you-'

Michel's fist came out of the shadows and sent Andy sprawling across the cell.

Andy shrieked for the guard, who came in almost immediately and dragged him out. The cell door slammed behind him.

At ten minutes to eleven Michel slipped out of his filthy, white t-shirt and jeans and put on the khaki tunic and shorts. They had a curious smell. He wondered where she had found them. In some stinking bazaar, probably.

He emptied the rest of the contents and found glue to fix the wig and beard. She had thought of everything. He put on the turban, fitting the elastic strap tight under his chin, and then the khaki puttees and sandals.

He was ready.

He waited.

After few minutes, he heard it. A car horn. One long blast, followed by two short ones.

He yelled for the guard to fetch the chief head warden. When they were alone in the cell, he gave him the twenty thousand rupees that Valentine had wrapped in the uniform jacket at the bottom of the box.

The warden was suitably impressed. The money was equivalent to six years' pay. He led Michel outside to the exercise yard.

It was quiet. A yellow moon hung low over the prison walls. Michel placed the military swagger stick under one arm. A nice touch that, he thought. Now to brazen it out.

He marched across the compound, tapping the swagger stick against his thigh. Two guards lounged at the inner gate, silhouetted by an oil-lamp. They snatched up their rifles and saluted when they saw him.

Michel barked in Hindi, 'Open the gate! Come on, hurry it up!'

One of them fumbled with a set of keys and the iron gate creaked open.

Michel waited. He didn't want to appear to be in too much of a hurry. He grabbed the other guard, snatched his rifle away and made a show of examining it under the light. Then he slammed it back into the startled soldier's arms. 'This rifle's filthy. Clean it!'

Then he walked out.

There was another compound between the inner and outer walls. A stone archway housed the main gates, which were iron-studded and massive, each forty feet high and ten feet across. They were rarely opened.

A small door had been cut into one of the larger gates, and it was through here that new prisoners were brought in and - more rarely - released.

A single guard stood in the shadows.

Michel spotted the glow of his cigarette. 'Attention!' he bellowed.

The man gasped and dropped the cigarette. His rifle clattered to the ground. He scrambled to retrieve it.

'What's your name?' Michel said.

'Corporal Shastri.'

'Report to the warden's office first thing in the morning. You are a disgrace to your uniform. Now open this gate!'

The guard did as he was told. Michel walked through. A moment later, he heard it slam behind him.

He looked along the deserted street. The van was parked about fifty yards away. It was similar to the jungle green bus he had ridden each day to the Tis Hizari courthouse - an ancient Bedford with no windows. It flashed its headlights at him. He ran towards it, spinning the swagger stick into the air in triumph. It clattered into the gutter.

Valentine jumped out and stood by the rear door, holding it open for him. 'Quick!' she said. 'Inside!'

He leapt in and heard her slam the door shut behind him.

Then he ripped off the fake beard and started to laugh.

CHAPTER 53

The van lurched through the old Delhi traffic. There was the usual din of taxis, trucks and motor rickshaws, even at this time of night.

You're a genius, Valentine, he thought. It's a pity I have to kill you.

He heard something move in the darkness. It was pitch-black and he couldn't see. There it was again, a rustling noise, like something heavy and wet dragging itself across the metal floor.

'Who's there?' he said.

He panicked and reached for the back door, looking for a handle. There wasn't one. He pushed against the door. Locked.

He heard the noise again and threw himself into the corner, making himself as small a target as possible. What the hell was that?

'Valentine!'

Don't panic. She wouldn't do anything to you. She just got you out of Tihar, for God's sake.

He crawled to the front of the van and beat his fist against the metal partition that separated him from the driver's cabin.

'Valentine!'

That noise again. It was getting closer.

He launched himself away from it, his body hammering into the other corner of the van. *Merde alors!* Whatever it was, it was stalking him.

'Valentine, stop the van!'

The serpent had been taken in Burma. It was a reticulated python, one of the largest of the python family, twenty feet of thick, sinuous coils.

It could not see Michel. It was the heat-sensitive organs in its facial pits that sensed him first, and then the darting tongue picked up the scent particles of the pork grease that had been smeared onto the tunic. Pigs were a favorite prey. It moved in, to attack.

Its hunger was excited by the strong vibrations that it picked up through the metal floor of the van. The sounds were transmitted to its ear drum through the huge bone of its lower jaw, and it knew that its quarry was helpless and terrified.

Its massive jaws opened, revealing over a hundred needle-sharp teeth, angled back towards its throat in six shining rows. But the teeth were not intended for biting or for chewing. They were used to anchor the victim while it used its coils to crush it to death.

Michel felt something clamp onto his leg and he screamed.

It wrapped itself around his shoulders, a massive tentacle as strong as a man's arm. He tried to pull away, but it was useless. A cold band of muscle gripped him in a merciless vice.

It pulled him across the floor, and he heard himself scream again. Another coil went around his waist. He tried to shout out, but there was no breath in his lungs. The steel bands were suffocating him.

One of his ribs cracked.

He suddenly knew with absolute clarity what Valentine had done.

Bright lights flashed in his head. He closed his eyes and saw Adrienne in her faded green dress, beckoning him to follow her down the wooden steps of the apartment into the Saigon streets.

This time she wasn't going to leave him behind.

Valentine listened to him die. His death throes gave her no satisfaction. She had thought it would be a moment to savor. She was wrong.

It was simply justice.

She thought about the Hôpital des Invalides, a quiet and secluded world where everyone wore masks and green sterile robes and even the air was filtered and purified. For the first two weeks, she had floated on the soft, white clouds of the morphine.

'Valentine!'

But then the pain had started. It had been like a hot sun burning down on her skinless flesh, undulating waves of agony that had left her screaming and sobbing until the duty nurse relented and brought her some more drugs.

She heard Michel call her name again. He was kicking the side of the van.

She thought about the day they had taken off the bandages, and she had been confronted with the nightmare stranger in the mirror.

The muffled sounds coming from behind her rose to a crescendo. 'Valentine, stop the van!'

She thought about her father.

She heard the whiplash hammering of the final struggle.

Then, silence.

CHAPTER 54

Outside Mathura, on the road to Agra

Constable Sunil Bose hefted the jemmy bar in his right hand and cautiously approached the van. He waited by the rear door.

Sergeant Jagdish Sharma checked the cabin. Empty.

'Get it open,' he said.

The villagers said the van had been there all day. They thought it must have been abandoned. There might be an innocent enough explanation. They would find out.

Bose wedged the tip of the jemmy between the back doors and levered it open. The lock snapped with a bang.

Sharma threw open the door.

At first, he thought he was looking at a coil of incredibly thick rope. Then he saw it move and realized what it was.

The python had tried to shape its meal first, disarticulating the joints at the shoulders.

But the meal had proved too large, and the lower half of the man's torso and legs still protruded from its mouth, coated in a sticky mess of saliva.

Its body obscenely bloated, the python stared back at him with unblinking eyes, helpless. A prisoner of its own victim.

Sharma gasped and took a step back. 'Shiva,' he whispered.

Paris

René Budjinski stood by the grave, his hands in his pockets. It was peaceful here, and the morning mist blanketed the noise of the city. Noelle had been buried under a young beech. On a clear day she had an uninterrupted view of the city skyline. She would have approved.

He knelt down, removed the old flowers from the vase at the foot of the headstone and replaced them with fresh red roses. His thick fingers were clumsy in their arrangement, and it was some while before he was finally satisfied.

'I have a girl staying with me now, Noelle,' he said. 'She has had a tough time. I am taking care of her. She needs someone to look after her before she is ready to go back into the world. I am trying my hand at being a father at last. I know you'll laugh at that. But I have potential, you know.'

He stood up, admiring his handiwork. 'You would have liked her. She is a lot like you.'

He reached into his pocket for his cigarettes, took one out, then changed his mind. He put it back in the pack. 'She's trying to make me give these up. I know you would have been with her in that. Goodbye sweetheart. Sleep well.'

He turned and walked towards the gates. The mist began to clear, and the morning air smelled sweet.

About the Author

I have been a writer all my life. It's all I ever wanted to do, except for a brief dream of being a pro footballer. I started out in advertising as a copywriter, then worked as a journalist, a magazine columnist and a script writer for radio and television before becoming a full-time novelist.

I love adventure and travel and that has shaped the kind of books I write. Early in my career I developed a passion for Wilbur Smith novels. I also love Cornwell and Follett. When I publish a book, I'm hoping to share it with other readers like me, who crave adventure, and stories with action and twists, but also love something else – exotic locations, long ago times and unforgettable characters. The kind of stories that stay with you long after you finish the last page. It's what I read and it's what inspires me to write.

I try to travel to all the places I write about to experience the smells and sounds that you just can't get from Google, and I have written many chapters in airports, on planes and in cafes in cities around the world. I am completely in my head when I'm writing and it doesn't matter where I'm sitting. Stories play like movies in my mind. I press play and pause as I write.

When not travelling or writing, my hobbies are India Pale Ale, the acoustic guitar and dogs.

I was born and raised in London, but these days I live in Fremantle, Australia, with my wife and spaniels. I post regularly on my Facebook page if you'd like to see behind the scenes or ask a question.

Thank you for reading my books and sharing my adventures.

Colin Falconer

About the Books

Special offers

Colin Falconer books are often selected by Amazon to be in Kindle deals. To stay in the loop on deals and new releases, sign up for his mailing list at colinfalconerbooks.com

Enjoy this book?

You can make a big difference by adding a rating or writing a short book or series review on Amazon. Thank you!

The Epic Adventure Series

Multi-bestselling historical adventure thrillers.

Stand-alone stories that can be read in any order.

30,000+ five-star Amazon reviews.

Exclusive to Amazon in Kindle, Kindle Unlimited and paperback.

Part thriller. Part history. All adventure.

Printed in Great Britain
by Amazon